# THE
# BANYAN
# TREE

# ALSO BY CHRISTOPHER NOLAN

*Dam-Burst of Dreams*

*Under the Eye of the Clock*

# THE
# BANYAN
# TREE

A NOVEL

---

# CHRISTOPHER
# NOLAN

ARCADE PUBLISHING · NEW YORK

FIRST U.S. EDITION 2000

First published in Great Britain by Phoenix House 1999

ISBN 1-55970-511-6
Library of Congress Catalog Card Number 99-76694
Library of Congress Cataloging-in-Publication information is available.

Published in the United States by Arcade Publishing, Inc., New York
Distributed by Time Warner Trade Publishing

Visit our Web site at www.arcadepub.com

10  9  8  7  6  5  4  3  2  1

BP

PRINTED IN THE UNITED STATES OF AMERICA

My grandfathers
Christy Nolan, a writer of the 1930s
John Martin, who dined on apple dumpling
in the Clarence Hotel in 1911

# THE
# BANYAN
# TREE

# CHAPTER I

That churn came out once a week, usually on a Friday. Big brown crocks of thickening cream stood there waiting for the fray. A great black kettle watched for its turn as it filibustered on the hot stove in the kitchen, while out in the drab dairy Minnie O'Brien fussed as she made ready to bring about a miracle.

The churn echoed in emptiness when she set it centre stage on the cold cement floor. A round-bellied barrel it was, its staves held together by four iron hoops. Eight days had passed since it was last used; its insides now waited their hot and cold baptism.

When Minnie felt that the churn was scrubbed enough, she set to next to sweeten its porous wood. At hand lay a bunch of freshly plucked hazel leaves, and those she thrust down inside it. Fetching then that big black kettle, she poured its boiling water in on top of the leaves. Scalded so, the leaves released their nutty sweet scent and the hot wood of the churn absorbed it into its druidic, dark drum.

Her hazel wand waved, Minnie disposed of the limp leaves before shocking the churn with, this time, icy cold water from the old spring well. Three white pails full it took to cool down the steaming hot wood, three whole pails full she used to freeze the churn in readiness for its sacramental rotations.

Nursing still their helium harvest the cataracted crocks waited, still playing their stoic games, but the moment they were lifted they yielded up their booty, listening in awe as their clotted cream dropped ploppingly down into the cold, damp coffin of dankness. There it lay fooling itself that it might yet escape, but then down slapped the lid, snap went the clamps, and up the churn was hoisted onto its stand. There in total darkness the cream lay while the churn hung where it swung, while Minnie geared herself up for the imponderables ahead.

Eventually, her state of play ready, her sleeves pushed up to her elbows, her feet planted firmly, her children somewhere within earshot, she gripped hold of that handle and sent the engine of the churn Sundaying into life.

Plumbing its cargo the churn end-over-ended, the billygoat of its sum slopping and slapping against either end. Twisting the handle to the rhythm of an old O'Brien chant the churn and churner gradually built up speed until the ginseng was singing:

'Going to Connecticut,
Going to Connecticut,
Going to Connecticut.'

There was, she knew, no great need for any member of the O'Brien family to emigrate, but with her hand still holding a loose grip of the handle, Ireland's long-ago potato famine but a memory, she activated the humbug until she had the rhythm reduced to:

'Conn-ect-i-cut,
Conn-ect-i-cut,
Conn-ect-i-cut.'

A sense of lonesomeness equal to the evidence of an unkindness of ravens usually, and for no obvious reason, crept over her every time she churned, and it was then that she'd be glad to rope in her children, their complaining an antidote to her sense of foreboding. 'Here Brendan, you take a turn,' she'd say as she slid her hand away, and when properly humoured off he'd set on his drum-drum route to Connecticut. Sheila, when her turn came, always spat in her hand before she gripped the handle and, being a girl, and to prove her worth, she'd never ever give in till her mother shouted 'Whoa'.

By then the helium would be knocking for release, and it was the littlest of the three children who'd be chosen for the special thumb-task. Lifting him up, his mother would stand him on an old wooden box from where he could stretch in to place his thumb on the silver escape-valve. His strength was never sufficient to depress the button, so his mother would place her thumb securely on top of Frankie's and, strengths combined, the little boy'd cheer as gas whistled from the churn. Minnie loved her littlest so, and making much of his miracle she'd hug him before lifting him down to the floor.

No time to let up. It'd be her turn again to grip the handle and set the churn in motion. Her right hand would grow weary and then her left as her journey upturned and turned up. Relief, though, would dawn when on stopping to examine the lid's little porthole window she'd discover that the cream had cracked and, yes, there they'd be, the little crumbs of butter sticking precariously to the round glass.

That would set her to change her tempo, for now she had to become as midwife to the crock of gold within the churn. Her hand rocking the cradle, she'd heel the churn over and back, see-sawing it until the butter gathered together into an island plashing around on a lake of blue-white milk.

Sesame-like she'd remove the lid, her eye taking in her harvest. Then, her hands washed, she'd lift up nuggets of the butter and hit them slap against the upturned and slanted lid. Milk hidden inside the butter would steal lava-like away and spill back down to swell the milk in the churn. She'd never stop until her hoard of butter was ready to be dropped into a crock of fresh water. There it'd bob up and down as she kneaded and pummelled it, her children all the while keeping her supplied with ever more spring water. It was only when the water remained clear as nectar that her job was done, and even then she'd have to salt the butter to each one's taste.

The day's churning would be drawing near its climax, but Minnie would have yet to factotum the job. Cutting off a portion from that butter mound she, like a juggler, would toss her prize

3

from one butter spade to another, slapping and slipping it, plopping and gripping it, until the golden butter was shaped to her mind's fancy and ready to be nudged onto a dark-green platter. There in its innocence it'd wait until, holding a spade pen-fashion, she'd inscribe her name upon it in a pattern of dots and dashes.

Fridays of yore worried, but seldom now. The dairy was the location of those far-flung human endeavours. It was still there, but now its whitewashed walls grew seas of black mildew. The big brown crocks which had once held cream no longer held butter's promise; now they were laden down with the years' rusted junk. Voices, the young voices which once complained of tired turning of the handle, were silent now, flown to the four winds. Panicking behind the dairy door the churn, the focal point of those distant Fridays, crouched yonder in its place. The hoops which held its varnished staves were still there, holding it intact. The plughole piece of wood, the spigot, starved of moisture and now dry as cork, slept senile-stressed sleep underneath the dairy table. The two handles which used to loiter waiting their part in the lifting of the churn hung down in idleness, no need now their hinting strength. Yes, the barrel still stood, but only just. Weary from the years' tomboy-thinking, it yet managed to hold its body together so that the round lid would have something to sit upon. Only the lid played God: there it sat upon its frame, a cobweb hiding its porthole window. Still waiting for the pressure of his thumb, its silver escape-valve damned well watched the door to see if the child might return to train his finger once again upon its button and allow it to whistle.

4

# CHAPTER 2

Minnie O'Brien, the star performer of those long-ago dairy miracles, was now but caretaker to this house and farm. Just like the air which stymied here, she too spent her waking hours in waiting. Nothing mattered but that the smoke would curl from her chimney during every daylight hour and that come nightfall a light would give off gumption in its beckoning from her kitchen window. Minding her minefield, she vexed her days. Hers was a hyphenated status, for her husband, Peter, slept now beneath the single yew up there in the village cemetery. His wait was indeed similar to hers, for never an hour passed by that he could unclench his teeth, for even in death he sensed the danger of allowing the yew's roots to steal into his mouth to water themselves from the trough where his tongue used to lie.

Weathering the years, the widow woman stood today leaning against the Snowcem-ed white wall. The relics of the old clematis still clung here to its fractured frame. Minnie played games as her mind set about remembering the morning when she asked her new husband to help her move the plant from its former site beside the turfshed to this hump of ground running alongside the new wall in front of the house. Peter had his doubts that it would take to its new bolthole. This morning her ears could hear again the ping of his spade in the early morning stillness. 'Here love, catch a holt of that,' his voice came back, and now touching the very leaves and tendrils of the plant her eyes undid time as they examined the blossom purpling there before her.

Pondering on her lean life now she left her place sideways to the wall and set off on her daily patrol of her land. She owned five fields in all, none of them special, none but the one in which the giant oaks clumped. The stumps of four of them, blackened by nature, stunted there still while to their right flourished four more, their branches strangling the skies with their canopy of conceit. Peter had been the surgeon who cut down the four oaks. He needed furniture for his new house, since the nest egg, the sovereigns willed to him by an old uncle, had been holed badly in the pursuit of his dream. But the oaks didn't figure in today's pilgrimage, neither did the sundry memories associated with the sour grass which grew around their roots. No, this sally was to find out at first hand if her gate had kept out the big foreign bullocks from loafing around her prize field.

Not able to stand the pressure any longer, Minnie had given in to her neighbour's offers and let four fields of grazing to the farmer on the other side of the mearing ditch. Jude Fortune, the widow of Michael J., had for ages had her designs on the old woman's place, but four fields were not what she was after: she wanted the run of the entire holding and then she could keep out that Protestant fellow, the man to whom Minnie each year sold her one field of meadow.

Swallowing up her neighbour's five fields into her own vast stretch of land was Jude Fortune's unspoken aim, but four years had now slipped by and her cattle had never once got a chance to graze in the field where words and wonders once twined together. Jude's resolve was durable and year after year she suggested the actual terms to her renewing the lease, but her pumice stone had minimal effect on the wodjous woman, Mrs Minnie O'Brien.

Today, then, was but another day at the battlements for Minnie. She had laid her groundwork the very day when, upon her instructions, her solicitor gave the go-ahead to Jude Fortune's leasing of four of the five fields. Down she went that May day to check out if the gate to the special field was closed, and not even satisfied with it being bolted she set about tying it. The bolt was already homed into its tunnel in the old railway sleeper but she tied it nonetheless. The thick strand of wire was hard to manoeuvre; her hands certainly felt the strain. She tried to imagine the cattle's strength as maybe rising on each other they might be forced against the gate, and so with that in mind she threaded the wire through the hole in the bolt, twanked it around the armiture, yellowed it around the plank before coaxing it back towards herself so that she could set about twisting the two ends together. 'Musha then, the Holy Spirit himself'd not get in nor get out through that gate,' she thought, and smiling to herself she stood there sizing up her handiwork.

Now Minnie could dream on. The four big oaks stood high and haughty; as for the grass growing around their feet, well, the tufts could be mowed just like the rest of the meadow and when mixed with the red poppies and white clover the coarse grass could then turn sweet – only the baking sun was needed. Thus was her thinking that May day, and when it came to the question of what to do with the meadow she somehow felt in her gut that George Hamilton would, under the wasps' sting, come in and take it so that it wouldn't be left on her hands.

The sun which shone down on her as she leaned on the white wall was now higher in the heavens and hotter on her back. She pulled along though, for her gate held a note longer than did her lungs. Her breathing was coming faster by the time she neared the iron gate, but when she saw what was there inside it and gazing out through its bars her heart almost stone dropped. 'Musha will you look, after all my time and years of trouble,' she thought, and the big round solemn eyes of the cattle gazed on her in rapt attention. Her eyes swept about her, searching for the dog, but he was off the far side of the third field trying to raise rabbits for his own excitement. Minnie hadn't the puff with which to whistle, so, trumpeting her hands around her mouth, she called out the dog's name and waited until he came bounding through a batch of thistles.

Ranting and raving, she urged the dog to get behind the bullocks, but the untrained urchin was wacky enough to keep attacking from the front. The cattle galloped rebelliously, the dog

7

circling before them, but they, the gung-ho foreigners, were but having high jinks. Five times, at least, they galloped past the gap in the hedge where that tree was tackled by the storm last November. A big ash tree cobbled with tons of ivy was brought down by the gale force winds, and the fencing which she herself had done the moment the tree was cut up had held the *bearna baol* unbreached till now. But strealing along, half trotting, her wish today was to force those cattle back out through the broken-down fence. With every last breath she shouted until one big fellow burst back to where he belonged, and his ten playmates then followed suit.

War had broken out between the bumsteers and the guardian of the field where the line of history had been conceived. Second-guessing now she, the Fenian woman, had to mend her fences. Soldiering on, she found branches and bushes and then like a crow she hit-or-missed until the gap was newly darned. By now, though, her old face was burning and her tired senses dithered from the cattle one moment to the whereabouts of Frankie the next.

'I'll go on as far as the river and then double back to see if they have forgotten the taste of my meadow,' she thought, but on reaching the rut between the fourth and fifth fields she found that last night's downpour had put a fillip of water struggling there. She stood for an age looking at the little trench and then, her breasts sagging, her legs slightly buckling, she gathered her skirt and made ready to jump. Pilate would have hopped it blindfolded, Peter would've stepped across as though it wasn't even there, in her heyday she'd have skipped across it, but that was then and this was now; now it took all her resolve. Her take-off was sudden when it came – the feet thieved the air and down they landed. It was only a little jump, a mind-over-matter jump, but as she walked towards the river now she smiled the schooled smile of a woman.

Red, flapper-faced, she eventually reached the innocence of the flowing river and kneeling down she cupped her hands together and threw water into her hungry notions. Handful after handful it took to cool her down. Now she just knelt there looking down at the maverick shimmering in the mirrored pool, trapped there where the cattle broke down the river bank. 'My! how time flies,' poured out its Lombard notions, while in its head burst now a rush of blood, the sound whirring like the noise from the circular blade of a bacon slicer. For what seemed an age she knelt, her gaze fixed on her reflection down there, but when her old knees began hinting that the damp was getting to them she got back on her feet and, though wobbling a little, she managed to how-an'-ever her way back from the deathtrap.

Returning from the river, Minnie took a hard look at her patchwork and decided gung-ho or no, those cattle were barred entry again. Tired now, she dragged herself along. Beside her trotted the collie, his tongue out, all but lapping the stoic air. Overhead swept dozens of swallows. The dog's eyes only glanced their way as they swept past his hunting festival. 'Yes indeedy me,' sighed Minnie, 'that job'll hold for now,' but at the same time her lips were whispering 'Ah! God help me, I wish he was back.'

Nearing home, she knew by the straight line of the smoke coming from the chimney that the kettle must surely be on the boil. 'Maybe the postman'll have come and gone,' she thought. 'Maybe he'll have written to say he's coming home. Aye indeed, Minnie Humphrey, and pigs might fly.'

The porch was hot as hell when she entered, so throwing the door wide open she continued on her way into the dark kitchen. The kettle was quietly singing on the stove but she knew she'd have time to remove her wellingtons while waiting for it to come to the boil. Returning to the porch she sat down and eased her feet from their boots, peeled off her socks and placed her clammy feet on the floor, noticing that the tiles still held a modicum of heat. Relaxing now, she felt satisfied with her ordeal down in the fey fields: her fencing had held intact and the last she saw of them the bullocks had mosied off to graze their four liberties.

# CHAPTER 3

Red-flowering geraniums sat on the sill all around the inside of the glass porch. Here and there on their big leaves stuck the odd red petal. Now and then a freebie of air blew in through the open door, rustling withered leaves which lay on the tiles near Minnie's feet. Slowly she stooped down and, gathering them, set about crunching the leaves inside her clenched fist. Then she deliberately opened wide her hand again, but the withered geranium leaves stirred as though trying to jurisprudence themselves. She smelt them, testing their mustiness. Her cupped hand was to her nose when for no reason at all a voice, a voice which she had heard last summer, came back now to taunt her. Perhaps it was that the lungs tumbrelled and brought it back, the foreboding voice of her next-door neighbour. Perhaps the tungsten today was the same only different, perhaps the cunning words then told still their taunt. 'Mind how you're going,' it said. 'Mind you don't get sunstroke or something, sitting there under the glass of a day like this ... I've come about the bit of meadow, how about giving me the grazing of it and you'll not have the bother of the mowing, and the saving, and the weather ... Just let my cattle have the run of it and sure I'll give you the same for the grass as George Hamilton gives you for the meadow ... Ye'know you're not able to be down there running after cattle.'

Minnie was flummoxed that day, but now she thought again of how she dealt with the woman. 'Musha-then, I beat about the bush a lot but how could I, then or now, have said "Not while grass grows, water flows or crows put out their tongue will that field be dumped upon by your Charolais and what's this the brown ones are called?"' The place of remembering didn't alter at all, for just like last time she now caught hold of her lubbard and, fingering its fat fold, she struggled yet again as waffling on from one breed to another she tried to conjure up that name, but sorra way could she, then or now, come up with the word 'Simmental'.

The afternoon seemed dead now compared with the morning's activities; how long she slept could best be gauged by the high price the kettle paid as it sat boiling its bellyful away. She had meant to go back in and make herself a mug of tea, but the intention got lost as her hands became shunt to her brain. Whenever she found herself feeling tense or worried she had a habit of sitting down and sliding her hands forwards and backwards on the arms of her chair, and now that that voice had come back to niggle at her, her hands got going at their toing and froing.

Plying their trade now, the fingers feeling for every whorl and grain, those hands soothed the old woman until her senses silenced and her body snapped slump. Soon a dribble slowly slithered from her loose lips and slid down onto her bib, the gunsmith's shape settling eventually in a puddle near her heart. Looked at from a faraway focus the spittle glistened, almost resembling a gemstone, but on close inspection her slightly open mouth spoiled the image with its slobbering.

Ransomed and breathing in slow tempo, her reflexes jumped to the sudden racket as the clock chimed in the kitchen. With an effort she stood up and, shuddering, tried to shake off her fatigue. Making her way she sloothered her steps along, and with one eye on the boiling kettle she fetched the teapot from its place on the seat of the dresser.

Pouring some boiling water into the pot, she tempered it before spilling its ablutions down the sink. Her movements almost automatic, she acted the part without even thinking. Two scoops of tea she tossed into the pot. Boiling water she heeled in on top. Hollow it sounded, the lid slapping down. Past caring, she set the tea to brew. A slice of soda bread to accompany the tea turned out too thick, but her hand didn't heed it as the butter was added. The mug was next. Hanging on show on a hook on the dresser it was, its public face showing a pink cabbage-rose. Over her feet wandered to fetch it, down on the table she set it.

Fetching the pot now, she filled the mug up as far as the little gold blob – the blob was but a speck of gold dropped there in the making, but now that blemish acted as a blessing. Words not necessary, 'thus far and no further' it suggested.

Fetching milk, she used it to stain the tea. Just a *braoneen*, thin-like in its pouring. Sugar to sweeten the brew, the wanton brew, two teaspoonsful stirred in in an absentminded swirl. And then just a few steps more as with the mug in one hand, bread in the other, she slackened down into her chair under the plain man's sky. But as she attacked the snack her hands began a game of chance. The one with the tea lorded it over the one with the bread, one plying its wound, the other stuck in her field of sense.

Planting her empty mug down upon the tiles she felt suddenly chilly. The porch had cooled and the tiles now felt uncomfortably crude. She pulled her socks back on – she evidently didn't need the wellingtons, but for now she was too lazy to get up and fetch her slippers.

Nearby lay the dog. He had the two crusts for his bother. His mistress, alert now, talked to him, praising him as befitted his deserts. 'Musha, you've a lot to learn yet ya bowdawn, ya going at their heads. Would you listen when I shouted, oh! no! You were too hellbent on your job.' She talked her secret lingo to Rover, and the dog wagged his tail, thinking he was being praised.

# CHAPTER 4

Minnie sat on in her chair until the slanting sun fettered her spirit, the subtlety banking her stolen years into a bunch of ramshackle lines. Nimble thoughts came still to strand her brain in feats of rescue. This stringed day held her senses together, and now sitting here her long-agos careered around her porch. High on a stepladder she put herself again to yearn for him, her hero. 'Musha-then, I was knackered,' she thought 'the night when Peter fell for me and me for him.' Her blue eyes looked out now between the geraniums at the orange light glancing off the apple trees in the orchard, but though her gaze glided over the scene her mind didn't register it, for it was unveiling a thumb-sized wink of strabismus.

Nine times at least did she doze off while her brain attempted to reconstruct the night of the occult. The sound of his steps beat solemn as they straddled her Nibelung of the five fields. He was the lad who inherited the homestead and land from his old uncle, and he strung his neighbours along when they quizzed him as to how he could be building such a fine new house and he so young.

His secret treasure was saved by the arthritic man who lived in the long thatched house down at the end of the boreen, the man almost curled up by crippling disease. He determined that his life would not be for nothing, so with his nephew in mind he plagued for the future, for he believed that his brother's son would do for him where he was himself denied.

Brendan O'Brien, that solitary, windswept man, was in his prime cheated out of the thing he most loved when his attractive girl was stolen from him by the enemy in pink, the *mí-ádh*. She survived but seven months from the day when the fever first struck to the day when she struggled no more. He never got over his loss; her burning cheeks and blood-plied lips stayed in his mind forever. He was in the planning stage of marriage when the tuberculosis first struck; he had bought the marriage bed, brought it home mattress one day, bed-ends and frame the next. He had such plans for him and her, but the haggard was robbed on him, the bride-to-be stolen by the cough. In death his Lily became as strumpet to his loneliness and though he did eventually use the bed frame he somehow could never bring himself to sleep upon the good, blue-striped mattress. By day he kept himself busy and bothered, but at night he lay in his half-caste bed, his mind tortured by silly dreams. Silly though they were, they nevertheless helped him as he watched the years steal up the boreen, and when he thought of his place being left without chick or child he started to winkle a sovereign from his earnings and salt it away. 'That's for him,' he'd say, 'Peadarín'll need that.'

The day was well gone, the world and his wife were, at this time, out and about their night-time business, but down in the glass porch where Minnie O'Brien sat, whole days, whole nights, whole worlds and their whole wives might as well not exist. For the old reliant here had, just a little while ago, heard a sound of footsteps as, marching Himmler-like, they foot-soldiered through her dreams.

Those long-ago, noisy steps belonged to an autumn evening in Drumhollow. Minnie Humphrey was working late in her father's huckster's shop, storing away all of the accoutrements belonging to her day in front of the customers. The doorbell dingled the arrival of a latecomer. A voice said 'Nice evening, Jack.'

Down along the boarded floor the footsteps nail-booted. She, sweeping her hands back across her hair, stood there waiting for them to come through the small Gothic archway which led into her mostly dark and shadowy glory-hole.

The lamp tagged to the wall was still lit and behind its flame plaqued a round, fluted, silver disc which refracted its silent lesson down and around the girl standing behind the counter. The counter itself was meant to front a tall, strapping fellow, but in Minnie's case it reached almost up to her breasts.

In a medley of stalactites the things of her shop hung from the boarded ceiling, all types of gadgets swinging their legs in watchfulness. The customer who strode through the archway glanced, as he often had before, at the girl standing waiting. He ducked this way and that for fear his head might crack against the utensils which sagged from separate cup hooks in the ceiling. Saucepans, frying pans, tin mugs, tundishes, heads for brushes, even two burdizzos hung there and, as though their meaning might be lost upon the customers, a flitch of bacon hung there beside them.

Although natural to the devotees of this glory-hole, the customers had also to be careful of where they put their feet, for the floor space was chock-a-block with bags and sacks, their turned-back collars revealing their honest guts. The established shelves placed from floor to ceiling were stothered with all kinds of things – anything which could turn a penny was housed there, just waiting for the need to arise.

Mimicking her father, Minnie's normal way was to set about chatting her customers into parting with their money. Having served her time with him, she would now almost try to sell gunsmoke rather than miss a sale.

'Musha, 'twas only a mousetrap he wanted, and me poor girl thinking he'd buy half the shop,' she laughed now as she tried to concoct the drama of that night, that nervous night when for all the world like the Statue of Liberty she stood right up on the topmost step of the folding, wooden stepladder. She was almost in shadow up there, but she could look down and size up her chimera below. He was the young man who was building the house out the road, that she knew, but suddenly her legs felt weak up there, for this handsome fellow had just now said something strange.

15

Their conversation had to do with the mouse coming in for the winter, dreaming of her nest, maybe, her vermin children'd have lots of shavings in which to hide when her path up the stairs was blocked by big bootcaps. The little mouse skedaddled but now, he, big bulldog, had reason to come here to Humphreys, boasting his glad-ragged house for this girl to hear. Her voice coming from up there near the ceiling told him that 'Nuala Lynam, you know Johnny's daughter, from there near the bridge on the road to Huntstown, was in here and talking about your new house. She climbed up on the high bank on the bend near your boreen so that she could get a good look down. She thought it was beautiful, the most beautiful new house for miles and miles.'

But the face looking up at her had changed somewhat, something was wrong. His expression had hardened and his eyes seemed almost cruel. His voice too seemed different; he spoke almost through his teeth. 'Nuala Lynam,' he said 'can look all she wants from the road, but from the inside she'll never look out. Now if it was a girl say like you, Minnie Humphrey,' and now his big plámásing smile was back on, 'the door would be flung wide open. Not that there is a door just yet,' he laughed 'but when there is,' and now he whispered, 'it'll be open wide if you should take it in your pretty head to come down to see a fellow's house.'

'As God is my judge I didn't say I would or I wouldn't, but the box with the word "mousetraps" written in my father's black letters thought I had the jitters for try as I could to steady my hand, sorra steady would it. Yes indeedy me, the box saved the day, 'cause when I turned around again his usual grin was back where it seemed right and though I said "catch" he missed the mousetrap I threw to him. Into a bag of bran it fell, and while he was fetching it I backed down, the floor never more welcome. I always since had a soft spot for a mouse.' She said the words so that her mind could listen and attire the image with what came next. 'Indeed'nd I knew only too well that he'd be back first thing Monday morning.' She smiled now and told herself to think of standing there several steps above him, and he looking up, sort of lost for words. 'A mousetrap, and it caught me a man and him a wife, that's why when he'd come stormin' in to give out about the "the damn mice eating the sacks, the corn all spilling out", I'd pacify him, get out the packing needle and mend the holes and then it'd all blow over. The mice knew I was beholden to them. And sure it was the least I could do for them.'

Thumb-working the past into the porch her feet started to cool down in company with the tiles. But she had ground still to cover, her husband only now had come back to gee her up. "Member the dress that night was the one I made myself from the heliotrope sparva, it looked just blue in the dim shop light but when the sun shone on it, musha wouldn't it come up almost mauve. Yes indeed, the fella fell for me that night and when I got to bed if I didn't kick m'heels in the air and tell the statue of Our Lady in the window nook that "I think I've met the father of my children, no, no thinking, I know I have."'

'After that I didn't care what my father felt about having to pay me. I just lived for the evening time when Peter'd call to walk me out. There he'd be all spick and span, the sawdust and the stains all done away with. The other girls had their caps set at him, but they were wasting their time 'cause him and me were, as they say, an item.'

'Aye indeed the mousetrap caught me a good man, a good honest man. He could be surly the odd time. The boots had to be ready for him going to town. "Shine them well" he'd say. Where would you be with the collars, I ask you, the stiff ones, 'member three to a shirt, then they softened a bit, the makers got sense, Lord I hated the starching and ironing. But then he looked so well. Listen though, poor little Sheila never knew how much he thought of her, the big fuss he'd make of her job on his boots. 'Member how she used spit on the leather, she swore it'd bring up the shine.

Sheila was his gem of the three. Ah! he was the broken man the day the bus pulled off from the gate, she off to be a nurse. 'She'll be able to nurse us if we ever get sick,' he'd say, and he barely hangin' on the best of times. Ah! but we had the good times too. Work was never that bad, the company the two of us were to each other at the turf or corn, hay or spuds, mangolds or turnips . . .' And now her old face broke into a smile: 'Turnips,' she said. 'Aye indeed, no wonder I'm here keepin' the smoke going up the chimney.'

It was late now, too late to be fumbling for the past, so heating some milk she fetched a biscuit, and soon that long-ago night stopped breathing for Minnie Humphrey-that-was.

## CHAPTER 5

Minnie Humphrey was the only child of Jack and Sally Humphrey. Her father had come into the village a stranger to the locality, but before the first six months of their married life had passed he had his name, curlicues and all, up over the door of the draper's shop. Sally, his wife, had been a Butler, the one to whom the family shop had come down, but when she fell in love with her haughty Dublin man she found herself giving in quite easily to the transfer of ownership. Her husband had only a small amount of money to invest, but with it he refurbished the shop and then, sin of sins, he built a lean-to on the back of the original house. Clothes had always been the things sold in Butler's shop, but now he wished to have the back broken through and a catchpenny cave built there. Never did an amount of money reap such rewards. Now his long counter ran its way, but down at its end was a Gothic archway, and when a customer needed something besides clothes all they had to do was walk through into Jack Humphrey's den of devices.

It was at the gymkhana in Archerstown that Jack Humphrey met Sally Butler. Sally had travelled to it by brake, only one of three women along with a party of thirteen men. She felt every mile of the journey, the sodden journey, for the eastern sky had hidden its indifference until the brake had gone past the point of no return.

When the rain did come it came ploughing through the clouds, thunderous it sounded on her big black umbrella. There she sat cutchying, her cousin, Tom, seated beside her, their heads and shoulders dry, their knees and feet scutched by the slanting rain.

As the brake approached Archerstown a watery sun broke through over Kilskeer, henpicking whether to stay or go, but the longer it hesitated the braver it became, the humble load of humanity helping it to hang under the humping sky.

The hungry, rambling road conquered, the group plied towards the field of vincibles, their hurry to get in hustling them along. 'We'll meet up again,' the man told his cousin, 'after the fifth. Remember, Sally, there's four races and a consolation one, and I'll be on the look-out for you near the tent.'

The thought of being alone was the very thing Sally needed, for her memory of her last trip here tormented her today. She remembered standing watching her father buy the doll for her, the victim doll, the one with the blessed dimpled smile, the creamy lace dress, the long black ringlets, her face set under a blunt fringe. She could see her even now, housed in a standing pose inside a cardboard box, a sheet of cellophane stretched taut before her. 'There now Sally,' her father said 'whenever you need a friend she'll be there to play with, so mind you don't drop her or she'll break like an egg.' She smiled a candid smile now, for his parable was indeed later proven, but the dress, the French lace dress, she still had kept as a memento of a benign man.

'It'll take two hours at the very least,' she reckoned as she thought about the running of the four races and the consolation one for the losers. They were, she surmised, in the process of starting that first one, judging by the excitement. Her interest, though, was in retracing the steps of her father, for it was the field's place of chancers with their stalls and see-nots which beckoned her today.

'For corns, bunions, calluses and chilblains, three drops of Rattlesnake Oil on toes last thing at night,' screamed the long-haired Indian. 'I'm a Chocktaw,' he boasted 'and in here I house my rattlesnakes.' The thing of the snakes was an old battered suitcase, and by times he startled his audience by pretending there was going to be a stampede of serpents from its old, worn frame. Sally, standing on the edge of the crowd, watched as he worked in a frenzy, trying to hold folks' attention, calling by times on his plant to act as guinea-pig to his cure. 'Do you have trouble with your feet?' was his opening, and there before their own eyes his circle of gawkers watched as he rubbed in the mandatory three drops through the scarified leather of his stooge's boots. 'Do you feel it working?' he'd enquire, but the miraculous cure was self-evident, the hobbling man now tiptoed and danced around in relief.

Now was his Rattlesnake Oil newly pressed: 'Only a ha' penny a bottle, will you buy sir?' His humanity never defeated, his wrinkled brown face smiled in dalliance as he tried and tried again. Now Sally joined in. Silently she egged him on as he became a gymnast cavorting around his imprisoned rattlers. His was an ancient race, he boasted. 'My Big Chief, Chief Wrinkle-Me, him one hundred and twenty-nine, can do the same as me and why, because of my Rattlesnake Oil.' Pleading as was his wont, the Indian was still claiming cures, but now her interest was waning so Sally stumbled on towards the next distraction.

The Cheapjohn was standing in front of his Aladdin's Cave, his stall built in terracing, each shelf a granary of geegaws. Cheek by jowl they stood, each thing hiding a secret price tag, nobody to say yea or nay to a bid, the genie himself absolute in his power. Sally stood shoulder to shoulder with the onlookers, her eyes running from one thing to another. In a humdrum box piled children's rubber balls, scarlet ones marbled in shades of blues and yellows.

Beside them stood fractious dolls, their beautiful dresses frilled and flounced, the gaze in their eyes fixed in resignation. Further along grouped other childish things: skipping ropes, mouth organs, spinning tops, trains, marbles, yo-yos, jew's harps and storybooks. There too the things of adults, country folks' needs – plates and cups, mugs and jugs, pots and pig rings, pliers and rope, there they sat, their guarantee their only limbs. But up on the topmost shelf, out of reach, this man set out his few things of value, devious things struck in gold or silver, dewy pearl or garish stone, things for folks' adornment, things held, hoult for hoult, until bargains were struck. Sally knew the thinking behind the out-of-reach-ness of his hoard, but it wasn't any of those trinkets which caught her imagination. Her heart was captured by the only thing out of kilter up there, the burnished violin, its belly just whining for her touch. It hung by its scroll from a no-longer young nail, and tied to its d-peg its bow hung dead beside it. She heard her nested tunes caterwauling for expression. Nobody was aware of her longing, nobody could feel her feverish touch as with her gaze she fondled that beautiful fiddle. 'How much for the violin?' she could hear herself asking, but outwardly a numb gunfire had failed to go off.

She was caught off guard though, for suddenly all hell broke loose when, with a rusty schoolbell in his lollypop grip, the Cheapjohn made thunder peal under the Archerstown sky, his din wilfully proclaiming that, like it or not, he had desperation to sell.

Sally smiled when she saw the first thing being held up for selling. No catchpenny this, the china chamberpot was gold-rimmed, a lily design upon it both inside and out. His fingertips balanced it and then spun it around, his voice like satin suggesting the comfort of a goes-under. 'Imagine, ladies, the cold frosty nights ahead' and now he winked in wickedness – 'but you won't feel the bite o'the night, the thing'll be there under the bed.' He now lined up his price only to reduce it, he coaxed for a bid and reduced again, he sighed in trepidation as he reached a giveaway figure but he was wrong, his weather eye watching the woman in black, for it was the wiry-haired man with the gaunt face who finally gave the nod, walking away then, the purchase parcelled up in a Dracula-shaped package.

Sally Butler glanced after the man with the chamberpot but nothing much stirred in her mind. Like him, she too wished to walk away, her fiddle humpbacked in her grasp. Like it or not the hawker, encouraged by getting shut of the chamberpot, was now rabbiting on about his next novelty. 'It'll shave any hog, dog or divil and after that a dragoon soldier,' he hollered, holding aloft his cut-throat razor. A spot of sunlight bounced off its steel blade and coursed from one face to another, his risen voice following it as he begged for a bid. He had to knock down his price, down until he reached panicking-god's money, and it was only then that the man in the cloth cap dug his fingers into his waistcoat pocket and without saying anything pressed his coppers into the city-slicker's palm. And so it wended its way, this Cheapjohn's pilgrimage, novelty followed pig rings, novelty followed plates, hands mesmerising his public, item in chase after item, his higgledy-piggledy items growing gradually thinner on his shelves.

Past endurance, Sally felt green in the face, for however long she waited the burnished thing never got an airing. Umpteen tunes had she already played upon it, an accompaniment to the Cheapjohn's every soldier, but now her ears began to heed another sound, the hum of it coming towards her from an underbelly somewhere away to her right.

As though gabbled mantras led her she walked along, her skirt growing damper from the *tráithníns* beating against it and her boots glistening in the wet grass. Nearer they brought her to the stall where an angry monkey heard nothing which was pleasing to him. Perched on his owner's shoulder the black monkey with the attitude sat, his neck in a hard leather minister, jabbering on in the only voice he had. The player was thin as a lath; his hair plaited down his back served as a ladder to the little monkey and the homburg on his head hid his old bald spot from the animal's sharp nails. Occasionally the little creature lunged at his strict hero, no human him, and then the hero, funny in the extreme, humpty-dumpty threatened him the role zealot. Now that the puny monkey was silenced the bully strutted his stuff as lining up his playground he attempted to draw his crowd. 'Come and have a go with your old pal Joe!' he hollered. 'Your mother won't know and I won't tell her.'

Standing on the rim of his circle of countryfolk, Sally watched the jester at play. Nearby he had set up his blackboard on a tripod and in white chalk had listed the lucky numbers for his next draw. Not satisfied with his congregation, he set about using the monkey as bait. 'Look't-the-monkey, look't-the-monkey,' he shouted, but the capuchin monkey only grimaced. Sally walked closer and now she could see what the hullabaloo was all about. In a small, plaid tin box the wheeler-dealer kept his tickets, each one rolled tight as tuppence, nothing to be seen, like quills packed in honeycomb mimicry. Swaying on his perch the monkey watched the tickets being sold, but though Sally bought three sets of tickets the gain belonged to the God-damned monkey and his manservant.

Embarrassment fanned her face as she pushed her way through the human chain dreading still around the wheeler-dealer. 'You've been taken for a montha, Sally Butler,' she scolded. 'Three times you got the cod, no wonder the monkey was jibbering.' Her disgust with herself was shortlived, though, for as she approached a blue-green tent she grew interested in the man standing in front of it, his brown shiny boots sturdy on top of an upturned butter box.

This hawker was dressed like a toff, hand holding a fat cigar, one gold tooth to be glimpsed behind his clipped moustache. He wore his bowler tilted at a rakish slant, and he shouted out his parable in an accent foreign to Sally's ears. 'New boots, old boots, strong boots, fine boots, boots for the laeedies, childreen's boots,' he sang, then slightly changing gear he steered ahead, logging his range of new and old clothes. Listening to his stylishly exaggerated voice Sally smiled as she tried hulling it in local jargon. It was, she noticed, mostly women who manhandled his rails of clothes, quietly fingering his fabrics and touching his silks and chiffons. 'If only he could see the few duds in my shop,' she thought, but the truth was she didn't see a market in Drumhollow for his finery.

As she moved away from the wheedling sellers' stalls she was chivvied again by the starter's pistol for the fourth race. Nervous now, she knew she should be heading back the way towards the tent inside the gate, but not able to forego the remaining attractions she decided to get a spurt on to the three-card trickster, the nearest now for evidence. At his table stood a small, lean man with a wooden leg. He had placed his bet on a card and stood waiting the outcome of the fall guy's gonorrhoea. Though a stranger to her, the small man, she felt, needed somebody at his elbow, somebody to stand by him. She was of no great good to him though, for when the actual cards were sleight-of-hand shuffled they fell face up and the little man's bet had bought no freedom for him, no Gunther's drim hunch.

Moving along again, Sally worked her way alongside the next few wags, where they were trying out their wiles on the local attaboys. She stopped soon again to marvel at the dexterity of a juggler who, disporting his legerdemain for those innocents looking on, windcharger-like lustred the air with highflying stars glinting off the silver discs which he sent soaring after each other into the high sky.

Where the trick o' the loop worked his ottava-rima, the bystanders and Sally were fooled as, time after time, the wizened old man smiled in *soi-disant* innocence as he unfolded the deception within his coiled leather belt. Sometimes he allowed fellows a free jab at the belt, the result rigged, but once money changed hands the gambler found to his cost that when the coiled belt was unwound it only revealed that the hand holding the jabber had been deceived.

There was but one more distraction worthy of note left in the triangle yet to be inspected. It was a name which caught Sally's attention. GYPSY JUNO it read. Two words waiting to trap a single person and a fortune teller inside a booth. The booth itself was painted bright yellow, and around its entrance was a breadline of flowers romancing with each other. Hanging down in the doorway itself dangled long strings of multi-coloured glass beads, and staring out from behind them was a funereal, kooky thing. Sally was tempted to go into the woman's web to have her humility strewn before her in this stranger's droll speech, but her violin suddenly played across her hearing, the vibrations of it no different from the cry of a rabbit in a snare.

'Of course it's still there,' she said to herself as, her visits to the other stalls behind her, Sally again approached the one where the fiddle feared sale at all. The sharp hawker immediately spotted her but continued his conversation with a dapper, dark-bearded man. After a short delay he sought her eyes and reacting to her enquiring gaze he said something to the man and came towards her. 'Can I show the nice lady something?' he enquired, and now she had to come clean and ask the price. 'How much do you want for the little fiddle?' her voice said out loud the question disporting all day, but the man of the stall knew his business better than to tell her. Stretching away up to the place where it hung he lifted the fiddle off the nail, almost rupturing himself, and turning towards her he stressed the violin into her hands. Her term of diminution not wasted on him, the Cheapjohn set about plying her with his usual huff and puff. 'Isn't it a beauty,' he said. 'Last one I've left, last of a box, came from Italy, sold like hot buns. What does madam think of it?'

'How much?' She was curt this time. He was so hoping to be shut of the fiddle that his price was honest when he said 'For you, one shilling.' He almost pleaded with her to buy it, for no one had ever before even asked its price, not ever, not since he himself bought it at the bazaar in Brighton.

The bargain settled at sixpence left Sally breathless, and though she tried to speak she couldn't, for now she was in a trance, the warm smell of the violin's belly drifting up her nostrils, the bow flexing in her hand, and her groin tightening in pure pleasure.

Sally's step was sweet as she set out to meet up again with her cousin. The journey on the brake all the way to Archerstown had not been for nothing. She now carried in her hand the black violin case, the fiddle inside: just like a body in a coffin it snuggled, its bow hiding in there with it. Nesting in her memory was a reservoir of music, tunes and airs which she had learnt from her father. Now she could hear that music as she held by its handle this violin case, *her* case, *her* fiddle, *her* hand, her — a single and singular old maid carrying a Stradivarius.

The fiddle now lay between her feet, its narrow end sticking out from underneath her full skirt. She and her cousin were having their snack — tea and a dry cheese sandwich. The tent was crowded, the fresh air a flyblown affair; nothing rose towards the supports of the marquee but smoke, steam, and bedfellows' breath. Tom was miserable, hadn't had a crumb of luck, four races and nothing either on the fifth, even the consolation went by the boards and he wouldn't mind but he knew the winner well, had watched her doing all the spring ploughing for her owner and here today her spavined feet threw clods as she won her race pulling up.

This wasn't the time to be boasting about her bargain, so there Sally stood munching her curled-up bread. The crowd strafed her and Tom as, either making their way out or elbowing to get in, they sometimes pushed against them. The ruddy-faced man apologised as he accidentally brushed against Tom's arm for the hot tea splashing from the full mug almost shot towards his cousin standing there, her mind miles away. She looked only briefly at this awkward neighbour as he stood in beside Tom, but through the massed crowd brushed another man, the dapper, bearded one whom she had noticed a very short time before. They, the two men, got into conversation with her cousin. She couldn't quite catch what they discussed but, pleased to have her space to herself, she stood at her ease while staccato-like crumbs from her bread dropped towards her fiddle.

She almost jumped when Tom spoke. 'Sally, I'd like you to meet Willie and Jack Humphrey,' he said. 'You know, Willie that runs the barge from Dublin.' The two strangers stepped slightly forward, the red-faced man saying that he was pleased to make her acquaintance. His brother, though, just lifted his hat and studied her with a full brown stare. Her smile diffident, she bowed to them both, noticing only the tall one's trim appearance. He had a curly brown beard tinged with grey, and two deep-set studious eyes. Watchful, that was her tag for him. Ignoring her then, the pair turned again to her cousin and took up their conversation. Just the odd time did she glance past Tom's shoulder, the thing which was now a source of fascination the big Adam's apple as it rode up and down the tall one's neck. It reminded her of her old yo-yo, that is the odd time when she could get it to rise and fall at the flick of her hand.

## CHAPTER 6

Three months had slipped on before the name Jack Humphrey was mentioned again, the name forged that day in Archerstown now strolled out in guarded lightness by the cousin Tom Browne. He glowed in acting as go-between, thinking he had found a husband for his solitary cousin.

The name of his Man Friday was barely recognisable to the girl in the clothes shop. Her memory had but dimly stored an image of this long-in-the-tooth man with nice eyes and a big, busy Adam's apple. That was all she remembered of him, for the man winding his way through the crowded tent had held no interest for her, for *she* had just joined an orchestra, the string section certainly nurturing itself as it housed its bomb in the case between her feet.

27

Yes, three months had slipped by since Sally had bought her fiddle, three months of nights when, her shop door closed for the day, she returned to her back kitchen to gremlin her tunes on her dying fiddle. Her chin resting on its black axle, she side-eyed at the strings; accounting for her bow's stroking she vibrated her nuances at the dead of night. Tunes which her father once played strolled now from her fumigation, she the only one left to give expression to his musical legacy. Deaf to outside sounds she, greedy for the hunt, fickled her music there on her new violin. She was rendering 'The Coulin', the beautiful melody which her father last played when, like a warning, a loud knocking started on her front door. Her bow finished in mid-air, the fright thieving it of its twang. Frantic to go on she yet had to leave her fiddle aside. The tune was now breached, her line of memory snapped.

'He wants to marry you.' The words fondled by her cousin's tongue sharded into her whole being. Her Sunday was wracked the nocturnal night. 'The Coulin' discarded but a few moments ago, hung now like dust particles in the room. Her dress became fevered tight to her figure, for she had become conscious of herself, of her age. She was thirty-five years old, an old maid in her neighbours' eyes. Now behold and be-damned if there wasn't a man wanting to know her hidey-hole, wanting to be a father to her children, now her whole stultifying life was going to be burst wide open to change, even to wonderment.

The marriage was fixed that night, the marriage which her head never conceived of nor her heart ever pleaded for. Matched by their go-between, the girl agreed to become wife to the man from the gymkhana at Archerstown. Love was never mentioned, never heard of, but her mind was nonetheless humming the street sound when she went to bed that night.

Hours, it had taken, to make the match. Long hours of talking before Tom Browne's cousin agreed to marry the man, Jack Humphrey, the man whom she had met only once before and whom she best remembered for his busy Adam's apple.

# CHAPTER 7

Drumhollow, head in the sand, kept its back to the sun all day long, but over on Humphrey's side the old houses bunched there squinting and seeking every gram of light which evidenced from the sky. The village consisted of a single street, a great burly nothingness of a street: the world passed through it without bothering to give it a glance. To the inhabitants themselves, though, the village was a metropolis. There each day it breathed in silent planning, breathing and gasping as though a length of purposeful wire kept the houses tied together in a single strand of woes and wishes. Fifteen houses in all stood there on that sunny side, fifteen, the middle one the clothes shop. Humphrey was the name roosting over the door, Humphrey where the villagers had ever before read Butler's.

The shop window beneath the name 'Humphrey' was now the window on Jack Humphrey's world. Across it ran a half curtain. In the window and facing his public, Jack displayed his goods, but inside the old man himself stood. Planked there all day long, his two brown eyebrows awned over his inquisitive eyes, as he watched and remembered everything and everyone that passed. If only he could have minded his own business he might have eventually found favour with his neighbours, but no, his gaze graced the cross-curtain from early morn until closing time at night. To a soul the locals dreaded his watching presence, the good-boys referring to his wiry visage as resembling 'a boiled shite in a huckster's window'.

The birth of their baby girl helped to soften the reaction of the locals to this cuckoo in their village: now that he had an offspring he had won his place among them. As much for Sally's sake as for his own they, the locals, shook his hand and wished him and his family well. 'Ah! she's the dead stamp of her mother,' the experts said, 'a Butler through and through.' Jack had to agree with their findings. Laughing it off, he chortled as he boasted that 'the next little fella'll have to be like me'.

It was at the dead of night the name came to Sally, the name which would grace her baby girl. The night was under the impression that something sad had occurred, for the skies had opened and torrential rain was battering down on the roof overhead. The baby was sound asleep in the little square room next door, to the front of the house and directly over the shop. Sally lay winding her clock of names, family names, saints' names, Irish names, but nothing sounded right, every name got stuck in her mud, every one of them thumbstuck until she mentioned MINNIE. She said the name so often that she glued it in her soul. Minnie would be the word to which this little girl would answer, it would be the word which from here on she'd murmur into her baby's head, into that lovely little smelly well sited in her skull. This name would always sound like magic. She said it again. 'Minnie, Minnie Humphrey, Jack and Sally Humphrey's daughter, Minnie.' Minnie, that was the name which her mind heaved up out of its haggard of history.

Before she could tell her husband of her brainwave she had to wait the notional hours till he woke up. In the meantime though, her mind was busy being grateful. Lined up beside her he lay, his face stunted by disappointment; he had wished for a boy child while she but wished for a live one. Now was her hour for reflection, for this, the moment of her mining a name for her baby, was the very same hour when her own baby sister was buried by men in unconsecrated ground, a gull-crying ground, a *cillín*, where in the space of time between dark and dawn the angels wept in mourning as the hungry ground golloped up in insulting ignominy the unbaptised baby of her own mother's sacred womb.

But the day of the new baby's christening was a dismal affair. Two sponsors stood for her; the postmistress would be her godmother, and her uncle, the bargeman, would be her godfather. Neither of them wanted to do this job, but when they were approached neither of them had the gall to refuse Sally.

The moment of the baby's christening was drab and brackled by her screams of attrition. Her mouth open to the elements, she wailed in protest. Fr Murphy, though, had his job to do, so ignoring her cranky behaviour he baptised her with the tools of the sacrament. Praying, he tested her with water, salt and spittle but it was only when he set her name in among the words of Latin that she suddenly clammed shut. Not another sound came from her as she set to gaze towards the candle flame. 'Minnie, Vis baptizari?' asked the priest. 'Vola,' the voiced stamp registered. Nine attitudes away waited Minnie's birth-mother. Her dreamchild was being christened in the place of men but she could not be present there, for she had seven times sinned in her dedication to her role and now awaited churching before she could again step into the holy church, the sterile church, the sinless church of savage bent.

# CHAPTER 8

Same room, same window tumbling spots of pink and blue, heralding a martyrdom by kindred-crying that this was her very last morning in her bedroom beneath the old slates, sitting just above the shop. Minnie had nested here for eighteen years, years when she played drag to her father's disappointment. For him the rot set in the very night she was born. His hopes that night were shattered, for he had convinced himself that the child his wife was carrying was going to be a boy, a son and heir to his newly acquired fun palace. This very idea was at the root of his every move, from lifting his hat to the solitary girl in the gymkhana to the made match and then the eventual marriage. The few quid he held in his hand enabled him to build on the lean-to to the house, and his courtship of his bride in those early months of marriage won her over to his idea of her changing her right of ownership to accommodate his name over the shop door. Now all that was needed was that this healthy woman would bear him a boy child. He had himself so convinced that when he stood gazing his frameworked ideas out over the racket in his shop window he would listen to himself as he mouthed the words 'Humphrey & Son'.

Now Minnie's days of neglect were over, her hulked days under the light from the wall lamp. She would never again weigh out those long rashers of bacon on the weighing scales, the rashers which she had cut on the red bacon slicer. Never again would she stand there white in the light, white from fatigue, from standing all those long hours in her father's glory-hole.

While she had barely any regrets about leaving her slave-driver father, the matter of leaving her mother's house brought tears gushing this very last morning, for out of a quagmire her mother had jonquiled the hubbub of normal living. Lonely though their set-up, her mother had seen to it that the little girl she brought into this world would know fun and love in some measure. And so when each birthday she brought Minnie to town, the day, wretched to start off with, would become marvellous when they set foot outside Drumhollow. Their ritual, though simple, was thought about and planned to the smallest detail. The daughter could never know how her mother gathered money for days such as these, she was never witness to the hiding place – a tear in the stiff paper backing of the picture of the Sacred Heart. Each time Sally refilled the lamp with oil was a chance to slip her siphoned pound note into her bank: each time she relit the wick and replaced the red globe saw the flame bend towards her, the full-blooded red colour echoing her sacrifice. That, then, was how her mother robbed Peter to pay Paul, and every so often she removed her hoard and lodged the money in her old family's account in Huntstown bank. Nothing changed on the ledger page but the surname, and when his old customer swore the manager to secrecy he agreed for old time's sake.

There was another day when mother and daughter swung from the beams of normality, always on a Thursday – the day when Jack Humphrey went to Huntstown and finished up in the shebeen on the way home. Then could they find time for their own devices, for they both loved the violin, the music lending strands of karma to their existence. Sally taught Minnie everything she had garnered from her own father, but she couldn't help noticing that her girl had a sense of tone which only the gods could teach.

But Thursdays and their music would never dream again, never again would the two women drown their sorrows in sirens of distress. Now her world would be somehow different, for this May morning was her last time to wonder here beneath the eaves.

The set of blue and pink curtains which she herself had made still languished the morning through, for now the glory-sun had risen early and was attempting to sneak in through their spotted sparva to kiss this Vestal a lobotomising kiss, the better to prepare her for the marriage ahead.

Minnie lay looking around her four-square cell, looking at the rig-out which she would wear for her marriage. The bridal suit hung on its hanger from the end of her wardrobe, a navy blue suit headstrong in its need for flattering relief. Now her eyes drifted towards her hat on the dressing table, her white hat, the thing which would tango-dance her towards the way of women. Sitting beside the hat was the item of luxury this Wednesday morning, the white orchid, the wold-fresh flower, the one newly arrived from Knowles. In an eggcupful of water it bathed its stem so that come ceremony time its lip would be pouched, its spirit dewy. Her missal with the mother-of-pearl cover lay waiting on the table beside her bed, its title forged in gold lettering, its gilt-edged pages just waiting to be disturbed. Her mother's drab suitcase sat on a chair, its lid flapping open. Watching, it waited to see if she needed anything from inside its old carcass. Viewing her Pandar-time, the bride-to-be gloated to herself before running through the morning's routine. Last night she had had her bath in the galvanised tub, her special soap used to lather every nook and cranny of her lithe body. She had washed her hair as well, and now the curls and ringlets scattered on her pillow. Her head though, ached this morning, the fast before Mass denying her even the relief of her morning cup of tea.

A knock on the floor beneath her bed made her jump with fright, but still she lay on in her virgin's palace. A dream which she had last night was back now to tease her. Yes, she could see him again, the bearded giant traipsing through fields, his eyes stuck upon the balls which he tossed into the air. Five balls in all she counted, four black and one pink. Up they went and down they fell, but the giant soon had them travelling so fast that she could see only a blur of black. The giant's face faded and drew near: far away it resembled that of her father, but each time it came close up the features dolloped her in drops of muddy syrup. The sticky syrup tasted sweet when she licked her upper lip, but then the sweetness turned rancid, the ugliness almost filling the wok in her young tongue. She was lying there wondering through her dream when the broom handle this time knocked agitatedly against the floor. She leaned out of her bed and with the heel of her new shoe knocked in reply a rat-tat-tat which said I'm awake and coming. But still it took some moments longer before her mother heard her drawing the chamber pot out from underneath her bed.

Out of bed she set about her toilet. Lifting the ewer she poured a big swoosh of water into the basin; now lifting the icy-cold water, she reasoned it into her smart pain, the chill easing her forehead for the bare moment. The toothbrush dipped now in soot and then salt, she polished her smile in readiness for her man. Looking into the mirror, she sized up her appearance before deciding to run downstairs to check out her parents' feelings.

When she ran into the kitchen she found an arresting quietness there. Her father stood with his back to the fire, his mouth set in a straight line. 'Have you everything in order, girl?' he asked, as though it was a business-as-usual day.

'Yeah,' she answered, 'everything's ready, where's Mam?'

'Oh, she's in there in the room,' he said, 'going over that table for the thousandth time, you'd swear the King of England was coming to breakfast with us.' Minnie didn't reply, didn't think that this was the time to debate such a topic.

The parlour looked resplendent, the white tablecloths uniting underneath two long common tables. The Butlers' best Royal Tara decked them. The yellow and white tulips, the ones which had accompanied the orchid on the train from Dublin, nestled together in a vase on the sideboard. A fire, not needed in May, stubbed its stride for now, knowing that it needed to be leppin' when the wedding party arrived for the feast. Decanters filled to just right stood beside the tulips, while over in one corner of the room the half-barrel waited, the porter which the men would slug long after the fledglings had flown.

'There's enough there to feed the five thousand,' Minnie said with a giggle.

'Aye,' replied her mother, 'and wait'll I place the wedding cake on its pillars. You know, love,' and now she smiled, 'this morning has been planned for almost since the day you were born. Nothing was too much trouble, all I wanted was to see you happy and married some day to a fellow who'd not turn out to be a glugger.'

Minnie didn't say anything, but gathering her mother in her baby arms she hugged the daylights out of her. Now it was that her raffish eye fell at her father's feet as he stood there framed in the doorway. His avoidance showed in his pleasant evidence. 'Come on, girl, you're going to be like all the women,' he scolded, but then almost at the last ditch he said 'Now amn't I going to give you the big send-off?' The words reminded him of his sacrifice. It was there in his inside pocket, the envelope, and in it the dowry for his daughter, the hard-won money, the stranded thing, now pressed against his left nipple. 'Get up there and get your things on,' he was ordering as she passed him by, but then just as though she were hinged to a sixpence she abruptly turned and kissed his hairy cheek.

Minnie was nervous when she entered her bedroom, so drawing back the curtains she flung open the window. Looking out into the clear sky she took a big deep breath of fresh air. The curtains, thinking that she was having doubts about her man, puckered themselves in preparation for a dance. They would do a polka-dot shimmy for her, a dance in which they would show how the self in woman is always sacrificed, always blood-let, always reneged on.

## CHAPTER 9

The guests were gathered, all thirteen of them. The two men of the nuptials were there in the front pew on the men's side; the mother of the bride had said her last cunning words to her daughter, and now sat on the women's side of the aisle and waited in loneliness for her beautiful daughter to arrive.

The clock in the sacristy had just struck eight. The altar boy had the candles lit. The tulips on the altar matched those on the sideboard at home. The sun shining through the window over the organ-loft crept ever so stealthily up through the church until, arriving at the white marble altar-rails, it set about bathing the whole sanctuary in a toying light.

Three minutes after the clock struck the father led his daughter towards her waiting man-of-war. There before the numb altar stone he left her, the gimleted girl of his groin; the tableau of Cana about to begin, he stood back and watched for his moment. The priest, the old breathless man who in his prime determinedly baptised the mewling baby girl and who later on frilled her tongue with her First Communion host, now stood again before her, this time to witness and bless this moment, the moment when, mouthing prayers, a man slipped his gold spancel in along and over the jungle-green hill of her young girl's ring finger.

Minnie Humphrey-that-was and her husband walked together down the aisle of the parish church and out into the startling air of the village of Drumhollow. The bridesmaid and best man led the rest of the guests in a trail after them. Hail-fellow-well-met that her husband proved, the bride now knew that with him at her side life would be golden indeed. Her husband, feeling her hand in the crook of his arm, now fanned himself in his own glory. He had discovered this beautiful girl hidden inside a glow-worm's cave and now today, here, he had her at his side, her face brimming in happiness and her full promise just a bus journey away.

The Humphreys' parlour was stuffed to the gills with an assortment of souls, some guests, some neighbouring women roped in to help. The room grew hot from the fire, and so too did the backs of the newly-weds as they sat at the centre of the banquet table, the mantelpiece directly behind them. They were first to be served by the women, their creatures respectable for this day. After all, herself and himself had done the decent thing, her lobby was still intact while he had somehow managed to hold fire until his *banbh*-pink intentions could this coming night be bejaysused in the Clarence Hotel. The bride and groom smiled till their faces thought they were evil, as bite by bite they nursed each other through the feast.

On their woodland plates lay rashers curled in thoughtful déjà-vu, black pudding circles full-stopped right where full stops were never intended, and sausages, tanned by the pan until golden, lay like sleeping piglets back to back and tight together.

Jack Humphrey, between mouthfuls, looked down the table at his new son-in-law, the hunter who had won his prize, and old man that the father now was, he knew that with Minnie gone he would from here on have to service his humbug all by himself.

Minnie's mother gulped down her food, for she was anxious to have the meal over and the wedding cake cut before the bridal couple had to depart. Giving the best edged carving knife into Minnie's hand she invited her daughter and her new husband to start the junta on the heebie-jeebies of a cake. Granted that her daughter would mill but the same plague as herself, the mother enthused *mar dhea* when it came to clapping the young couple's first incision. Now with a deliberate smile she passed around the fruit cake, its icing jubilant, its dreams a possibility stillborn.

# CHAPTER 10

The smart-stepping pony set out with a spanking stride towards Huntstown, a bow to her neck and a certain Fenian defiance in her eyes. Her ligaments thong-in-boot gathered her limbs into a great human-like ploy and her silver mane imitated her mind's arrogance by seeming to wash back over her body, blowing as though it thought that she had over-pulled on the reins. The trap sped along behind the steed, the iron wheel-rims grating on the hard gravel road. Its three passengers, two facing one, sat behind the pony's tail, Minnie closest on one side, Ned Naylor on the other. Ned, his duty as best man played out in the church, was there lying by waiting to act as hackney-man to this couple. He was now driving them to the depot in Huntstown to catch the blue bus to Dublin, his whip held aloft like the Olympic torch. He didn't dare drop its lash on the pony's haunches, for he knew too well that if he hit her she'd fart, and not today of all days did he want her to embarrass his passengers.

Ned Naylor deposited his wax models in Huntstown and, having time to spare, brought them into Barry's Bar to treat them. He enticed the bride to have something on him, and though not yet hen-thirsty she tried her hand at a glass of port wine. Her stance in the snug was cosy and almost darkly private, so relaxing she sat back and sipped at her fear. His male model, the ham-fisted hero, the friend who had married the very girl he himself had set his cap at, clouded the day under a moustache stained by creamy froth which he filtered from the pool of bogwater mirroring in his hand. For himself Ned chose Paddy, whimsical whiskey to whet his hurt, for he was a maverick, surplus in this hothouse.

The window of the snug was frosted up as high as the midline, and in the centre was an oval of clear glass on which the name 'Barry' was written in frost. Minnie was sitting sizing it up when through the insignia she saw the suggestion of blue. 'Here's the bus, here it is,' she said, and jumped to her feet, but the men stayed put, for they still had the dregs of their drinks to toss back, and old hand that Ned Naylor was, he knew precisely the length of time the bus would stand its ground.

Peter O'Brien ushered his new missus up the steps into the bus, and as it edged out into the road the going-away couple waved a last wave at Ned. The spluttering engine gradually got up speed and moments as moments go turned now this whole onion into a dumb-waiter. The newly-weds grabbed hold of the seat in front of them as the axle now hurled them about in higgledy-piggledy gamesmanship. They sometimes bumped against each other for great lurched seconds. Loving the nearness of touch, they yet never gave credence to the fact that their lonely place technically waited. Minnie, numb with nerves, whispered that she loved this fellow beside her and he, Peter, numb with longing, told her that he was absolutely wild for her. But unbeknownst to either of them the bus, the blue banker, nursed this bacarrat game until the series of noughts and crosses were filled, and showed the girl coming out the winner.

39

# CHAPTER II

Nobody even noticed the young couple as they walked their ransomed path towards O'Connell Bridge. The young man stepped terra-firma steps beside his slender wife: she, though, smiled awhile with each step of hers, as like a team of ploughman's horses they now lunched upon the towpaths. All around them was an orchestra of new sounds: the hulking of rabid trams, the constipated horns of motor cars, the clip-clop of hallmarking horses, the bicycle bells of frenzied cyclists and the voices of Dublin's nunnery of novices.

Dublin, the city of just about right, the city where sirens and sinners are somehow saints, welcomed the bog-trotters to its bare bosom. As they struck along they couldn't help noticing this city's bad-toothed smile, its gaps where the foreigner blew out its teeth and tried to plunder its respectability. The man of this couple fought his own fight, buried his own brother the cold day in hell, but he was not for remembering those things in this street; rather he was asking his wonderful girl to muck in with him in the life which his dead brother could not ever tread.

Peter, as usual, was nervous as he guided his stellar-vagrant down Bachelors Walk. He knew his way about, he had oftentimes come here with his father. He had been with him the day when he bought the little yellow ducklings in the shop with the cockydoodle logo. He told Minnie his story, showed her where Nolan's 'Noah's Ark' once stood, and he remembered for her his utter disappointment when, sinning, his little jaundiced ducklings grew up to be big white ducks sporting yellow beaks and matching legs. Now, though, he had other things to be going on with, for he was under Pandarus's snivelling orders and he, like Troilus before him, set off now down the tunnelled tomb's fairway.

Dublin's Liffey lapped along beside the lovers, its Ha'penny

Bridge waiting to help the couple arrive at their hunting lodge. This huckster's Moll, though, had never crossed an iron bridge before, nor yet a wide, wild river. Minnie held on tightly to Peter's arm as she glimpsed the river through the railings and her fear built up. Underfoot the structure pulsated under its trafficking feet; hers, though, were waffling on a red-hot plate. Her man, sensing her utter nervousness, hesitated in his stride. Line by line he held on to her until, greeting her gumption with a smile, he yielded when they both stepped together down the last step.

The evening sun washed over them in umber tones as they manoeuvred down Wellington Quay. Really they weren't even thinking of it when she noticed the sign for the 'Up-to-date Studio'. They entered young in heart, and when the photographer viewed them from under his black cloth he stumm-saw something for posterity. 'Smile,' the muffled voice eddied, and begod, smile they would if they could, but like it or not the fear of the unknown lulled them to but grimace.

## CHAPTER 12

Peter held back with fear the heavy oak door of the Clarence Hotel. His timid girl walked through. Young and awkwardly, they approached the little old lady in the desk, but now that he had to sign the book the country bloke froze. 'Just sign here,' the receptionist suggested but, pen in hand, all he could manage was to skirt around the space, his hand shivering the leaves on the birch. Minnie felt for him at the moment but the receptionist came to his rescue. 'Are ye on yer honeymoon, luv?' she asked the girl in tow. The girl didn't need to reply, for now this old wiseacre of a woman was saying, 'My, how time flies! It seems like only yesterday that my man and me were on our honeymoon and now, luv, we have nine grown-ups.' Minnie smiled her shy acknowledgement while the man with the pen found his resolve and managed to land his name on the ledger.

The porter set off carrying Minnie's suitcase, leading the way to the couple's bedroom, which was situated to the front of the hotel and looking out on the Tiber of his old city. The door just now opened by his key revealed a vivid bridal room, in its centre a self-conscious bed all dickied-up in pink quilted satin. Matching the pink bedspread, drapes hung in gathers at the window, while towards the glass itself lace curtains hung handsomely in white. Opposite the bed a black cast-iron fireplace stood, its grate empty save for some scrunched up red tissue paper. The only other items in the room were a mahogany wardrobe, matching dressing table, and a shy pink chamberpot barely hidden beneath the high fourposter bed.

'So you're from Westmeath?' the wily porter stated, as deliberately and delicately he placed Minnie's suitcase on the floor. He didn't want a reply; forging ahead to tell the newly-weds the timetable of the hotel. 'Dinner'll be served almost any minute now,' he was elaborating, but the coin which Peter pressed into his palm sent him hustling away.

Now the bog-trotters were on their own, their singular own, so, hats abandoned, they grabbed each other to kiss and hug away the silence of their loveless day. Nothing now could separate them, they felt, but that was before they heard the dinner-gong as, booming in busy butting-in, it called them back again from behind their closed door, back to figure yet again in the higgledy-piggledy of this hotel's public arena.

# CHAPTER 13

Victorious morning shinned up over the horizon, bringing in its crested dawn jaws a big orange; it held its jaws closed on the sphere until the skies had anointed this city of Dublin. As it songed the reading of the streets, it honey-coated the facade of the hotel on the quays by lustring it in tones of saffron. Swinging about then the sphere eyed the morning's linen sheets, as bluffing and blowing they stealthily soaked up any broken-veined clouds which dared to be present. There was one black cloud hovering over the Clarence and for now it ignored it, but attack could only be stifled for so long and if results didn't come hackneying soon it very much feared that it might have to bomb it apart.

Trestled by her husband's crooked body, Minnie lay freshening her vulved awareness. The high ceiling hied her from its ornate height. 'Thy will be done' was not her maiden's findings: her experience last night had been both terrific and terrible. Outside her window hullabaloo was ding-donging on the morning quays; river boats hooted their mournful sirens, great Clydesdales clip-clopped on the cobbles while iron wheel-rims murdered the shape on the stones. Whistling men looked at the river, working out their chances of a dockers' dig. Pushcarts bearing fruit and vegetables barrow-wheeled towards street stalls as vendors hailed each other in robbers' greetings. Such were the sounds plastering her consciousness as she stirred in her bed of bothering.

She turned her head now towards her husband of one night. 'Peter, love, are you awake?' she said, her words worming. But his face lay there all flat and misshapen near her. He was deep in sleep, his he-man's lovemaking fabling his dreams. She lay awhile sizing up the man, but a crick in her neck made her turn her head to face forward again. She ascribed several reasons for her feeling so

43

cheated, and then, as though guilty about sharing a man's bed, she turned back the bedclothes and stole quietly from the warm sheets. For a moment she stood gazing masterfully at her bed of marriage.

'Myhowtimeflieshowareya,' she lipped as she surveyed her nasturtium-red mystery.

Minnie O'Brien walked slowly towards the window and, separating the two sets of curtains, she stepped between them to look out on the green river of dunces. Standing thus, she watched the old river dumb its way out to sea, this old river which had pocketed insults and curses, had had green goliers spat in its face, and had even wombed stiff corpses under its skirts. Here it slupped this very morning, its head held high though its lungs were lined by grey history. Paying no attention to anything, it almost missed the she-Gulliver up there in the window of the hotel. Villain though she looked the river seemed to have pity on her, for wave after wave it ran towards her as it tried to comfort her. Really, it didn't know the answer to this girl's problem, but slurping and sloughing it tried to tell her that time was on her side and that time, the old tinder-box, held all the answers.

Breath eventually misted the window before her but she fingered a patch until she could see the river again. She wondered about the brides who had possibly stood where she now stood, and mused on what they might have thought about this marriage bed. She established there and then that her feelings had to come into the question, and as her self-satisfied man turned from her last night she, wilful in her pride, would not admit that her experience was one of makeshift happiness. She was thinking in her plight of how her scheme might work when the noise on the quays sinned its way into her pellicle of hurt. She pressed nearer to the glass in order to inspect thin slices of folk as they fretted their route up or down the street. Nine o'clock in the morning they told themselves, but she in the window was only now about to go to bed.

Minnie looped back through the bedroom curtains to stand now looking at him in the bed. She was goose-pimpled by the cold.

44

There her husband lay in his sleep while his young wife sought tinder for her listing fire. His head moved slightly on his pillow, his eyes slitting open, but then as though to focus better he lifted his head to stare at the vision before him: white flesh stubbled by full-grown locks of foolishness clad its mole-in-the-hole; ringlets of blonde curls tossed over its shoulders; its tomboy's breasts playing brave games pointed accusingly at him in the bejaysussing bed and bluebag-blue eyes factotumed his drowsy stare. 'Minnie, love, what the hell are you doing standing there like the Blessed Virgin?' said the startled man in the bed as, turning back the bedclothes, he waited for her to slide into his arms.

Peter found that his bride was shivering with cold when, folding her to his hot body, he attempted to light her dead fire. The heavy touch of his hands as he massaged her limbs brought hot blood deluging from her funky heart. Putty in his hands his girl became this numbing morning, and though he funnily enjoyed his labour she, his savage, butted in never. Tyburn-timing, her husband five-fingered her flesh until her rosy tundish was quivering, and now on this morning of 18 May 1922, as the clock faces of the city showed twenty minutes past nine o'clock, down in the bridal room in the Clarence Hotel, Peter O'Brien and his bride, Minnie, made lynching love, yes, sighing, lying, lynching love, down there where the belly of stones flowed by.

# CHAPTER 14

Hot off the press, the hero of the sullen hour was first to set off to the bathroom located five doors down from the scene of the crime. Breakfast aromas run amok drove his stomach wild with longing. Minnie, though, didn't smell what he smelt, didn't even plan on her next meal, for now that her dinnerthing was placated all she wanted was to lie on and, tame now, to savour the novelty of this morning's vanquishing.

'Yes,' she sighed out loud as five doors down she now fed herself into the ass's milk. Gingerly she slipped down. The water – 'Oh! my God' – gushed up between her legs and almost heeled her up entirely. The buoyancy frightened her and brought a blush to her face. Now, though, she started to master the fine-tuning, and lay there as the soft warm water ebbed and slurped at her every lifting. At rest, her body luxuriated, its natural curls surfacing only maybe. She stretched to the soap dish and picking up the primrose-scented soap she set about bombarding her crevices with its lather. Frivolously she linseeded it through her dyke, dredging her mole-in-the-hole with its healing dolours. Stretching out one arm after the other she soaped them, but when she attempted to sit up her slippery body all but heeled up again. Activating the soap anew, she did contortions trying to reach areas deemed out of sight and therefore out of mind. Ahoying her progress she told herself that she was fierce lucky, for just a little while ago she had changed from girl to woman and as if that was not wonderful enough, here she was now in the Clarence Hotel sitting and sometimes lying in its white hope, and view it how she would, she had come a very long way from the young girl who had duck-bathed in the little tin bathtub at home. As though shy about her carry-on in Dublin she now let the soap slip from her grasp, but she, ploughing omelettes,

46

had the fun as, playing ducks and drakes, the soap brackled every unkind orifice. The giggles were at her as lying back for the very last time she said, 'Minnie Humphrey, you'll remember this Thursday morning for as long as you live.' Her eyes closed now, she just lay there in wet happiness, blissfully unaware of the greasy mirage surfacing on the water.

The clock in the Clarence was chin-wagging the hours when, breakfast over, the blooded couple descended the stairs. The wiseacre at the desk turned her old amber eyes upon them to see if they had known failure, but with her hand sliding down the brass balustrade the girl looked triumphant, for upstairs this very morning she had dispatched her Tarzan and now was in fact sampling the aura of walking in the footsteps of wacky Jane.

## CHAPTER 15

Peter checked out for them both and together then they walked through the lunatic-quietness out the door into the furore of Wellington Quay. 'Let's just take a gander down this end first,' suggested Peter as he led Minnie to the left. Down the cobbled city quay, down the drenching wind-home they strolled, each trying greedily to Tyburn the streets of Dublin in their soul. Watching the pair of montha-knowalls stood a grey building around whose granite framework ran a series of terracotta friezes. Almost jaywalking, the couple found themselves edging out into the path of big-time traffic, attempting to decipher the story which was glued up there on the building. Minnie was taken with the washerwomen elbow-deep in suds, advertising the newly invented Sunlight Soap. Peter too was interested. He didn't quite see the connection, but he was nevertheless taken with the two big white

47

horses, ploughing a scrape while standing still, a scrape which he surmised they'd never have to harrow, sited as they were high up on a tall building, on a wall which they could never climb, in a city which was just now escaping from a foreign king's grasp.

Barely glancing at their hotel the couple walked back along by the Liffey side, nosing nearer to their bridge of sighs. The vomit-green water flowed freely now, as a purloined boat sat heaving and nutcracking the dredged loot from the river's bottomless hoard.

Reaching the bridge of her noble crossing last night Peter headed Minnie in the opposite direction. They crossed the busy thoroughfare and together mounted the steps which led to Merchant's Arch. Passing under the tall granite archway he brought his girl through a tunnel and out into a village which, like a snail on a wall, clung to a hill. Here now he had her standing in the human heart of Dublin city, in the very site where in days long ago men wearing horns on their heads had turned a slimy swamp and jungled hill into a labyrinth of craftsmen's homes and gimleted stone streets. Here each of their streets acted as guardian to its own tackle or trade, here cheek by jowl those foreigners had worked in gold or silver, jasper or jade, clockmaking or printing, bookbinding or bellmaking, candlemaking or tanning.

Peter was at home to a peg, for this was his village of boyhood memory. He recalled days on the wing spent in the company of his late grand-uncle from that sunny place, and his own father who, carting his load of turnips to the city markets, had often brought him with him, seated in a special hollow made amongst the turnips. The joy was his when they stayed overnight in Mrs Molloy's lodging house in the Haymarket, for next day they planned to meet up with the visitor from South Africa.

Jack O'Brien had emigrated to Connecticut along with his brother and sister, three O'Briens jumping ship so that those left behind could still manage to eat from the one pot. The other two long since dead, the old survivor was back, doing his best to hearse his life for as long as he could. He hadn't stayed put with the others in Connecticut, but instead joined a cargo boat to South Africa. For years he worked in the gold mines, but when the yellow stain reached his lungs he left the mines and joined three hardchaws working the ivory trade. Peter as a small boy was mystified by the swank of the old grand-uncle, from his bowler hat to his gaiters, his monocle to his big, gold pocket watch. The merchant always licked his lips when he had his cargo of elephants' tusks and ivory ornaments disposed of, his wealth derived from a game plan liveried by innocents' pain.

A mizzle started as the honeymooners moved up along Crown Alley. Neither of them bothered to comment on it; neither, it seemed, was even aware that it was raining. Minnie, the new wife, nursed her steps along beside Peter, her hand hooked in his elbow's plan, her joy in being with him, no playing now to his gallery.

Peter was silent. For a few seconds he was stopped in his tracks, memories suddenly surfacing. A presence seemed to be in step with him and her. Silly sounds from his boyhood nosed in on this his moment of manly lightening. Back, for all the world as though it had happened five minutes ago, came the picture of the hot tearooms in the Clarence. He, a small gosoon, was sitting at the table with the two men. He was eating a pointy-ended pastry, its jam pooled in the centre, sugar granules coating it, the whole baked brown, only the jam held true to itself. There was one bun still left on the plate in the centre of the table, and he remembered how he eyed it, feeling that the bun was waiting for him, waiting as though vampire-lonely for the touch of his teeth. He looked in front of him now but there it smiled, its sticky brown roof trying yet again to flog him to death. The bun nudged him to remember how, his last jumbo-mouthful swallowed, the men moved off, he traipsing after them. Before he could say aught they had climbed the seven steps to the men's toilet and, ordered to urinate, he lined up beside the two gents, his little teapot snug beside their kettles.

His father's horse was stabled over in the Haymarket and the time to harness him was near. Saying farewell to Jack O'Brien that

49

day, they, himself and his father, stood watching as the South African disappeared down the quays, his bowler hat tinting the sky. He never once looked back. It was as though he didn't need to; his gait said it all, the determined gait which seemed to stumble forward, hill-climbing where no incline stretched.

His envelope with its green-ink-scrawled address never came again. Jack O'Brien's boat which, at its last sighting, had been there evening on the resting tide funnel up, delved into the cola-sea somewhere around the equator. His ragbag crew had struggled to the brig's end but, gllomp, the sea swallowed it down, down into her splanchnocele. All that remained was an Irishman's voice, drake-planned in a boreen of bubbles.

Peter's reverie took but a second, his mind swiftly reverting to his whereabouts. Back it came to this village which had always held him in thrall. He had always planned to come back to this very place but he never made it, not until today. Today, though, he was being the big fellow; today he was breathing love in this storybook-story in Temple Bar.

## CHAPTER 16

It took hours for this couple of logarithms to wind their way through this maze's every turn. They were in fact so contented that, though the streets and city waited their pleasure, those cunning lanes and alleys here had somehow managed to mesmerise them. Together they walked, she sometimes noticing the green pistols in her undercarriage, he only sensing his own pilgrimage as, haughty in his planned intuition, he just sessioned his coulter through this, his village of reason and yenning.

'Crow Street,' said Minnie, as she glanced up at the street name on the bricks above her head. 'Crow Street,' she said again, fascinated by the fresh image from those rookery sounds heard every springtime in the clump of trees in the field to the back of her huckster's shop away down home in Drumhollow. Strange as it seemed, a feeling of belonging came to her as she strolled along this narrow street which ran away towards a busy sounding thoroughfare. Peter joined in her passing reference to the name, wondering why the natives christened this little hop-along street so. They were each light-heartedly suggesting possible explanations when without any forethought her husband led his wife up two granite steps into a buff-painted shop, so suddenly it seemed almost as though he were under some spell. He said nothing, but just left her standing all lost and disorientated. Sounds came towards her in agitated waggery, and no matter which way she turned her eye was forced to fix on some shape or make of a clock, all of them womanising together in a chorus of thingumajigging.

'Now you're talking,' she heard herself say as, turning a Hun's pirouette, she studied the guggenheim streeted all around her. Her hearing getting used to the nuances of this chattering assembly, she became aware of a hearsed voice which came to her from somewhere near the door. Acting as though she were still single she walked towards that sound, a breathing sound, stealing out from deep inside a clock standing under the planked mezzanine. The clock was tall, its femoral bones forcing it to stand proud and erect. From under its skirt glanced two neat feet, and like a snowman its head just sat there all squat upon its polished mahogany trunk. Stylishly, figures and diggers were strutted there upon its white-as-death face and, beautifully modest, its sundial hinted only of life, of a long life underneath her stairs.

Minnie smiled a quiet smile while she got up the nerve to turn the key jutting from the clock's belly. Under the eye of her husband she gingerly turned it. Now, gently, she opened the door and looked inside at the bowels of this humming giant. Pensively she looked at the heavy pendulum as over and back it panicked, over and back, yessing a she-god's questions before she could even ask them.

'Can we afford this?' she whispered, and moving nearer her man of this morning's pyre stole a march on her father by saying the thing she most wanted to hear. 'Of course we can afford it,' his voice said, as if just for once he was going to be a gold, gold god to her woman's illogicality.

The grandfather clock was fitted into its box and made ready for the next day's barge to Westmeath. It took the silver-haired salesman with the tonsured head and his boy assistant to lift it into place. They mercilessly removed its innards and placed them alongside the body in the box, the only sound of protest the tinkling bell which, full of wondering, wondered why its days in Frengley's shop had had to come to an end.

'That should reach Huntstown by Friday the twenty-sixth,' forecast the old salesman as, placing the lid on the box, he set to with strong string. The long string stole from a hole in the lid of an old tobacco tin, the noise sounding like a war-dance going on inside. 'You've a fine clock there,' he boasted. 'Sure we're famous for good clocks, send them all over the country we do, and that one'll see ye out no matter how long ye live.' He smiled up into their faces, kneeling on the floor stacking the odds against the clock ever escaping from its land-lock.

Peter started to ask about a luck-penny, but seeing the hard look he got from the fanatic he dropped the subject and waited for his docket to be filled out. He counted out the four pounds and two shillings, the furniture of his pocket, brackled now before he could ever store it away for herself for a rainy day. Dublin city would witness the dispatch of this artfully tied-up box. Fixed to its lid would be a white label, a scarlet-framed label, and written on it would be the words:

Mr Peter O'Brien
Drumhollow
Huntstown
Co. Westmeath

Friday's traffic would wind it along on the first stage of its journey towards the Royal Canal barge, the boat which would limb the clock all the way to its destination.

The deal done, the couple from Drumhollow bumbled from Frengley's out into the hum of Temple Bar. The little streeteen was chock-a-block with aimless folk and foraging traffic. Horses waited to draw their drays up or down the dream, but no limericks flowed from the bog-trotters' lips for today they weren't noticing horses' hooves, too engrossed in each other to heed the dumb animals. Reckoning on what Jack Humphrey might think of the hole in his brown envelope's dowry Peter smirked, jousting he had broken into the money to buy his girl the hulking clock. They laughed in excitement as they folded up the receipt, she saying that it was when the man moved the hands to twelve and the plant hammered the bell that she in fact fell for the clock, fell for its January-bell, fell for every tinkle from it, its seeds coming at her not from inside the buff-painted dream in Crow Street but, like it or not, from a spot under a staircase in a house rescuing itself down at home in Westmeath.

## CHAPTER 17

Back down the street of their first melting the O'Briens strolled. At ease with the world, they decided on having a snack: lunchtime had come and gone but they hadn't even noticed. Now they went seeking out a tearoom where they could sit and greet each other across a table.

Gilchrists of Angelsea Street was recommended to them for

afternoon tea. They found it there on a corner, a dairy-cum-tearoom, the dairy next to the street with its shop window full of eggs, butter, cheese and homemade cakes and bread. The tearoom was to the back, just a big square room dolorously dark and stuffed to the gills with tables and chairs. Minnie and Peter found a table for two vacant in a corner and inside this holy cave they sat, their knees wedged against each other under the oilclothed table.

It was the cakestand which marked their visit to Gilchrists' tearoom. Their order had been a simple request; 'Tea and buns,' was what Peter ordered. The teapot when it came was just ordinary, the usual run o'the mill type, a Carlton four-cup size. Nothing though, could have prepared them for the cakestand. Delicately in the centre of their table the young waitress set it, the cakestand, the tiered cakestand, the fancifulness of it spoiling their view of each other, the hessian-backed tablecovering fumbling under its Sunday. On its bottom tier the songed cakes sat — curranty buns and eccles cakes; the middle tier was decorated with puff pastries some of which had jam and cream oozing from their privates; but the fanciest items of all were kept to adorn the top tier, the littlest plate, the one closest to the opulent gilt handle. Placed there, inside corrugated paper cases, sat four icing-covered delicacies, each one dolled-up in a different colour — orange, bitter brown, white and green the rainbow was painted, and so as not to be jealous, each fancy cake had a common touch to its icing, in the form of a curlicue woven from chocolate-brown innocence.

Peter was first to break the spell. Minnie never would; she was in her element sitting somnolent drinking in every word which gubbed from his lips. It was his taking out his silver pocket watch which destroyed the lullaby, the very action sending crestfallen feelings creeping all over her, yes, the itch of it almost sundering her body. 'Good God,' he gasped. 'It's nearly four o'clock and we have to go to Kelly's Steam Mills, remember me telling you that I want a few boards of Cuban mahogany?' She did indeed remember, and was on her feet while he gold-peddled. He listened to the sound from his trouser's pocket as he felt for his money and approached the counter to settle for the tea and buns. Without remembering to find a thimbleful of relief for herself, she stood beside him, there ready at his beck and call.

# CHAPTER 18

Sad thoughts were not in evidence this day of days as, standing in Dame Street, Minnie was going to have another first. In dread, she waited with him for the next tram. Only certain of one thing, she stood stoic beside him as he smoked his Wills Wild Woodbine. Naturally, her eyes sought out the approaching tram, she diminutive now. Grandly it halted, some folks disembarking, others like herself, but not like herself, going to board it. But this was a new stunt which had to be addressed by her and smartly she stepped on board, her husband behind her. Their fares paid, Peter hustled her along, the stairs waiting, though her hunch was for downstairs; she didn't feel a need to become airborne.

Up the tram's stirruping steps her husband urged her and then further along the aisle until, reaching the very front, he ushered her into the first seat. Sitting down she now felt all excited, for from this great vantage point she was going to view the Dublin of her recent daydreams.

Ponds of sunshine washed over the tram as with a wobble here or a rattle there it advanced along Dame Street. Peter, squeezing her hand, sat there, his craftsman's eyes drinking in the game facades of this street's buildings. Guilty about taking up Minnie's time going to look for timber he again squeezed her hand, but she herself was by now busy as a nailer, jam-packing her gombeen's silent film. Her hand holed up in her husband's, she Cyclops-eyed at *and* into shops and offices, gavelling people into dimwit forms.

Busy, her eye homed in on the work in progress inside a shop window, a man in white cutting off a wedge of butter from an iceberg of butter; in every detail she filmed it, herself playing the narrator. 'Liptons,' her lips undertoned, 'lips, I'll just remember lips and then I'll have the name.' Now she was looking into the tobacconist's where Peter had bought twenty cigarettes (he had only ever before bought the bare-backside packet five-strong, but today he was sinning on the side of riches). Her individual eye noticed the scripted lettering over the tobacconist's door: v. SANDERSON it read, but she would only ever rill the ornamental pleasantry around the two capital letters. Nimroding down into a hollow she kimboed cunningly to see if her artist's lens might credential something else, and no sooner ready than her eye landed on the Empire Theatre, its billpost fanfaring the 'Enormous Success. HART AND O'BRIAN. In laughs till off!' She realised that she'd easily remember the poster. 'Just the same initials as me and Peter,' she said, and so saying she smeared the letters across her mind's eye; life must not forget those initials, she almost said. In her innocence she wondered if they might attend but then, feeling guilty for even thinking like that, she busied herself instead filming a horse down below beside the tram, trying to find grip for his toes on the shiny cobblestones. Twice he plunged, his shoes knocking sparks from the stones, his dray of Guinness barrels milking his every ounce of strength. 'Pull,' she encouraged, 'pull attaboy, pull,' and as though he heard her voice the big brawth of a horse pulled, the load of sixteen barrels swirling their bogwater behind him. For all the world as though she were the man holding the reins she filled each barrel with creamy froth, wishing to hunt the weight from off the horse's breast. 'You'll remember the sparks,' she fumed, filing the moment for future reference.

It took the tram a minute or so to climb the steep hill, and there her hologram pinholed the big church, the church of Paradise and Hell and the divil as well. Like a citadel it stood, the junta-funded church, but she didn't know that aspect of it: all she would remember was that this dramatic edifice stood on a hill just up the street from where she bought the clock. 'Yes,' the tram seemed to say before heading off in a Cromwellian gallop.

Peter's hand was getting edgy so she glanced at him to see if he was planning to go. 'Just a few yards more,' he whispered into her ear and she, still stringing her film, grew anxious now, seeing hurriedly, trapping swiftly some children leppin' under a skipping rope, young babies in mothers' arms, women hanging out of windows side-eyeing down towards the pavements, whether at the children playing or watching until a drunken husband blundered homewards, or the coal man was calling, that she couldn't know; this part of her film would depend on her intuition and only in time would the mind strut out its speculations. 'Come on Minnie,' the man's voice broke in on her soundtrack and abruptly she shut the lens on the gull's line of flight, her valiant eye afforded no more gallivanting.

Like it or not, he had to leave her, knowing that the timber yard was no place for a young woman on honeymoon. They had dropped into a church to say a prayer before the Blessed Sacrament. But Peter, though praying, could only see the cabinet in his mind's eye: he needed Cuban mahogany for it and the sawmills waited. Making a hurried sign of the cross he whispered, 'I'll nip over to Kelly's, won't be a minute, you can wait here.' She, wishing to please him, whispered that she'd be all right. 'You go off and get your boards,' she said. With a genuflexion he hurried away, the swing door continuing its song as he walked out into Thomas Street.

# CHAPTER 19

Minnie O'Brien stared up towards the tabernacle. From inside its folded gold door her Creator watched. Now she was on her own. Just Him and her, God and woman. Her new status had just been stamped upon her but her aloneness now was palpable. Seeing that He wasn't saying aught she began to pray. She thanked Him for putting Peter her way and thanked Him too for getting her out of her father's clutches. 'Please give me the grace to be a good wife to Peter,' she said, and the reference to her husband brought a blush to her cheek, she just lately having seen things never before revealed to her. Longing for another go, her conscience bugged her. 'What a thing to be thinking,' her mind hinted. 'It was all new to me,' she said, despite His listening presence, 'all new to me, Peter's thing.' Her eyes galloping in tune with her heart, she glanced up along the acres of wooden pews, up along the nave. Her head three times solemnly bowed, the word Jesus tripping off her tongue, but it was mechanical, her bowing, her mind hundred-legged all about the church. Pythagoras had linked the ceiling into a fulcrum of breathtaking height – her highest point ever was standing once on the very top of the stepladder in the shop.

Now her foolish heart sensed her distraction, and stretching for her handbag she rummaged for her rosary beads shying in the bottom. Touching it, her fingers drew it out. Blessing herself she kissed the crucifix, now ready for some down-to-earth praying. 'What's the day?' she wondered, and then it all came back again: she had married yesterday, so it must be Thursday. Thursday the Joyful mysteries, she roted, first mystery The Annunciation that Mary was chosen to be the Mother of God. Beads oiled by her skin now slid by, the Our Father separated from the Glory Be by ten Hail Marys. Her lips moving in unison with her fingers, her imagination lending the image to that long-ago announcement, she could well see the young Jewish virgin being told that she was going to be the mother of God-made-man. Indeed she felt at one with the virgin; the solemn place of incision was common to them both. The newness of Minnie's findings uppermost, she felt in her heart an affinity with Mary.

Five decades totalled her one rosary, and still she waited for Peter's return. Twice more did she finger the round of the beads and at no time was he the soul who entered through those swing doors. Worried now, she was just worked up to the stage of going in search of him when, like a frightened rabbit, he peeped in at her. Starting, almost, she was on her feet in a flash, and forgetting the tabernacle she turned on her heel, eloping then with her new god.

Hemlock she had drunk there in the aloneness of the big church, but now her man was back beside her. Together with him she dipped her finger into the holy water font and, making her Germanic symbol of faith, she ilked beside him and walked out into Thomas Street.

Famished from this their first ever separation, the O'Briens made their way up along the street and, reaching The Clock, pushed open the door on this plaid kingdom. Peter had once before supped at this humans' counter, had studied the gangland stressed here in mirrors, but today he was all eyes searching for the snug, and the moment he spotted it he pursued it for her sake.

The small nook of a room was vacant, so they settled down safely. She removed her hat and placed it on the streeted velvet seat. He didn't remove his, only set it back on his head so that the restricted bloodflow might gush freely about his forehead.

At the mention of drink she asked the question which had been gnawing for hours, and finding the dingy toilet she was more than happy to relieve herself. She returned to the snug in time to see the barman arrive carrying his round tin tray. 'What'll you have, love?' Peter had asked, and her trembling lips had asked for her usual libation. 'But, Minnie, you're on honeymoon,' he said, smiling, 'and I'd like to treat you to something better.' Now, next to his tumbler of porter sat her treat from her new husband, a glass of port wine, ruby in colour, and when she tasted it it scolded her palate in wort. The strict privacy of the snug brought them close again, she whispering, he jolly and talkative. Five times did the barman carry in his tray but now her drink was red lemonade, safe red lemonade; his, still, tumblersful of his favourite bogwater with there the essence of Holly Bog steady as she goes rising up the cream in little droplets, gathering like ingots till the collar round the neck was fluffy cotton actuality.

The red velvet snug stole their dream from them for, prating now, they grew more carefree, the genie allowed to second guess his way from their turnpike bottle. Peter was under the influence when she noticed the change come over her man. She, though, kept her head yessing his ramblings, while at the same time wishing that she could somehow work him back again into talking and teasing about him and her and the night still before them.

But no holds barred this fellow from the country sinned as, stung in his softest spot, he now began remembering his sadnesses. It started out with his regret that his own brother couldn't be best man yesterday. 'Indeed, he was before me eyes all through the Mass, I could see again us lowering him down into the grave. Y'know it took two full wheelbarrowfuls of moss to line his grave. We had to scour half the country searching for it, we gathered it from rocks and from under ditches, two whole barrows. Lord, but it was lovely when we finally got it done, the four sides, even the floor of it was green soft moss. Do y'know what, Minnie, he'd have loved you, he'd like you like I do, but if you only saw his face after the cordite, sort of burned, ould black carbon blown up along it from his throat. Through his throat, that's where it went, the shot, but we made sure the mother didn't see it, pulled his uniform up tight under his chin, his face clean as a whistle by the time she got to see him. John'd have been me best man yesterday, me eldest brother, and now he's below in the cemetery in Meedin.' Peter

O'Brien, the brand new married man now began to cry, there before his new wife he began crying, crying in the place of young love. Minnie Humphrey-that-was couldn't stop him, hadn't a clue what to do, didn't know how to throw his brake. She attempted to shush him but each time she tried he only repeated the whole, and he wanting to say sorry to her.

It was only when the *olagóning* had gone three rounds on his brother the young Irish Volunteer, and a further four on his arthritic uncle, that she asked him the time. 'We'll have just one more drink,' he said, 'and then we'll push off.' But with gusts of lemonade gas playing up her gullet and down her nose Minnie had had enough, so, lifting her hat off the velvet seat, she deliberately placed it on her head. The tears from his tales still petered down into his tumbler, shores of tears, but now he saw that she had the going on her so, lifting his glass to his mouth, he drank deeply till nothing remained but the stain on the tumbler and the scum on his moustache.

Minnie it was who dabbed his eyes and kissed his cheek, the brine from his tears salting her lips, but he had to blow his nose into his own big white handkerchief before he could walk out into the public bar. His hat had to be placed back on properly on his forehead, and this time he had to tilt it well down over his eyes.

The pair that left the snug was not the pair that went in. She held her head as snug as ever as she walked back out through the public bar of The Clock, but the drab-coated fellow behind her looked straight ahead. She bowed briefly to the staff behind the counter; her husband, though, didn't nod his thanks until he reached the door.

Peter was the one to shiver slightly when he stepped out into the street; his pores wide open, he felt the wind cresting his sweat. Incense from the nearby brewery tried to balm his reverie but, his dander up, he simply sat his head the better to face down his foolish thinking. Under his hat the brother's face still kept flitting and racketing: it hardly seemed proper to want to win more

61

regretting. It was just as well, then, that he didn't notice the attitude of the cold grey building on the far side of the street, that old church over there where the Irish patriot Robert Emmet was hanged. It was in fact carpenters just like himself who had constructed a gallows outside its gate. Its viaduct was not used to hang a giant alone, but, guilty by association, seven carpenters were also hanged, swinging their last gamble upon the hanging tree so expertly planked by fellow tradesmen in wood.

## CHAPTER 20

At the stroke of eight o'clock they descended the stairs of the Clarence Hotel to the dining room, and there their table stood waiting, its white damask cloth showing soft fold marks. In its centre and about to play gooseberry nestled a stunted pink candle, its wick motionless, its flame attracting every or any whiff of air. Herself, seated first, looked radiant in a bottle-green dress with a bertha-style lace collar. Her fair curls and ringlets she had piled up high on her head, so just the odd curl stole loose and fell down to touch her cheeks, and her blue eyes, blue as the bluebag of washdays, danced tonight, their happiness strangulating the candle flame every time she happened to glance its way. Himself, his hair and moustache almost the colour of raisins, his honest eyes deep-set and brown, his face with its dimpled chin and plum-purple lips, sat opposite, his fresh cream shirt relieved tonight by a maroon tie. His dark grey suit played second fiddle to its waistcoat, for from the vest-pocket on one side to the pocket on the other side stretched an ornamental silver-linked watch-chain, its sterling silver glinting every time he moved in this tramp's light. They studied the menu, she being choosy where last night she had been petrified.

For the main course she chose fresh salmon, he deciding on chicken, but when he pinpointed his choice of dessert tonight he went again for last night's choice — apple dumpling.

For all that the waiter noticed, he attended this pair from the country with his usual line of chatter, asked their opinion of Dublin and what of it they had seen today. As he talked he ceremoniously poured white wine from a common-or-garden bottle; the girl bowled over, almost, by her husband's extravagance. It was she, though, who answered tonight, telling of the day in the village just up from the hotel and how they purchased a clock in Frengley's.

The vegetable broth was delicious. They made a meal of it, the soup and rolls filling their empty stomachs. They conversed this time as though used to the intimate atmosphere. Pleasing themselves, they lingered over each course, their smiles streamlining the tablecloth. When their desserts arrived they looked at them with interest: her lemon meringue pie cut in a triangle-shaped portion, his choice served on a decorated dish deep blue in colour, the dumpling's steam curling in the candle light. The golden dumpling, old-fashioned though it was, seemed the volcano now as hot creamy custard dribbled down its sides. He slid his fork through the pastry shell and exposed the baked whole apple, a clove sundering him in it attesting insights. Digging deeper he lifted a forkful and, dipping it in the custard, lifted it to his mouth. He chewed the dumpling and tasted its hot floury apple then he let it slide down his throat, waves of saliva in company.

A pot of tea was the last thing served to their table, and as they supped they felt almost drowsy. Peter waited for this still moment, until she was lulled in conversation, before stretching over and placing a little black box into her left hand's grasp.

'Minnie, love, that's what really delayed me today when you were there in the church. It's just a little present for you to remember today by. Every time you look at it you'll think of now, me and you here in the Clarence and me giving this to my one and only girl.'

She came over all shy and, foostering with the clasp, failed to open it. He reached over and flicked it with his thumbnail and now opening the lid she looked at a brooch, its gooseberry-green stone set in a surround of gold filigree.

'Take it out love,' he whispered, and lifting it she laid it on the palm of her hand. Her voice, when it did manage to speak, sounded tragic.

'Where in heaven's name did you find it?' she said. 'It's the most beautiful thing I ever got, look't the candlelight shining off the stone, look love.' He laughed lightly, reminding her of her long wait in the church. 'I was on my way back,' he said, 'when I spotted a shoal of things in a shop window, and spoiled for choice I couldn't make up my mind what to buy you. I wanted to get something that you'd have forever. And then I spotted it in its little box, can't remember the name, it's Gilbert something, look, there in the lid.' And she, holding the box between them, read out the gold writing, 'Gilbert Friedberg & Company.'

## CHAPTER 21

The countryside breathed easily as it cast an especially wise eye on the couple, back from Dublin and dismounting now from Ned Naylor's round trap. Ned wanted to drive his friends right down to their front door, but they had other ideas. Opening the road gate which Peter had only recently erected there, the bridal pair ventured into the boreen, into the little curling road which cantered down to the newly-built house.

Gethsemane pitted the air in the boreen with stillness, the only disturbance the sound of their footsteps fashioning their hold. The narrow gravelled road was bordered on either side by a hedge of hawthorn, its white swathes of blossom playing babbyhouse as they adorned sloping branches. As though released from muteness the couple now dangerously talked, their voices striking the stillness here, the goat's cabbage listening. A faraway lamb tried to distract them with his plaintive bleat, and the man of the couple cocked his farmer's ear, but the bride didn't notice the nursery sound. Her mind was preoccupied for she had, just now, through the one and only gap in the hedge, got her first glimpse of the house, noticing the smoke which lackadaisically wormed from its chimney.

The waiting house watched the couple as they approached the wicket gate but the moment they walked duck-fashion through it, the house eliminated one for the other as, very curious, it chanced assessing them. Nothing stirred inside its hulk, its black windows just gazed and gazed. Minnie, as though sensing the watching presence, laughed her nervous laugh, her voice breathless though she but sauntered along the path towards the light-filled porch.

Time noticed nothing, the dimwit time; it just holed up in its recess while Peter O'Brien carried his pretty wife across the threshold and into his breastplated kingdom. As he carried her he laughed his caveman's laugh and she, hunted down by nature, played into his hands, not lonely yet.

Inside, the kitchen was innocently minding its business, the black range giving off a sultry heat. No fresh air had circulated these past few days, head man away, the minder didn't bother until today. Ned Naylor had acted for Peter while he was on his honeymoon, and never caring about the kitchen he only had eyes for the farmyard and fields. But his mother couthered him to have the kitchen warm for the new woman, and giving him an especially baked cake she ordered that it be put standing 'where that little girl will find it.'

They, Minnie and Peter, almost tripped each other up in their anxiety to act normal, and when he had shown her where everything could be found, he excused himself to go out inspecting Ned Naylor's handiwork. She, left alone now, sized up her kitchen, her gaze not missing the oilcloth on the table, its all-over pattern

65

showing a brown fox hiding in a clump of grass. The dresser was laden down with delph; every hook sticking from its shelves carried either a sundry mug or a willow-patterned cup. But she of this new house was not going to hum tea into cups trolled by any other woman. Her best china, Ned Naylor's wedding present, was going to deck her table for this their first suppertime in Drumhollow.

Minnie set Ned's square box on the table and, opening it, rummaged through the long straws of woodshavings until she found her first cup. Settling it in her clasp she began to study the scene painted on its near side. It showed a little sandy cove with tiny boats pulled in at rest. Overhead the sky was high and blue, with cirrus blowing in white puffs. Up there too flew swallows, their forked tails their trademarks. At the sea's edge rose a high cliff with red-roofed houses looking out on two little yellow-sailed boats farther out on the water. Inside the cup where, when she would drink her tea, her eyes could study them, flew yet two more swallows, full of gracefulness as they swept towards where freedom called them. Immediately she went searching for the saucers and plates, those other items belonging to Ned Naylor's set, and when she had them all unveiled she stood, her eyes admiring their first glimpse of reveried peace captured there on each item of the china which the bachelor man had especially chosen for the girl who would never now be his.

When she had the china washed she set two places at the table, Peter at the head, she sideways to him. The clash of the gold-rimmed china with the greasy oilcloth covering could not be missed, so she went outside to find some flowers, returning with a bunch of hawthorn blossoms, unaware of the ill-fortune attached to their ever being brought inside.

The table standing at ease now even looked resplendent, as moments stimulated the hunchback on horseback who galloped around outside. The special meal was going to be just that, she felt,

66

as, fetching Mrs Naylor's big cartwheel of a cake, she went in search of a knife to cut it into slices.

Minnie was kneeling in front of the firebox making toast from a hard-as-the-hob-of-hell half loaf which she found in the bread bin when Peter elbowed his way through the door into the kitchen. In his arms he carried a heavy chair, its seat cushioned in velvet. Planking it down on the floor near the range he said, 'Don't mind the toast for a minute, just get your rump into this chair.'

'Who's it for?' she asked, and handing him the slice of bread on the head of a fork, got to her feet.

'It's for the girl I married,' he said. 'I knew you were used to comfort, sitting down all day and your father working his fingers to the bone for you.'

They laughed together, she sitting in the new chair, her face the match for the ruby velvet. Peter stood sizing up how she fitted in his creation, but she sat there, her scorched face lit up in smiles, her hands sliding forwards and backwards along the wooden armrests. 'The beautiful brooch in Dublin and now this,' she said. 'You had it ready for me, and not a thing did I have for you.'

'Aye indeed,' he teased her, 'that's what a fella gets when he marries a pauper.' She was still blathering on with her disbelieving thanks. 'You're too good,' she continued. 'It's too much, you didn't need to, sure didn't you know I fell for you that night on the ladder?'

The chair over which he had struggled the long winter nights before his wedding became now the distraction to this couple's first suppertime in Drumhollow. The teatable was completely derailed, its futility forged into oblivion. The hot toast was left to stiffen, the gingerbread left uneaten, the hawthorn blossoms, like it or not, were all but welcome; in fact everything was abandoned, now that his chair had her trapped in his man's myselfing artifice.

## CHAPTER 22

At a gallop Peter ran back down the stairs, he a farmer getting from his bed and it way past evening milking time. But the pair had forgotten the time; their new bed in their new house at the same time as he gave her a new chair had strenuously given them a new intimacy, now completely thuled in this setting at the end of the boreen.

An old hand with the mood swings of the range, he soon had the kettle jizzed up for the second time, but when Minnie joined him they only took time to grab a cup of tea and a piece of Ned Naylor's mother's gingerbread.

The cows stood aghast at the lateness of the hour; one had in desperation begun to run her milk. The inquisitive beasts were googy-eyed at this newcomer, but her strict thinking was now to watch her husband as he set about his chores.

Down along the platform in the cow byre stood the four cows fresh in from the fields. Minnie sitting at the doorstep watched as Peter set about the milking. Her hunter's eyes watched the cows' concerted breathing under this tin roof, but her man was busy pinging their milk against the bottom of his galvanised bucket. The avalanche was slow in coming, but as each cow let down her milk every squirt changed tune until the bucket was filled to the brim with froth-covered milk. Their reward was but an unspoken blessing as, dipping his thumb in the white world of froth, the milker made a bluff of a cross on the loom of each cow's flank. Every time he filled a bucket, every time he emptied it, filtering its magical yield through a veil of muslin, he listening, and she learning to listen, as the milk folded through into the silver can below.

The milking completed, the harvest stood waiting to be allotted. Some milk was poured into brown crocks where its brashness would eventually surface, to be skimmed and set aside for Friday; some was reserved for household needs; and with hungry calves kicking up millimurder, some was apportioned into individual buckets for them to drink. Though country born and bred, Minnie was not prepared for the antics of the calves. She had to help hold buckets steady while the six calves dodged and knocked spots from their tin mothers. Great torrents of sucking accompanied their gulping and though their milk was devoured, the calves still retained their urge to suck. Their buckets taken away they sucked each other's ears, each other's navels, some even settling on sucking the iron bars of the haggard gate. Minnie, the sightseer, rankled though when she found her husband's cure: dipping his sally rod in fresh dung, he daubed it on every saliva-clad place of the calves's desiring. 'Have to stop them,' he said laughingly, explaining that their sucking might inflame or damage one another's genitals.

Peter, the ready man of ready methods, set off now for the pigsty. His wife, dressed in a set of his dungarees and wearing a pair of his wellingtons, big-booted her steps after him. Now though, life was going to give her its second lie, as standing at the pigsty's door she watched every momentous move made by five pink bonhams as they fought to be first into the trough which Peter filled with milky mash. Her nervous hands tilted an imaginary trough as she attempted to remedy the *rí-rá* going on before her. Golden yellow straw was the pigs' bedding, their Mafia the food which they, like fools, shoved from the trough with their snouts. Nothing would satisfy them if they could not stand four feet planted in the food while they fought to fill their hearty stomachs. Nothing could have prepared her for this display; indeed, as she watched the five Bonhams her feelings from her red bacon-slicer days came back to haunt her. How could she slice from little fellows like those before her? But time would roll like a bastard ball over her memory of this evening and pigs, big and baffled, would leave her shed as though lines of lemmings heading for a cliff face.

'Ne'er a need to rub dung on those greedy urchins,' she was thinking as, moving away, she followed to see himself bed down the poultry for the night. 'They go by union rules, the ould hens, they quit early,' he said by way of explaining why he didn't need to give food to his poultry. Quietness wafted towards her when she stood to size up the hens perched in grand rows of headless bodies, those old derelicts from his uncle's day, dreaming. 'Are any of them laying?' she asked and he, imitating their cheers when they lay, said, 'Only two at the moment go "fuck, fuck, fuck, fuck off," but then sure, two is all we need, an egg for you and one for me.'

## CHAPTER 23

The oil-lamp stood at ease on the centre of the kitchen table as this farmer and his wife came in for the night. Word of mouth hung like tired ether in the light which dropped from the glass shade. The attractive pair were spent both mentally and physically, for their day which had begun in the Clarence Hotel was now about to wind down here in this majority tied together under a blue-slate roof.

Gingerbread at the very least, the fresh-baked bread from Mrs Naylor, came to the rescue once again but this time they had butter, the butter which only Peter knew about, hiding in the green pin-holed food safe out on the scullery wall. They ate at their ease, he drinking cup after cup at Minnie's coaxing. She strengthened her hold on him by feeding him titbits, the meal so scant, yet she made of it a play.

The china too was there making play, numb now in the everything under the grass. Pity this feast knew not, for Minnie, the housewife, seemed now a winner, sitting here with her new husband radiating a she-god's hands-on approach to married life.

'Minnie, will you set a match to that candle there before I blow out the lamp,' suggested Peter as bedtime came around. The candlelight was drab when it had to do the work of the lamp, but easy to handle. They brought it with them up the stairs to the bedroom.

The playful candle, standing in its stirrups, brought its own mystery to the room upstairs, its tiny flame spurting the moment the room's resting air hit it. Around the walls it ran shadows, until the hungry foursome became their own magic lantern show. The bed, the place of their earlier tryst, lay all dishevelled, its brass bedposts stealing light from the candle's flame. Minnie listed in the light as, standing between the two naked windows, she viewed her innocent image in her every furtive glance.

'Can we put out the candle?' she asked before taking off any of her clothes, and Peter strangulating her shadow, laughed at her nervousness, knowing full well their isolation. 'Put it out love, if that's what you prefer,' he said as he nosedived into the heap of bedclothes, back in his own bed for the second time on this, the third day of Holy Week.

# CHAPTER 24

Friday and Friday, eight, counted Minnie as she calculated that today was the date when the clock, her clock, would be set into its space under the stairs. She felt she should be up, felt that dawn had broken, but though her thews tried to best her eyes open she stayed put, her body not yet ready to stir itself.

Yes, the stairs seemed to say as eventually she crept down them, four steps first, then the landing, and finally the nine which led to the kitchen. Carefully she counted them, one two three four five (ten past five, her brain teased) six seven eight nine, nine wooden steps had Fenian-fetched her down just in time to see the sun rise over the otiose townland of Drumhollow.

The kitchen was quiet, the black stove still and silent; just like a warm-blooded corpse, it needed attention before rigor mortis set in. Minnie glanced at its numb condition before opening its doors to the firebox and ashpit. There was the possibility of life, but it was hidden within a sea of ochre ashes. Her hands grew busy rattling away the loose ashes, and she didn't stop until the hopes for the new day's fire remained within the grate. The damper pulled out, she encouraged eddies of air to run through the chimney and blow fresh life into the *griosach* of last night's banked turf. When the embers grew red-red, she scooped up handfuls of curly shavings from Peter's workshop and dropped them in on top. Hesitating a moment, she waited until they ignited, and then added her next ingredients, some *cipíns* and small clods of brown turf. Now, her stove set sail for the day and its fire burning red, she filled the kettle from the immaculate white enamel bucket and set it down to boil on top of the firebox fool.

A mug of tea soon created drama in the kitchen. It was her own childhood's mug, bought in Devaney's shop in Huntstown when she was five, and it had survived many mishaps to be here in her hands today. It arrived out to her here in her new home tied to the handle of the old trunk, the homely mug tied on by a mother who was missing her only child. It was as though Sally Humphrey wanted to let her daughter know that though she couldn't break with tradition, she wanted to look at the child-bride to see with her own eyes how Peter O'Brien was treating his wife of nigh a fortnight.

She now cupped the mug in her hands like a brandy balloon, sitting sipping sometimes, her mind going over all her losses. Nearby, the trunk which belonged to her mother's family lay open, half emptied. The Butlers had had the old trunk for aeons, but her mother had said that she would like Minnie to have it, to bring her luck. There it played on the floor when Peter went in to bring her out her trousseau, holding in its cold cavities all the bits and bobs which she had placed there in the months leading up to her marriage. Giving the lie to that Hun of long ago, he drove to her old home in the village, returning with the Butlers' trunk sitting on the seat opposite him, a common mug acting as its label.

The pony, her tacklings removed, was tumbling in the dust pit and Peter must surely have hit the fourth field by the time Minnie had unpacked the top compartment of the old trunk – clothes mostly, her frocks and bibs, her punter's things for wearing on the farm. Together the couple had carried it into the parlour and placed it in the middle of the floor, Peter laughing at its isolation, it being, along with the Up-to-date Studio's photograph of their likenesses on the mantelpiece, one of the only two items in the square room. 'Don't you worry, love,' he promised her, 'it won't always be this bare. Just gimme time and I'll knock together the things you need for here.'

But furniture was soon forgotten, for on removing things from the second cavity of the trunk she came across the violin, the ominous blackness of its case sanded by the years. The discovery stopped her in her tracks, for now she had to thump the violin case on the floor and rescue the fiddle from within its hump-backed hold. Bringing it with her, she took her place in her new chair in the kitchen and began to limber up her fingers and bowing arm. How long she sat could only be measured by the sounds of a cow lowing near the haggard gate. Her fingers froze in lightness, her heart holding still. She hadn't completed her unpacking and now, with the fire burnt out, she knew that there was no likelihood of grub being ready for the evening meal.

This morning, this early morning, she minded again how Peter, hearing the music pouring from the open windows, abandoned the cows and making a beeline for the kitchen burst in, his face agog with interest. She started to put away the violin but he begged her to go on. He sat himself on the second step of the stairs, his nailed boot ready to stress the cement floor, his freshly lit Woodbine curling limbs of smoke from between his fingers.

Quietly she sat down again. Sitting on the edge of her seat she was shy now, as an audience sat there watching. Bent low, he pretended he was just listening but the moment she got up steam, he was seven steps ahead of her, his nail boot his *bodhrán*. Scutching along, she drabbed her dance tunes for her husband, but at the end of her recital waited a great treat.

'I'll have to stand up for this next thing,' she said. 'It's for you, it's a tune I only learnt lately, and I want to get it right.' Her cheeks grew flushed and he, noticing, said, 'B'japers, this sounds mysterious.' Looking at her, he drew miserly on his little biteen of his second fag and waited.

She, the praying-mantis of her mother's rood-screen, ignored his banter for, caught up now in her music, she started to play 'She Moved Through The Fair'. A look of bafflement crept over Peter

74

O'Brien's face. He never knew she could play like this. She had only ever mentioned it in passing. 'I play a bit on the fiddle,' that was all she had said, but now she had stunned him and he grew shy at his discovery. As though the truth lay secretly hidden elsewhere, that look on her husband's face wildly flitted before her eyes and, remembering where she was, she somehow moved the mug a little and as though she didn't see the scum on the dregs of her tea said, 'Lord above, will you look't the time, and me with no stirabout ready for the breakfast.'

## CHAPTER 25

The pony's racket was wrong. Saturday, Saturday, Saturday, was the rhythm of her gait as she trotted along the road. The young whipper-snapper couldn't get her two-beat stride right for she added lucky-strike methods to her every step. Wanting her to smarten up her pace was but Peter's aggravation for as Minnie sat in the trap this exciting day she didn't notice anything the matter with the pony's trot. All she could think of was her clock under its lid lying waiting where the barge dropped it off, the sin waiting patiently for her to come and claim it.

Despite the fumble in the pony's gait, the trap nevertheless moved ever onwards. As she trotted her ears stood cocked and her eyes set themselves on the horizon ahead. The thought of her failing to arrive in Huntstown never crossed her mind; more likely would be the worry that she might shy at a flying paper.

Peter was as happy as the day's long, sitting opposite Minnie as he encouraged the pony along. The day was fine, though a breeze blew straight into their faces. They chatted about the family farms and cottage houses on either side of the road, but once

75

Drumhollow was left behind Minnie found that she ran out of information. Her husband, though, could give the seed, breed and generation of every family, and sometimes he drew her attention to houses tucked away behind shelter belts or perched tightly on a distant hill. She only knew one other holding, situated close by the bridge which they were now approaching. 'Isn't that there the house where Nuala Lynam comes from? Remember she came all the way out to see your new house? She told me that day that she lived in the house near the bridge,' and she pointed at the long single-storeyed house with its corrugated tin roof.

'Yea, that's Johnny Lynam's place,' said Peter. 'Johnny has a big crowd of them there. You're right, that's where Nuala lived, but I heard lately that she's gone now, to live with an aunt and uncle in Birmingham.'

His answer was straightforward enough, but still Minnie detected an edge in his voice, the sound bringing her slap-bang back to the night when she sold him the mousetrap. She held her whisht, though, and instead, sizing up the sky, she said, 'I hope the day holds out till we get the clock home.'

'Backitup, backitup,' called Peter as he backed the pony until the trap was near to the big door of the stone shed which acted as the dropping-off stage for the barge from Dublin. The depot hand saw him approaching and noticed that in place of his usual common cart he drove today a nice round trap. 'Who's the young girl?' he asked when Peter came in, and with a bragging smile his customer replied that he had married since last he saw him. They chatted amicably; they knew each other well. Peter had oftentimes come to collect goods ferried from Dublin, and the man was always ready to help him with the loading.

In a matter of minutes the men emerged carrying the long cardboard container out towards the trap. Minnie dismounted the moment she saw them coming. 'Good day ma'am,' the stranger said by way of signalling that he knew her status, and she, bowing, smiled his way. The men lifted the box up into the trap and, jockeying it this way and that, decided to let it run the whole length of one seat. Now they went to fetch the mahogany planks and, returning, set about tying them into place alongside the clock. The load left little space for the two dreamers, but with a board pushed along a bit Minnie managed to wedge into her seat, and climbing on board Peter sat down beside her, trying his damnedest to double back his legs in the space left to him for manoeuvring.

It was duskiss by the time they set out for home. The clock and planks still sat where they had been secured, but down on the floor of the trap sat a supply of groceries and set there too, with its long blade sticking up through the space behind the pony's rump, was a new scythe for cutting thistles and docks or even meadow in places where the straitlaced blade of the mowing machine couldn't easily go.

The load was heavy and the salt-and-pepper pony's pace was snail-slow. The road was deserted and even seemed slippery, for sometimes the pony's hooves seemed to snap in their footwork. All around her the countryside, sly in gut, listened, stringing her hoofbeats into its maw. It even noticed that when her driver urged her on, his voice seemed preoccupied, his sentences hanging themselves as though ether. 'Gid up there, attagirl,' he said quite often, but the countryside was right in its suspicions, for despite the cosy image depicted by this moving white hope, the sadness of a memory was back to haunt. Across the hedges lay old lights and safe houses, stacks of turf and haggard cocks of hay, grazing livestock and barking dogs. But there too, in this Irish landfall-struck-silent, lurked bad feelings, as brother got up charges against brother, father against son, nephew against uncle, all in the cause of holy hell. Peter stirred his pony homewards but in between conversations with his wife, he was plodding those fields, himself and his volunteer comrades, his brother the captain of their brigade. Indeed it was just over from here that he and John had spent their last night together. They had hidden in their safe house beside the rescuing ricefield, and old Sarah Lynch had given them her last farl of griddle-bread and a Baby Power. Between them they shared it as they hid low in a dyke. The taste of the whiskey burned now in his mouth, the memory fussing, but John and he were brothers together, not like now. Now the fear for the future emptied his full mouth in one sharp swallow.

They were about halfway home when Peter dismouted to light the trap's lamp. Cracking a match, he held it cupped near the candle wick. The flame jittered until he closed the lamp door, and now as the trap slowcoached homewards, the lamp heralded its coming in a white light and its going on in red.

Though the sun had long since gone down, the new moon stole across the heavens, her fast light hidden behind her placid presence. Minnie oftentimes glanced up at her, wanting some light to fall on her cargo, on her clock which had journeyed through day and night through acres of Ireland, through Sinn Fein fields and through gladiators' haunts, to be here in their trap tonight. Her notions numbered the bridges under which it likely struggled, the simple swans which must have beaten wings before slipping way, the scent of flowers and grasses through which it must have meandered, as stumbling by city and towns it crept along at a hoof's clip-clop. The hill O'Down it would have passed, and Kilcock too, as the barge which wombed it preyed it along the fleshy waters of the Royal Canal.

## CHAPTER 26

The gate was shut tight as tuppence when they got back from Huntstown, so Peter had to extricate himself from his gombeen's confinement before he could hobble towards the bolt and draw it back. 'Drive her in, love,' he said as with a flourish he swung the gate wide open and the woman, taking the shrewd reins in her hands, drove the pony and trap, and clock as well, through into the boreen inside.

Darkness, the darkness which accompanied them all the way home, now drunk with power, enveloped them even more drastically the duration as they lessened themselves down the little road towards the house. Nothing had readily kicked over the traces while they were absent, but the moment they drove into the yard the natives all became notorious, their voices harmonising the hunger which by now gnawed at their vitals.

Where the pigs had slept all day, stunting their hunger, they now screeched as they made known their appetites. The sucking calves denied their tin mothers, started to suntan the air with their plaintive attentions. The four cows, three heavy with milk, stood chewing their cud, dilapidated from waiting, but the moment they sensed a touch of hands on their paps they began to orchestrate their voices to echo each other as they lowed their point of view. Only the hens had given up on their fool's pickings. Thumbnosing at the big Rhode Island Red cock who heaved his stubborn, last-minute crow, they hen-stepped off to their perches, hen-brained enough to know that sleep is food and greatness can do without it.

When he had the animals seen to, Peter struggled to drag the mahogany planks from where they sat exacting a shower of May rain. In a pile he pegged them down, stained by big splatters of rain. Kicking them idly he was at the same time picturing the cabinet which he planned to make and his eyes, though looking vacantly at them, were in fact intriguing a stylish piece of furniture. He could picture it now, standing in its graveyard of shavings and sawdust, the favourite held together with dowels. Yes, he'd hold each dowel in his mouth till the saliva would moisten it and then, with a groove already cut in its sides he'd home it, slippy and easily driven in, and the air which it'd displace could then escape back out through the groove. His chosen cabinet would have chamfering, concaving, carving and even some inlay as well. Umpteen designs floated to the surface of his brain as he stood there in his workshop, but he continued to shoo them off for the fume wasn't right yet. The artist in him wouldn't sing out till the time was ripe and the tune was sweet.

## CHAPTER 27

When Peter settled how the cabinet might stooge for him, he returned to the kitchen: he knew Minnie would be on tenterhooks, waiting to erect the clock in its pet place. She had already removed the tyings and set the lid standing against the dresser, feeling the mistress of the kitchen every time her steely look glanced into the box. There as though shy the clock lay, its body trim, its hands joined still at twelve o'clock. The voice in its throat was completely still; a foible would be needed to get it to speak. Where she had stood that day in Crow Street and on opening the door of its belly had seen its guts going and coming when needed, she saw now but a great nothingness, for, dreadfully, with its innards removed its belly held nothing now but wind. It was as if pabulum had eaten its Julian's thumbs and left a scarecrow there to play dead rather than let her see the future.

Big Bullavander, the hectoring clock, was at last fitted in underneath the seventh step of the stairs. Room had to be left so that his hat containing his glass eye could be fitted down over his brains and face. The weights were so heavy that Peter didn't trust Minnie to hold them, causing the very first row here in the new kitchen. The disagreement which began over the weights spilled over into an argument about how to regulate the pendulum. If it was hung high up, it meant the clock could be made to run faster, and hung lower the clock could be made to run slower, but the balance was hard to find, the hanging went on for ages. Peter was tired from his day's grafting, Minnie was weary from being idle all day, even the pony in the field only now felt relief following her long Saturday, Saturday, Saturday journey into town and her foot-snapping journey home. But the new inhabitant, relishing walls around him in place of that cardboard coffin, stood devil-may-care there, the very centre of attention.

For all the world as though it were a game of ping-pong, the couple gregged each other. Minne was anxious to see the pendulum swinging but Peter, with an eye for detail, was waiting until he felt sure before even setting the hands at the correct time. Quietly the clock stood waiting the outcome, its doors open wide, its face hungry as whiteness, its tomboy-hands black as lies. Sometimes the bell in its brain tinkled madly, their fleshy hands driving it wild, but still and all, it comforted itself by reasoning that its moment for off was nearing, yes, the pendulum in its middle now hung steady, its balance gauged exactly right.

After what seemed an age Peter looked at his pocket watch and began to set the time. He fixed the hour hand exactly at eleven, and then moving the big hand he worked it all around its orbit until it rested at the figure nine. Now the stage was set, so taking a last glance at his watch, he tipped the pendulum, sending it swinging over and back on the caffeine clock, the clock which was going to farm the future for simpletons.

Peter fell asleep that night before Minnie ever came to bed, for she stayed below in the kitchen assembling her thoughts as she heron-watched the clock. As she listened and learned from this Nathaniel Hodges clock, she found herself thinking of her mother, her own strength came from watching how that woman cadenced joy where only slavery stumbled. Suddenly, though, those voices from the past vacated the kitchen, for now this clock's song would hear her silent note, plotting to afford her a sunny tenor to her violin's concerto.

The clock chimed twice as she climbed the stairs to bed. She was tired out from her long day's fling. Undressing, she draped her clothes across the back of a chair before sliding her body in alongside her husband's, her mole-in-the-hole stumbling at the touch of him in his dreams.


CHAPTER 28


Holly Bog, the flint of winter's fire, belonged to the inhabitants of Drumhollow and its environs. It was divided into turf banks, each bank forming turbary attaching to each neighbour's holding. The bog was located about two miles away by road, but as the crow flies it was a mere two fields and a birch wood away. Generations of O'Briens had cut their bank each year, and now it was the turn of Peter O'Brien to cut and come again, for as long as he lived.

Thursday, June-day, saw him set off for the bog, to prepare the O'Briens' bank for cutting. He drove his donkey and cart, for he had to bring his bog-barrows and tools to the place where he planned a victory.

He was all alone as he stood up there in the purple heather cutting great sunders from the high virgin bank, which he then pushed over to drop down into the waiting bogholes below. Last year's site of unearthing was now full to the brim with brown bogwater, but as each sunder fell that water became dislodged. The placid waters broken from their confines flowed and leaked into dividing drains, each time a sunder fell down, each time a sturdy foothold drew nearer. Pillar after pillar, the sunders dropped until the water had been driven away, and now with further additions of birch branches, heather and wobbly boards Peter made a floor where the water had only lately reigned. He tramped and stamped it until he knew that the surface could hold the heavy-laden barrows. He never halted the face-saving until he saw the thankless bank stage-managing to become a limerick to his winter's fire.

The long drawn-out road to the bog was a must when ass and cart brought folks' barrows and implements to the bog, but later, when the two desperadoes set out to cut their turf, they took the shortcut through their neighbours' fields. As they wended their way, he carried the basket of grub and the three-quart can of spring water. Minnie bested along beside him, free to be herself until they arrived at the site which Peter had readied for harvesting.

Minnie O'Brien had never stood in a bog before, much less acquired the knack of gripping soft mushy sods of wet peat. After some rehearsal, though, the play between the turfcutter and his catcher began to come almost naturally to her. She started off by quite wildly missing the sods coming towards her, and even the ones which she did manage to catch broke in her hands and dropped in a heap at her feet. Peter, though, was encouraging: the girl from the huckster's shop would soon learn her art, he felt, and as though anxious to prove him right, before very long she began to feel confident as sod after sod was caught, and, still intact, was left down to camp upon the barrow.

The dress rehearsal over, the O'Briens were ready to start. Out of the June sky the sun beat down. Orchestral manoeuvres in the dark-brown secrets of Holly Bog were about to begin. The mesmeric floor faced them both. Board after board, each a foot deep, was about to be cut from the turf mass. Peter the sleansman, was tackled and ready; Minnie the catcher, holding her stance, stood waiting. He stood at the turf-face, symbolizing all that was free and flowing in his masculinity. She stood there on the new stage, ready, willing, and receptive to any flung sods of wet turf. He set up the ballet, she became his ballerina. Slean in hands, he sliced off the first sod. Now his slean swung towards her, and yielding him a catcher's grasp she clutched his sod, swung around and slapped it down onto the slatted barrow. Nervous at the start, here they stood, Nijinsky and Pavlova, now stealing the limelight from an uncle and aunt who never got their chance to jump an *entrechat*.

No words needed to be spoken on Holly Bog that day, the only friction to be heard from the slap of the slean against the next sod, and the sound of the caught sod being slapped against those sitting on the barrow. Minnie's strength allowed her to catch and wheel away eighteen sods but, deeming her man to have almost double her strength, she, when she filled his barrowload, piled on the agony to the tune of two rows and a rider. Thus they worked each livelong day until Peter found himself working down the depth of a grave but doubled, and finding himself down at this depth he had no choice but to leave all the catching and wheeling to his girl. Her strength ebbing, he advised her to 'Load light and go often', his mantra his only help to her, his reassurances ringing out from the floor on which he now stood, below there where air and keebs trapped in the time of Stone Age man now eased from the peat which his slean gutted.

It took in all ten days to murder the turf bank, ten less than lonely days when Minnie, her hands blistered from clutching the barrow handles near the umbo, wheeled and wheeled away the lunula of turf bank and heeled it up on the forest floor of old, there to let it breathe the foulness of the twentieth century.

The tenth day was in fact the best day of all. It was the day when the last barrowful of turf lay heeled up at the very edge of the fast-filling bogholes. And there, away up on the high bank, the place of next year's cutting, stood Minnie, her face freckled by bog-brown spatters as shoulder to shoulder with her husband she looked down at their handiwork, at the entrails of this Irish monster which between them they had slain and laid out to toast on the strumpet ground.

## CHAPTER 29

That turf lay weathering down in Holly Bog, the crust on the sods battening down while the heavy shower fell, but up in the village this Sunday morning the dreadful rain caused a flood of despair. It was while the priest was still inside in the sacristy that the darkness engulfed the church and its waiting congregation. Vesting for Mass, the curate was in a world of his own. Not for him the damper of torrential rain on a team's hopes. No, he was standing in front of a large crucifix, praying his awe as he put on the amice and alb, and tied the cincture around his waist. Picking up the stole, he kissed the cross on it and haltered it around his neck. Then slipping his head through the opening of the chasuble he let it fall down to hang like a sandwich-board front and back of his body. Finally he lifted the maniple, and sliding his hand through it let it hang there from his fore-arm. Now, fully robed, he stood in Drumhollow Church ready to approach the altar to offer a mystical enactment of the Passion and Death of Christ.

A tinkle of the bell at the sacristy door signalled his arrival in the sanctuary, his acolytes, two young village lads, preceding him as he advanced towards the altar. At the very sound of the warning bell, his congregation rose to their feet and stood in respectful silence. They watched him place the draped chalice down upon the cold table and waited until he kissed the altar stone before they dropped to their knees again.

Mass was in progress when the noise began. Latin words were firing the air. 'Credo in Deum, Patrem omnipotentem, Creatorem caeli et terrae,' prayed the priest as he declared the faith of him and his people. The tinpan-tittling came slowly at first, striking the roof and windows, just tinpan-tittling then suddenly a downpour, belting blazes out of everything it struck. The sound was eerie and the darkness almost that of the catacombs. The only relief was the light stolen from the two candles on the altar. The sound of the torrential rain dressed the congregation in misgivings about today's match and, more importantly, today's victory. 'We'll be damned well washed out of it,' thought the fifteen hurlers to a man, but over in their corral on the other side of the aisle the women were optimistic. 'It's only a shower,' they surmised. 'It'll be over again before we get out.'

Communion time came and went, and though the men received the Eucharist and whispered the weather forecast into God's ear, the rain still battered down. It lasted right the way through Mass, right up to the last Gospel. 'In the beginning was the word,' the priest was saying in Latin, his congregation listening in silence. Suddenly the din switched off and a welcoming slight light began to filter in through the stained glass windows. Peter standing there noticed the change and, squaring his shoulders, he thanked God, for it looked like the match could go ahead today. Minnie, sited amongst the women but back a distance from him, could see his lifted stance, and she knew by the gimp of him what he was thinking about. Her thoughts, though, could never be his. She was

86

at this very moment planning on lighting three candles for the Holy Souls in Purgatory. She had already told God of her discovery this morning, told him how bilious she felt, told him she hadn't a clue what to do; she was, she told him, depending on Him and His holy mother to get her through. She was waiting for this Mass to end and then, when the neighbours filed out, she'd light those candles.

She tried walking on eggshells as she approached the side altar, but the board floor echoed her every step. Her coppers too made a din, as down they dropped into the money box beneath the candelabrum. Despite the distraction, she stooped down and fetched three candles from the little basket on the floor, and lighting each one of them from one already lit and burning, she placed her three in a grouping for themselves. Now she knelt down beside them, her eyes fixed on their flames, and filled the void between them and heaven with her words and worries. Three Hail Marys, that was the quota by which to bring relief to those souls trapped in the no-man's land of Purgatory where, unable to help themselves, they yet could pray for others in distress. Minnie was now banking on that ages-old belief, for to tell the truth she felt at this very moment she needed all the help she could get for her cratered land, she being the only one to know that a baby teed there.

# CHAPTER 30

To a soul, the creatures of fortune turned up at the field singled out as being flat enough for a hurling pitch. Larkin's sheep had done the needful, grazed it to the quick, and now the sun highlighted a nice green down on which the game could be played. The two goals were high in their uprights — Peter no doubt had high soaring balls in mind when he constructed the capital H's. There was no such thing as a changing room; the opposing teams togged out behind two different bushes, their look-outs anxious that their team's mickies could not be viewed by enemy eyes or God forbid, by women. Inside their own coveys, the two captains gave last-minute instructions to their sides. 'Mark your man, stick to him like a barnacle to a boat,' was Peter's advice, and 'Remember,' he added, 'always to face the puck out.' Those were the last words his men heard, for the referee's whistle sounded and sprung them into action.

The coin which the referee tossed into the air fell face down into the green cradle, choosing to give choice of ends to the captain of the visiting team. Ballyduff in their red jerseys settled on playing with the breeze on their backs in the first half, knowing from experience that the dilly-dallying wind might have changed course before the start of the second half.

Though fate had banjaxed the toss of the penny, the village lads were far from be't as they moved to take up their positions, their new jerseys of black with bands of white being worn for the first time today. Nerves, though, played havoc with their senses. Holding their hurleys they fielded out, some swinging on imaginary objects, others gripped by sudden shivers, their whole skins quivering as though they were horses cooling their pelts.

Others still stood relaxed *mar dhea*, but in truth only the start of the game could bring relief from this torture.

White as death, his face a mask, the captain of the Drumhollow team soft-shoe-shuffled in anticipation as he waited the throw-in of the ball. Partnering him at centre-field was his mate Ned Naylor. Ned, totally unfazed by folks' excitement, now and then leaned his whole strength on his hurley, seeming intent on breaking it before ever the match began.

There, then, before an audience of wholly biased spectators, the year's county final was just about to begin. The referee from neutral Brownstown stood with the ball clutched in his hand. The moment his watch read three o'clock he blew the whistle, threw in the *sliothar*, and it was a hurley with tin strips binding its boss which was first to make contact, its owner sending the charred emblem songing its first venture down towards the Ballyduff goalmouth.

Minnie, standing among the Drumhollow spectators, plumbed her hopes for her man and his team-mates. She had watched him last night as he bound strips of tin around the boss of his hurley. 'It'll strengthen it for when it comes to head-on battle for possession,' he laughed, adding, 'in a mêlée of hurls it'll stand up to every abuse.'

Now she noticed that those tin strips glinted in the sunlight as time and time again at midfield that hurley pulled back the scores of Ballyduff. She pursued it for the whole length of the game and watched it balancing the ball as, running the dream of Gerontius, it mulled it over the bar for a point, or het up the opposition by shimmering it beneath the crossbar for a humdinger of a goal.

And when the power was long since gone from her neighbours' lungs she especially watched when — it looking as though the fat was in the fire, the time almost up, a draw in sight, the threatening whistle in the referee's mouth — that creatured hurley with her husband attached stole the ball off a rival's hurley, and velcro-holding it ran ten, twenty, thirty, forty yards before tipping it into the air and clouting it one final wallop, which sent it winging straight as a die between the high uprights to win the foolish match for Drumhollow.

When that final whistle did shrill through the evening, the supporters milled onto the pitch, all high with pity for Ballyduff, but licking their lips with pure delight for their team's win. Regal he seemed, seated up on the villagers' shoulders, the captain who stole victory from the fingers of failure. Minnie, carried along with the crowd rushing towards the team, stood back now on the fringe of the manhandling, being careful of herself. Her sebaceous finding was so new that she felt shy almost, but still she hung on there waiting, waiting to connect with her man. Gradually his gaze wandered from face to face, and then he saw her, and once their eyes met, sorra the one else existed for that split second. He swung away then, his body slithering this way and that, but he had in that one contact yoked his wife into his moment of victory.

## CHAPTER 31

The long five miles strung out before them as, with Minnie in tow, the crowd straggled along on their return trip to the village. 'Up Drumhollow,' the cads cheered with every hill they climbed. Their voices echoed and re-echoed as they seared the prime of the lazy lands which stretched on either side of them, for time, the guardian of their locality's entrenched mentality, had only ever witnessed defeat at the hands of jildy Ballyduff. Minnie, though, hearing their bragging cheers, had her own know. 'Maybe it was their new jerseys which brought them luck,' she surmised, but they, the locals, thought it was all the doing of her husband. 'Only for him we were be't,' they said. 'It was him who snatched the game out of the fire.'

Out in front and still playing captain, Peter led the victorious mob all the way back to Drumhollow. His head in the clouds, he walked on air. He deduced that his team could from here out do full justice to themselves, for now that they had broken the Ballyduff jinx they could beat anyone. Behind him, and mixed in with the crowd, he knew his wife drifted, but this evening he had his hour to savour, his new fame to experience.

Minnie was indeed behind him, working her way homewards, her neighbours all over and about her now that her husband had stolen victory for them. Gradually, though, she fell back until she could manage to slip off without being noticed, for she had her morning's suspicions to think about, and the boreen called to her once she neared the gate.

Once the gate was closed behind her, the flurry started in her mind. Back it came, the innocent of this morning's findings. 'Wait'll he hears there's a babby on the way, he'll be over the moon,' she told herself. Donning the mantle of mother-to-be she strolled along, comfortable looking at, and listening to, the carry-on of the nature within the boreen. Yes, the white blossoms of May were a thing of the past, the colours of autumn now beginning to no longer hide and wait. But she didn't care about any changes like that, conscious there and then of the bubbling innocence, still green as it was within her own womb. Timing her nature, she moved further along, the yaw in the road correcting itself as she advanced.

Sometimes she stopped there to listen to that other new thing, the sound of the brouhaha as the victorious Drumhollow team neared the village. She stopped again when she reached the wicket gate and, leaning on it awhile, imagined what her man's reaction would be to the great news which she had been keeping on the back burner all day.

Hot fried golden rolls of boxty with a ham and onion filling were there on the plate before him when he sat at the table. 'If I don't have spuds for him in some shape or form he'd think he'll die,' she had told herself as she rasped the raw potatoes. Now she was glad she had gone to the trouble, for he was indeed starving after his fierce day. Two tumblersful of porter was all that had passed his lips since breakfast, and now he sat and savoured his tea-dinner. Cup after cup of tea she poured for him, and all the while she poured it her idle hand caressed the nape of his neck. Her touch, though gentle, was desperate to be noticed but he, thin in his dibble's pour, felt that she too was fussing as, full now of his own importance, he believed that she hero-worshipped him too.

The match had been played in Larkin's field, but now every twist and turn of it was re-enacted in the O'Briens' kitchen. As he ate his meal, Peter talked his wife through all of the details of his win. 'Ah, will you shush, love,' she at last said. 'Sure I played a harder match on the sideline than you did out on the field, and when you went, love, on that solo-run, my God, my tummy was in a knot, what if you put that ball wide, what then? I know I'd have died there on the spot.'

'So would I, love,' he admitted, and for the first time since he arrived home he grew humble. 'Sure Minnie, that's the luck o'the game,' he said. 'The ball went right for me today, but it could have gone wide just as easy.'

Tiredness struck once he had his belly full. Four cups of tea, the whole plate of boxty, and two helpings of apple pie with cream from the dairy puddled around it, it took to satisfy his hunger. 'That boxty did the trick,' he said as he patted his stomach. 'Tell us, Minnie Humphrey,' he said, 'how's a fella going to dance at the *ceilidh* tonight and you having him full as a tick?' She laughed as he hugged her, and shooed him off to get his chores done.

The farmyard's circus never got a quicker run-through than it did that evening. This farmer had a kick in him now which the animals had never before witnessed. Milking was done rapidly, calves once fed were left to their own afters, and the hungry pigs, though still squealing and shoving, were given their mash. What they did with it was their own business, for their owner had been quite a wizard today and now, the hero of the hour, he was to be one of the victims at the shenanigans in the village school.

It was black as pitch, the slothful night, when, the chores done, the couple set out for the *ceilidh* and the presentation of the cup and medals. At death's door, cradled the moon in the lifeless sky. They stepped gingerly at first, but then growing accustomed to the darkness they strode along more surely. When they reached the gate he stopped her, whispering, 'This medal tonight is for you, my first hurling medal, you can keep it and maybe some day give it to a son of ours. Anyhow love, it's for you, before we go out on the road I wanted to tell you that.' Then he kissed her and held so, her lips sealed, she couldn't say aught, anyhow the moment wasn't right, it was *his* really. The syndicate which ruled her body knew that, knew the hearsay of men, knew that she couldn't pierce his bubble, not now when he was being hailed as a saviour. His say said, they readied themselves again and cautiously opened the gate.

## CHAPTER 32

Set in the very street itself, the school tonight housed almost every man, woman and child for miles. Nothing more exciting had this school seen before, and such was the wildness that the old parish priest himself, and he on his last legs, vowed that he'd be there tonight if it so happened that Drumhollow hurlers scooped their first ever County Final.

Old daylight had long since gone and black myths' assembly aggravated the street by the time the look-out heard the heavy clip-clopping of the approaching horse. Running to the gate, the captain and his mates took up their position, and there in the light of two lanterns they stood waiting, so proud of what they had achieved.

Now, though, their pride was of a different hue, for the fact was that their answer to the rich horse-Protestants of the locality, their own parish priest, his driver plying onwards the big black horse with the bald white face pulling the large tub-trap, was coming to add distinction to their achievement of today.

Though used to seeing this horse and trap, the men still stood in admiration as the great brute beast came to a halt beside them, his driver shouting 'Whoa there!' in pleading bravado. His grooming was the last word in perfection: even his hooves caught the light, being polished black for effect. Though he now stood still, his harness continued on its journey, the leather crunching and complaining as was its style. The owner, dressed in his black garb, with a white collar hunting at his throat, dismounted stiffly from the trap, while the driver, making certain that the horse didn't giddy onwards, stood resolutely holding his bowing head.

His congratulations offered to this welcoming party, the priest set out with them for the schoolroom where the dancing was now in progress, leaning with every arthritic step he took on his polished blackthorn cane. His position secretly winnowed him from the supple activities inside, and as his ear picked up the music, he nodded to himself, his face smiling his aged smile of lonely resignation.

The band, which had been at full throttle, came to a sudden halt, the billy being given to the squeezeboxes, the spoons and the fiddle by the look-out on the door. The board floor which for the hour had been franked, now famished, as hundreds of feet yielded up a roadway to an old man's steps as he made his way towards the improvised stage. Here the silver trophy stood all isolated, looking as though it was waiting for the touch of this priest's thin, ivory hands.

Quietness descended as the warring Firbolgs turned a turn-about on the pages of the Annals of Westmeath. Yes, they thought, we dreaded the entry for today. 'I feel a great delight in being here with you tonight,' the priest said, glancing at the envelope in his hand to remind himself of what he wished to say. 'I've been watching this team build up,' he said, 'and know well the long hours of practice it took to bring yourselves this far. I'd be pleased if it was a football match which you all won today, but hurling' — and now he stopped and, ignoring the words on the envelope, looked around at them and, smiling, said — 'Hurling is the most skilful game in the world. You all know from your schoolbooks that the game of hurling goes back as far as Setanta, or Cuchulainn as he became known, and here you saw today the hurlers to whom the skill has come down.'

His every sentence was met with a round of applause, but when he lifted the trophy to present it to the captain his action brought the place down. He stood there too and joined in the applause as Peter lifted high the cup, the cup held up so that the stars this night could be reflected in its silver skin.

But it was when the captain stepped forward to receive his medal that the wolf-whistles fried the atmosphere; long timely whistles coupled with lusty cheering broke out, for this crowd knew only too well that but for him they'd have had to wait for another day.

It took Peter some minutes before he arrived back to Minnie but true to his word she was first to hold it, and first to study its design. The silver medal was in the shape of a shield: ornamental tracery ran around its rim, curling in loops and knots, punching sometimes stopping it from running too far. In the very centre of the design bulged a circle of bronze, and carved on it was two hurleys crossed in relief and a ball sited there between their handles. 'It's beautiful,' said Minnie, 'it's really exquisite,' the delicateness of the medal's tracery appealing to her eye. 'You know what I told you,' the hero of the hour whispered and she, glancing sideways at him, smiled and nodded in self-conscious delight.

One, two, three, four, five, six, seven sidestepped the dancers as, the presentations over with, they got down to their night of celebrations. Only the priest had walked away from the victory scene, and now, as the heavy clopping horse headed back to

Huntstown, he carried in his wagon of pity, a prick at the reins and a saint sitting opposite, waffling in his sleep.


# CHAPTER 33


The *ceilidh* ended in pleasant weariness, and then the revellers moved on to where the bonfire was burning on the *plásán* near the forge, its flames and sparks bursting into the night's blackness. Neighbours taffrailed around it, talking the talk of tiredness. The young bloods of the townland, who had spent hours building it, now cheered to send the signal of their magic into the strutting sky. Minnie stood beside her husband, the light catching her face in its fun palace of shapes. She had, like a hen on a nest, stayed hatching her secret all day, but now as she coaxed her man to come on home, she had decided that her wait was over. Tonight she was going to be true to herself.

He made an awful eejit of himself when he heard that his bride was going to have his baby. 'Me going to be a father!' he said as, hugging and kissing Minnie, he swung her around, her feet sometimes hitting the floor, but most times not, waltzing her all around the kitchen table. 'God, I'll be so proud of him,' he boasted. 'Wonder will he look like me or like you – God forbid, but wouldn't it be shockin' if he looked like the "boiled shite" himself!' They laughed uproariously, neither meaning to belittle the other. Sighing and then taking a whit to cheer again, he masqueraded the daddy image, always referring to the baby as 'he'. He was still at it as he mounted the stairs to bed, saying 'daddy' with almost every step; he was still at it as he lay in his marriage bed, but when his pregnant wife climbed in beside him, the daddy bit was soon

96

forgotten, the lover taking over until this clocker's angst was but a lackadaisical sigh.

## CHAPTER 34

Three months had slipped away before the news announced itself to her mother. It was Sunday dinner which did it. Throughout her childhood her tastes had never once been catered for, her notions had no bearing on the dinner menu. 'Pig's bum, cabbage and potatoes' she hated with a vengeance, but her mother, victim that she was, cooked the salty bacon especially to please her husband's taste. The bacon always put an edge to his thirst, so when he went to the shebeen just short of five o'clock, his need for porter was akin to that of a desert nomad. The more he drank, the thirstier he got. The more he satisfied his need, the drunker he became. The never, never, thought-about wife stayed at home with her daughter, liking the freedom to be themselves until lang-go-lee his staggering footsteps could be heard somehow shuffling towards them, come closing time each Sunday night.

Today would be no different; the dinner would be the same, but today her mother would have put four names in the pot but only three would dine from it. Today the very smell was indeed enough to make Minnie feel sick. She had to yield to her nose and about turn to go outside for fresh air.

'Is it what I think it is?' whispered Sally Humphrey as she joined her girl at the front door. Now she and her daughter snuggled in an embrace of wily understanding. They whispered, though there was no reason; they giggled, the mother no better than her nineteen-year-old daughter; but the moment they joined Jack and Peter in the kitchen they came over all decorous as the daughter broke her news to her own father.

'That calls for a drink,' her hungry father bragged as his future solemnly seemed strangely poor. Turning an about turn, he went to the parlour and, fetching his bottle of whiskey, began rostering panicking God's names, ones he thought suitable for a grandson of his. Whiskey for himself and his son-in-law he heeled out into the glasses and, Tolstoys both, they drank in celebration of their will and deeds' name. 'Here's to the new babby,' the grandfather-to-be said, and his son-in-law, touching his glass with his one, replied: 'Aye please God, it's great news, isn't it?'

## CHAPTER 35

As was usual nowadays, Peter O'Brien woke before the clock. After all, he was now going to be a father, and in his mind this child his wife was carrying was, in a manner of speaking, going to pay the ransom which he felt he owed his late uncle, the crabbed westerner, who straddled loneliness here after the decline snuck away his girl. If only he could come back, he'd get the land of his life, for now his old green-stained thatched house was gone, and standing in its frolicking foundations stood a gem of his own nephew's creation.

Two storeys tall the new house stood, the windows big and running wide. Assessing he'd need several rooms for his offspring, he thought up three more rooms for them. For all the world as though he feared a neighbour's avarice, he built on a fine sturdy roof to it. Beginning at the wallboard, he nailed on layer after layer of blue slates, stopping only when space ran out, and not be't even then, he capped the whole scenario with a cartwheel of brownish-red earthenware ridge tiles.

In his element he was, up there on the new roof that April day when the Black and Tans drove down the boreen. He was fitting the flashing around the chimneys and, determined not to panic, he stood his ground, the faces of the 'Tans the only thing out of kilter down in his front yard. 'Getting married, are we?' was their first parry; 'See any Shinners?' their next.

He looked down at them and, pretending he couldn't hear, held his left hand open at his ear. 'See any Sinn Fein Fenians?' they shouted, their mocking tones turned ratty, a rifle in their midst. But he, a living breathing Sinn Fein suspect, took his time before replying. Panning around the surrounding fields, he then decided to look back down at the rabble, the picture of innocence as he shook his head.

In a cloud of black exhaust fumes they drove away, their pot-shot target still kneeling where he was. 'God Above, but that was the close call,' he thought as he remembered the three lads who just a few moments ago had been filling a bottle of milk in his dairy. Liam Mellows had in fact even waited back to shout up instructions about the funeral of a friend before taking to his heels, the three heading off towards Holly Bog.

The sound of the Crossley tender had vanished into the stung countryside by the time he dared be seen dismounting from his perch. 'One son under a heap of clay in Meeden is enough for any mother,' he was thinking, 'another up here in the cemetery would be the last straw.' He thanked his lucky stars, for he could well imagine his mother's reactions if she could have seen the sitting duck he was just now, rifles trained on him. Now he calmed down again, and the chat last night came back to him. The news arriving by bush telegraph was hinting that Britain was nearly ready to cut her stick and even their own side was second thinking, had their bellyful, there was word of maybe a truce. 'Wouldn't it be just my luck,' he thought, 'like Francis Ledwidge, I'd be smigged, and the end of the war in sight.'

His step was nervous as he walked towards the turf shed where he had stored some of his furniture, and in at the back of the dresser press he had the naggen of whiskey, but the men had had a swig last night and now there was just a mouthful or two for him. Battening down his nerves was his intention as he walked towards the steps leading up to the calves' hill. Sitting down on them, he took a gulp of whiskey from the bottle and swallowed it down in a hurry. He stressed the need for it in his stomach as he sat there thinking, a thread of gumption still holding sway. Wise now after the fact, he nursed the last of the whiskey, his hands stunning the bottle with their attention.

A full twenty minutes slipped by before he gradually came to and began thinking of his house again. The windows were next for fitting. He had already red-leaded them, and the new door which he had made was leaning against the workbench in his shed. 'I'll fit them all in the next few days,' he said, 'and then I can go to Huntstown to have a look at paint.' Nothing more, he decided, could be done this evening; his mind wasn't on it any more. Only one more mouthful remained in the bottle, and, taking stock, he now put the bottle on his head, and down his gullet tumbled the hot humour.

His fields evidenced his greased steps as he set off for the river. In the mearing ditch birds sang, gloating over his escape. The cattle grazing in the fourth field were faced homewards, their ringleader a few paces in front, her head down, biting the clay in her anxiety to chop grass. He, though, was not for noticing things of the fresh evening. He strolled along, his hands in his trouser pockets, he thinking of his brother. The gun which had killed him might soon be silenced for good and all, for ever, but the harm was done: the croppy boy lay muted by human hand.

When Peter reached the river he sat down on the bank, his boots hanging just clear of the flowing water. For what seemed an age he continued to sit there, his eyes vacantly watching the ripples whisper along. Down beneath the tinted water lay the bed of stones, still and silent despite the ever-moving river. As though wishing to add to the volume of the water, he cast in his dewdrops of history, his brother's name first in his funeral, respectable in its description. Truce was another idea which he cast in, the sound of the ponderous vision taking time to move off. Lucky that he was to be still alive, he threw in his words of gratitude to mingle with the truce wake. 'Yes,' he thought, 'I'm steeped to be still here and building my own house,' and now he began to storybook the countless blank faces of local Volunteers all gone from the countryside. 'Yes,' he told the river, 'they're all gone, milked through the gap opened by the boys in Dublin. It was madness,' and now he absolutely whispered it, 'madness to take on an empire with nothing but our bare hands.' Now he began his roll-call again, the names of his comrades dropping from his heart. They were only country fellows, none of them warlords; they didn't know they were in fact being led by a group of innocents who believed in their ability to take on an empire by splaying their poets' dreams through the dry masonry of Gulliver's city. He bowed now as he folded each martyr's name where water waited. The O'Rahilly sank first, solemnly sank, then in dropped Plunket, McDonagh, and the others, but when he came to that 'prince of men P. H. Pearse', his lips moved in reverence for there, echoing echoes, the stoicism which was Pearse's secret weapon tinkled through to him before it finally folded itself into the soft water and headed off towards Huntstown. Guerrilla warfare might have won the day, he reasoned, but the strength of them and their eight hundred Volunteers taking on seventy thousand British soldiers was, he knew, a dream freewheeling towards annihilation. But with that thought came another dating back to his schooldays. Remembering his old teacher's words he now started to think of what the foreigners had done as turn and turn about they raped his beloved country. Thanks to his schoolmaster's lessons he saw Partholan buried, his newly-murdered hound buried alongside him. Where he came from, nobody could tell. Then came the Firbolgs, then the Tuatha de Danan; Nemedians came too, maybe before the Celts or maybe after the Norsemen, he couldn't remember. And then there was the Fomorians, the pirate giants, was it the south of the country which experienced their piracy or maybe the west? And did it matter in which order or from what direction they all came? All it proved was that their master was right when he told them that their bear-shaped island had more foreign blood in its clay than the whole of Europe combined. The history lesson had almost flowed away, but then up cropped Cromwell. He, the last to come, did the most destruction, banjaxed everything standing, and as though that was not enough he then planted his own bully boys there in the north. 'The Fardowns'll never come in with us, never join in with us,' he told the river. 'They'll not, not while there's life left in the kick of an ass.'

Growing cold now as he sat there in his hunched form on the river bank, he heaved a deep moan and, as though it were an omen of things to come, he thought of where he had been just two nights ago. They had both lain nearby where the brown bracken used to stand, and he could even now feel again the long strands of wavy hair sliding through his fingers. He smiled as he remembered the yes of her body to his, the whispered words of love from the girl, his own lusty feelings stringing words for the moment. His guilty feelings forced his mind into thinking of the girl: no great mind reader she, her innocence swallowed his flummery, heeded his wants.

He was caught off guard now by the resting image of a human face cackling at him from the clay bank opposite him. Two holes made by birds, perhaps, sat close together, spilled clay resembling traces of dried up tears falling from their sockets. A dirty-white sinew of some hidden root stuck out from the bank and then buried itself again just where a nose would sit. The gash in the place suitable for a mouth could have been her mouth, hung there wide open as though hesitating to find out if a gun could blow out her breath. And framing the guilty image opposite hung grass browned by winter frosts. Red, the grass should be, he thought, for Nuala Lynam, the poor girl, had the most stunning hair of any easy girl round Huntstown. He sniggered now at having had his way the free night, but the girl his heart played for had not yet flickered in his eyeline. He'd know her when he found her, but the daughter of the poor carter near the bridge could never fill his head with virginal imaginings.

## CHAPTER 36

Searching doesn't always mean finding, but under the maxim that 'the divil's children have the divil's luck' he gadded for a few months more and then she happened, the girl, the umbilical thing to which he thought he'd like to be tied down the enemy lifetime.

Nearby his past licked along. The carter's girl, spirited away by her father, had gone to stay the duration with her aunt and uncle in Birmingham. Dreadful, her going away in shame, her sadness compounded by the doubting words of her baby's plaster-cast father, but then her clumped baby thought nothing of the journey, but lay low until he landed in a barren couple's nest. There he made them feel respectable, became their cuckoo, though his song was ever fierce as he sang his notes towards Ireland.

A plaster-cast father to one baby didn't mean that he was going to fail the one bejaysused in the marriage bed, so up he got at sparrow-fart each morning, wanting to keep his eye on the future. His new wife expecting her new baby had him all a-dither. She, with her woman's common sense, coursed full steam ahead while he continued to thumbsuck in worry, worrying that he might have left something undone, something to chance.

This March night in Drumhollow sensed something, for like a stymied monster the countryside froze, frost hoaring uliginious ale and vacant secrets. Not about to fail, not now when Minnie needed

103

him most, Peter O'Brien cycled pell-mell towards the doctor's house. Recycling his guilt for the past, he pedalled, up one side, down the other, the pedals went, he quaking with fear of what was due to him. As though fate wished to rub his nose in it, the trip was all for nothing: Dr Tom Lane was away from home and wasn't due back till late that night. His wife promised that she would try and get in touch with him, and failing that, she promised she'd dispatch him the moment he showed his nose, whatever the time.

Like the hammers o'hell he turned those pedals, the house down the bog road his next port of call. The old resident there was the local handywoman, but now folk seldom bothered her as her years were filling up with *síor-rá*. 'Beggars can't be choosers,' he said the moment her house came into view and yes, the lamp was still lit in her kitchen. The old woman had the hot-water bottle in the bed, the cat let in for the night, the Sacred Heart lamp burning red, and she was just about to light the candle when the awful knocking came to galvanise her.

Never one to choose her steps, Maggie Dempsey steered her way down the boreen to the house of high drama. Her groundwork was laid out for Peter before she sent him hurrying home to break the news that she'd be there in ten minutes. 'Ten minutes,' she laughed now, as with her breath in her fist, she half ran and half stumbled the route which she could one time have travelled in ten minutes. 'Twill keep her heart up,' she said out loud as her own heart ticked in rebellion. Now, though, she had reached the wicket gate, and was telling herself that this was but another babby, no doubt the head must be ready by now.

The stairs nearly took away the last breath from her body, but her best foot was forward as she walked into the well-lit bedroom. One glance at the girl in the bed, though, was all that was needed to make her bones shudder, for in that one glance she sensed trouble. The girl's own mother was by the bedside, her hands dampening her daughter's forehead with a cold damp cloth. Maggie Dempsey, this new servant to the cause, cowering, almost stamped around the room as she tried to cover up her fear. Hands washed, she tied on her old white calico apron, and moving towards the bed, she was the soul of discretion as she examined the fine-boned mother-to-be. Scanning the bulging hill before her, her aged hands searched for the lie of the baby. 'Yes,' she thought, 'the head is down.' Now her hands were seeking some stirring, but all was placid, all as quiet as death inside. She took her wooden ear-trumpet and, desperate for a heartbeat, reddened it against the taut skin but all she could hear was the mother's thumps: the harder she trained her hearing the more unsure she became. Then, as though the baby wished to signal, she thought she heard a lavabo-like murmur, just a faint faintness but it was all she needed. Now she set her path inwards, going after that faint yes.

Clearing the bedroom, she gave important orders. Hot water stood beside the table near the lit fire but still she ordered more. 'Wet a pot of tea,' her voice called after Peter and his mother-in-law, but her eyes were seeing a huge crisis before them. Now her wise voice began to coax the forcing girl, trying to direct her, encouragement her greatest style as she stood praising and smiling through her huge dilemma. 'I can see the head,' she boasted, though none was visible, but her experience sensed that the girl's hopes needed expressing.

Hour after long hour passed by before Maggie Dempsey glimpsed the tiny patch of hair and boasted of its beautiful blackness. Boasting, cajoling, praising, but never panicking, she talked until the last two lock-gates were breached and the honest head brackled out.

Now, cheering her young mother's victory, she dragged him out, bloody, blue and silent. The scissors severed him from his jonquil's lottery and, as though his body was a hot cake straight from the oven, she ran with him and, placing him on the big white towel on the table, rooted in his throat looking for the glug-glag, that soft resin which now held his silence. The air passage cleared, she held him upside down, and as though it was all his fault, gave him a sharp slap on the scalded bum. He gasped as though he had died, but she attacked him again. The wail was sorrowful when it came, the siren wrenching those down in the kitchen, but everyone had to stay at their posts until this woman said otherwise. She, though, was working. The umbilical chord hung and swung until it was tied down, and now her hands almost took on a life of their own as they began sugaring his lungs, heart, limbs, working him over till they felt that this babby was here to stay.

'It's a boy, Minnie,' boasted the handywoman, her voice now feeling free to make the planned insinuation. In the bed lay the heroine: barely able to breathe, she just listened to the grief of her finesse. The head of the bed yessed in a big bow to the good news, the lily-white sheets winked their red establishment, and the young girl, the manikin of the altar, packed her thanks into a flesh-covered chalice and grinding her teeth in a last desperate effort, lifting her eyes towards heaven offered up her planned sacrifice.

Maggie Dempsey was the first to congratulate the father when he stepped across the threshold into his bedroom to see at first hand the son born to him of Minnie Humphrey-that-was. He had been down at the foot of the stairs fretting and fandangoing when his decorated dumb doll, the new arrival, broke the silence of the house.

Father and grandmother grafted together as they burst up the stairs, the call from Maggie their lunacy, but once they reached the bedroom door the grandmother yielded place to her son-in-law. The new father was rightly comforted by the scene he saw, for there in the bed lay Minnie, her baby close to her breast. Standing now as though decorated by palsy, he couldn't for the life of him walk those last few steps. Maggie, the old navvy of his son's birth, eased his nervousness by gently lifting his baby and placing him in his arms. 'There now is your fine babby,' she said, 'and that girl there in the bed is the best I've come across.' Peter, looking down now at the weather-beaten face of his son, smiled in delight, for his farmer's hands which had dabbed life into baby calves, lambs, pigs, even a kid goat, now held a baby of his seed, freshly measured, green in devotion, new in sound, never heard before in earth's eye-opening atmosphere, breathing and exhaling in a place devoid of his presence just one hour ago, spitting in lipped disgust at having to mesmerise himself as he passed through every single one of the nine locks on the canal before nosing out into life between the gentle handholds of a local handywoman.

Maggie Dempsey had been going to bed when the knock came to her door, but now the dreams which had escaped her pillow became the handsome baby of her sleepless nightmare. Her feet were tired and swollen, her eyes heavy-lidded, even her gracious hands were avoiding her gaze as they nested in the folds of her heavy black skirt. The firebox door flung open wide, she sat in the chair staring into the scarlet-red-vivid-purple as helium from the kitchen's supply torpedoed the flames coming from the turf and wood. Maggie was indeed very weary after her ordeal, and her senses knew full well that this night's drama could have ended badly. 'I never thought he'd make it,' she cackled as the filtering light from the still-drawn curtains stilled the kitchen. No other light was there except that from the Sacred Heart lamp, but distance into the new day dimmed even that. The happy woman needed no fag-end of candle or dollop of Haifa's oil to light up her uniqueness, all she really needed was some shut-eye, just forty winks, so that come a gaffer's cry she'd be ready to climb those stairs again to help this young mother to let down her beestings the better to feed the gigolo of last night's cha-cha. Game plan on hold she soon fell asleep, her head hanging hinged to her neck, him under the stairs her only companion.

# CHAPTER 37

A great peace enveloped the house and five fields which yellowed here in the virgin's gravelled yard. The struggling farmer had said his gratitude before throwing himself down on the old uncle's mattress in the new bedroom on the planned backlands. Vainly he tried to get to sleep, but all he could think of was the gravedigger's nearness this night. He sobbed fractured fears into the coat folded now as a winsome pillow beneath his head. What would've become of him if he had lost his Minnie and her son? Hearing still her cries, which the hip-locked labour forced, he knew that the doctor would have excused himself come what may. He absolutely streamed blessings now upon Maggie Dempsey. She had devoted herself this whole night to bringing the boy baby bravely through the pins and into the space awaiting him. Breathing, the feeble place now kindred-straddled him with sleep and, new father that he was, his back rested easy. His hearing numbed, he breathed in and out, unaware of that other woman who braved her altar for him, unaware that she was likely dancing a new hornpipe, dancing it at such a rate that even dead limbs would get up and join in with her. The pillow under his head, though, heard nothing, for no doubts seemed to niggle at his sleeping brain, and lumber, heavy with name tags, seemed far from his dreams, for names, those names from his conscious haggard now seemed as though they had never existed, mined now beneath his cranium, mined at least nineteen names away.

Quasi-peace was shot to smithereens when the baby's cries burst from his polished wood crib, the frenzy only of terror hue. His mode of conduct left a lot to be desired, but his voice didn't care about niceties. He screamed with hunger, the gravity fever pitching from his lungs. Frantically, his mother struggled to sit up but the effort was better left for now, for here she came, her messenger of bragging, she would know what to do. Her hands would lift this little bounder, her fingers would find him the fragmented funnel and her bubbling certitude would guide the young mother as she attempted to let go her colostrum.

'Now, now, now,' shushed the handywoman as she entered the bedroom. 'You've got to give your mother a chance to get ready for you,' her voice advised him, and then with the hands which first fondled him she gripped him soundly and, carrying him to his mother, settled him down to his gravy train.

Minnie took a little while to relax but he feared he'd starve. Eventually though, his feed came, his little lips guzzling the beestings into him. Maggie showed his mother how to finger her breast so that he might latch on better and now, after what seemed an age, he turned away, his belly full, his eyes closing in sleep. Maggie and Minnie, Minnie and Maggie – the new baby already knew the difference, as he lay all drunken and dilapidated between his mother's breasts.

## CHAPTER 38

Minnie joined her hands beneath the blankets, trying to keep warm against the chill in the bedroom. Her mind was slowly forgetting the ferocity of last night's horrible fear. 'God, thank you for my beautiful little boy,' she whispered, the prayer coming as often as her breaths. Her mouth told Him of her thanks, but her eyes were playing a different game entirely. They studied the wooden cradle, Peter's cradle, the honesty of the man carved in every detail of its polished wood. But then her gaze fell upon the child within the cradle and her hands automatically moved to feel the deflated belly beneath the bedclothes.

Breathing soundlessly, the baby slept as though he had been there since the house was built. Waves of tenderness winked from her immaculate eyes as she facted where her baby but slept away his drabness. Precious, she called him, as she felt his very being thinking through her. Sweetness sprang next and, humming its potluckness, her mind sugared the honesty of his round facial repose. Live, he was alive, sands-in-the-desert-quiet, but alive, and under the blankets her hands moved and joined in again with her mind's whispering. She rid herself of all feeling for her sacrifice, and instead thought about his lustred music. His minutes were building into hours and his plumbed hours were nearing that transom hour, that bragging hour, when he might bubble burst just to hymn his daylong lifetime.

The baby strolled his estate unaware of his mother's gaze. He bivouaced now, waiting still on the nine bells from him beneath the stairs. Here he belonged. Here he slung his tent not feeling that he needed permission to be linked to this family. He was here, momented here, his newness strange only to his parents. He didn't mistake his target, he was just establishing the right to be here. No, nine bells didn't mean he'd go away, but his heart greatly needed the rhythm in order that it would beat in time. Monetary stiles would one day hurdle before him: for now, though, he just slept, for come transom hour he would wake up and tell the lonely room that he respected its white walls, its two windows, its brass-knobbed bed, its black mantelpiece, its pink gingham curtains, even its old wooden box. As though wishing to be there to gild his thinking, penury, the ponded sun's lunchbox, never hunted gold light from new promise, and so this daytime's sun draped the house — old house, new house, white house, fresh house, stale house, thatched house, slated house — with decanted light.

# CHAPTER 39

Saturday was saddening the pony, for despite the big celestial event at the boreen's end last night her footwork this new day still wouldn't come right. Yes, the Saturday Saturday Saturday Saturdays were there large as life, but she had a job to do, and the handywoman deserved her very best efforts. So, head held fearlessly high, she delivered her passenger to her home down the bog road.

Saturday of Saturdays it was, and delinquent that she was she travelled back home every ditch being inspected, every yoke being shied at. Dactylic steps didn't mean an inane sense of whimsical behaviour: no, she was doing her best to even out her spanking stride. Her driver this morning never noticed the gait and behaviour of his pony and her hooves, for, his fetters sawn, he sat there in his trap, the happiest 'virgin soldier' on Planet Earth. Containing himself had been his job all night through. He had wanted to witness his baby being born into the place his old uncle knew, but, his job done a long nine months before, he was superfluous to the solemn struggling handywoman. That door of the bedroom was closed tightly while the baby catted his way through his nine stiles, but his cry when it came electrified him, as though a she-god had prodded him with her neutron's finger. And those volcanic yells which erupted from that silence sweetened the struggling girl's freshness, but for him they sounded but the lava-words of underplay. Now though, his stoicism was back intact, and as he drove along the road this day his face was but a mask to his being.

The houses of the locality, some thatched, some slated, stood there in their isolation like shebeens' tired secrets. Whiskey hid weasel-like in the odd cupboard press, but this morning, this themed morning, he didn't need whiskey to wave with glum glee. Those householders didn't know his news, didn't know that he was now the same as them, one of the crowd, could father a child, a son, someone to work for, someone to die for, someone who would be here to fire the name, never to let it die out.

Seeing Peter O'Brien's trap scudding along by gaps in the roadside hedges, folk could never imagine the mind at play there behind the pony's tail. Fatherhood was, for this first time, actually hurting in his belly. Beckoning him homewards, this new vivid baby tickled his mind with surmises and worries: 'Will he feed for her when she's without Maggie Dempsey? – The length of his body – Would he be half a stone? Ah no, more than that – I think he'd bring the auncels down to eight pounds, or maybe six ounces more – He has big bones for a slender girl, he'll be a tall fella – What would Jack Humphrey say if he could be there last night? It's well I have the rifle up above the rafters, he'd shoot me – He'll be all brag now, a grandson – poor Sally, nearly as bad as meself, being all full of confidence she'll not remember the pain – like hell she'll not – for me to have me own child! I didn't care boy or girl, well, not a lot, just a teenshieweenshie bit – a boy for his sake, he'd be so happy. "Gad," he'd say, "there'll be an O'Brien now in my place, none of yer milkywatery lads, one of us." Aye, Brendan – aye, it was herself said it: "If it's a boy, and if it's a girl we'll call her after his girl in the grave – either way we'll pay him back." Lord, she's some girl, how was I so lucky after – bloody lucky – No good now, him and her's gone. Now, it's only him – Poor auld Maggie, didn't make any barbubble, just came – great auld woman, didn't wait to judge. Now he's here, he'll be a credit to us. Will we be able to rear him right? School, and maybe he'll be a teacher or a doctor, or maybe if he has the hands he can be a carpenter like me. I'll show him everything – how to keep the nail going in straight – the roars of him when he hits his thumb for the first time! Oh, there'll be conabun! – How to judge with his eye, turn a leg, maybe a bit of fluting, aye, and carving maybe godroons even – To dry boxwood for the inlaying — Aye but who knows, maybe he'll be a farmer with the five fields — ah, he'd need something else with the five — not to mind, there'll be three now. We'll bring him down the fields, her holding one hand, me the other, him swingin' between us — Mind the river, or an ould cow might kick, dung and he'd step in it, squashing up between his toes — diggin' worms, searching mushrooms, birds' nests, robbin' honey, frogspawn in a jam jar, aye indeed — The bog'll be the man, what's this, what's that — no I won't, shake o'the head defyin', she'll have her work cut out — Blessin' himself, little pudgy hands, left or right, will he know or care? The neighbours — "He's that young fella O'Brien, a hurler yet, aye, maybe for the Poc Fada Larkin's" — The dog wranglin' this way and that — put weight over the well — road gate — ah no, not for ages, tie the wicket gate, though — O'Briens now maybe change — ah no, never lighter, dark, dark always, maybe darker — for all the world like — She'd be delighted, coughin' away, "He's like you, the livin' image." Pity he never lived to see and spoil him — She brought up the blood — blood — see the blood I've seen forced up outa the ears — More to come — The madness when you compare her last night — The gun no good. Shockin', shockin' the pain, exhaustion. Wonder what now? Cryin' maybe, or her feedin' him, breast full as a tick, him guzzlin' — Get up his wind, says Maggie — Lots of fun ahead but no uncle John — dreadful. Myself and her and him — Auld Jack Humphrey'll not spoil him, hold his hand tightly but put nothin' in — likely rob the child of his penny. Ah, not fair they had Minnie, damnit — herself'll be countin' the minutes listenin' for the pony.'

# CHAPTER 40

The pony looked happy to be nearly home as, having entered on her last lap of the journey, she stood waiting for her master to fret the gate closed, then, with the bit between her teeth, bungled her hooves down the boreen towards the house. Yawning from his night's missed sleep, the driver sat gazing from every gap in the hedge towards the house waiting there below. The style and presence of it was ever of interest to the builder, but today he only had eyes for the middle upstairs window. Mundane though it was, black glass though it exhibited, the grey mind thought it a great avenue to Hollywood. In its hump it stored his human happiness. The Hundred Years' War had been dramatically fought there, behind its Pliny glass yolk. He couldn't describe the scene that hummocked inside just now, but his baby had visited last night, and he knew full well that herself and himself now had the boy child of their dreams, yet a scald from God where a night's sleep might be planned.

The man in the trap brought the wheels to a halt. No more revolutions after the pony stood still. 'Whoa,' he had said to her unheeding, but still she heard the command, the word which led to 'stop'. Thinking only of his new baby, he didn't even wait to unyoke his horse, but headed instead for the back door. Three steps at a time brought him to the bedroom, to the yellow eminence where with Minnie he could find happiness, and where, beside herself with joy, she waited to wreathe his head with hinny-pearls.

But now that he reached the place he barely glanced at her, just a flit in her direction before those eyes of his were feeling out his son. He hunched his shoulders the better to stoop in over the cradle, and, thinking of his fatherhood, felt his penis gunfiring anew; mule that he was, he boldly plunged his straddle in mustylimbed nothingness as, punishing himself, he gnomed the gas in his stomach. Grinning now, he at last turned to Minnie and she, likening him to God, climbed slowly from her bed and, joining him, soldiered a voice which was saying, 'My! how time flies.'

Peter avoided Minnie's eyes as she eased herself back into bed, almost ashamed of having created her tired, painful condition, but she was enthusiastic that by evening she'd be up and moving about. He still lingered by his son's side, drooling over his sleeping figure. He tenderly touched his head, licking the crop of hair with his finger's touch. He suddenly came to himself and, realising that they had neither of them eaten since the early hours, he hugged his girl and trotted downstairs to hurry up the kettle. Quietness now caved under the roof of this new house, as the baby rested where he had been littered and his mother axled in her bed. Downstairs, the father made cheese milk all over golden-toasted bread. Tea drew its linament limbs and stood waiting to be poured into Ned Naylor's cups. The whole scheme was lined up and ready, but a car's foghorn up there at the road gate made mucheen of the scenario.

## CHAPTER 41

The motor car stopped where the wicket gate stood waiting. Noticing nothing different, the doctor stepped down from his vehicle and, vesting himself with his Gladstone, made his way to the front door. Peter saw his thundering figure step the fillgap distance, but he waited until the medic windfalled the knocker.

'Yes yes yes,' the father's voice said as, now sure of himself, he walked the tiles of the glass porch and opened the door. 'No need to hurry now,' he said. 'Thanks to Maggie Dempsey, she had her baby last night. You forgot your promise to her that you'd be here to help her, off you went to Dublin to dinner with your butties.'

'When did she deliver?' the doctor cut across, but Peter, drawing himself up to his full height, said, 'At past hope o'clock, and but for poor Maggie I'd be burying them both.'

Leading the way, Peter climbed the stairs, the doctor following with excuses to dress every step, but the moment the men reached the bedroom the Mecca of birth took over, and in a she-god's presence they summed soldiers of lousy pestilence. Minnie had been listening to the conversation on the stairs, but when her gaze met that of the doctor she smiled, for as far as she was concerned her baby was landed, was alive, and to make matters even better, there was nothing either man could do to add to or take from her human timebomb. So her smile was secret, yet manifest of her happiness when she took the doctor's hand. Her words, though, afforded the credit to the touch of another woman. Her baby was next to feel the touch of his hand but he, sound asleep, just squirmed when his gubby stylus read the doctor's unease.

Dr Tom Lane was a man in his late fifties, a big tall man once but now stooped slightly, his head seeming too heavy for him to hold his spine straight. His complexion was ruddy from years of good living, as a connoisseur of good wine. His eyes, when he steadied them, were calculating, and his teeth, when he smiled — and did he smile — were long and yellow and hungry for the respect of the gentry. He looked now at the baby, the muchness of his large persona almost shadowing the cradle. Humming his grandeur, he examined his hunted avoidance, scrutinising the handywoman's work for any sign of infection. His stethoscope looked magical when he fed it between him and the mite lying sleeping, and now he began nodding as he declared baby O'Brien, 'A fine staving chap. Well done, you pair, you have a fierce healthy chap here. He'll be a credit to you some day,' said the wily doctor, and turning then to the mother, hovered until the husband felt superfluous.

Steering his steps to the landing, the father descended the stairs until he came to the spot of last night's fandango, and here he stood himself winning at the post where hindered fear beckoned death. 'A fierce healthy chap, the doctor said, and he should know,' smiled the superfluous father and, feeling he had backed a winner in his Minnie, set about filling the empty kettle with fresh spring water from the white enamel bucket.

Dr Tom Lane drove at a snail's pace towards the road gate and, easing the car through the open gate, stopped. Getting out of it and standing clear, he gripped the five-barred gate and with a swing of his arm brought it clanging against the step of the pillar. Rattling and shuddering, the gate gave up every fight, and Tom Lane shot the bolt securely home. A feeling of great relief swam over him, and walking away he juggernauted his grey gaze back down the boreen towards the sedate house. He still rankled from the abuse which the strident father had levelled at him. In fact he wasn't used to having his profession challenged by simple folk. He had given his usual flummery of excuses, suggesting that his absence had more to do with Minnie's having got her dates wrong, but Peter O'Brien wasn't having any of it. He was articulate and hard-hitting, and even now the doctor was reminding himself to be on his guard in the future. 'I'll have to watch that O'Brien fellow,' he said. 'He's a jildy boyo if ever I saw one.' He turned then to open the car door, and was just about to climb in when a flash of movement caught his eye. He glanced in its direction but all he could see was a twig shivering. He stood awhile looking all around, and then caught sight of it – a little robin standing on a briar which was reddened by frost. The small familiar bird nodded as his one eye sieved the glance from Tom Lane's two. His feathers fluffed in the sharp breeze and viewing this site as his territory, he clung to the briar and gave his watch-winding warning to the stranger. His notes galvanised the doctor, whose mind hurtled back to those mornings long ago when he'd sit in the big farmhouse kitchen with his grandfather, eating frosty, late-hanging apples, while outside, without fail, would sound the watch-winding noise. 'Do you hear the little robin?' his grandfather'd say, and he always had to go searching to find the perch where the bird chivvied from. 'It worked every time,' he laughed as, his foot now hard on the pedal, he drove back to his surgery in Huntstown. Nimrod in his hands, the car chugged along. The bird, though, still timed his memory, and smiling again he remembered the fable from his boy's reader about the robin's breast being stained red by blood which spurted from the head when, tiny though he was, he tugged the thorns all by himself from the victim's Crown Of Thorns. His mind on his childhood, the miracle which was Maggie Dempsey's didn't even signify in his stupid world of self-importance.

The doctor had barely set out for home when all hell broke out down in Minnie's bedroom. The baby was now hungry, and yelled the place down. While she fed him, Peter once again attempted to ready some food. Trying to be imaginative, he made a mound of scrambled egg and this time, not wanting to let it grow cold, he raced up and down the stairs until Minnie suggested that he sit down beside her and they eat their first proper meal of the day together. Outside, though, the hens still waited for their scratchers' feed, the calves still minced around their sheds waiting for their bucket drinks, the pigs squealed their chorus of panic, and worst of all was the plight of the cows as, straining at their tyings, they hooved from foot to foot, morosely waiting for the touch of a milker's hands.

But that first baby and even those restless cows in fact belonged to history. The recalling of them was but a waiting woman's ploy. The only thing belonging to the present were the geraniums around the windows of the porch, still dragging their roots for old times' sake, and the woman, the graffiti-writer herself. Tomorrow would be another day for her. Tomorrow her geraniums would again keep her company if it so happened that something clicked where her mind freewheeled, and then with their big green leaves would cushion her voice if it so happened that she managed to link the present to the past.

## CHAPTER 42

'Ah! those were the days, when if I wanted a jug of milk all I had to do was go out to the dairy and there I had milk from my own cows,' she told the dog as, having gained home, Minnie attempted to open her two-litre carton of pasteurised milk. TEAR TO HERE the instructions read, an arrow indicating the dotted line along which the scissors should cut their path through the thick, waxed, cardboard carton. 'Sorra word it says here about where a body might find the scissors,' she remonstrated, as rummaging through her forest of clutter she almost every time failed to remember to hang them back on the hook where she'd find them. This cranky evening it took an absolute shakedown of the joint before she found them, and then she suffered the haggard of pains as, dying for her fix, her tea all brewed and ready, her hands failed to make fast enough headway with the blunt scissors.

The clock striking six o'clock disturbed the mug of tea, for now having won the battle with the carton she sat swigging her dominance. Her clock was nowadays a minute or so fast for she never took it upon herself to remedy it but now it thieved her teatime by hinting at news in train. So over her drab figure trundled and switched on her new transistor. Her sight not able to gremlin the wavebands, she, from her years of listening, searched through the streams of talking and music until she happened on the voice she thought suitable. Of late she sought out none but the home news. Bong, bong, bong, pealed the Angelus bell from her radio: not liking the druidic sound, she blessed herself nonetheless. But no sooner had she begun her titular prayer than back went her mind to the days when, as a young girl, she took turns ringing out the church bell in the village. Three threes and a fifteen, her format in those days, a musical sound which she relished in sending out all through the golden evening in dumb folklore. Tacking along now with the newsreader, she followed the actuality of her bunty world, but sorra thing registered in her mind. It wasn't until the man was reading the sports results that her nelly copped on to her guggenheim. It was, in fact, his mention of the Indy Car Rally which summoned her daughter Sheila back into her brain. 'What's the way it went?' she palavered as now, her consciousness suspended, she was back, away back, in the haggard, the children giving out the tig. She heard the young girl's voice frazzling, and joining in she began velcroing it out from where it stranded, the only barbubble, would she remember it all. Then it came it tumbling in ecstasy, things not even packaged, things-words:

> Indy tindy
> Terry berry
> Bumpty seedy
> Over Dover
> Dick Mullann
> Tom thrush
> 'ere o'er ire
> OUT

Frenetic the sum of her thinking, yet greedily she tried the same again, stutters studding her hereabouts. Yes, the voice belonged to her little girl, her girl born of the nest, the nest he built in the top of the oak trees. Yes, the girl born to her and himself, the girl with the brown nocturnal eyes – yes, she resembled her, all bar the eyes, fresh eyes she herself had, eyes blue as the bluebag she wet in order to blue-bleach her white sheets each washday when as she jettied her washtub the blue steeped into her sheets. But her baby, in fact, started life at the brown cusp of nightfall.

Playing tricks on the inhabitants of Drumhollow that long-ago night, the night before baby Sheila was born, the sky turned the townland into a white nightmare. Nothing, the morning revealed, was now the same, for the snow which had dredged down all night long jinxed every landmark under its white anointing. There Minnie stood looking out at the still picture, her lonely seven-stage job, hill upon hill, waiting. Absentmindedly she had drawn back the blinds, and found herself almost startled by the harsh light. 'God above, will ye look?' she found herself saying. For what seemed an age she stood there wool-gathering, her hand sliding in circles all around her bulging body. She smiled now for down below her in the yard she saw their cat, his mien so obviously disdainful as, surreptitiously striking towards the house, he had to high-step and sometimes even jump to make his way through the deep snow. Another contraction, though, galvanised her into thinking of herself. Her labour had hours yet to go but she knew that come late evening there would be a new arrival on this white landscape – a scarlet life would be stamped here before this day was through. A shiver suddenly shuddered and, turning away from the window, she gathered up her day duds and brought them with her down to dress in front of the warm stove in the kitchen. The house was quiet, for baby Brendan was already dispatched to stay with his grandparents. She missed him now with every article of clothing she put on but he was safe, she knew, and the child sent away was better than she having to fob him off when her waters broke.

The warmth of the kitchen soon enveloped her and as she dressed she listened to the rammattack out in the yard. Peter was there, running through his morning's work. He was, after all, going to be ready when she needed him inside.

Minnie sang quietly as her feet strangulated the stairs. Ten times did she climb up and back, checking on things prior to Maggie Dempsey's arrival. She had the fire blazing in the grate, the cradle ready, its satin lining aired. Two candles stood one at either end of the mantelpiece, and on the windowsill beside the bed, stuck stoutly in a jamjar of sand, she had set the thick stump of the red Christmas candle, holding promise of lasting longer than the two slim white ones. Yesterday, baby or no baby, she had got down on her knees and washed the linoleum on her bedroom floor, adding a drop of disinfectant to the water. She didn't follow up her job by polishing the lino, preferring instead to retain the healthy disinfectant smell. Now the bed was set in readiness for her delivery, the white sheets revealed as she folded back the counterpane. Viewing the room she was well pleased, and with its door kept closed she knew that by the time her baby was here, the heat would be just right for the dénouement.

A white body plagued by bloodstains, the baby girl arrived in a hurry, for her brother, the first-born, had done the donkey work when with his head bent down he scavenged his way through dam after dam as he swam towards Drumhollow. Adder-like, this female child now slid into the breached gateway, the hour seven o'clock. The moment she smelt danger, though, she screamed for, wise before her time, shrieks of styled guilt revved from her voicebox, sounding as though her throat desired to oil itself by hat-in-hand regretting her membership of Eve's fold.

The symmetry of her scene soon soothed her cries to a murmur as hands-on life stringed her belly-button for her. Her father was called on immediately, for this time the new baby was well fit to be seen. Soon his great hands circled Eve's dredged line, but the baby didn't need him as she, a baby fish out of water, curled her toes in readiness for a life of only second-class importance. Under his blankets she had been conceived; now over the binary of nine the joyous stillness yielded her up, baby O'Brien, the new ling of love.

Wondering the weight, the proud father rushed downstairs and, rummaging in the dresser drawers, found the turkey auncels. By the time he ran back upstairs the handywoman had the baby parcelled in the big blue towel. Taking the auncels, she hooked the hook in through the towel and, holding her prey aloft, tried to read the hand's route. Quietly the black hand descended, but her tender gaze couldn't dissect the stony drop. 'Here Peter, you have good eyesight,' she said, 'see what the scales says.' As though he were shortsighted too, the father brought the red candle with him, and while its waxen tears drunkenly heeled over the rim and crept down its sides, the light from the wick winked sending fire into the dot-dash arcade, until the soliloquy stopped at the dot below the number six.

'Six pounds eight ounces,' boasted the proud father, and his mouthed words wafted the flame, sending a shiver to agitate on the shiny brass face of the German auncels. 'Six and a half pounds,' he said again. 'God, we have a fine little girl now.' Smiling then in a striking frankness he turned and gazed at herself in the bed and between them passed a runcible look, she Fenian, he swinging free. Yes as free as a bird, écluse that he was, he plimsolled the mouth which she had just now given him to feed.

White as the countryside was, it became still whiter that brazen night. A whistling wind strutted fresh snow into, and evidently over, every footprint and wheeltrack in the yard outside. Peter gave his dilapidated handywoman a schlep of whiskey before she took on the journey home, and looking at her as she seven-sipped it, he knew in his gut that tonight was the last time Maggie Dempsey would do a good turn for him and Minnie.

White worlds yielded when the pony stumbled her way towards the road gate, her farting the only sound, cunning in the dabbed air. Quietly the driver touched her with the reins as he urged her through the blizzard, sure of himself this new night. Sitting in the shelter of his body Maggie, her black shawl wound around her head and shoulders, didn't feel the lash of the wind. All she was conscious of was the whiskey smell of her breath as, trapped inside the cloth, it hung beneath her nose. Feeling hot in her gut, she sometimes hiccupped but, satisfied with a job well done, she nodded off, her body heeling this way and that.

Back in the bedroom the new baby hiccupped and grimaced the night away in the cradle beside her mother's bed. The beestings, whole beestings, disported inside her Jill's gorged body. She had drunk and guzzled on the denial, aeons-old and fashioned from jasper. Now, while the world outside lay sleeping beneath its blanket, the baby inside dressed herself as she set about forging her tools in preparation for her tiny soul's minioned journey.


## CHAPTER 43


Under its carpet of white the countryside settled, the snow lasting a whole week. Frost each night guaranteed its stay. All around there was comparative quietness. Cows allowed out to drink from the river sallied home again as soon as their thirst was quenched. Occasionally a bawling low crested on the air, Michael John Fortune's bull scoffing at the snow. Of recent years Michael John had decided to run a bull with a herd of pedigree cows. He bought him at the Spring Show in Dublin, where he chose only the very best specimen. Exhibiting was his hobby; his red, white-headed Herefords stole the trophies each year. He'd have his herdsman groom them till their hair curled like a baby's and then, as their white dewlaps hung and swung just at their knees and their prime leading article revelled between their hind legs, he'd lead them round while he watched as the judges hokey-pokey fingered them, but ne'er a fault would they find. Now, though, this had been his last year for showing. He was phasing out his pedigrees: the lands would instead carry herds of rougher cattle bought in for fattening, and the moment they were mud-fat he'd cart them off by train and sell them in the Dublin Cattle Market.

Next door to Peter and Minnie's smallholding stretched Michael John's vast estate, both families sharing a mearing. The O'Briens' portion led down as far as the furthest end of the third field, Fortune's running from that spot down to the river. Never did Michael John Fortune have words with an O'Brien about rogue animals; he maintained his mearing, the O'Briens theirs. Any time he did have occasion to talk to Peter or Minnie he was frank and courteous to them. They in their turn respected him for the half-sir he was. They knew he was the last surviving son of an old, once noble, family that came to Drumhollow three hundred years back, and now the future reign of a Fortune was Michael John's responsibility.

Where local farmers sowed their wild oats the neighbours likely knew, but in Michael John Fortune's case they were out by the side of it, for he, being gentry, mixed with his own ilk. He never was seen to chat up a local girl, in fact was never even seen in a girl's company. 'Jaysus, do yees think he might be one of dem lads?' the goodboys oftentimes asked as, sitting in the shebeen slugging stout, they wondered and sometimes even suggested likely sexual peccadilloes for their swanky, aloof neighbour.

But all the speculations came to an abrupt end when Jude Fortune stole like a fog over the village and countryside of Drumhollow. Peter O'Brien was first to be told. He was passing one day by the big black wrought-iron gates when Michael John's car nosed through. The driver jumped out and called him. Just for a moment he delayed to enquire about Minnie and the children. Then, the ice broken, he told his next-door neighbour of his marriage plans, 'in Rome, next month'. Peter was genuinely happy to hear his news. He didn't have many dealings with him, but he looked forward to seeing Derby House come to life again.

# CHAPTER 44

Michael John Fortune got the heebie-jeebies on his honeymoon. He and his new bride spent their very first night together in a big hotel facing out onto the ancient Sallustian Gardens. At a snail's pace the cab taxied them up the steep streets and there before them, right at the kerb's edge, was the hotel, its deserted attitude swinging nonetheless behind acres of mullioned windows. His marriage that glorious sunny day had been a lily-white affair. His uncle the Dominican had married them, marvelling, in his innocence, how his nephew had ever been smart enough to capture this haughty, beautiful girl. The old monk was captivated by this green-eyed goddess, and silently thanked God in advance for the handsome boys which she would likely give to the family name. He steered the couple through the exchange of their marriage vows, the man with the altarboy image, the girl with the grand gaze. He had carried out this killjoy coupling many times before, but today he was witnessing a ceremony where his own bloodline was involved. Today as he stood in his fagging penguin colours he was happy, his umpire-only smile had a warmth to it, for he was seeing to it that his nephew's children would enter this world blessedly legitimate.

The cry broke in the dead of the night. Reverberating, it tried to drop down along the facade of the hotel, its destination Via Colonna. It was a cry which strangulated from her throat, made her sit bolt upright in the bed, still asleep, as though trying to free a word from her jailhouse, the effort shaking the bed. Grabbing her, her new husband tried to shut her up, tried to stifle her hesitating tremors, tried to 'there-there-now' her absolute hurt, freckles the only colour winking from her skin. His comforting voice soon tore her slumber from her body, and now Jude was awake and coming

126

over all embarrassed. 'Was I talking in my sleep?' she asked, but he folded her tighter in his embrace, telling her, 'Twas only a nightmare.' Nightmare it really was, and for all that he could now surmise, it seemed but a single bad dream which tonight had vexed itself the moment his bride fell soundly asleep.

Jude Fortune's pole-star screamed that night for the first time in her married life. It gathered sirens from her dreamworld and, as though wishing to greg her new status, set them at her husband of one night. Hers was the star which juddered over the hotel ponded near the Piazza Fiume, and under her tutelage it would follow her right the way back to Derby House.

Derby House stood gathering itself in readiness to welcome home the boss and his bride. The sun had hidden behind the hump-backed hills as the setting drew up a plan for the arrival of the owners. Finding the gates closed, Michael John declined Jude's offer to get out to open them, and instead jumped out himself and threw open the entrance to his home.

The motor car agitated the avenue away as it was driven towards the house. The hell of a lawn on either side guffawed. Here and there the grand guards of mushroom-shaped chestnut trees growled as they stood there, adept at their waiting game. The lady in the front seat devoured them with her gaze. Her stead would judge them later when she settled herself in here. For now, though, her eyes looked in between them one and all but, het up enough by this young man for all seasons and all reasons beside her, she now became victim, here on this avenue, to a storybook ending.

The lonesome court, lucky to have a new woman to guide its days, jitterbugged as the boss attempted to carry his bride in across the big heel of its front door. Annoyed by the disturbance, the Alsatian dog arrived on the scene. He looked moidered by temptation as he greeted Michael John with a dog's joyfulness, but when his pine-tinted eyes fastened on her there in his hall he, cunning in bitter notions, sensed only locking up at her newcomer's hands. His owner absentmindedly patted his head while the bride, who had bought no gin for baptising such a head-on melting, linked her hand in that of her husband and allowed herself to be favoured right the way through her new home. As she was led along, she saw two girls waiting to welcome her, at an arch which led towards the kitchen. Relics of oul' god's time, the girls were not the stuff of servant and mistress style; they were employed to see to the cleaning and cooking. Menfolk in this family tolerated their best efforts, but now they stood there under the green gaze of Jude Fortune. Dinner was served by them at the stroke of eight o'clock, but cunning though they were, they could not read the new woman's face in the manner of her eating.

Servants' rooms down in the basement waited, but the quitting time tonight set a different pattern. Jude Fortune gave the staff the night off. Welcoming the seemingly friendly act, they smiled and sniggered, nudging each other as they surmised about her motives. Bold now, they agonised their way home down the back lane, wondering with every step how dreams might change. By morning, though, she the newcomer, had news for them. Rostering showed her new schedule, 'eight till eight', and come their quitting time she sent them away to their own houses in the village.

# CHAPTER 45

Derby House grew to recognise the sound of a new set of footsteps. It noticed the footfall of someone desperate to better her lot as Mrs Jude Fortune's driven feet tracked their winding war through rooms which in recent times had only ever heard the sound of careless feet. She summed up the contents inside each room, telling herself that all was now hers. The walls hung with portraits of family all long since dead, bar two in the library, of Michael John's brothers, one a doctor hit by a shell in Gallipoli, the other an officer become cannonfodder at the Battle of the Somme. But she was not for regretting their passing; she dismissed them as but dead-heads to her new name.

Next for withering examination was the upstairs of her stately home. Last night she had climbed the stairs, but with her husband all over and about her she did not manage to take in her surroundings. He played husband, lover and host, the real McCoy to her bride's dreams, and when he brought her into their bedroom he pointed to the bed which the servant girls had rigged especially for the new lady of Derby House.

But today was different. She was on her own as she decoded the have and have-not of her domain. Fanning her footsteps, she stepped into every single room, scrutinising their heirlooms with a valuer's glance. Never hesitating too long in any room she came at last to the master bedroom, her room of the night, the one where every other Fortune copulated with his bride. Gravely she looked at her bed of last night. The bedclothes were folded back, the white sheet tucked in around the thick mattress, the grace of the him and her there to be seen, right in the middle of the bed. It was only fun, the ingredient of just such a frippery was numb now. Clicking her tongue she reversed from the doorway and, as though shutting in a demon, sharply banged the door shut and set off with square steps across the landing which led to the back stairs. When she reached the kitchen her tour of the house was over, all that remained for her to judge the swaddling ply outside in the sturdy yard.

The great square yard was gravelled, and right around its perimeter stood stone outbuildings. The coach-house, the dairy, the old wash-house were all still standing, but now they found themselves used for disparate purposes. The fumes from the motor car's exhaust had blackened the walls of the coach-house. No longer needed, the dairy was chock-a-block with large crates for preserving fruit. In the wash-house hung bric-a-brac of former days: wash-tubs, a mangle, storm lanterns, coach-lamps, even a copper budget can, but insensible to their past glory she looked at them only with regard to their possible value.

Singing to herself, her footwork strode on now towards the high-walled gardens. As she approached the entrance the clock in the dome over the archway began to racket as it engaged to strike three o'clock. She, the griffin here now, glanced up at the timepiece and, freeing herself to act the second in rank here, her eyes took in the *tráithníns* growing from the tiles roofing the dome. 'Come springtime and that'll get cleared,' she planned, but once into the garden she became worried as she witnessed the staff working the place. Three swarthy men plucked apples into hanging containers and three more worked among the vegetables. Killing time, they didn't see her stand watching, blaming them for the seeming chaos in the long drawn-out vegetable plots.

Away beyond the boxwood hedges stood a large greenhouse, its door hanging wide open. 'I'll bet there's a waster or two over there as well,' she was thinking as she struck out towards that open door. She walked along a path which crisscrossed with other paths and then, where she was least expecting it, she came upon a grassy circle on which was sited a weather-beaten statue of the youthful Imogen reading the oracles. She gave it only a furtive look, for at this moment she was hellbent on sussing out how many men whiled their time away in the greenhouse.

Inside, where she had expected to find another dosser or two, she saw Michael John working among the heavy-hanging tomato crop. 'Oh there you are, dear,' she said, and he, full of glee at seeing her come looking for him, came to meet her, his brow dripping beads of sweat. 'It's hot as hell in here,' he said and she, smiling in spite of herself, took her hanky from her sleeve, and with a steady look in her green eyes dabbed his brow for him. Her gesture delighted him so much that there, in full view of his workmen, and in the presence of the red witnessing tomatoes, he swept her into his arms and hungrily kissed her.

Gardening was soon left behind as this pair went walkabout. Michael John was as usual taken in when Jude requested that he bring her on a tour of his land. As he led her from field to field of his estate, he told her the history of the land, linking his family, the men particularly, to its fields and fables. 'Yes,' she agreed. She remembered each portrait but, though she was vocalising agreement, her hopes were in fact blinding her in each field's tombing. Her feet had never before walked those creamy pastures, yet despite their previous and noble ownership she now devoured the ground as her steps hunted for gold.

Michael John's stock were scattered through the whole farm. Cattle were to be found in great sweeping fields, only the dividing ditches separating the different droves. In the square horsepark, four hunters bad-mouthed the grass, set here in his assembly, jumpers one and all. Further over, on a far distant hill, he showed her his flock of sheep, hundreds of them, some lying down, others nibbling the dawn, this very day speckling that hill like mushroom spawn.

Next to the mearing which divided his estate from that of his next-door neighbours' lay the swipe of arable land where last spring he had sown his corn. Now Jude, walking along beside him, found herself treading on grim polished stubble; guillotined at ground level, the corn stubble sprang under as she stepped on the raw straw.

Their survey was almost over, but Michael John felt he'd show his new wife where the nearest neighbour lived. Leading her to the mearing, he pointed down to the house and fields across from where they stood. She, standing on tiptoes, looked across at Peter and Minnie O'Brien's farm and, everything taken in in that one searching glance, she joined up with her husband again, a secret stylish smile hovering at her merciless lips.

'Now that you've seen my home and lands, what does my bride think?' he asked as he slipped his arm tightly around Jude's waist. The person walking beside him only pretended to yield to his loving protective arm. Touching his cheek with a brush of a kiss, she whispered, 'It's more beautiful than ever I could imagine. Your house is a dream and those fields seem to welcome me. It's just as though they need me to get to know each one of them, so I'll ride out with you when you go herding in the mornings, or if needs be I'll go on my own.' Michael John loved her for her enthusiasm, now promising her he'd build a dynasty here for her. She nodded in agreement to his every boast, but his new missus had a mind of her own, and even now though this was but her first day, her entrepreneurial gut told her that much more could be done with those rolling acres. She kept her thoughts to herself, though, for she had lessons to learn, the first having to do with how to produce beef cattle. The second had nothing to do with herself, yet had everything to do with her.

# CHAPTER 46

Minnie O'Brien stood outside the church in all innocence, waiting for the Fortunes to emerge. Up in the gallery they had sat, in their usual earmarked seat. Since turning over to the Papists' ruin all of sixty years ago, the Fortunes had ever since sat where the scrubbers could not infect them, and today, no different, Michael John Fortune and his new wife sat up there. Going by custom, the neighbours didn't dare climb those stairs and sit in that seat; neither did they move to receive communion until the Fortunes descended the steps and approached the altar-rails. When Mass was finished, though, they all left the church for they knew, as everyone must, that the Fortunes would be last to leave their rarefied seat.

'Congratulations and welcome to Drumhollow, I'm your next-door neighbour,' said Minnie as she extended her warm-blooded hand to the new lady of Derby House. Jude Fortune stopped momentarily and, running her green gaze over this countrywoman, a coldness crossed her face. Taking the proffered hand, her kid-gloved shake was cold and limp. 'Thank you,' was all she managed to say before she moved away, but Michael John, feeling for the smarting expression on Minnie's face, took her hand now and said, 'It's so kind of you, Mrs O'Brien, to wait back to give us your congratulations.' Doffing his hat then, he hurried away to catch up with his wife.

The coldness of that encounter stayed with Minnie from that very day to this. Her hand could still feel the frigidity of that touch. Today though, things were different. Today Jude Fortune could wave a greeting from over on the far side of the street in Huntstown and Minnie, her mind on the new spectacles she was just about to collect, could still manage to return that greeting prior to going in the optician's door to talk to Mr Murray.

'Round your neck, that's where to keep them,' was the optician's advice to Minnie. 'Tie them on with a bit of string and then you won't plop down and make smithereens of them.' She agreed with him, for she had sat on her old tin-rimmed ones, the ones which she discovered all of sixty years ago.

She had been standing that day whitewashing the slob-boards which sheeted the cowshed, the rock lime bubbling in the bucket beside her. Occasionally she stirred it and then, dipping her brush in the liquid, hurriedly applied the lime-wash to the porous boards. On first painting the wash left little impression, but when it dried out the effect was dazzlingly white. Almost every slob had a blemish of some sort: some had hollowed spaces where light now entered, some had knots, and some had drips of resin drooling down their grains. There were just a few short boards left to finish that day, the ones up over the door. She moved the barrel on which she stood over to the spot at the door and, placing the bucket on top of it, climbed on board. Resting her fingers on the beam over the door, she was just about to stretch up to begin her downward stroke when her fingers on the crossbeam felt something yield, something move, something soft. She jumped down off the barrel in her fright, but eventually her curiosity won out; she climbed back again and now examined the scary thing. It was covered in black cobwebs, but when she stirred it a hint of silver glinted. Now she lifted it and discovered a pair of tin-rimmed spectacles. Her hands got busy cleaning them and, the temptation too much, she fitted them on, tucking the fine silver wires behind her ears. The lenses were so strong that she almost lost balance, but her joy in finding such an unusual object sent her hurrying to Peter's workshop.

'What in heaven's name are you saying?' said Peter when he heard Minnie's story. 'How could glasses get up there over the door in the cowshed?'

'Well that's where I found them,' she answered as she placed them in his hand. 'They must've been there for years, judging by the dust and cobwebs, and who put them there I wouldn't know.'

Peter tested them out on the label of a turpentine bottle, but they only made the writing swim and blur. They wondered together, trying to figure out who might have owned them, but Peter gave up. He couldn't remember an O'Brien who wore spectacles.

The useless glasses were thrown in the back of the dresser drawer and for decades they hid there, rubbing shoulders with the mousetrap, the clothes-brush, the shoehorn, the packing needle, tins of boot-polish, a spare hatpin or two, a buckle belonging to the belt of a man's raincoat, a corkscrew and the turkey auncels. Every time the drawer was pulled forth, every time the items stumbled about, but there the spectacles second-homed until the day when Minnie found her sight was failing. Her rubbish had by now grown and filled the drawer to the brim, but still she rummaged until her hand fixed on them. Their lenses were badly scarified, but breathing on them she shone them before trying them out on the *Westmeath Examiner*. She was delighted with her discovery, and knew now why her mother used say 'never throw anything out for seven years'. 'Seventy, more likely,' she smiled as, bringing the newspaper with her, she went to sit down and read at her ease for the first time in months.

Despite their grazed lenses, she got many solitary years of reading from the tin-rimmed spectacles, but now bifocals made letters leap from the page as she glanced through the lenses of her new tortoiseshell-framed glasses. Now when she read, newspaper stories of Westmeath people leapt from the columns. Now she was able to scrutinise those pages of words, had comfort when with yesterday's eyes she searched for the mention of a name. Her bifocals, though, failed to find the wretched name. It wasn't there among the death notices. It wasn't mentioned in the society columns. Reports telling news from abroad didn't seem to have heard of it. 'No,' she said resignedly, 'whatever about his brother or sister, they didn't hear anything of him in Dominic Street or he'd appear somewhere there.'

Dread always came creeping as she left down the *Westmeath Examiner*. Nothing could she do to henpick elsewhere. No doubt she would hear again this very night the owner of that name come stomping through her bent brain, and too well she knew that come azure-dawn he would be there again, stepping stones laid down before her, he arrested in his approach, stunning in a donkey-jacket, as she saw him silhouetted in the wicket gate, his mouth pursed, whistling to the sky.

## CHAPTER 47

That son of sodomy was born on a cold blustery day at the end of March, attired in skin of blush-pink and hailed as a boy hero. The white-veiled nurses joked about the march which he stole on his parents, they having had their last child all of nine years before. Minnie, though, was smitten the moment her eyes caught their first glimpse, but being the sensible woman she was she never hinted of this baby's vanguarded conception. Now she watched as the nurses deftly carried out their surgical strike, watched them stringing him up and watched them as they weighed him, the plant lying in the chromium well of the hospital's weighing scales.

Francis Peter O'Brien was born to a couple who initially sorrowed for his coming. They had their family, and felt cheated by the new pregnancy. It was all his fault, Minnie told herself over and over again, but she wasn't complaining the day they took the break from thinning the turnips. Bringing two drills each they knelt with a drill on either side of them, their hands busily winkling out gaps in the thick rows of turnip seedlings. 'Leave the length of your hand between each seedling,' she had been told the first time she ever helped in the tillage field. Now as her hand chucked out fistfuls of seedlings and dumped them in the hard, clayed valley between the drills she didn't need further tuition, for her eyes measured the gap where future turnips would grow and swell, pushing against their neighbours, trying every which way to corner the sunshine and garner the rain. She seldom glanced back at the lonely plight of the single seedlings left standing now in the hump-backed drills: no, her farmer's eyes had to size up their next flagbearer. If the seedling bore any sign of malformation, any sign of finger-and-toe disease, she turned it down, as farmers knew it could never become a full-bodied globular specimen.

Working as a team, the couple thinned the crop of turnips, sun bearing down on them from a high sky. 'We'll take a breather now,' suggested Peter from his vantage point ahead of herself. He headed away towards the shelter beneath the oak trees, and threw himself down in the bumstalks beneath their branches. Quietly, he lingered resting on his elbows as he watched Minnie prowling Eve's stoicism through the turnip drills, and knew that with her at his back as he kaffired he could never fail.

Minnie finished out her two drills before joining him, but she never guessed that the shade was timing her moment to perfection. She and Peter lay together in the great universe under the giant oaks and laughed and talked about their children. They were content with their lot, and both felt satisfied with the number of drills thinned. It was so simple lining up their achievements, but when she lifted herself up on one elbow to say something to him she found that he too was in the process of sitting up to make some point to her. The joint movements set them laughing, he claiming he was the expert in telepathy.

That was how the gnome's game started that day, and that was how she now recalled it. Her resin oozing from her brain, she was dreaming though conscious. As she glanced she funnelled her

137

notions, her eyes seeing their dreams. Peter's dungarees were stained by yellow clay dust. Two knee stains. Her best bib was ruined. She had started out kneeling on a folded sack, but she wished to keep level with himself to nag or banter and found the cushion more a hindrance than a help, so she abandoned it, the bib having to take the brunt of her every inch forward. She couldn't now remember the trading in words, but could only waver in remembering. The will-o'-the-wisp was under the yew, his love-making added up in stones. The straight back of him returning to his drills. The dreadful daylight of their lust. Their lack of blankets under which she could have numbed their stern sound. The bother she experienced trying to adjust her clothes. The sign of his high-water mark. She shy going on home, afraid that a neighbour might have happened by, or even farsighted from some vantage point. The sign of their stint on the sedge. Her deviousness all the way home. How she strealed her steps back towards the haggard. How the sheets on the line never stirred, never hubbubed. How she fumbled with the gate before lavishing her steps towards their harbour.

Sunny and sweet, the June which witnessed the buffer's sin, she reckoned, but he never gave it a second thought. The turnips, vile as they were, cellophaned her blushes onto their skins, and in the months following the fun they gradually wet themselves as, swelling and bloating, they jungle-skinned themselves into lordly, globular roots. Sometimes when she went for the cows she walked heavy steps past the drills of turnip-tops and, shy, she found her face growing red in camaraderie with the dinner things. Now poor Peter trekked in to the hospital and a hungry son yelled dolefully from the nursery at the very far end of the corridor. Sacked by her sense of strangeness, she now lay in her bed listening to his call, while on the windowsill near her elbow strutted a bowl of hob-nobbing hyacinths.

Peter bragged while in Minnie's hearing, but as he cycled home each night from the hospital fears hung around his neck. Like an incubus they were, and like an incubus they hid themselves while he got on with his guardian angel's help. It was the image of the new baby which fumed his fears, the baby never quite expected. 'Herself must never know,' he warned himself. 'Her life has precious little comfort; she doesn't need to hear, she must never guess.'

Caws from the rookery on the Fortunes' land broke his silence next morning. He lay there on the workshop floor, the disinfectant smell of the shavings breathing through his fan-shaped nostrils. His body was cold as ice. He struggled to get up and found he was stiff in the legs. He thumped his shins and revved the blood-flow in his veins. By the time he had that done he found his brain turning over the scheme from last night. The drink which he had when he left the hospital surfaced for consideration. The tightness in his chest as he cycled home. The gradual build-up of the stitch in his heart, the shaft of pain running down his arm. He could remember now the time it happened; the hucklebuck happened the time he was sandpapering a thing in his stung honesty.

Though Minnie couldn't be aware of her husband's thinking, she knew a bungle played him when he saw the nurses flitting here and there through the hospital. 'He's terrible shy, God love him,' she thought. 'He misses poor auld Maggie and never thought at his age to be coming in here. Dreading it, he is,' she said as he walked down the long ward towards her bed next the window. But hiding her intuitions she cackled and cooed, her husband being made much of the moment he lit down near her pygmy-son's cradle. Cuggering together each night, they streamed names from which to choose one for their son. She was the one who had final say, and every time she pinholed junior's name she came up with Francis, and for himself's surprise she added on Peter.

The children squabbled about the trap going to town without them. They couldn't see why they couldn't be on hand to bring home the new baby. Wilfully they begged and cajoled their father to let them come too, but nothing doing; he had his orders and they didn't figure in Minnie's coming out. He was to get provisions for the special homecoming this evening, the welcome home to the turnip playboy, but though she called out the shopping to be done she never mentioned that he was to bring Brendan and Sheila to Huntstown.

'Keep the fire in and the house cosy for when the baby comes,' their father called as he drove away.

'Don't forget to bring us home something from town,' was their joint reply. Both had given their word on not fighting until he got back; they promised they would have the table set, the turf in for the night, the sheds bedded and the cows in, the slide closed on the hens' shed door. Attempts at baking were even promised, but as he neared the final corner on the boreen he took one look back and started to smile, for they had already disappeared back into the yard. 'They're not bad kids at all,' he thought. 'They'll have themselves all fagged out trying to have things ready for their mother's return.'

Turning out onto the tar road, the winsome pony attacked the journey with an air of playfulness. The oats this morning had given her a fillip, and now she wanted to display her pent-up power. Head held tilted to the right, she egged for the off, but her driver suspected that it was the oats talking. He knew that nothing could change her Saturday palaver.

No one would ever suspect that the man had anything on his mind as he went from shop to shop buying his list of provisions, and when he was finished fitted them into a cardboard box which he housed up near the front of the trap. The item sticking up like a steeple from the box was a bottle of raspberry cordial. Minnie had suggested it: she knew it would look well in the handsome glasses which she had inherited from her parents. 'The heirloom,' Peter titled them, the times when he poured the *deorem* of whiskey for the visitor, but when wetting the baby's head this evening, Brendan and Sheila would feel special with the red cordial prized in their glass menagerie. Peter was careful, though, of the parcel of fresh meat. The brown paper around it was beginning to show brines of blood, so he knew he had to keep the plagued package away from the other foodstuffs, and with herself needing space for her baby and bag he decided that when he got them loaded he'd place the meat up beside him. The old raincoat which he usually sat upon could now sit beneath the parcel and thus protect the trap's cushions.

He was all *a gliondar* when he arrived down to her bed. His step was light. He knew the whole row of women in their beds were measuring him up, but he completely ignored them, and instead fixed his weather-eye on Minnie.

'Are you kill't waiting?' he asked, but so relieved was she to have it all over, to have the baby tanked up and ready for off, that ignoring his fuss she stood up and without uttering a word stretched up and gave him a kiss, there in front of everybody. He got all embarrassed, but handing him her case she stooped in over the cot and, gripping hold of her baby, said, 'Come on now, love, we'll head off.' She waved little royal waves at the sightseers: 'Goodbye,' her voice was saying over and over. Peter didn't say a word, but on reaching the door he doffed his hat at the full winestock. Carefully now, he fell into step with her and together they checked out at the office, the nurses gamely wishing them well.

The bellyband slapped up tight against the pony's underbelly the moment Minnie and her baby stepped up on the trap's iron step, but then down chucked the shafts, bringing the strain slap against the straddle the moment the family spread their weight on the floor inside. The pony, dreaming there, lifted her head only slightly, as though she was measuring the arrival of this new simian soul. Minnie, conscious of the biting cold, snuggled the baby ever so tightly to her body, and now Peter was fussing as he wrapped the old uncle's travelling rug tightly around them both. 'There now, try and stay as you are and it'll keep out the breeze,' he off-handedly suggested, and then, picking up the reins and drooping them onto the pony's back, he called 'G'up there', and steered her where she was going as, trundling along, they set out on their footloose journey home.

For all she was worth the pony trotted towards Drumhollow, attracting God's notice to the fact that she dragged and fondled a family behind her. Life softly locked them together inside in her tub-shaped blood group: none of them wondered why or whinged wherefore. There they rolled, droll inside their cocoon, with Minnie never stonewalling and Peter, Trojan horse, foraging a slow desert. At the edge of the town was a drinking trough, and there the driver stopped and let the pony drink. Slurping her grizzled credentials, she effected a long draught. The darkness was all about them as she shunted to go again, and where the sun had slowly headed westwards a sliver of moon came stealing now, funding this theatre below with no light at all.

Listening out for the sound of the pony, the children knew that once the bolt shot home on the gate she'd put on her final spurt. Like the proud girl she was, she'd sally home at a jog-trot. The moment they heard her tick-tack-tick they were out the door and running, each endeavouring to be the first to see him. The pony had to abandon her grand plan, for now the children blocked her avenue. Up they climbed on board her bounty-bus, wild to see the little person parcelled up inside his wrap. There she patiently stood, waiving her purpose. At last the reins dropped again on her back, and thespian that she was she, lifting high her head, manoeuvred her hooves in this final curtain call to the homecoming of Francis Peter O'Brien, the third leaf of the O'Brien shamrock.

No homecoming to compare with, the new baby bawled the moment he was carried into the kitchen. He couldn't realise the scene scaped here in his honour. He didn't appreciate the warm kitchen, the cot aired beside the clock, the solemn faces of his big brother and sister as they watched to see how he'd fit in to a family's shanty. Whomsoever was watching didn't matter to him. He only knew hunger, fretting now for his feed.

# CHAPTER 48

Tin tacks were all that held the school together by the time young
Francis Peter O'Brien enrolled in Drumhollow National School.
Today the schoolhouse, such as it was, was gone: there was
neither hide nor hair of it now. The spot where it had stood for all
those years was flat as a pancake. The ditch with its high bushes,
and that lone beech which used to argue with the rote learning
emitting from the chimney, was gone too, pulled from the soil, clay
clinging to roots, birds' nest skeletons clinging to high branches,
crater marks tampered in beech bark. The whole lot was blitzed
away and now this open-plan area dressed naked but for a pile of
cement blocks, a scattered heap of timber, rolls of fibreglass and
long black plastic pipes.

'Wouldn't you think they were going to build a cathedral,' said
the old woman as she stood sort of lost on the street where her
three kids had been schooled. 'A cathedral,' she said again out
loud. Now her eyes wandered over to the right-hand corner where
the hopscotch beds used be, and there saw a gulag of green roofing
tiles. 'Green tiles, no less,' she smiled at the swank of it. 'Musha
then, slates are a thing of the past, I suppose.' Minding her
business, though, she eventually moved on, her shopping bag
straining with the weight of her groceries.

Ghosts of her past accompanied her on the way home. She,
listening, heard them say things, and now, rescuing their voices,
she structured human beings through whom she could give life to
her loneliness. This manner of atavism kept her at attention when
all else about her seemed at variance: plans voiced on her own
territory comforted her in moments of jim-jams. Today was no
different. At her own pace, glancing this way and that, she made
her voyage home. One minute she was at the church lighting her

candles for the holy souls in Purgatory, the next she was ball-and-chained, her phantom lubbard-pulling at her noggin. One of those candles back there in the church was in fact standing lopsided, but she hadn't noticed it. She was nowadays too busy fabling her list of names in camera, for her safe God seemed to be backing down now, just when she most needed his jubilation.

Vine-like, straggling briars tormented her almost every time she walked up or down the boreen nowadays. She had to leave her messages down on the ground now, so that a briar could be coaxed from the knit stitches of her hat. 'God be with the days,' she thought, 'when himself was here. No way would he have those things grabbing hold of me. He'd be there slashers in hand, and boy' would he cut them back! He'd cut them to the very quick.' Her chosen one was never far away. Like the bad shilling, he groped maverick-like for resurrection the moment her nerves jarred or her stern sense of duty wavered.

The wicket gate was wide open panicking, whereas she had closed it on her way to the village. Noticing every distraction to her homeland, she nevertheless tried once again to be her Manchestering self. Humming to herself, she braved it along the path and round the gable-end to the back door. The tune she was singing was her old violin's scherzo, but the moment her hand turned the knob on the back door her voice began to sing out:

> 'The people were saying no two were e'er wed
> But one has a sorrow that never was said.'

The farce ended the moment she stepped inside into the kitchen. The musty kitchen, unlike her heart, held no threat, no libido log-jammed in the lunatic inside its mind.

The relief almost palpable, she walked to the table and placed her heavy satchel on it. Taking out her groceries her hands felt steady again. Full-blown pork sausages looked moist as she set them in a plastic box. In alongside them she curled her half-ring of white pudding and just a small portion of black. The clingfilm was the same bit she used over and over again. 'Sure, it's only to keep out the cold draught,' she thought as she tautened it across the rim of the box before storing it in the fridge. By the time she came to store the barmbrack in the bread bin, the hunger had begun gnawing, and even though she hadn't yet sliced it she could already almost taste the fruit and candied peel, and visualise her nose inhaling the smell of the spices and the dreadful, several scents of the brack's yeast.

The clock struck four as, a mug of tea at her elbow, she planted herself in her chair. Her barmbrack echoed as she started to eat the nuisance slice, her senses nursing the fear that she should be on her guard for the ring: the fact that it was only September didn't seem to dawn just now. Once past that hurdle, she began to enjoy the taste of the lovely soldier's tinkling inside the sultanas. She thought as she chewed and chewed as she thought, and every time she swallowed her banyan tree grew in desperation. Her singing a few moments ago had reveried himself sitting on the second step of the stairs, she back there again playing her gadfly tune on the violin, gadflying that honeymoon fortnight. Now, though, the barm was busy working, for as she savoured it the banyan tree sent down more roots and the moment they hit the floor up sprang three children, her three children, playing a game of snap-apple this Hallowe'en in September. Her eyes attracted them towards her, her hands all but extended themselves to hand pick them for a hug, but they, stressed in their play, were trying to grab a hold with their chins of the shiny, swinging, Bloody Butcher. Suddenly everything changed, everything blurred, and from the pell-melling blur advanced a child's face. Her eldest boy, his tousled hair spilling onto his forehead, drew near and, staring into her keenness, spat at her, his white juice coming plash against her immaculate face. Right away it began to run in runes down towards her chin, the tickle of it staving her consciousness until with a start she came to. Her vagary now gone, she found her empty mug sleeping in the hammock of her skirt.

Standing up she headed for the sink, but before doing anything with the mug she rubbed her damp tears away from the chub of her chin. She didn't see a simsam in what she did, for her eyes were now busy sizing up the refuse coating the inside of her mug. Second-guessing, Minnie knew a letter was due from Brendan, for the long tealeaf at the handle had tiny dust eaves framing it. And to tell the truth she wasn't at all pushed about a letter winging its way from him, from a bishop no less, for too well she knew the track of his tongue, his religiosity, always promising to 'remember you in my Masses'. No, she'd far rather have him a priest, an ordinary five/eight, down where families struggle, where human beings need a whisper of love, a word of praise, a crank of their wheel, a forgiving and a blessing.

But all the neighbours thought it was an honour to have a bishop selected from their locality, and going by their judgement it was. For Minnie, though, it didn't feel anything different. She could still remember the day when, down in the third field, her son, her first-born, told her that he wanted to be a priest.

## CHAPTER 49

It was an ordinary pot-walloping day in summer, the day when, her end-over-end churning done, Minnie set off to check how the in-calf cow was looking. Her husband had gone to the forge and his orders to her were, 'Keep an eye on the cow in case she drops her calf in the river.' Slow to answer back, she never in her hard-pressed years once questioned his thinking, and today being no different she set her sights on the fields. Brendan floundered playfully along with her, leppin' thistles one moment and walking composedly the next. The cow had struck out on her own, her tail to them as she wolfed the grass into her. Hearing their voices she stopped in her tracks and glanced back at them, but recognising the two humans went back to her grazing. By the time they had reached her, though, she had swung around to face them, her big soulful eyes sizing them up. Minnie, the expert by now, examined her, but the signs of calving were not on her. 'Sure, she's not even down in the pins yet,' she told her son. He was not quite sure what he was supposed to be looking for, but accepting that his mother was the one in the know he turned away and headed off towards the double ditch.

The double ditch ran almost the whole width of the O'Briens' stretch of land, but stopped short on the right-hand side, where it left a gap through which access could be gained to the fifth field, the river field. The entrance to the double ditch was almost closed off by stones, a mound of stones picked off whenever the plough exposed them to the weather. Inside the double ditch, between the two tall rows of bushes, was a high-floored bank of clay covered with straggly moss, dead leaves, tracks of cattle hooves and here and there the odd stupid cowpat. A canopy of thorns and thinkers were interwoven overhead, blackthorns and elders hemming in one spot, hawthorns and hazels another. The odd ash tree jutted up through the roof and, wily, a black briar or two hung down like stalactites, dangling there as though awaiting a collapsing pine. In where even the air stymied, the remnants of a babby-house still thought thoughts. There was the thing which started off as a wooden horse, but now had no head and only one leg. Frankie's duck was still tied to a branch, his red head peeling paint, his varnished body scurvied from the elements. A doll's leg, pink in the main, grew from the moss, and near it on the ground was an empty porter bottle, its placket choked with black dross. Up wedged in the bones of the hazel tree was a two-pound jamjar, their pinkeen jar, but now it was full to the brim with dead leaves and sleeping snails.

Brendan hesitated for a moment before he climbed up over the stones and entered the Aladdin's cave. Devouring its pathway, his humped back had to brush and drag through the renegade things. Every time a cowpat surprised him, every time he cursed, in his mind the numerous evenings when he came down to bring home the late-grazing cows, and the work he sometimes had trying to wrest a cow from this bland cul-de-sac. As where silence dares, the thing concealed in his groin began now to feel as though it needed attention. The fright of his secret started to gnaw. His tongue thonged now a dreadful fragrance, and his mouth became so pregnant with words that he eventually felt almost sick. 'I'll have to tell them,' he said, 'that it's a priest I want to be, not serve my time to Daddy in the workshop.'

What he wanted to do came from the pictures the missionary had showed in school, all the little black children in Africa, smiles from ear to ear, the priest in his white soutane teaching them about God. Yes, that's what set the mills of his mind working, the vision of the chalice the resulting image. Now he had to break the news because his letter had to go before this month was out, the address of the school written in the missionary's copperplate, hidden underneath the statue of the Child Jesus of Prague.

Brendan chose Minnie to be the one to hear his confession. She, though, was in no fit state to hear it. Her migraine headache was playing noughts and crosses before her eyes. She was breasting along through the third field when he caught up with her, but he felt then that he had to wait until the right moment came. They were in the course of talking about him getting a pair of new boots, his bare feet now all stained by those cowpats back there when, dreadfully, it all came out, his sentence all bald and illogical. 'I'm going to be a priest,' his voice stillbirthed.

Her ears heard the sentence but failed to receive the sentencing. He said it again. 'Mam, I'm going to be priest.'

She heard it this time but pretended she hadn't, the fun gone out of her day. 'Mam, did you hear me? I'm going to be a priest,' her son said again.

'Ah, g'ou'o' that,' she said. 'You going to be a priest? Sure you're too young to know what you want.' Now, though, she glanced at her boy and their eyes met – the stream dried up before her. The timespan of her son's announcement was but a minute, yet the piercing stab stretched the moment right the way back to her labour in her new bed.

'I know we haven't any money,' he continued as though the cost was the bogeyman, 'but the missionary said the order'll help us out.'

'Did you ever hear the likes?' she said as, taking him by the hand, she led him towards the banked mearing, and there stage by stage heard how and why he felt himself called to be a missionary's human. 'Good to be sitting down for this,' she thought as, stroking his hand, she listened and listened.

Pasture land felt rock-hard under her feet that day as she tramped back home. Brendan, mocking her mercy, skidded stones along the field before him. They had had the drama of their odyssey lurexed by cobwebbed immolation. Now, hunting for honesty, she dreamed up how her boy might be if he turned out to be a priest.

Nearing the house, the mother seized her son's arm and, whispering, cuthered him on how best to break the news to his father. 'Wait'll he's in good humour,' she suggested. 'Be very careful to break it to him gently, you know your daddy has you earmarked for the workshop.' Brendan, though, had his own plan of campaign set up, and now he reassured Minnie by telling her that he planned to tell his *úrscéal* to his father when they were at the milking.

The striking milk had already struck rebelliously against the bottom of the two white enamel buckets, the cows had finished the swishing of their tails, their milk had strained through the filtering muslin cloth and lay wombed inside the tall silver can when what needed to be said came blurting out. All conversation had just a short while back been emancipated: now the two nomads stood

149

there, each humpbacked in his own attitude, each held as though in a trance. Wallop, the heavy clanger fell.

'Daddy, I'm going to be a priest.' Wallop, the story sank in a forged sound. 'The missionary said a fellow like me can be helped through school, cause priests can do that sort of thing if a boy's parents are poor and not able to pay for him themselves.'

After some seconds the father swung around and without straightening said, 'Brendan, will you not be talking shite. "I'm going to be a priest," and you only a gosoon, what would you know about what you want.' His son tried to butt in but the father wasn't having any of it as, putting up his hand, he held sway, swatting a fret which could not be aired this side of Sunday. 'Where you're worrying about what'll pay for you to be a priest, I'm telling you it's no go. I want you to help me in the shed, the others have to be looked after you know. Don't you be minding the missionary, they only think of numbers for the vineyard, as they say. Where you're wanted is here. Anyway, who's this missionary that you're goin' on about?' And walking away, he picked up a three-legged stool and, bringing it back with him, sat down heavily at his son's bare feet.

Brendan, quashing the desire to bawl crying, began at the beginning and stashed his story, stubbing his toe into the clay platform with every full stop. The story, full-blown that it was, came thithering from the boy's mouth. Seeing his father's face, he laughed as he childishly described the Sibylline photographs which the missionary passed around the class, using each photo to help him point a raffed-whilesome picture of how a priest saves pagans from the fires of hell. 'The pictures showed a woodwork class with a priest teaching the boys to be carpenters. Another was of a class out in the shade of a tree, learning their alphabet from the blackboard. Others showed Mass being said with all the people kneeling on the ground, y'see it's so hot and anyhow they have to build a new church, the missionary said. It looked lovely and I was the first to put up my hand when he said "Who'd like to be a priest?" and there was five more as well. It's for Africa, so it is, that we're wanted he said, the African province or something like that. He wants us to tell our parents first and then write to his order of priests. Money wouldn't stop ya being a priest, he said too. And Daddy do y'know what, his eyes were grey and so was his face, y'know dried cow-dung colour it looked, he says it was the sun.'

While the father and son ruminated on the mouthful which the son had said, the dumb cows just chewed the cud, their big-bellied belches bringing up their goodgeens for still another chew. Their ears cocked, they heard the unspoken fright there in the father's anxiousness. He was telling his son that the priests had a habit of choosing none but the very best and the very healthiest boy in a family and 'we have TB on the grandfather's side in ours,' he said, 'so don't be at all surprised if they shoot you down. You know Brendie, they're sons of ghosts for diggin' in folks' cupboards,' and as he spoke a migratory smell of bracken tickled up his nostrils. He laughed now at the news he was going to tell Minnie as he said, 'Brendie, would you like me to break the news to your mammy?'

The cows, sensing they were coming near their time for letting out, started to move from foot to foot. Bright, right there through the slits between the slatted sheeting of their shed, stole the slanting sun's light. Only their ears quietly stood listening, their hearing now picking up the sound of footsteps coming through the grass and weeds at the end of their shed.

True to their hearing, the mother stole with bated breath through the nettles towards the knot-hole in the boards sheeting the end of the shed. She put her one eye to the hole and looked down along the clay floor behind the cows. The man and boy were laughing together. Which of them created the joke she couldn't tell, so taking her eye from its winking hole she instead placed her ear on the space to hear how the form was. 'He's taking it well,' she summarised, more in confirmation of her ears' hotness than of her eyes' straggling detective work. Minding the silent nettles, she stepped back again from the hole, and stealing away she told herself that 'yes, himself sounds happy, lighthearted even.' The path back to the house was humming as she hurried along, but when she reached the security of her kitchen she sat down and, joining her hands in her lap, prayed 'Ah! God help me, it's all before me yet.'


## CHAPTER 50


Brendan ceased to worry that night, now he had unloaded himself. He hesitated to fall asleep, though, for he had the past month's events to mull over. He relived now the moment when the missionary walked into the classroom. He grew red again as he sensed once more the priest's weighing up of him with those calculating grey eyes. 'Hands up any boy who'd like to be a priest?': the words newly reverberated in his mind. Now he remembered that it was an evening after that when he was truly nabbed. Yes, there it was precisely as it had been. He could now hear again the scampering of the playful dog as she raced to fetch the stick which he had thrown for her. He could still feel the saliva-chewed stick which she'd yield back to him. Now he studied the image, the image which that evening just flitted across his eyeline. The playful dog didn't see it, but the image came hurtling back almost as often as did the dog. It was a chalice, a see-through chalice, the wine inside blood-red in colour. On top of the wine floated a little white tuft, just the size of a cuckoo-spit, and two hands lifted up the chalice as though in offering. Two hands was all he saw there holding the chalice, no body at all, just two hands. He had barely taken in the image when back came the enquiry: 'Hands up any boy who'd like to be a priest?'

Numerous times since had his brain re-run the image, the

beckoning persisting despite his young boy's efforts to ignore it. He failed now just as he had that first evening, when he sat on the garden steps trying to continue playing with the dog despite the butting-in thing with the white fluff. Many was the time he tried to forget it but the sound of a flurry of paws, a stick lying against a wall, even the silly smile on the dog's face, and back it'd come, that damned annoying picture, that forget-me-not of his brain, back to goad him into remembering.

It was the horse fair in Huntstown, and he decided to stroll around and have a gawk at everything to be seen. His father's year-and-a-half stood waiting to be eyed up and down by farmers looking for a haughty, high-headed filly. He stepped smartly from the artful design of a puddle of piss and almost bumped headlong into the missionary. The bearded monk bowed slightly and strode on. His victim, this young boy, turned and, running after him, said, 'Father, I want to be a priest. Remember, you asked in Drumhollow School.'

But the old street-wise monk was not impressed. 'Hold on, hold on,' he said. 'You're going too fast, you can't just collar me like that. Who're you with in town?'

'I'm with my Daddy,' said Brendan, 'but he's minding the year-and-a-half he's trying to sell today, he knows I'm having a look round.'

'Come on, so,' said the priest, 'and I'll get you a glass of lemonade, and then you can tell me what's bothering you.'

The fizzy drink, he remembered now, made an absolute eejit of him, coming gushing back down his nose so he had to brush it away with his sleeve. The missionary pretended not to notice, busying himself drinking his tea. 'Now boy, let's hear the story of why you think you want to be a priest,' and so saying he smiled for the first time – a frigid smile, but it helped Brendan to relax.

They were on fairly friendly terms, him and the missionary, when they left Greene's Hotel. He could hear himself now as he told the priest that day how he had found out what he wanted to be, and though the great one didn't say yea or nay, he still wrote down his order's address on the scrap of paper with his copperplate, which until today had lain hidden underneath the statue of the Child Jesus of Prague.

Peter and Minnie stayed downstairs for a long time that night. They talked and worried at the obelisk now standing before them. Minnie's migraine throbbed and Peter's heart fibrillated. 'Imagine us having a son a priest,' said Peter and Minnie nodded, almost afraid to answer. 'You'd wonder,' said Peter, 'might he be mistaken about him having a vocation?'

Minnie answered, voicing the one thing which bothered her. 'Jesus,' she said, 'he's very young to be knowing what he wants to be, sure when it's all said and done he's only a child. I know it's only secondary school he's going to first, but once he's gone he's gone.'

They tried every ploy as they attempted to ease their plight, but it was Peter who gave in first. 'Look't the time,' he suggested. 'Come on to bed. Don't you and I know we can't stand in His way – if the Man Above wants him, that's that.'

'Aye indeed,' said Minnie, 'that's that, but sure we have him for a couple of months yet.'

## CHAPTER 51

The pony stood daydreaming, her head hanging down, her eyes closed. Three of her hooves were planted firmly in the gravel yard; the fourth lay heeled up, resting on its toe. She stood between the shafts of the round trap waiting to be called into action but the signal hadn't come yet, the cargo wasn't ready.

Inside in the O'Brien kitchen all hell had broken loose, for this very morning one of the O'Brien chicks was about to fly the nest. The father sat polishing his black boots – the fact that they didn't need polishing was nobody's business but his. His wife was sewing on a button to his shirt. If only he had behaved like all other days the button would have slipped through the hole, but they all heard his cry, 'The curse o'shite on it, there's the bloody button after flyin' o'me shirt.' Minnie called up the stairs for him to throw it down and she'd stitch it back on. Now, though, he couldn't 'find the damned button.' But down the stairs he brought the shirt to find her with the entire contents of the cracked blue-banded quart jug heeled out on the kitchen table. Rummaging through the debris she eventually found a shirt button, and threading a needle set to to stitch it on. As she sewed she side-eyed over at her husband, trying to see how he was making out, but at his expression her tongue sat back in salty drowning. Tears brimmed, but she brushed them away. 'Make your daddy a nice cup of tea,' she called to Sheila but he, never able to read her state of play, echoed the refusal she didn't want to hear. 'Well make it for me, anyhow,' she added, for she was playing her usual role in keeping the extraordinary ordinary. As she stitched now she knew Brendan was upstairs in his bedroom getting used to fear, and Frankie, feeling left out, was accommodated under the stairs, he and the collie. He stroked the dog's head but then turned her ears inside out, trying to blame her for smiling in the face of tramp's treatment.

Nine o'clock chimed in the freezing kitchen. Over beside the hot range waited the new trunk, nice-smelling clothes hidden inside it. As though he hadn't heard the chimes, the father glanced at the clock before lifting the trunk and stepping with it towards the yard, Minnie traipsing after him. When he reached the trap he slid the trunk in along the seat. Concerned for his efforts she said, 'Careful love, careful,' as, barely breathing, she sanguinely sampled the slipping away of her Fenian ghost.

'Come on now, Brendan, or we'll miss the train,' said the father, having returned to the kitchen where he stood nursing his hat.

'Will you have a cup of tea for the road, Brendan?' asked the mother, her hand on the kettle. 'Can I sleep in your room till you come home on the holidays?' pleaded Sheila. 'Look't what Frankie has done to the dog's ears,' laughed Brendan. Frankie, shedding his hands away from the dog, ran out of the kitchen and Petal, shaking her ears back into shape, ran after him.

'Come on, we're going to miss the train,' Peter said again as he headed out the door. 'Aye, and we up all night,' added Minnie. 'Are you sure you have everything?' she asked for the fortieth time, and for the fortieth time he nodded. Now it was time to say goodbye, and taking the boy in her arms she kissed him and, hugging him tight as tuppence, took a final inventory of his body. Up and down her hands slid, decorating secret furrows on her boy's back. Now she touched his ribcage, his shoulderblades, even his spine, getting a last touch of him before the stranger took him off her. 'Goodbye Brendie,' she said. 'You take care of yourself and write often.'

'I will, Mammy, if I'm let,' promised Brendan, but he didn't hear himself speak. Away up at the bend in the boreen waited Sheila and Frankie, Sheila ready to shout her goodbye, Frankie only waiting for a jaunt.

Tears blinded the mother as she followed the trap out as far as the boreen itself. There the two sat, the trunk keeping the distance between them. Himself looked back at her but didn't seem to recognise her, demented, feeling only for his own heart. Her hand waved at Brendan for as long as she could see him and then, when nobody was there to see her, her sobs escaped their confinement. 'And all the times I kissed him better, his tears pouring down his little fat cheeks,' she prayed, 'and now he's gone, gone with the new trunk and all we have in this world gone with him.' The testament came from her very soul. Her devotion to duty seemed but to have won failure and torment.

Sheila shilly-shallied in the wake of the pony and trap all the way up to the road gate, but the mother, not able to stir an inch, stood back there where she was in the boreen, her body all-yielding and her heart luxuriating in her woebegone. The time of morning became a time of mourning as her ears listened to the pony's steps changing gear from a soft gravel sound to a hard beat on the road to Huntstown. The Church had stolen one of her chicks, and though she had been an accessory to the fact she now blamed herself for having been caught off guard. She was just about to return to her post when she noticed Sheila wending her way back. Suddenly she thought of Frankie, and shouted towards her daughter, 'Sheila, go after the child in case he gets out on the road.'

Tick tock, tick tock, laughed the grandfather clock. The sound syrupped her state. Nothing else in the haunted kitchen felt like singing, only the clock, the pendulum-regulated clock. Minnie didn't find solace despite the loyalty of her chum, her heart out of mood with the swinging song. Looking all around her now, her ferret's eyes dredged the dresser, the long envelope still stuck out from behind the plates. She took it down and, drawing out its contents, began to read it all again. The typewriting was actually spelling out the route ahead for her son. The academic subjects ran like columns of soldiers down the page. Listed there were Latin and Greek, subjects which she, the huckster's Moll, found strange and secretly grandiose, and streets away from her son's hesitating story down in the third field. 'Ah! they'll make gumgee of him, teaching him things he'll never need,' she said, but despite her misgivings she thanked God for choosing her son to be His priest, for she knew as of this newborn instant that her son would survive the course. But the tears which continued to fall down and make the pages in her hand all soggy were still tears of hurt. She brought the letter with her now, and as she climbed the stairs she felt and sounded like an old woman. Opening the door of his room, she went in and sat down on his bed, as though she was needing to be where he last lay free, and lying back against the pillow she glanced around the room, her bleary eyes looking and looking at what he last looked at, the night before the day of reckoning.

Life had to go on, though, so when she heard the pair of escapees coming near the house she was off that bed like a flash. Drying her eyes, she stamped down the stairs: she was going to be master of her ship, and she intended to man the bridge until her husband returned from his holy jaunt. 'Did you shut the road gate?' she asked Sheila, as though the gate held back some monster. The naturalness of her question spread normality through the kitchen, and in no time at all she was chatting to her two remaining chicks, sounding as though she had but a hen's brain.


## CHAPTER 52


The plaid tablecloth was dressing the table. Ned Naylor's china asked the reason for this evening's celebration. The clock smiled in fat, five-timed strokes of luck. The children were being boisterous over a game of hide and seek. Weathered for autumn, the skies fidgeted with accumulating goat's whiskers. The boreen had strangulated sound by carpeting itself with windblown leaves. The coins of candour feverishly jangled at the bottom of her apron pocket whenever she walked to or fro in her endless journeying. Over and back, over and back, Minnie's feet fined the floor, over and back to that dresser, for in its shelves and cupboard nested the bones and bread for every occasion. The big black boss bade hello to her hot linseed hopes when he blew his whistle upon her as she played cheerleader to the Man Above's damnedest. Mighty effort was she putting into this counter-action, the kettle hurling credit where it thought credit was due. Her face bloomed in her rosy-cheeked battle as her hidden resources hand-picked this grim evening for family rejoicing.

Playing still, the three inmates never heard the trap's arrival. Tethering the pony, Peter called out the kids' names. They heard him yell just like the rats did in Hamlyn, and pushing changed to shoving as the two O'Briens dived for fresh air. Minnie was last to emerge, but her greed for a glance at her golden love's face was smashed to smithereens when her eyes dwelt upon the trap. There it stood, its glistening handlebars upstirring the heart with gluggered sound. Sheila screamed in joyous delight when she saw the new girl's bike. 'Red is my favourite colour,' she screeched.

Peter carefully withdrew the lovely shining bike and, handing it over to his daughter, told her to 'give a jaunt to Frankie when you get back from your first ride.' Her bicycle had a carrier, and that was to be the child's seat for now. The father knew the child would be in a pucker when he saw his sister's bike, and so with that in mind he got the carrier thrown in for luck.

Both of the children ploughed dreadful excitement as, now loaded behind his sister, young Frankie was advised to hold on tightly to his sister's waist. The red bike brought them in wobbling freakishness up towards the road gate. Now on their own, the two others looked the look that they were longing to look, and the truth lay in the faces facing them. 'I got it on tick,' the lonely man said, 'and he threw in the carrier.'

'You're a great man,' gloated his wife, as together they didn't react to the question burning all day. 'And he never looked back,' Peter blurted out, 'and he had time and to spare, and Michael Mahon's daughter was going too, to England, to nurse I think she said. He wasn't lonely at all. In the best of humour, like he was going on his holidays. Me standing on the platform thinking he might change his mind or something. No bother on him. "I'll see you at Christmas," he said. Wonder does he realise what he's taken on, but I got the bike anyway. The others matter too, and I said this'll get them going. She must feel bad, they had each other to play with for so long. But he's okay, gone off on the train like he was tired of us. You know he's shockin' intelligent, but he'll learn.'

Minnie never interrupted her husband. She walked before him into the kitchen and then said, 'He'll know in the night how far he's gone and he'll know in the morning he's there for good.' But Peter was standing looking at the table, and he smiled when he saw what she had been up to. 'Begod,' he said, 'if the two of us weren't up to the same game,' and now they both laughed, himself and herself, in grand relief.

The oil-lamp burned as usual in the big front window of the house down the boreen. The family were at home. The fact that one chick had flown the nest did not mean that the house was gone into mourning. Inside in the kitchen, the O'Briens sat before the black range.

The man of the house dozed after his pitiful day. His wife was darning a sock, running a needle and yarn across and back, over and under, up and down, gradually filling in the big spud-hole in her husband's sock. Every time she wove the thread she reminisced about Brendan. Every time the yarn ran out she mentioned his name. At every knot she tied his baby's laces and when she finished she tucked the sock into its match and remembered the times when she had tucked her first-born inside his baby blanket. Cutting her plaything she measured how much thread she'd need to mend the next boy's little stocking but then, glancing at the time, noticed that the clock was moving on. Tipping Peter's black boots with her brown boot, she greatly nodded towards the clock. Her husband bestirred himself and, stretching, yawned. 'I wonder if he's asleep,' he said, but his wife didn't answer, didn't trust herself to say what her wondering mind was thinking.

Minnie put away her mending and sat down to wait for her husband to bank down the fire. He placed clods of turf in on top of the now deadening embers. Filling up the firebox, he finished off by placing two damp sods on top. 'Now that should hold it,' he said. His hands looked clean, but still he washed them in the basin

160

on the small table inside the scullery door. Now he looked at Minnie and, coming towards her, gently took her hand and drawing her from her chair said, 'This was one of the "for worse" days. Remember "for better, for worse" up there in the church.'

She looked up into his face, and her voice was slow and hot-spud-in-the-mouth slurred as she said, 'Petie, if only we knew then what those words meant.' But he was butting in. 'Ah! love, if only we knew then what we were really promising. Aye, that's for sure,' he sighed as, securing her steps to his, he as it were led her into a new scrape, he the leading horse of the team, his groin grumbling with every step they mounted, on their cinder-track towards bed.

## CHAPTER 53

True to form, the druid fell asleep the moment his lovemaking machinations were through, but the mother, the fund, yes the fund, lay the night through, her vigil the only thing possible under her roof. She wasn't the only woman wintering in Drumhollow that night. No, yonder in the neighbouring house lay Jude Fortune, her beggar secret as the derrick at night's fall. There she lay, awaiting the mucous thing which would tell her that her first-born was about to be prised out into its welcoming niche. Her merchant's heart told her her little mite would be rollercoasted into its family's home, but the unease this night still kept her awake, still kept coming at her in furtive hands-on lifetimes.

It was in fact the day the swans' nest was plundered that Felix Fortune was born. As Michael John drove Jude to hospital he noticed the knot of people standing on the canal bank, there on the Drumhollow end of Huntstown. His fleeting glance told him the swans were most likely the cause of excitement, but his wife was noticing nothing, for her contractions were breathing fear through her every fibre.

Cunningly, though, Jude Fortune got it in one, for despite her strains she brought everything hidden into one concerted drive and the final push, when it did come, dromedaried a boy into the dressed womb of Fortune joy. 'Never again,' she never-agained until her hesitating heart knew the rhyme by rote. Now she lay in her cunning, before-and-after bed, bragging to herself that this birthing of an heir to her husband allowed her off the nest; saw to it, in fact, that she would never again be involved in the hunt and fright of having folk drying up her hole with greedy stunts.

Michael John had hung on the livelong hours until time yielded up his baby. His time spent in the waiting room was murder on his nerves. He had retraced his steps through all of the willows, grunting sometimes at the prospect of his life. He was almost there, almost home and dry, but still he thought that his wife might yet run into difficulties. Her cries of night were not now to be heard, but swinging echoes stole by times into the no longer humid place. 'It's a boy, Mr Fortune,' his mind heard so many times that when he eventually did hear the astonishing news from the sedate nurse he was dumbstruck, and could only gawk at her as though he couldn't bear to understand her words.

When sleep eventually stole in and ran amok through his golden loot, Michael John tiptoed away. Mephisto-like he strode along, the night before him one of victory. A great deed had been done, he had secured the continuation of the Fortunes' bloodline. Felix was the name chosen for the little son which now gunwaled back there in his frolicking craft. He didn't care whether or not his son might someday have a playmate. He just followed his hunch, the one under his belt, its nobility sagging as, housed now, it crunched in brunt sins of thought.

The journey homewards played triumphantly through his hands as, gripping the steering wheel, he sometimes lightly turned it or swung hard on it to round a bend. Umbilically tied to his baby boy, he was still picturing his little scalded face and he felt red now in the warmth of himself. His mind wasn't even on his thoughts but, as though a magnet drew him, he suddenly found himself re-running the fever of the morning's canal bank. In no time at all he had stolen all the hilltops, and now here he found himself stopping to investigate.

When he got his night-eyes he sized up his plight. Seven faces of night-time grinned into his green devastation. Gone were the two regal birds, gone their flat thunderstruck nest, dreadfully gone was their setting of eggs with their seven settings of little birds scrunched up tight inside their nurseries. All was gone, gone before even the starter's pistol could give the signal to them to come breasting into the waters of the Royal Canal.

As though under sentence, a long stick stumbled at his feet, the flow of the water making it jolt against the clay bank; no longer old in history, the stick cowered there, its guilt trembling under its style. 'How could they do it?' he hasped as he lifted the stick from the water, but the limb o'the devil that it was, it steered clear of any blame. 'I'll bet it was a bunch of snotty-nosed brats who did it,' he thought as he broke the stick over his knee and, throwing it back in the water, watched as the future flowed away.

## CHAPTER 54

Felix Fortune found his feet the first time he rode on his father's shoulders. High up there he sat, holding onto his father's hair, feeling like any little boy should. Playing ducks and drakes with all of his mother's rules, the boy fun-filled his days in the company of his father. Together they explored the fons of farming, the little boy fed enemy images under his father's guidance. Whenever they grew lonely they jumbled their yolks and made fresh frying, their flummery thundered by nonentities. Time led them to go farther with each new sally. They frolicked in the river, patted the drim and drew horses on their velvet muzzles, listened to the beat of wild geese wings, watched rabbits crest grass at evening time and, day of all days, they climbed the stile in the mearing, and together made their path towards their next-door neighbour's house.

Together they neared their driftwood, each one of their steps a standby to its neighbouring one, each one desperate to taste liberty, each real severe. In outlook where east meets west each was timid, but when each step neared the den the fiddling heard coming from inside the house freshened their resolve; wassails lit up as they celebrated in advance freedom, the father's rescue of his lonely little son.

The O'Briens were unaware of the approaching Fortunes. Inside their house they were fighting their usual battles. Minnie had just settled her tart in the oven, its filling of red rhubarb and white sugar melting with every truculent minute. Sheila, the young girl of this family, was sawing on a fiddle, her tune echoing her story, the house trembling with the rhythm. Frankie, the child, was baiting the stumbling dog, as holding the sweeping brush as a hurdle he coaxed the dog over and back across the hedonistic handle. Peter was not at home; he was away where the men were buying and selling pigs. His fat ones likely sold, he was due home, and where earlier the fat pigs had trundled he'd surely have four or five *banbhs* which, stolen in their prime and denied any reprieve, would likely be hiding in the pile of straw on the floor in the bottom of the cart.

It was Minnie who answered the firm knock on the back door. Hands all covered in flour, she hailed her visitors. 'Come away in and sit down, Mr Fortune,' she said as, hurriedly rubbing her hand clean on the skirt of her apron, she thrust it forward to shake her visitor's.

Now the man came over all awkward. 'I don't know why I'm

here,' he said, 'but my little son has been agitating to get over this long time. He hears your children playing and will stand for ages listening.'

'And why wouldn't he come over and play?' said Minnie, fondling his curls, crediting him with human intelligence. 'You'd like some tea?' she coaxed the boy, and ignoring his father the child gave a solemn nod of his head. 'Well that settles it,' said the father, smiling, and before too long the rhubarb tart was told to cool, the visiting child going to be the first to taste it.

Inside this secret kitchen Felix Fortune was fed rhubarb tart, the beckoning smile of the mother here making the runcible spoon feel greasy in his young hand. On his father's lap he sat, the better to size up sentences before whole fun could be destroyed. The bunch of rhubarb which fed the evoked tart had its severe sourness hidden well by sugar, and as the little boy grew, stumbling, in his freedom, he began, with each new spoonful, tasting the cream which Minnie had ponded all around his helping.

'Would you like a swing on our swing?' asked Sheila as she watched Felix finish the last spoonful of tart. He nodded again, heartened now in this company. 'Come on,' she coaxed, and taking his grand little hand in hers she led him towards the back door. No longer feeling the nearness of his father, the little boy followed after the girl. His weather eye, though, kept glancing backwards.

The swing there before him hung hangdog, but the moment he saw Sheila swinging in it he became interested. 'I'll hold you on my lap and we'll swing together,' suggested Sheila, and once he got the furnace lit he forgot all about his father. Up in the air he felt himself soaring, holding a death's grip on the ropes now he had conquered his initial fears and trusted the girl who was flying him sky high. 'Tell daddy to come quick,' he bragged as the art of flying gripped him, and now, sitting all by himself, he gradually festered sureness with every rise and fall.

The father jumped to attention when Sheila called his name — indeed every time he heard the shrieks of his son he had mentally jumped for joy. Now he followed the girl, Minnie in train, and the fun he witnessed in the O'Briens' haggard brought the feline greenery alive in his hunted heart.

Junior Fortune thought that once escaped from frowning faces he had escaped every obstacle, but when he eventually reached the stile where he and his father had crossed into O'Briens' set-up he found today's barrier an entirely different hurdle. The stile, he discovered now, had big gaping spaces waiting for his little bare legs to slip through. All at sea he was as he stood there fretting, but this stile could not fetter that high-flying swing. Trying not to be afraid he began climbing, almost counting every rescuing inch. Keeping his eye on the where or wherefore, he thought his way forward until, in a snail slither, he mastered the topmost thorns. Everything went well on the downward slope, for now he could see the end in sight, but once his feet hit terra firma he found himself confronted by giant-sized bogeymen, frightening him as they swayed and jitterbugged before him.

Refuge was nowhere to be found for little Felix Fortune, for the stile over which he had climbed seemed dreadful now, looked at from where he newly stood. In front of him, too, lurked great new threats, for in their millions tall cocksfoot and rye grasses tried their damnedest to frighten him, all the time seeming to want to swallow him up in a frenzy.

His hand it was which came to his rescue. Hinting he'd be all right, it took a stunted hold of one of his baby curls, and together he and it hightailed it through the tall meadow, neither ever once faltering till they saw Minnie O'Brien's house standing beckoning.

Minnie O'Brien was in the course of rolling out her spud cake when her eye detected the movement of the handle of the kitchen door. She stood riveted, watching. The door opened a slim gap but the eye peering in didn't belong to any of her children. The door was closing again by the time she reached it, but the boy was still there when she gently opened it back. Grinning her amazed delight, she welcomed this little tub o'guts into her fanshape of caring. Making much of his being such a brave fellow, she led him towards the chair sold out at the end of the table, and fetching him into her arms she settled him in place. The evening was made morning of by this visitor and the tea, when she set it before him, now became Never-Never-Land, laced with just enough milk to be bubbly in free love.

## CHAPTER 55

Derby House, the little boy's own home, was sited between two yew trees. There where it had stood for centuries it still stood, like it or not, playing weather games as it loitered. On its face the verdant creeper breasted along, munching on the mortar, its crying leaves wind-sterned each night by haunted screams.

'Half-sirs' was the term which the neighbours used to describe the status of the Fortune family, as through the front gates they studied the big house set up there at the end of the great avenue. To them, and for most of the year, it looked lonely and forbidding, but come the autumn when the creeper put on its rouge the house became almost inviting as it stood there in a semblance of peacefulness, seranading the contrast between its happy family history and the dreadful solemn green of the funereal yews.

But peace has many deceptive colours simmering where a house thinks itself happy, and that was in fact the story inside the lovely-looking, red-faced house. 'Butter wouldn't melt in her mouth' was the impression playing from the owner's plagued wife, but the story was all wrong, for the woman who stomped around the rooms of Derby House was to all intents and purposes a caged animal who couldn't trust herself to not bite the hand of the husband who wanted to make love to her.

Handicapped by her secrets, her game plan always in vogue, the mistress of Derby House made sure that every chance where an eavesdropper might hear her cry was frankly choked off. Today, though, the long avenue knew ominous strings of funeral coaches before the woman herself could even herald them, for despite her best laid plans her little bird had flown away to find love in another woman's nest.

Jude, the housewife, was here and there the thumb-nailed afternoon, her little boy no less than an half dozen whats and whys behind her. Her attention wavered though, as she stood leafing through a ledger on her husband's desk, figures her placebo, dreaming her distraction. 'Come on Felix, we'll go down, the dinner won't be long now,' she said, but where she last saw him was bare, the only evidence stacked in the fire-irons which hung there as though dead.

When the search for Felix failed to find him, his mother displayed fecund-madness, as veritable night descended on her nested behaviour. Foul-mouthed, she blamed everyone in sight. Her husband, now on the scene, tried to calm her lapse into nightmare.

They were all standing there blaming and being blamed when Frankie O'Brien coursed into the backyard, his foolish running body seeming at once as though trespassing on grief. But when he spoke his tongue gave out the grim news. 'Yer Felix is over in our house eating bread and jam. Mammy sent me over, she said to tell ye not to worry, she'll get me to bring him home after he's finished playing.'

'She will, will she?' said Jude, her fears stressed in lapsed intuition. But right on the heels of her word-jigs she played the grateful mother, relieved that her boy played holy games in finders' fields. Now she changed tack and, turning her green gaze on the next-door neighbour's son she said, 'You're a great boy to pelt all the way over here in case we were anxious and worried. As long as he's safe sitting over there in your house, as long as he's okay, that's all that really matters.'

Noticing his wife's hell, her husband boasted of his little son's bravery. 'Going all that distance by himself,' he gloated, but when Jude finally rolled her eyes towards him, he found his nightmare holding him by the short of his findings.

## CHAPTER 56

Felix Fortune was only ten years old when his daddy died, killed when his horse, Tuppence, refused to jump a high stone wall. That morning he had ridden out with the Ballyspit Hunt and was pitched head over heels, his neck broken in the hard fall. Nothing could be done for him. He was dead as a doornail by the time the tragic news reached Derby House.

The day of Michael John Fortune's funeral was horrid in his boy's face as, wound up like a tin soldier he stood there, baffled, at the graveside, his black-decked mother beside him. Her words of last night were uppermost in his mind, when he had stood being couthered by her as she laid down the standards for today's funeral. 'Hands down by your sides,' was her first command. 'No tears, no snots, 'cause when you're a Fortune you never snivel.' Always remember that, remember who you are, she insinuated, and now as he stood there his body was following her instructions but his mind, rebelling, wandered and worried and yes, even secretly wailed. His eyes glancing at his father's coffin didn't bother to study its furniture. All he could see was the nuisance which hid his gob-stopped father from him, for, puzzled, he had watched last night as the mortician pulled that white veil right up over his daddy's face. He had wanted, even then, to plank himself between his father, lying still, and the hangers-on who plumped for that fashion of blinding where eyes couldn't see.

'I am the resurrection and the life,' the priest was intoning when suddenly Felix jolted back to reality, just in time to hear the sound of the clay hitting his father's coffin. He would have loved to have hidden his face in his mother's coat, but he knew his mother better than that. He would have loved to have been able even to look up into her face, but he knew that was out too. Instead he kept his stare fixed down below there, down in the womb, down where his daddy heard nothing.

It was while he was schooling himself to remember who he was that his boy's terror took root, and now he found himself looking around him in distraction. His eyes vacantly met the stare of those on the opposite side of the grave. Suddenly, though, he got undone by the tears which he saw hurrying down the face of his neighbour and now, eye contact made with Mrs O'Brien, he somehow drew comfort from the look of love which she gave him.

He was in his bed, the darkness hounding him, when he saw and felt again that look which he harvested in the cemetery. The night, open to his notions, yielded up the look again. He saw the tears which flowed down Minnie O'Brien's cheeks, and knew they were meant for him, in his child's justice knew that it was the sight of his face which had acted as spur to his neighbour's grief. 'The poor, poor boy,' she was in fact thinking when they made that eye contact, and now, in his hot-tiled prison, he fed again on the gold which skulked in his friend's enema.

Further along the corridor, his mother lay relaxing after her day in the public eye. Groaning never, she now devoted her time to planning for the future. Her tears at the graveside were a success, her green eyes flooded in regretting. She looked out at sympathisers as they dutifully queued to offer their condolences. Her nerve held today, the journey from here on would be easy, her mind told her. Now to find a boarding school for Felix, was her shut-eyed resolve.

Next morning saw Jude up and making headway with her new spite. She had no regrets about her dead husband. Her duty to him lay still asleep upstairs. She had martyred herself for long enough but acting, she felt, could not go on for ever.

Listing the good and bad points of boarding schools did not play any part in her choice of place for her son. He'd go where the Fortunes always went since finding the faith. She'd pack him off to St Fechin's, sure they'd make as much out of him as they did his father.

# CHAPTER 57

It was seven years since Jude Fortune's own father had died, and now with Michael John gone she was shut of the two men who had had an input into her life. The men were as different as chalk and cheese. The father, the bluebottle of her childhood, had infested her every struggling dream; her husband, the gadfly to her married life, had at times seemed almost as bewildered as she, for through no fault of his own he found that their weald and wasteland of a marriage was ruined before it could ever be happy.

Jude's reality lay somewhere between a father's commerce and a husband's love, but to her haunted gaze there was no difference. To her there was no such thing as love. Cone-shaped need, yes, but then needs must when the devil drives, and she was on first-name terms with the devil for many's the long, long year.

Jude Fortune, the woman now widowed, had heard schoolboys chant a bawdy rhyme when she was just eleven years old. 'In eighteen hundred and ten,' they ranted, 'When women chased after men / The men, the fools, took out their tools / And chased them back again.' The boys hadn't a clue of its meaning, but she heard and fully understood. Never the child, she never joined in the chant; she sent them packing, for they and their games never held any interest at all. Even when she joined in the girls' frantic games of tig, hopscotch or skipping, hers was but a fury, a game within a game; she only ever regained her breath at, first, last and always, sums. Her female mind dredged down deep as she walked home from school, and no sooner had she parted with the last pupil than she spent the remainder of the journey gubbing figures. She had still a three-mile journey before her and it was then she got down to her calculations. Vastly complicated sums she devised, all the better if copious figures fumed before her eyes. 'Awkward little gits,' she called nine, thirteen, and underarm decimal points, but as an added spoiler, she always conjured up bastardised fractions, their numerators smaller than their denominators, and then her hands would dredge scorn on the dregs which she worked out to a final answer.

The widow Fortune thought like a farmer but grafted like a whore. From early dawn till close of day, she schemed the enemy route ahead. Her son was now lined up for rescue by the priests in St Fechin's, though she herself stank in sins of omission. Feverish vengeance had no need of a god, no need either of a living soul.

Michael John had taught her how to drive the car, and now his lessons were going to pay dividends. Her black and bottle-green car could be spotted yards away. Its driver, sitting square behind the wheel, seldom if ever acknowledged a salute from a passer-by.

Hy-Brazil – the Isle of the Blest, bilateral and lateral, became her hallmark. Money was her phantom, and she used and abused everyone in pursuit of her goal. Bystanders gaped at this sturdy widow woman; the cute hoors of bachelors for whom nobody had been good enough now rummaged in their castration, each wondering if by any chance they might make a new playboy in this barren woman's bed.

Trestle-high, her gates kept out the riff-raff and kept in her business dealings. The bank manager, for whom she had a modicum of respect, sat down with her in his sanctuary, and though she did seem to know her markets, he knew that come what may she'd number her successes or losses, whilst he would always be on the winning side, would always come in with the whip in his mouth.

Changes began to reap rewards where Jude was concerned. The big horses who grazed her fields within an inch of their lives were first for dispatch. In their place came hungry rooks of cattle, their ribs showing, but as long as their eye was lively she knew she'd be able to graze them until, come market day, they'd wobble with flesh, their hind quarters taut inside their overstretched skins.

The poor hard-working farmers from the neighbourhood, and indeed for miles around, became almost dependent upon the widow woman for their annual harvest. If they were quick off the mark they sold in October or November, but if they held out for a few quid extra, they likely found themselves missing the sale, and to make matters worse they found that come springtime they sold her their specimens for the same money or sometimes for even less than she had offered last time round.

Like something possessed, the luck ran Jude Fortune's way. She bought from a kitty looped in greed and when she sold for a great profit, she nested herself with the bank manager in Huntstown and, drunk on power, gambled on her luck holding out as her stocks and shares, listed and unlisted, grew firm comfort for her in sometimes faraway territories.

There was, however, one farmer who held his whisht and never once got involved with his next-door neighbour's funeral. He held on to his cattle until they were fit for the market. 'Butcher's bullocks,' he classed them. 'Marbled flesh, that's what the housewife needs,' he told Harry Fletcher, but the butcher in Huntstown only ever had need of two of his cattle. The others he walked as far as the fair in Oldcastle rather than be compromised by a drag broad.

Jude Fortune didn't pretend to notice the strategy at play next door to her. She, in fact, put herself out to bow to Peter O'Brien whenever she met him cycling to or from town. When it so happened that his wife cycled alongside him, or shared the pony-trap with him, her action was different. She just beeped her horn and passed on without either a smile or a nod. For all the attention which she denied her neighbours on the road, her scheme out in the fields mearing the O'Briens' was different. The workmen were ordered to top-dress those fields, so that come growth in springtime her hills would be green to the hilt, when almost everyone else's fields were grey and bearded.

Housed for the winter, Peter O'Brien's four or five dry cattle found themselves at large again come the first sign of softness in the weather. Hanging on their haunches would be rattlers of old dried dung. The fields into which they'd straggle would be still tired from the harsh winds of March, and when they'd cast their bovine glances across the hills beside them they'd low in hungry desolation.

Right on cue, Jude Fortune would smile when she heard the dirge off-loading where she had set their downfall. It came as a satisfaction to her to be somehow in the position of needling her neighbours. Really, her bank balance was such that she didn't need to do business with Peter O'Brien, but the gnaw in her groin could only be satisfied if she found she had each and every one of the riff-raff under her thumb.

# CHAPTER 58

Minnie O'Brien was startled out of her wits when Jude Fortune, on her way home from the mart in Huntstown, sounded her horn at her as she passed by in her 1987 registered gold-coloured Mercedes. Her brand new car and the swank of it was wasted on her old neighbour, for nowadays the stumbling-along renegade of the past was but fearing for the state of her health, as she struggled to continue her watch in hopes that her gone-away son might venture home to his birthplace in Drumhollow.

By nightfall, though, Minnie had long since forgotten the fright she got on her way home after collecting her pension. Now she sat thinking-through her notions of this new rave, her mess o'pottage simmering at such a rate that not even the clock chiming could frank a full stop to her flowing gallop. 'Was Brendan finished and gone to the seminary when Sheila took the whit to go nursing?' she asked herself. The dog Do-be, habit-knowing, just raised an eye, glanced at the voice and returned to his dreaming before the fire. Shelter was caffeine to his blood, while silence tooled his mistress's house. 'All the do-be's and the does-be's are dead,' said the teacher of yore, and when Felix gave her this present dog she buried her memories of her down-the-years collies, and named him 'Do-be', the better to restore her youth and her intelligence. 'Aye, they got two first places, he got his when he did his leaving whatyamacallit, and she got hers for coming first in her finals. Ah, himself was so proud of her, all in white, the veil on her head hiding her beautiful hair. "You'd swear she was a nun only better," he claimed, "Maybe she'll nurse us when we heel up," he said. But then again we'd hate to bother her, she always was his pet of the three. Ah, will you listen to me going on, when the stream hasn't even reached the bridge much less be gone under it. But himself was the same, he

175

had the brains but didn't have the dough. Between you, me and the gatepost, the best of them all was himself, and he without a brag in him, all day every day working, if he wasn't at the furniture he was out in the fields, out there come spring, following the horses until he had ploughed the country for the kids. Now where's he and where's them, nobody holding back Judas Jude but me and you Do-be, and don't we know that you're already dead, so that leaves me, aye indeedy me, the one that learnt nothing but how to work the bacon slicer and fill the old tin box for him. Yes indeedy, the miser that he was, and now he's mushroom compost, as they say, up there in Glasnevin. Twas good he got back to where he came from, and you wouldn't blame him, that was a lovely place where he was born in Phibsboro, and wasn't it a good one, he homing back like the swallow, can you beat it, but she was sorta lost, didn't care much for the traffic, spent all her time looking out the window, the big buses, all they got for the shop going in the rent on that house, and then when he got laid up he had to have the nurses coming in, but sure 'twas good they had the savings, it saw them out, the two misfits. Only visited a few times, and then three days when he went, and four for her funeral. Sure it was a release to her, she was be't up terrible with the ould rheumatism. Ah 'twas a grand place, there on the North Circular, the big rooms and the lovely fireplaces. Twas hard, you know, to come back, never see her again this side of heaven, never see inside that house again, never look up at them fancy ceilings. Himself never knew I was so taken with the redbrick houses, 'member the brass bar inside the door to hold on to while you changed your shoes, so they said anyhow. Brass bar how are ya, we were damn lucky to have a pair of shoes for Sunday. 'Member Sheila had to get white ones for the nursing. 'Member me and her bringing the cow to Hamilton's bull but the ould devil wouldn't serve her, mustna ha' wanted to perform in front of three females, but I think he was off the boil. Himself was shocked at me and her daring to go to the bull, but what was the big deal, she saw much worse, I'm telling you, in the nursing, ah, you can bet on that, ould dirty men in their todd. The bishop too, can you imagine the things he heard in confession, isn't it an awful life sitting in the dark in the poky confession box listening to shite of every sort and giving absolution, knowing the poor sods'd be back again, the same ould story ad infinitum as they say, leading-article trouble the bane of every man, causes all the damnation in the world, morning to night, night till morning, what's this they say, Do-be, the hormones is it, but men isn't the only ones to enjoy sex, sure the honeymoon was nearly a disaster but we got it right eventually. Musha, all I can say is we were like kids, knew nothing, had to learn as we went, member the woman at the desk saying "My, how time flies". Musha, if she could have foretold my life, bringing up three kids, and now they don't bother sending the thirty pieces of silver like in the Bible, but sure the Man Above said we should forgive, what was it Do-be, seven times seven and seventy-seven times more, something like so, and if He can forgive so can I. Listen here, m'poor ould Do-be, Peter m'husband was the salt o'the earth, look, he had the place willed to me and I never knew nothing until the letter came from – now if I can remember the name, well anyhow, oh yea Groans, that's them – Hubert Groan sent me the letter, he did, to come in to hear his last will and testament. But wasn't himself the honestest husband a woman could have, a damn good man he was, everything left safe for me, you'd swear someone was going to come out of the woodwork, as they say, to claim a share of here. He musta known the heart'd whip him, he keeping it all to himself. I couldn't believe it, and to think I couldn't even thank him, but that was the sort he was, that was him always, trying to fix things up to suit me. 'Member too his first attempt at making a toilet, all he had was four sheets of tin and a bit of a board for the seat, out behind the sheds out there in the nettles he made it. Come to think of it, Do-be, he made two toilets, the second was all swish, a water closet as they say, a tank built up on the roof of the scullery, or the utility room as Sheila calls it now, the water when it rained filled up the tank and then we could flush away our doosie. Do-be, it was America at home, let me tell you, but then when the fine weather came it was up the ladder and down, bringing pump water up to fill the tank, but between ourselves it's always the dry toilet I think of when I go through the haggard, himself tramping down the nettles for yards round it, and then in he comes and brings me out to sit on his throne. He made it out of a bit of mahogany, the kids were afraid they'd fall in, but I had to sit on it, he saying his oul' skit:

> In days of old when knights were bold
> And lavatories hadn't been invented
> Men left their load upon the road
> And walked off quite contented.

'The kids used be saying it for ages after and y'know, Do-be, about then it was a sin to be vulgar, but musha, doesn't it sound harmless now. He had a great laugh, and after it I was afraid goin' to confession in case the priest asked to hear the vulgarity. 'Member too the little lad down beside Maggie Dempsey's, making up his sins he was for his first confession, "Father," he said, "I said arsey arsey arsey three times" and the priest said, "That's the good boy, now don't ever say it four, and for your penance say three Hail Marys." Ah sure we hadn't a clue, informed conscience how are ya, but the Man Above had mercy on us and then picked our boy for Himself. My how time flies, member him up there on the altar saying his first Mass, the sunlight catching him in a big broad beam. Ah Do-be, y'should see him standing there where Christ Himself stood, he looked – what's this the word is, transparent is it, no, no, that's not the word I want, trans- trans- translucent, isn't that it, y'know like a ghost – that's how he looked, my boy the new priest, me and himself were numb from nerves. Sheila telling Frankie how to behave, if ye pass out I'll revive ye she says, still when it came to the time she was no better nor us, they were sorta moidered too at their brother standing up there where before the parish priest was always standing.'

While Minnie's body relaxed in the heart of time, her mind attaboyed where the future had played out its damnedest and for all she knew a future, snared even now, at least gave her gravy for her dinner-plate and feasting for her dessert. The quaint images belonging to that future strutted now in her kitchen, the altar of that ordination morning not up there in the village, but now stood rigged out before her, the character standing at its white sepulchre was still her son, her first-born.

Brass candlesticks, sugarbarleyed where they stood now on the back of the white marble altar. Tall candles grew from their twisted stands, only to end in fact or fancy flames. Flowers lent some colour to the marble theme, and a lonely soul stood vested upon the hanging hill. Naturally nervous, the voice rang out in Latin language, seed of man festering in head instead of street. Myriad feats of booklearning had led to this mysterious moment and now he, the celebrant, freed himself to absolve his brethren. Fr Brendan O'Brien fractured the air with a fine young-man's voice. Listening, his father beat his breast, *mea culpa, mea culpa, mea maxima culpa,* he confessed. His mother didn't pray at all, but knelt looking up at the altar's priest, his vestments all white and gold, his hair shining in the sunbeam, his voice disporting itself in church language. The voiceless mother created her own faith in her heathen heart. 'My son, my son', she boasted, plagiarising someone else's words, as, natural in heart but proud in mind, she looked and listened. Sheila and Frankie stared and stared at the back of their brother. His fringed maniple hung from his left arm. His voice never hesitated. Struck dumb at his hearsayed power, they felt that this Mass was different, very different, for now they had Brendie up there representing them. Beckoning them to witness his new, absolute power, he heard the warning bell ring. Then he said his mantra words. Nothing visibly happened. Nom-de-plumed nothing. But faithful everything. Now he had performed his miracle. Now bread was no longer bread but flesh of the word. Wine, red in colour, trembled but slightly and became blood of beast. Nursing this

179

harvest the arms lifted, the eyes looked up and adored, then the knee genuflected in humble salutation. Communion soon joined son to God and God and son to family when Peter headed up to receive Him, high Him, from the hand of his boy-priest. Minnie, the mother, nimbly stepped nine steps towards her son and, watching him lift the host from the ciborium, closed her eyes in utter disbelief where then she opened her mouth and felt the him at her breast now feeding her on manna from heaven. Next to receive was Sheila, the sister of like brainpower, but her receiving his host on her tongue, though religiously awe-inspiring, was yet something which she, despite her brains, could never humbly create for him. Last of the full-blooded family was Frankie, who strode self-consciously towards Brendan, Fr Brendan, and in his presence nonchalantly received communion just as he would any Sunday from any priest. He blessed himself hurriedly and, humped shoulders high round his ears, hollow-stepped back to his seat.

Communion lasted for ever as the very village itself turned out, its inhabitants, man, woman and seven-year-olds receiving the host from the newly anointed hands of a villager like themselves. He placed communion bread on tongues which hesitated in nervousness, on tongues belonging to beautiful young girls, on tested tongues of village blokes and on the tiny, pink tongues of small village children. All came, all saw, all – nearly all – received, and all – nearly all – were humbly thankful. He thanked heaven, this new priest did. His parents he thanked, for he knew he had almost bled them white. His sister and brother he thanked, for keeping him humble, for didn't he remember their fights on the turf bank of Holly Bog. The villagers he thanked, for being kind and supportive to him during his time among and with them. Last of all he thanked the altarboys, those heathen helpers at the foot of the altar. Now he was ready, willing and wanting to give his first blessing to those souls before him, his breathing congregation of religious catch-alls.

# CHAPTER 59

Religion exhausted, the short holiday at home with his family nearing an end, the villagers set to to give this young priest of theirs a send-off to remember. On the night the schoolhouse became the glow worm in Drumhollow, for the place was ablaze with lamps and lanterns and lighting from left-over Christmas candles. In one room the ladies set out the food and beverages, the men nudging in the odd half-barrel of porter. Out in the other room the men were the masters, setting up a stage upon which the night's musicians would play and upon which the teacher would make the farewell speech to one of his best ever pupils.

Brendan, the new priest, arrived on cue, his reception akin to that laid on for the bishop. He had come a long way from the day in the third field when he blurted out his pay-later story. Now here he stood in his classroom of old, a hero in black and a hunch of white.

There was only so much a person could devour, so the night eventually swung over to the other classroom, the juniors' one, where Humpty Dumpty still sat bravely on the wall and the cat still sat on the mat while the witch got on with her journey on her broomstick, all that was missing her mangy tub o'guts of a cat. The pictures on the walls, though, had no bearing on this night, for in here the music acted like a magnet, for the full-bellied tricksters were now drooling to shake a leg or two to the band's best *bodhránning*.

Nobody cried halt, yet a break came in the music, the interval now going to be allocated to others to do their bit for Fr Brendan's night. Sheila led off with her recitation of 'The Croppy Boy'. Sheila, cat o'nine tails, recited it the way the nuns had taught her to do it. Encore, encore, the crowds lauded, and shyly she once again obliged her brother but this time she chose his favourite poem 'The Ballad of Father Gilligan' by W B Yeats.

The show-stopper of the night, though, involved the parents of the new young priest. As if it was all planned, the band skedaddled and there was a void to be filled. 'They have no wine', his mother could have complained to her son but Brendan, only too aware of the hiccup, broached the subject of her playing her party piece. She had brought her fiddle and hidden it underneath the school press. Now her steps hurried towards it, and stooping down she hauled it into view. She opened the old shook case and withdrew her fiddle and then, as though it were the *Feis Ceoil*, advanced towards the stage. Nervously she gave a smile at everyone before she ruined her face and, stepping into a comfortable stance, began tuning up. Great hopes rode on her playing something nice for the neighbours, but then she almost gave up her spot when himself suddenly joined her where she stood. 'I've learnt the words off by heart, you know, your special tune,' he whispered. 'Give us a hand and I'll sing to your fiddling. Just gimme the billie when to begin,' he begged and now, her face full of fright, she began to play. As though he were an eunuch, his first words shrilled out but then, having got his breath, he began doing justice to the song. By the time he came to the end, his beautiful tenor voice had more than made up for his false start, and the audience were enraptured with their first hearing of 'She Moved Through The Fair'.

They pulled the place down at the surprise of seeing the O'Briens performing together: now they begged and cajoled for them to oblige again. Peter, though, hadn't prepared anything else: learning the words from the new songsheet which he had found in Day's Bazaar had been the job of weeks. Now he looked at Minnie for guidance and she, knowing well how well he knew the songs on the gramophone records at home, began to play 'Danny Boy'. It took one more song before the audience gave in and now, with his adrenalin bubbling, it was Peter himself who this time chose to sing 'Kevin Barry'.

# CHAPTER 60

At first sight the natives were inclined to stand back from this new white man, this blue-eyed foreigner who had just arrived on their African soil. They had, after all, grown used to their old bearded priest. For years and years he had rubbed away their sins for them, and for years and years they in turn loved him just as though he were a farmer like themselves. He was wise enough to know that he was but a human being added to human beings as, here in the bush, he tried to humanise a man-sized God for folks' understanding. He had always hacked away at their tribal gods as he tried to supplant their jumping Jesus with his kind of a white man's Jesus. But now he was gone. Gone down river. Handcuffed by his rosary beads.

His flock had noticed death creeping nearer to their beloved priest. If the milk of human kindness could have beaten it away, their baskets of fruit and food would have kept him alive. But high in the indigo sky, five stars had appeared in the firmament, and though the stars held the shape of a plough, there too unbeknownst to the shepherd crouched death, a face of hunger on it, waiting to nab the unsuspecting priest.

His sad flock strewed the waters with flowers as down the river chugged the boat bearing his coffin to the order's graveyard downstream. Great crowds cluttered the riverbanks as the boat moved away. There were no Irishwomen there to keen his passing, but his flock had their women, and at the dramatic moment they stood there ululating in unison their grief and loss.

The boat which had taken away all that remained of the old wizened man was the very same boat which, today, chugged upstream bringing in its bow the church's replacement for him. This newcomer appeared to be all that the old spent man was not, for this man now approaching was a hale and hearty young man.

He was as yet unknown to the watching people but soon they'd be calling out his name, their soft burr intoning the word Brendan.

White, he sat there in the boat, having already crossed lands and thunderous oceans to be here, to step now onto the stubbed land of Africa. A holy beginner, he was. He thought that his arrival in this new land was but the realisation of the hallucination which began that day in the National School in Drumhollow when, caught in the headlights of an old missionary's gaze, he had felt drawn, drawn towards this very site, to this group of huts nestling together, his folded in, in their circle. Now that he was here, he moved towards them, a child here on a fool's errand.

Day after day, the days grew hotter, then came Sunday, his first day to say Mass for his parishioners. On a makeshift altar he stood, and when it came to the elevation he lifted aloft his round white host, his God in disguise. At the same time fashionable chieftains with their fashionable families raised aloft their eyes to look into their sun's light, there to stye their thinking about this new white man and his new white god. Believers, though, came forward to receive communion, and he placed host after host full down on their tongues. He gave his final blessing at the end of his Mass. He gave it to those who crossed themselves and to those who didn't as he stood there facing them in the burning place, his vestments frogmarching the sweat from his shoulders and chest, his sturdy back and ribs, to drip from their binding down onto the red clay of Africa.

At the end of his first month in Africa he wrote home to his family and, disguising his loneliness, filled page after page with dreadful stories from his dreamworld. Folded inside their envelope they homed to Drumhollow, everything on the page a lie, every animal described a voiced nightmare. When he described the linseed-oil quality of blackest night he was in fact just weaving a carpet upon which he could place his struggling conscience as, far away from home, he wrote dog-in-the-manger-minding something for which he had no lord and master to further. When he described his tin whistle playing he said his music filled the whole countryside, but what he didn't describe was the sound, which was gull-lonely enough to send dogs to bay the moon. Graphic descriptions he gave, too, of the hand-beat on a tom-tom, and as he did so he cackled to himself while with his boned hands he actually beat the rhythm before then wording it for them. 'So as you can see I'm happy as Larry,' he told them, as with a lick of his tongue he folded down the flap on his envelope to Ireland.

Minnie's letters – it was always Minnie who replied – crossed from no-man's land to flint-dry lane by boat and train. She posted them in the village letterbox, and as she slipped them through its open mouth she smiled in happiness at the thought of him standing out there in that bushy place, hand holding that which her hand held, as she carried it towards the village post office. It was always an event worthy of chatter. Her voice would sound pleasurable when she'd ask for the stamp. 'He'll be pleased to hear from home,' the old postmistress would venture as, smiling, she'd remember his touch on her head the day she knelt before him for his first blessing. His name would look at her from the envelope and, making much of his mother, she'd lick the stamp herself and affix it to its hilltop. Despite herself there'd be a hesitancy in her hand as she'd hand the envelope back to Minnie, who would then nest it against her bosom before going outside to slide it into the letterbox to the waiting trap within.

# CHAPTER 61

Peter never told his wife about his bad heart. He didn't wish to burden her with his pain. From the night when the pain first struck to the day when the pain last struck, he managed to master the grinding sign of trouble in his heart. He fell on the plan of gearing himself below the level of his own strength, and by so doing he somehow learned to live with the grip in his chest which then spread to his arms. He oftentimes had to lie down on his stomach in a muddy field or on the turf bank in Holly Bog as the pain held him in its vice, but he knew from experience that with rest and quiet senses would come back, and eventually he would be able to mosey on with the work in hand. He never feared for himself, but had nightmares about the widow and children who needed his fearful earnings. As the years minded he gave displays of everything being normal but, noticing a change in the severity of an attack, he had the gumption to go to Hugh Groan, the solicitor, and there in his presence he put into writing the last things which he could have a say about. 'You'll not add or deduct one day of your life,' encouraged the solicitor, 'but should anything happen to you, the family and the place'll be safe in your wife's hands.' All that was needed then was his signature, and as he skirted to sign his last will and testament two clerks made light of being present to witness it.

The thresher told the story with stomach-turning sounds. Peter had fractured his usual rule by rashly piking heavy sheaves of corn from the stack on which he stood up onto the work surface of the mill. He forgot his slow-down method of practice, and instead pitched sheaf after sheaf to beat the band. The farmers feeding the sheaves into the big pink mill were always ready and willing to take the best that he could heave towards them. He worked as though he were back with Minnie cutting their first bank of turf.

He swung his body with an almost mesmeric rhythm. He felt wonderful, and enjoyed the verbal exchanges between the men at work with him. They slagged him about his having the son the priest in Africa and the daughter the nurse in London, 'And sure you'll never feel,' they laughed, 'till that young fella of yours brings home a woman.' The big mug of tea which George Hamilton's wife gave him decreed that his heart could keep up this pace forever. He sat on a barrelbag of barley and breathed in grand hearty timing. He ate three cheese sandwiches; he was hungry and needed to refurnish his strength. Back he returned then to his voluntary work and, starting on stack number four, the wheat, he hurled the topmost sheaves down to the band-cutters on the mouth's edge. He listened almost unconsciously to the play of the tumblers inside the thresher's belly. 'Wing-a-ning, wing-a-ning, wing-a-nign NURRNNN' sang the big pink mill's innards as it chewed up the actual umpire of associated granaries the wheat, the dream-filled wheat. It shook and shivered in the throes of threshing before then sending millions of single denizens into the chutes for sacking. Nesting still the straw, it blew and bloated until, chin-wagging, it worked the yellow straw out into Hamilton's haggard. Now its established echoed job complete, it eddied the chaff, the wrappings of the grains, out on to the grass beneath its body. Music only stopped when Peter, standing now on tiptoes, thrust the last heavy sheaf up towards the hands stretched and waiting. The job which George Hamilton had allotted to him was now done.

Carts laden with brown hessian sacks filled with barley, wheat and oats meandered along dirt tracks towards Hamilton's granary. Fellows walked behind, rescuing their strength after their day's work. Among them walked Peter O'Brien, chatting as was his wont. Pulverised by pain, he suddenly slumped to the ground and, holding his chest, lay there before his neighbours. They, to a man, lifted him and propped him in an alcove of bulging sacks, his head falling to one side and then towards the other.

The driver whipped up the heavy-laden horse and headed towards the weak man's house. Minnie actually watched the load of corn coming hurriedly down the boreen. She saw the men carry someone towards the yard. She made to meet them, but when she saw whom they carried she screeched in furious desperation.

'What happened? What happened?' she crazed as she tried to get to touch his face, but the carriers found his bodyweight heavy, and besting along they cried, 'He just got suddenly weak and fell on his face down on Hamiltons' lane. George's gone for the doctor and the priest.'

'Priest?' she screamed. 'Why priest, sure he's not going to die?' But the men said 'Lead on to his bed, willya, like a good woman.' They carried him into the kitchen, past the lamp lit inside its red globe. She kept ahead of the sagging body and, looking back in her walking, searched him of the Clarence, looking to see if he even remembered. His brown eyes looked, oh how they looked, but no sign of his darling Minnie did he see, dead hills denied him a view.

The men trudged, trundled and tramped up the creaky stairs and, coming over all gentle now, eased him up onto the pillows. They fussed taking off his boots, but she fast-gripped his face screaming, 'Peter, Peter, can you hear me? for God's sake will you answer!' Her hands cupped his face, felt his forehead, washed his face in hot tears, but the brown eyes seemed more interested in the ceiling.

Minnie's cries were cartwheeling around the room when through the din nudged the name Frankie. 'Someone should go to meet him and break the news about his dad,' suggested a man's voice. She heard the name and, swinging around, looked hysterical looks to see if he had come, but the men were scouting out the window and then she saw him too. She sacked her voice of screams, stood straight, and with a last look at Peter she walked out of the room, down the stairs, and the men could see her drying her eyes on her apron as she headed up the boreen to be the one to break the news to the child.

A habit of dark brown clothed his last remains. Tumblers of brown Guinness toasted his grand name. Tea, freshly made, was downed by the potful as around his bed the neighbours moved as though playing musical chairs. The priest had been too late to witness his soul's going. The doctor could not bring him back. Telegrams had broken hearts in Africa and London, as news of the sudden death described how a farmer had devoted his last efforts to the thresher. Minnie and Frankie were the only family for now. Sheila, on hearing the news, had left Guy's Hospital and was hurrying home. Brendan, every father's dream-son, only newly arrived at his post, could not shut up shop and come home to bury his father. No, he could only sting the days and nights with the venom of his heartbreak.

For all she was worth, the new widow-woman saw to it that her neighbours had full and plenty as hour after hour they kept watch around her husband's corpse. All night long she plied them with food and drink, all the while passing round her plateful of ham sandwiches, the bacon slicer's helpings here now to haunt her, she who in her father's shop sold all the necessaries for every village wake.

Now it was her own turn tonight. Her dear Peter, him whom she needed, was up in their marital bed all agonised and mute, and she of his soul was performing the miraculous loaves and fishes re-enactment. How could strangers know what she needed to whisper to this man of the Clarence Hotel? Her hands wanted to feel him just once more. Her eyes wanted to count the hairs on his head. Her jolly tundish would never again lift in union with him at play. Her safety in the night would now be haphazard and solitary. She wanted to say all the praises that had bubbled up in regretting, but now all she could do was smile, graciously smile, and see to the needs of every Tom, Dick and Harry.

189

# CHAPTER 62

Minnie was last to stoop down and kiss the face of Peter, laying her hot cheek against his menial marble. 'Goodbye love unt'l we meet in heaven,' she barely whispered. 'You were the very best, the only one for me.' Hinged to her cold-as-ice hilltop, it was Sheila who eased her joints away. Looking her last look down upon him there, fevered tears still continued to fall and mingle on his huntsman's jowl, the drops striking him like May rain. The glad lid, though, lent no more time for crying: down it settled itself to await the sounds of the screws erring as they turned this coffin into a box of ligamented lonesomeness.

The coffin, carried by Frankie and Ned Naylor at the head and two neighbours at the feet, wandered down the stairs. The man who had made those very stairs could not now take a step; there he lay in his oak overcoat playing the role of corpse. Down the stairs the steps carried him, the song of silence broken by prayers and sobs. Under the archway into the kitchen passed the man of the house, his being quiet beyond words, his body stiff beyond awkwardness. Naturally the clock glued its bell so that Minnie would not in future remember the hour when her love was wanted pitifully, wanted but not able to be asked for. Nasty death, the hoor, had gathered its ransom, and now the penniless widow tramped out to follow its cortège of triumph.

Two gleaming black horses drew the hearse towards the village church. Hawthorn bushes dressed themselves in red and yellow leaves. They bowed as he who had planted them passed, and promised to remember by garnering his blood to colour their haws. Bantering their famishing loyalty, the cows and calves approached the hedge to look in googy-eyed goggling at all this stir upon the boreen. The hearse rumbled along, inside its glass snare the object of the best of lunches, pivot now to all eyes and death's dance. Minnie wandered just behind, her arms supported by Sheila and Frankie. Her head was dressed in a black hat, its net hindering her eyes. She peeped through this black barrier to feast on him, holy, lying him, and her feet moved one after the other as she bashfully followed.

Bowing in chorus, the horses approached the village. Their black plumes trembled in the evening breeze. The hard black hat of the driver seemed to be bowing too as he drove his glass menagerie towards the waiting parish priest.

Minnie O'Brien stood between her daughter Sheila and son Frankie on the edge of the grave. Six feet down for fear'd of dogs, that was how deep the gravediggers dug. The void waited. The clay, all yellow, was dauby following the torrential shower of rain. Shy where it usually bragged, the sun stole through the grey clouds and shed a Hepplewhite shine on the coffin, just about still above ground. The priest prayed. The coffin, high-powered by human strength, hovered over the grave and then, as though willing to be sacrificed, clattered and clanged its rasping ropeway down, dead-down into the royal earth. Holy water spattered the coffin's lid. Clay stuck there, too, in dauby stress. Hail Marys entwined themselves around the cross down there upon the breastplate. Finally, the shovels shovelled the close of play. Peter O'Brien, the soldier of nothing, was for the worms.

Minnie, Sheila and Frankie had just witnessed hallmarked death being stamped upon the name O'Brien. Frankie had even aided and abetted it by shovelling one shovelful of clay in on top of his father's remains. Head bowed Minnie stood, tears scalding her stomach's rawness. Sheila, the nurse, had seen stiffs by the score, some packaged in sheets, others framed in tin boxes, as they were carted away, dispatched for final disposal. But now her own father had become one of the brigade of stiffs, her own dear father, the fisherman to her ling's catching, she hung there in a state of bewilderment. This burial had brought its own trauma, and the tears which petered down her night-duty-plighted face and fell on her hands were tears of futility, for she knew only too well that things would never be the same again. Her mind pinpointed her last image of her father. It was the last day of her holiday at home. The departure had come. He wondered if he was clean enough to see her off on the Dublin bus. He helped her board the two steps and awkwardly, laughingly, said, 'Don't stay away too long,' but he didn't know that she didn't catch what he said, for the bus just then blew a big belch of black fumes which playfully carried those words away. She could see him now as, glancing out the back window, she blew him a final kiss. He looked up into the window at her and highed his eyes heavenwards in mocking, laughing fun.

Francis Peter O'Brien, where he stood, was only standing in for himself, and for his eldest brother. Without any of the magnetism of Brendan, he yet stood there, his hands clean even though he had navvied the sticky clay in on top of his godsend of a father's remains. As the neighbours approached to shake hands and sympathise with the O'Briens, he to their every 'Sorryforyour-trouble' rescued his brother's silence by replying, 'Iknowthat. Iknowthat.' But what he didn't know was that, though he might forget the date on which his father died, the day even, he, like a horse with a stop in him, would never again be able to run past the spot on the boreen without hesitating to recall the awful sudden news which his mother broke to him, that his father was dead, killed himself piking sheaves down at the threshing in the Hamiltons' haggard.

Eventually the O'Briens were free to look at the mound of misery before them and to talk about the member missing from this damned dance. His name was breathed by Minnie as the three worried for him and his purgatory. It was the family doctor who banished them from the graveyard. He fadded concern for Minnie by ordering her daughter and son to take her home so that her poor body might get a bit of sit-down. Her children said 'Come on, mam, do as the doctor says.' Tackling her poison cup, she flung a last long look at the heap of clay and, turning away, she whispered: 'Ah, 'tis himself that has got the sit-down.'

## CHAPTER 63

As the months passed Minnie got used to lying at death's door. She got used to feeling the damp coldness of her late husband's pillow when time and again she rescued it as, lemming-like, it attempted to drop over the edge of the bed. Her ear got used to having the stapes moving in and out of the oval window as the sound of him that used to call her name echoed moideredly where the ear that was uppermost heard still the pronunciation of his voiced word 'Minnie'. Her body, the casket of her being, got used now to being only that, just her own creature of conned comfort as there it lay, flat as a pancake on her own side of the big bed. 'My, how time flies,' the second noise from the Clarence, was gone with her husband to the grave. Now as she lay through the dead of night her words of desperation became a prayer as she whispered, 'God, how I miss him.' Numb from head to place was now her commonplace as for all she was worth she gravedug her future days and days. Nobody, next to nobody, knew silence as she felt it – nobody that is except God, and 'big help He is,' she countered, the sighing coming from the place of her dirge. Same as yesterday, same as tomorrow, was her thinking as she stretched her body down and up the whole length of the bed, but even that cunning certainty was disturbed by the sound of some pot-walloping down below in the kitchen.

With all the delicacy of a chef, Frankie was downstairs making the stirabout. Lumpy, it'd be, from his heeling in the oatmeal without bothering to stir it in gradually. She didn't mind now. She had minded for donkey's years but 'look what it got me,' she grumbled. 'Come on down, I've got it ready,' called her youngest son and, wishing to be helpful, she heeded his call by shouting 'I'm coming, son, in a minute.' But it was all a lie. She didn't need lumpy porridge. For years, in fact since old gods' time, she had been a desirable housewife. Now it didn't seem to matter whether she got up or stayed on in bed, either place only reminded her of Peter. She lay on thinking of her last twelve months of torturous loneliness. Will it ever get easier? she wondered. The hawthorns were again changing colour, so her luck might begin to change too. Her family had now accepted that life in Drumhollow would be different. Brendan had accepted her news about his father's death. His faith in the Man Above seemed to console him when he most needed it. Sheila had settled back at work, her latest conquest now taking her mind off her father's death.

The bill for the funeral expenses had been cleared, and only yesterday her hands had settled flowers on his sunken grave. He seemed to be still in charge though she was now in the driving seat. She had tried to tame Frankie into taking on his role as heir apparent. His wanting to head off to seek his fortune was but more sorrow waiting for to happen. Her poor boy's hands were not gifted like his father's, so the carpenter's workshop had no hands-on staff to run it. She, of course, had her five-fielded farm, the running of it her sole right, thanks to her low-lying love in the grave. She had still got four bullocks and four cows, her pony trap and pony. Her farmhorse was a mare, and she had seen to it that Frankie brought her in season to Caulfield's entire horse. The mainstay was the donkey, who anointed his position by being such a drawer of wood and a drinker of water. He served as companion to the mare and bearer of burdens to the family now left. 'All is not lost,' she heard herself thinking. Peter's anniversary would be on Monday. The reds and yellows would be hawthorning their memorial to him. She thanked the Man Above for all His blessings. Her black clothes had eventually eased to grey, but as she sought around for her bedroom slippers she was now planning to vie with the hawthorns and dress in her best puce mohair jumper, the one which Sheila had brought her from London, in on the top shelf of the wardrobe.

Breakfast became appealing now that she felt she could jenny-goat her life. So thinking, she tied back her curly hair with a rubber band. She wore her ankle-length skirts shorter now, so when she slid her feet into the hungry interior of her red slippers she felt that she was about to take a step in the right direction.

When she did join Frankie at breakfast, she smiled as she downed his lumpy porridge. This morning she wasn't for highlighting his faults. After all, she had begun to look ahead now, and today her boy was going to begin the big job of drawing home the harvest of hard, dry turf from their bank in Holly Bog.

The breakfast over, she cleared the table. Her home was now going to be run differently. Her life had to go on, that she knew, the days when she seed carried and seed-birthed were now no more, and this new morning her mind riz, she was helping herself as she got on with her numb nothing of a menu. Thinking ahead, she parcelled up a few wedges of loaf for Frankie; filled a bottle of milk, and brought them out to the cart. He was all set for a day drawing turf out from the bank to rick it on the roadside in readiness for carting home. The final load of the day he'd bring on home so that she could test it out in the stove. 'If it's dry enough it'll bring up the heat quickly,' she thought as she listened to the iron-shod wheels grating up the boreen towards the road gate. 'What'll I do when he goes off to hunt for gold?' she sombrely asked herself. What could she do to stop him going, she asked as well, but being but barely in charge she fobbed off her no longer lonely worries, or just barely lunchboxed worries, and planned instead to bygone black-dressed despair by giving her home a golden spring-clean in Autumn.

Minnie tried to sing that billhooked day, but her famished voice didn't remember, couldn't alliterate, wouldn't echo, for her epiglottis stayed closed astride her windpipe, a stunt which gagged sound, sold out on her jugular vein, and in all sternum-stopped her singing. Now she needed the butter churn to bring her to Connecticut, so that there she might loose her loitering ham-pink tongue.

The stubborn milk, filtered and separated, awaited her touch. Churning nowadays was done by her alone. Nowadays even the gas depended on her thumb for its route of escape, and the butter ball bearings, giddy though they were, suspected that they glossed the window not like long ago, but totally at her mercy, as they stuck there like leeches to the monocle. A basket case, she almost was, by the time she got her churning finished, for when she addressed the butter mountain she today had trouble as, seduce it how she would, her fingers could not free the secrets still trapped inside the Hill O'Down shaped mound of butter. But yielding to her constancy, the sea of blue, spent milk began to encourage her, singing its own sly song in five festivaled farthings. Just for the jig o'the thing she butted in and now, warming to her new feelings, began to improvise as she sang her rendition of the blues in five/four time. Not for nothing did she learn the ins and outs of her mother's music; now her mind grew excited as she rigged a timpani for hammer in her scat version of the song 'Under the Bloke 'neath the Oak'. Now she found that her veins coursed blood again. Now her heart was in fact mega-pumping. Now her being never needed to voice a moan, for her ears heard a born-again voice, the voice of Minnie Humphrey-that-was, as jumpin' and jivin' it skewered the glory trapped here despite her fuckless life.

# CHAPTER 64

Frankie schooled the ass, weary from the work, down the boreen towards the thatched, open turf-shed. He walked along beside his ass's head, the loop of reins hanging from his casual grasp. The actual turf, piled sod upon sod into a pyramid, had settled down nicely on its jaunt home to Drumhollow. The young man sling-gadded along, his feet yielding to the drawing ass's gait. He was weary from his solitary job lifting and throwing sods the livelong day. Butterfingered never, he accounted for his every grip on a hard-skinned sod of turf. His back was solid but supple, and while he stopped, gripped hold, and stood slightly up to throw each sod his mind was busy where-ing and what-ing his destiny. The idea that his mother needed him was to the forefront of his mind. He knew she needed him to act as stand-in for his father. He knew that her five fields would one day fall to him but he needed, he felt, to be given his head. He knew that there was a place out there in the big beyond where he might heed his own common sense and earn enough to keep a shirt on his back and a spud in his pot.

Glumly he threw the sods into the blank shed's place, now throwing the same sods for the second time this evening. As he worked, he reasoned that he was just back from the lid of the great brown bog, yet all around him here the animals fought in their anxiety to leach his life from him. He knew that they and their ilk would eventually wear him down. Where his mother might benefit from his labouring, he knew he'd have little or nothing to show for his young life. 'I'll have to be like a shadow,' he thought, 'when I creep up on Mammy with my news. Sure she'll hit the roof when I say I'm going, but going I am and that's for sure.' Like the proverbial soot drop, he had a few months back mentioned his plans but she didn't react much then, she just thought he was in some sort of shock following Peter's sudden death. But now he was, in a manner of speaking, primed for off. When he had her turf supply home and clamped into the shed, the drills of potatoes dug out of the ground and pitted, and the turnips pulled and snigged, he would be off, off on his *giolladeachair*-road to the Irishman's hunting grounds.

Light was fading by the last sod's flight into the shed. The ass, the whole day's sweat stamped in tackling-traces on his shaggy body, had done his tumbling routine as he set about reverting to his Gunther's habit. Inside, Frankie's supper was ready and waiting, a mound of scrambled egg and sausages piled high on top of a slice of batch loaf. She, who had churned today, would have baked fresh bread as well but she needed turf, hard turf, to burn red in order to bring up the heat inside the dark cavern of the stove, so it was toasted loaf bread which assumed the base beneath the scrambled egg. Minnie, shaping it for its purpose, had removed both the Catholic and the Protestant crusts from either end of the doorstep-thick slice. Throwing the two crusts out to her hungry poultry she had watched them as, running amok, they squabbled over who should claim which. It was the Rhode Island Red cockerel, the know-all, who come dawn each morning, lost no time in thieving everyone else's sleep, that grabbed the curving, black, burnt Catholic crust and made off with it to his dunghill. The straight pale-brown crust from the bottom of the loaf, the Protestant one, was hungrily picked up by two hens, one a White Wyandotte, the other a chequered Barred Rock. They, holding hoult for hoult, darted every which way until, at last, the crust broke, and the White Wyandotte, selling dummies, managed to make her getaway with at least two-thirds of the crust held tight in her beak.

'The lot of ye are no better than the rest of us,' she thought. 'All ye want is yer crust, the whole jing bang lot of it, and to hell with who else wants a bit.' Those hens that got nothing side-eyed at her in hopes that she might have more, but when she went back inside and closed the door they scurried after the two victors, all heads focussing straight ahead to see if the spoils were still there where the scallywags were seeking minutiae from the prize which they had won.

Neither hen nor crust held sway where the two dummies set to to sort out the matter of the going or staying of the child. The mother sat at one side of the table, the son opposite her. The thing which acted as umpire was the bowl of butter balls, sitting there crying though a cross word hadn't yet invaded their space. When the opening severance came it came echoing innocence. The mother came out with the first sally. Her elbows rested on the table. 'How was Holly Bog? Bet you had plenty of time to think down there in all that quiet.'

'She must have guessed what I was at,' the son threatened. He stayed silent until he had the forkful of egg and sausage in his mouth and chewed. 'Aye indeed, the bog is the last place God made. There wasn't a soul down there bar myself. All I saw all day was an aeroplane away in the distance, and then it went behind a big cloud.'

The mother nibbled again by telling of the very first time she ever wheeled a bogbarrow, in fact any barrow. She told him for the hundredth time how the barrow on her return journeys used to clip her on the heels, until she wised up to it. He laughed to oblige her.

'Twill all be yours someday, and then you can work it like your dad and me,' she suggested. He placed his mug back down on the table and without looking across it he said, 'I'll not. I'm going to England as soon as I get the jobs done up here. There's nothing here but work and shit and no money on a Saturday night.'

Now she tried to hobble him. She drew down the subject of how brainy the two others had been, how the teacher said that Brendan could be anything he liked and how, for a girl, Sheila could beat the best of the boys at anything he set out for them to do. 'She was even cleverer than Brendan, it's a doctor she should be, but how-an'ever she loves what she's at. Now Frankie, you're the makings of a farmer, from the word go that's what your father laid out for you and someday maybe you could buy another bit of land, you know, extend here.' All the while she was talking he was wolfing grub into him. Now, as if to put a halt to her gallop, he got up from the table, got the teapot, filled up his mug again, cut another slice of bread before sitting down and saying, 'The pigs aren't fed, d'you hear them, they'll eat each other. I suppose you didn't get anything ready for them?'

If that was how he wanted to change the subject, well then, it'd be still OK by her. 'Yes, of course I have the pot boiled for the pigs,' she said. 'It should be cooled by now. And I've the milking done as well.'

Her son was cutting when he said, 'Don't you think yourself that it's gone a bit late for feeding them pigs? Sure, it wouldn't have killed you to have thrown them in a bucket of grub.'

Minnie knew he was right but she didn't admit it; didn't admit, either, that of late she was inclined to leave all those jobs to him.

The pigs put a stop to the debate, but when Frankie got back in the couple took up where they left off. This time, though, everything bar the pigs' pot itself got thrown into the planned row. Holly got mentioned time and time again, and it wasn't even Christmas. Five, the number five, became the crux between them. He didn't want to be a farmer. He wasn't interested in the workshop either. Not able to scratch, wasn't that what ye cuggered about? Ye didn't think I heard. You've a proud name. Don't let it die out. Humphrey did, why not O'Brien? Brendan is off saving souls, Sheila over there saving lives. Aye, isn't it gas, her saving English lives? You know what they did for m'uncle. They're both a credit to your Dad and me. Both suiting themselves. Two outta three not good enough. I won't be stuck in the mud, hands or not. You're only a gossoon, too young. What would you be knowin' at your age? A big bad world out there. He married. But he was twenty-five. You weren't then. Eighteen. Aye, but only moving down the road. Only eighteen, seventeen goin' on eighteen.

Eighteen, but I had my nest egg. Big deal. Much good it did. Church got it. Nothing left for her and me. We didn't matter. Nothing left then, nothing left now. When the lid closed. Paying oul' bills. No help from priest or nurse. Skypilot or pan handler. Yea she told me. Shit's shit. No one now except me and you. The widow and her innocent Charlie. Isn't that it. Wait a few years. Time enough. Save a bit of money. But there's a hole in the bucket, dear Liza. Don't be so smart. Your own boss now. Working for the stranger. Imagine leaving home. At seventeen. Goin' on eighteen. Have to go. Have to earn me living. Imagine leaving Ireland. Your father'd turn in his grave. He barely cold in it and you want out. After the price that was paid. Your poor uncle. The volunteer. Shot through the neck. Black gunpowder all over his poor face. They lined the grave with moss. But the worms got him, moss or no moss. What a way to be talking, and your Dad's Mass Monday.

But have your way. Think twice. Have thought. Hills are green far away. Same as here. Nothing needed but fare to Dublin and boat fare to Holyhead. Look't all that went before me. Look't Sheila. Better here. The electricity coming. Night into day, isn't that what we're promised. Life getting easier. Get a tractor. But there's a hole in the bucket, dear Liza. Lord you're provoking. Cause I've a mind o'my own. Think well. Sleep on it. In the morning. Talk again. Nothing to talk about. Nothing more to say. Her food out the door to the dog. Tension in O'Briens' kitchen was so thick that you could churn it and make, at the very least, vinegar.

Frankie O'Brien was up with the crows. He felt bad this new morning, almost hated himself for bringing the fight to his mother. When he arose he didn't bother to boil the kettle and make the mandatory mug of tea, and now, his jobs nearly done, his stomach was full of emptiness. 'How will I face her?' was his only daylight concern as he hackneyed his boots towards the back door.

Minnie acted cool, calm and collected. 'So what,' she suggested.

'If he wants to go, don't you dare stop him. He'll be back, you wait and see. He hasn't a hand to scratch himself with and now he knows it himself. He's neat, though, in himself, he'd have made a shopboy, but now the going's on him, his mind is riz. Minnie, there's nothing for it but to offer it up.'

Breakfast went down a treat. The porridge tasted like honey. The boiled eggs, buttered and salted, turned the meal into the equivalent of the Last Supper. 'Hunger is great sauce,' she said, and they both laughed outright and things got okay, sort of all right for now. As they ate they avoided the contentious issue and chose instead to talk of Peter's anniversary Mass.

The Mass for Peter O'Brien's first anniversary was just a family occasion. A few neighbours located themselves here and there in the church, but up in the front pew knelt the widow and her son, side by side for the last time. The Mass themed remembrance. Now, this time, the widow could pray. Her bold soul hulled her love lying in the graveyard with pleas for his new place up there in the company of saints. Her mind wandered. She could just imagine him socialising with her own mother and father and with the old stooped man, Brendan, and his own brother with the gunshot; they'd be all together now, lording it up there with the Man Above. Frankie, though, was on a different tack altogether. He begged for mercy for his father's soul, but with the thunder now taken from his mother's sails he began to pray for her, for her plight when, with him gone, she'd find herself totally alone.

# CHAPTER 65

Time flew by, the jobs were all finished, and now the not-quite-eighteen-year-old son of the widow woman was ready to fly the coop. His mother, stranded though she was going to be, yet stilled her heart and stole from herself where he was concerned. All of her four pigs were sold, the going price of the day accepted, no bringing them back until the prices were better, for she told her son, 'Take what you can get and we'll split it down the middle.'

True to her word, she handed half the money to Frankie, but out of her own half she bought him a new Crombie overcoat, two sets of underpants, two pairs of socks and a tie to remind him of spring in Drumhollow. It was a sludge-green tie with primrose-yellow stripes, the nicest one hanging on the bar that day. There were others there which were frumpy and sensible, but every time her hand felt this particular one she found herself drawn to it; she in fact felt she had to choose it just for the sake of her het-upness. She thought now that her purchases would see her son right for his stepping onto foreign soil. He would be wearing no hand-me-downs at all, no, he had the best she could buy in his suitcase, but she reasoned why shouldn't he after all, when all was said and done, he was her child, the turnip field's best, the fellow the oak trees stunted that day when lunchtime came early.

When today was gone the way all days go, he, she felt, would remember the final breakfast in her kitchen. She was, where she now stood, a farmer, finished her chores and setting about cooking breakfast. 'I'll show him how much in charge I am,' she scolded herself as, the morning dew still on the grass, she was out and about doing the jobs. Her hands washed, she had a bowl of batter ready and waiting. The moment she heard her son releasing the bathwater she'd begin on her first pancake. Two eggs she had whisked into the flour, and a pinch of salt, milk added then to make the consistency fluid. Melted butter she stirred in at the last minute, and now the sound of that water rushing down the plughole and out into the grating outside the bathroom window saw her spooning a big spoonful of the creamy-white batter onto the sizzling hot pan. Tilting the pan, she let the batter cover the whole base of it. As it cooked she watched the air bubbles rising and spitting. Now she turned it, her first golden pancake. He'd not leave one behind, she felt, as she started about building a pyramid for him.

A whole bowl of butter balls was used that morning to glaze each and every pancake. Every one of them set about leaking the melted butter whenever he rolled them up to take a bite. Butter got on his fingers and dribbled down his chin and she, worried for his new tie, took a clean tea-towel from the drawer and, tying it napkin-like, watched until he set about eating the first pancake last.

All the while he sat there having his breakfast she, nursing a mug of tea, sat opposite him, her mother's eyes doing their final countdown on his features. He was all of six foot tall, his body lithe and loose-limbed. His blue eyes were as blue as her own on washday. His sandy hair, fringed in his boyhood, was now swept back in a cow's-lick wave held so with brilliantine. His face was pale, with the odd scattered freckle; his nose was his father's, straight and regular, and his mouth, framing a perfect set of teeth, was fairly comfortably full so that when he smiled, his smile was wide, white teeth showing in their feeble pleasantness.

'Sheila'd meet you when you get to London,' suggested Minnie as for the umpteenth time she sought to establish whether or not he planned to go to that city. 'Here,' she said, as fetching an envelope she wrote down the telephone number of the hospital where Sheila nursed, and also the address of the nurses' home where she lived. 'You well know she'd look after you,' she coaxed, but he just took the envelope and slipped it into his inside pocket.

The site of the wicket gate became the graveyard of Minnie's farewell to her youngest child. There he was walking the path towards it, she like a whelp, game at his heels. 'You're getting a grand day for travelling,' she was saying, as though the weather had any say in the matter, and her son, glancing up into the sky, saw the sun blinding him with its brilliance.

When he passed through the gateway she said, 'Stop for a minute till I give you a hug, cause you know you're not too big for that.' He, swinging around, stood down his suitcase, and everything in the boreen stopped to watch as he surrendered to his mother's arms. He wanted to say how brave she was now that he was going, but the words were set in stone down beneath his belly button. She too wanted to admire his grit, tell him she was as proud of him as she was of the two others, maybe even more so, but all either of them could now do was hug each other, whin and bush. 'You mind yourself, son,' came her words. 'You get only two pigs next time,' and, 'Don't be killin' yourself lifting off that heavy pot by yourself,' was his love that sunny day. Her eyes, a sea of sorrow, looked up into his three-dimensional face, and his eyes, moist as her wash-tub on laundry Mondays, glanced down into the wounded die-and-die-again face steadfastly set at his chest. Into his pocket he felt her hand slipping, and gripping it he pleaded for her to take it away. She did, when she had dropped in all that she had in this world's money, and, 'Remember,' she shook him as she said it, 'if ever you need anything let me know. If it's on the top shelf of the wardrobe you'll get it, and, son, you need never be afeard to ask.'

'Bye now, and don't worry, I'll be OK, you look out for yourself and eat plenty,' he said as he cleaned away her arms from around his body. Picking up the suitcase, he turned around to start walking into his unknown. His mother, still feeling the tightness of his hug and the feel of his new coat against her cheek, now decided to have her last say. 'Listen Frankie, don't forget to bless yourself every morning, and don't forget to write often, and look't your belt dragging, you're going to lose it,' she shouted after him as there the belt dragged its feet along the ground, all that was holding it in place its brown, leather-covered buckle.

Stead for stead he distanced himself, fingers holding the belt buckle. He drew it forward and then, changing hands on the handle of the suitcase, set about threading the other end of the belt through the eyelet of his coat. By now he had reached the bend on the boreen, the spot where she broke the news last year. He stopped dead and, turning around now, walked backwards, his fingers wounding a wave back towards his mother.

'Go on, you'll miss the bus,' she bravely indicated as she shouted after him and he, the child, nub of butter that he was, swung around and faced forward again. Her hand was still waving though he was vanished from sight, and when she took it back to where it belonged she started to churn her thumbs for the very first time.

She stood sampling salt as she waited to hear the bus pull up above at the road. She, who had shed tears for days, had to lick her top lip, the tears were coming so hot still. When the bus did eventually screech to a halt she heard herself saying, 'Sure, God go with him anyhow, he's only a boy.'

Where she loitered the wicket gate waited, but still she wanted to hear the bus pulling away. She imagined she was there with him as he boarded the two steps, and she walked down the aisle when he went to select a seat. Going, though, belonged to Frankie, staying at home belonged to her; himself up there in the graveyard knew nothing. She was all that now mattered, where the house down the boreen was concerned.

# CHAPTER 66

The debonair clock, the waste peas of dinnertime's plate and the dog, were all that Minnie had left as, grieving for her bloodgroup, she sat dumbfounded in her kitchen. Dying had removed her great lover, the church had broken her bond with her eldest son, nursing had plagiarised her link with her dressed-dumb daughter, and her youngest, sundering his link with his five fields, had left her to drop his sweat in other fields of brown-green grass, or green fields greener than he had ever seen in his role as farmer's son in Drumhollow.

The mocking clock got on with its fugue, the dog got on with what her instincts told her and the lone woman sat wrapped against the November day, her cloak scanty, for she had given her best one to her youngest son, the one who emigrated just recently. As she sat there she reasoned with herself. 'It's the not knowing that worries me,' she thought. 'If only I could see him making out, having a bed to lie in, a bit of food in his mouth and a bob in his pocket, then I'd be at ease and content to wait until the day comes when he'll sling-gad down the boreen, his travels over.'

So saying, she became satisfied with her cross. Her better senses told her that her lot wasn't that bad at all. Hers was a gravelled yard, though here and there a weed grew, but come springtime her flowers would bloom up there in the garden, and the old tea rose with the exquisite scent would fill her kitchen with mercy whenever she chose to cut one of its blooms to set there in the window nook.

Wanting to carry on as would be expected of her, she set about seeing to the foddering. 'Was that the wind rising?' she worried as she glanced out the window. Where she stood she could see the evening closing in around her, the sky leaden with the weight of grey.

Pulling on her wellingtons, she was almost ready to face the hungry night. Where the cattle waited, they lowed in menacing tones. Their hay waited cock-high in the haggard, its east coast cut away, the other half now to be carved bench by bench by her sharpened hayknife.

Trundling along through the first field, her bundle on her back, she searched out a sheltered fold in which she could lay down her load. Dividing it, she allotted the hay in four separate heaps. Accepting that she was for some and against others, the four bullocks dragged from the open plan, and mingling it all together mussed up her stressed piles.

By now snow had started to fall, the flakes coming thick and fast, blown by a strong wind. Her commonsense warned that this was going to be a bad snowstorm and, thinking of her stock, she brought another bundle of hay to the bullocks and yet another to the three idlers closed off in the third field, and there she divvied it up between them, the mare, the pony, and the ass.

The clock was belittling when it struck dead on seven o'clock. Time had dreaded while Minnie worked outside. Now she was in for the night, she had seen to everything living outside, now the turn was hers as, famished, she set about warming herself in front of the fire.

The house heard her thinking and she heard it shunting whenever the great gusts of wind echoed down the chimneys. New to this blizzard tonight she jumped at almost every sudden sound. The sound, when it came, of the black kettle boiling was – along with the chiming clock – the only friendly sound in the lung-hollow hell here tonight.

# CHAPTER 67

'Ah! will you look, God, he wrote at last,' she said as she stooped down and picked up what the postman had dropped in. It was a postcard from England, from Frankie. The picture was of a range of mountains with down deep in a valley a grand little feck-echo house. His small boyish writing told her he had got work after only five days looking. 'I'm working as a farmhand for this farmer here in Chesterfield,' he wrote. 'See, you needn't worry about me,' he suggested, the writing getting smaller still for the space was randomly running out. Then where he should have been winding down his talking he wrote his best bit of all – 'I'll write again when I've good news,' it said. Only a little space was all he now needed but the stumbling block was there before him, for where he should sign his name was gone with his flow of news, and all he could do now was send his love instead.

The day was going to be a red-letter one for Minnie but then her hand turned the postcard skew-ways and she read his postscript in tiny writing up the side. 'I'll not stay too long in this country,' it threatened, and his final folly where he stuck it came in the form of a rubber-johnnie letter, a symbolic gesture, a fearless, decoded letter, 'F'.

Outside the day was spitting frost, the cold, lifeless sky looming overhead. Her news had come to thunder-roll in her kitchen and now she stood transfixed, nibbling at the corner of the card. 'And all the times I ran to rescue him as he came waddling like Frankenstein,' she smiled, 'and see now where he is,' she laughed. 'Still and all though, he kept his word,' she seven-seas-told herself as, new to this game, she felt that she and he might yet be great penpals. The freedom which she had given to Frankie might yet give him his freedom too, but for now the bit about him 'not staying' brought a conundrum to her, the great woman, here in Drumhollow boreen.

Worrying about her sanity, Minnie now told herself that she could session her life to suit her needs. Oftentimes she sat at night theming what she'd do with her stock. She dreaded the fairs till her senses rebelled, and then she'd fiercely describe what she could do. Her bullocks had to be sold, and in order to sell them she had to resign herself to the fact that 'every aul' scour of a tangler' would be there eyeing her up and down to gauge how big an *amadán* she was and how low a bid could he humiliate her with. Her years behind the bacon slicer had never prepared her for doing deals with this mafia. Her cattle could not be faulted, but when she stood in Huntstown on the fair day she stood in a man's world, a world which viewed her as a little woman with a little womb but not much brains. She knew all that, and still she dared to confound them. There she'd ring her squad of red whiteheads. Her pride would be equal to that of the biggest farmer. Her mind would have a shrewd idea of her cattle's worth, and piebald men were not going to beat her down. At first she recoiled against all the hand-slapping, spitting and leave-it-there hand-clasping, but after a few years she didn't care how or what spittin' the buyers did, there she was in the thick of the cowshite, spitting and leave-it-thereing with the cute hoors of farmers and dealers. She grew to love it, and when it came to her having to buy back some weanlings she was now as big a tangler as the best of them.

Minnie O'Brien's nonchalance, though, had a hell of a birthing. She could in fact remember every detail of its inception. It was preceded by a testing time of indecision, a time when she didn't know whether she was coming or going, going or staying put. But a hungry Thursday came, as hungry Thursdays do, and there was nothing for it, she found, but to put her best foot forward and take the first step.

That hungry Thursday was a day to be reckoned with, for that was the day on which she set out on her maiden voyage to the graveyard of chance. Togged out in her old gaberdine raincoat and black wellington boots, and with a black beret pulled well down over her ears, to make her appear a man, she rounded up her four beautiful bullocks, and with ashplant in hand she eased them towards the already opened road gate.

Greyhounds, they became, the moment the road opened up before them, running as though they smelt victory around the next bend. Her steps no match for those of the wild bullocks, she could only hope that they'd get sense yet.

Eventually she caught up with the mob, but now they were dachshunds in her sight for not only had they run themselves ragged, but they had splashed their dung all over their behinds.

Mercy was her bill o'fare as she sized up the drim and drew lot of cattle. 'What'll they look like,' she thought, 'by the time they trot the miles yet ahead?' But no farmer would judge them by her standards, she reasoned, the wisdom still hers though her boots had now got a fume in them which could not, even at this stage, match the opinions boring through her head.

Placidly, the cattle moved along before her. Running sometimes, walking others, they were now going along the road beside Gavigans' land. The morning was brightening somewhat when a voice suddenly spoke from a gap in Gavigans' hedge. 'How much for the steers, young man?' the voice asked as it and its Sten gun sat there upon a railway sleeper which the farmer had placed right across the space in his hedge. She got the fright of her fresh life with the suddenness of his question, and despite her beret a shriek escaped from her young man's mouth. 'Sorry, mam, if I frightened you,' the stranger said, and how well he knew that he had made a hole in this charade of hers. She, too, knew that she had failed at this her first hurdle as, game, set, and match, had just now handed him the fact that she was but a woman with a shout.

Hurriedly now, his plant held stoutly, the stranger got into step beside her. 'How much for the steers, I asked you,' he said, 'but now that I'm near them they're only piners, I'm afraid.' Under the impression that they indeed lost some of their pizzazz she, without any backing, failed to defend her cattle, failed to stick up for them, failed to say that they 'were outta the best cows in the country.' But it didn't matter in the least for, unbeknownst to her, he had his own plan of campaign. 'Are you from hereabouts?' he asked her and she, like a patsy, told him who she was. 'Ah, he was a grand decent man was your husband,' the man now said, sadness creeping into his voice. 'And for his sake, sure I'd like to help you out, not have you bringing them lock of cattle all the way to the fair and maybe get ne'er a bid at all. Just for his sake mam, I'll take them off your hands – that is, of course, if the asking price is right.'

'Thin aul' cattle,' she heard him saying. 'Light aul' cattle, look't them hind quarters,' he scoffed. 'Peter'd like me to treat you decent.' he told her, 'Sure a woman like you would be lost in the fair,' he said.

Her faith dented, Minnie began to stumble. 'Forty pounds I'm asking, and not a penny less,' was her answer to his now badgering questions.

'Forty pounds for them piners.' He now began laughing himself near to death. They had by this time reached Pooka's Corner, his hobnailed boots striding along beside her rubber-soled steps. Every so often he swiped at the tall margin grasses with his ash plant. His name was Paul Smallpot, he said.

Smallpot bid Minnie O'Brien thirty-one pounds apiece for her four cattle. 'It's just for his sake I'm bidding you,' he said. 'Now when I was a boy . . . one hundred and twenty-four quid I'm givin' you, and you know you won't do better,' he said.

Minnie hugged her stick to her body. Defiantly she mustered, 'They're worth forty if they live as far as the fair.'

Smallpot howled again in mock laughter. 'Look't here,' he said, and grabbing hold of her hand he spat upon his own and upped his bid to thirty-one pounds ten shillings. 'You'll o'course gimme a luck penny outta that,' he coaxed as he shook her hand, and peeling off one hundred and twenty-six pounds from a big roll of banknotes, he shoved them into her shaky hands.

Minnie O'Brien's joy in selling was in humpty-dumpty excitement. Her hand held out a quivering quid. He spat on the green note, too, and then shoved it and the whole roll back into his inside breast pocket. She, fixing him now with a lifeless look, no longer wished to talk. He had plenty more to say, but the cattle had moved on. He shook her hand again as he told her, 'We'll do business the future.'

Smallpot's shiny brown boots glinted in the early morning sunshine as he hurried away to join his cattle, and Minnie, turning for home, began to plan on what she'd lush her money. Reaching her gate, still open, her urge was, as it always was, to stand on the bottom bar and give a jaunt to herself as the gate swung to. She hummed now as she homed the bolt, and set off down the boreen to her home in one-by-one steps. The dog heard her approaching and, fed up with being locked in during all of the excitement, sent the hens flying as a way of celebrating its release from the shed. Stone hard was the money now in her pocket, as the deb and her dog made their way in the back door to the kitchen and the clock.

Nothing in the house for the dinner sent the woman with the money to the village shop. Her list – table salt, rashers, today's sausages and black pudding – solved her shopping needs. 'A boiled spud for myself and two for the dog'll leave almost an entire potful for the pigs and poultry,' she thought. She knew that with an apple for dessert her meal today would be complete.

She was thinking on those very lines when she met local farmer, Harold Heather himself, driving home a batch of cattle. Her gaze fell upon his purchases. Suddenly her feet stopped still for there, head up and facing her, was her own brackledy-head bullock with the piece missing from his left ear, the ear which he caught in the barbed wire when, as a yearling, he broke into the haggard.

'You've got money's worth there, Harold,' she said as she stood to make conversation with the farmer.

'Aye, they were pricey today,' he answered.

'How about that fella there with the hole in his lug?' enquired Minnie.

Harold had to think a while. Then the mind recalled. 'Him there, he was one of four I bought off that fellow Smallpot. I made him give me two quid back out of a hundred and sixty.'

Moaning inwardly, but pleasant to Harold's face, the highway-robbed widow wished the buyer well with his drove of beauties.

Looking back now, her feet moving forward, her mind on Pooka's Corner, Minnie felt cheated up to her place. 'Just cause I'm a woman, you bastard,' she said as she hunkered behind her female status. 'No doubt you're sinking big tumblers to celebrate the eejit you made of me.' Her heart felt hollowed out at the news that Smallpot had deceived her, her that was the widow of that man whose passing he had lamented the morning. Minding now how he had undermined her, she frothed at the mouth with pure temper. 'He done me for thirty-four pounds,' she calculated. Second time round he wouldn't, she promised. 'Fool me once, shame on you, you bum, but fool me twice, fool me' — twenty thousand times she said those words, the better to heal her hurt, the better too to remember as she tied those twenty thousand warnings to her fife.

As though the pony knew that her owner now had some money in the hollow of her fist, she chose that very night to frame her death there in the fields of Babylon. Faffing, she sought a space whereon she might surrender up her soul. She that had sundered herself for folks named O'Brien was now wasting strangling dreams, trying to come as near to her owner as possible.

The night was black as make-believe when her head began nudging at the gate. Nudge after nudge she nudged, until the gate eased open. Then, as though drunk, she fondled her last hunger as down the farm she meandered, looking for a funeral.

Jaded, so jaded was she that she sensed she'd soon have to give in. The new ESB pole stood beckoning to her. 'I'll be your tombstone if you make it this far,' it hinted, and she, hearing her own whinnying now gurgling in her neck, stopped when she reached the tall lollipop stick.

Dread made her pause there in the first field. Down she lessened herself on the soft dewy grass. Then, her head heavy, she stretched it from her and voicing a plaintive breath cushioned it, cushioned the head that would never learn new tricks ever again.

Where the salt-and-pepper pony had lain the grass now stood up again. Lovely green grass, its memory remembering nothing. Yes, mouths would graze each blade there growing, fresh green grass, it tasting juicy on the tongue.

The new arrival knew nothing of the whin and bush cycle here in Drumhollow boreen. The new arrival knew nothing of death. The new arrival was red with a white star in the middle of her forehead, but when she trotted the fields or the boreen her hooves were linseed where heretofore hooves had Saturdayed and died.

## CHAPTER 68

Mrs O'Brien, the widow woman driving the new flash pony, was seen as a snug farmer with a grand little place. Many's the eye was cast on her and it. She, though, saw to it that the locals knew that she regarded herself as being but a caretaker to the holding until, his travels finished, her Frankie would return to run the place himself.

Come Saturdays, her trap brought her and her farm's produce to Huntstown. Opposite her on the seat rested her basket of butter pounds and her box of eggs. Sometimes cockerels, some white, some blood-red and some chequered, would lie, pry in the eye, prone on the floor, legs tied together, down at her feet. 'Isn't it a caution how a body can manage to make out,' she'd often tell herself as, the pony trotting smartly towards the town, she'd sit there roly-poly moving on Peter's old raincoat, spread under her on the seat. Her butter had the reputation of being tasty and pure, so her customers would meander her way the moment she'd pull up in the market square. The eggs she'd sell in dozens and half dozens until there'd be nothing left in the box but the hay in which she had cushioned them. The chickens, though, would have many a breast-pinching before bargains could be struck for them, and the sale made she'd stand there looking after them, her hand-reared chickens as, their heads hanging in humiliation, they'd head off to cook their goose in some other woman's Sunday pot.

But where Saturdays of the past saw commerce where-withalling, this one heralded new beforing and aftering for, satisfied with this Saturday's earnings from her minesweeper's butter, her hens' torpedoes and Gulliver's chickens, Minnie moved away from the marketplace and set about buying the essentials for her solitary plainsman's place. Determinedly, she carried them back and placed them on the floor. But today her load was different, for not only had she bought her usual line in groceries and even a tin of red paint to paint the road gate, but there on the very top of everything else, and in a cushy safe spot, she set two glass bulbs which she had bought, needed as spares for her brand new inferno, back at home in her house in Drumhollow.

Yes, yin had met yang and echo followed echo the moment the electric light wired itself to the house she inherited from her husband. Now, as though she were Astra, she had but to put her finger on her new switch and gone was the golden age of ignorance, and here instead was her stubborn light of learning, the glow brilliant, the promise unheard-of though she attired herself as a widow of funerals and a Messiah sans equal. Now she wouldn't ever again carry paraffin oil in a can; never, either would she clean her tall glass lamp-chimney, nor gauge whether her wick was cut level. No, she need only touch her finger against the thumb sticking to the wall and the moment she gave it the thumbs down on would come electric light the likes of which she had never before imagined for this house down the boreen built by a bread-binned man, his belly full of stones.

With the coming of the light came the power of the word. Rural electrification assumed a dreadful force for good where Minnie was concerned. Her rescuing had been druidic. For years and years now the gulag had been illuminated from the outside in, but drumbeating her route ahead she now brought about her own education.

The day when the new electric-powered radio came quietly down the boreen was the day when Minnie became a student of hungry hunger. Voices never before heard could now ask her did she see what they could see. Seeing but not believing it possible, she fed her brain upon every word which proceeded from the mouth of God. Declaring her faith she drank it in, but only when her mind could conjure up images with which to match the words could she see how unique was her own brain, her burr in sound, her burr in farsightedness.

Nuts fell from her hazel trees down in the cul de sac between the fourth and fifth fields, and seeing as she couldn't crack them with her slow teeth she chose instead to gather words as they dropped from her ever-present radio up on the shelf latched to the wall near the back window in her kitchen. A Cossor make, it was, and every time she switched it on she whispered its name. Frugal were her thoughts of former glory now her stung head was being filled instead at every twist and turn of the radio's knobs. She loved the drunken sounds from foreign stations as she tuned the night-time away, but when she stumbled upon the World Service at midnight her severe hunger ran on and on every inch of the way, until near dawn she fell asleep to dream upon the glum Gwyn, the frugal Defoe or the Dickens of dilemma.

# CHAPTER 69

Dreadful was the knowledge gained from those years of nights when she lay quietly in the bed, where he should still be, listening all or most of the dark hours to the second-hand Philips, the radio which she bought especially for her bedroom. A luxury it seemed, but to her it was the comforter par excellence. There each night it thieved quietness from her bedroom as through its speaker sound waves crept through the air and into her soul. Peace, cunt that it now was, hunted for satisfaction, now her facts totted up her good times and silence drowned her bad times. Hers was the house of sounds, for all day long the wireless chattered or made music, but night-time was the daddy of all times, for it was then that surrealism fronted the back windows in stressed glory, while the front ones grew dreadful nightmares in nesting now human and thunderous.

From stunts like that came her relief and mornings found her trying to remember and distinguish which was which. Did she dream or was it her imagination, did she hear thin lies on the nightime radio waves or rant the thoughts herself? 'Never a dull moment,' she oftentimes said, the day ahead beckoning her downstairs to listen to the news on Radio Eireann.

The kitchen was her favourite place of all. There in her own room in the house her jolly life went on as usual. Nowadays when the kettle boiled on the stove the heat underneath it came from oil, but when her hands edged the kettle away from the hot plate the teapot never bothered to look to its laurels for now the teabag had stolen a march on it as there in the mug it lay, waiting its bulldog of boiling water to rule on the strength of its brew for Minnie's eye-opener.

This morning's news was over by the time she moved with the

mug to the table and, picking up her spoon, tried to drown the floating teabag. Down she'd press it and up it'd pop. 'Musha, gimme back the old loose tea,' she swore as with her drowned teabag fished out on her spoon she made her way towards the pedal-bin. In she dropped it, the little miserable thing, and turning set about adding some sugar and milk to her mug. She was there standing stirring when out of nowhere came a thought. Maybe it was the quality of the amber-coloured tea which, when the milk was added, turned a lovely creamy colour that set her thinking, but be that as it may, back went her mind to the days of the Emergency when everything worth eating was rationed. She could only buy a half ounce of tea per person per week then, but so hooked was she on her favourite beverage that she, in her innocence, tried to manufacture something which might pass for tea.

Word of mouth had it that carrots could be turned into a passable tea so she set out to create it. The griddle had to be very hot. The carrots had to be grated very finely. Nothing was to distract her while she stood there roasting the golden gratings for she had to see to it that each little bit baked brown.

Where the whole thing collapsed, though, was on the day when she dreamt up her tasting. 'Look at the colour,' she said as the striking amber juice poured from the teapot. Milk and some but not much sugar was added, then all that was needed was to taste it herself.

She took a mouthful, her smile still lurking at her lips. Round her mouth it ran, her tongue in revolt. Out she had to spit it, the jalap par excellence, disgust hovering where lately satisfaction strayed.

'Musha shortages were all we had to suffer back then,' she reasoned. 'Sleep for us was safe and undisturbed. Not like over there in England and Europe, there they quaked with Hitler on the march.

'"The devil incarnate" that's what Peter said he was, and sure who could contradict him don't I know, him with his "Heil Hitler" and his hand out, stupid, stupid arrogance was all he knew. Ah the poor Jews, he eyed them first, then anyone with a certain square jaw, next was the Romany gypsies, and last of all the cripples, big and small. Musha, wouldn't you wonder what he had for supper, how he could sleep the long night through, when all he thought of other mother's babbies, the stupid, stupid soap he made of them.'

The sound of water boiling onto the hot stove jolted her from Dachau back to her cosy kitchen. 'Ah will you look, m'egg'll be hard as a bullet,' she complained. Fetching it from the pot she set it down upon her plate and now, history evidently forgotten, she began to eat her dreadful egg, her brown bread and the liquid cold tea. So she ate while at the same time listening to her busy, venial radio. Her ear picked up the Boomtown Rats with Bob Geldof singing 'I Don't Like Mondays'. 'Ah, he only has Mondays to worry about,' she thought as, chew how she would, the rough meal from the bread undermined her dentures. 'Sorra use ye are either,' she said as, moving over to the sink, she showered her teeth under the tap. It was the grand sound of the gate opening that sent the electric tremor through her heart, and ramming the dentures back in place she stood listening for the flap from the letterbox. Her mind hurriedly sent her to pick up the letter but her heart warned, "tis only maybe the ESB bill.' Nudging forward, she tamed her steps towards the porch and there on the tiles it lay, not the real writing, tongue-held, childishly-small style, but a blue envelope stylishly addressed, the hand a finished hand. The letter from Sheila was secondhand welcome, respectable though her daughter was, for this mother of the churning, sowed seed from a granary gradually growing sparse in grain. Clutching the letter on the tiles, she held it tightly clasped in the stack between the line of life and plain of Mars. She searched for her reading glasses, and flopping into her chair she flittered open the envelope. 'Three pages,' she said as she sized up the letter. Now her gaze destroyed the secrecy of the ciphered code. 'Johnathan is settled down at Harvard,' her heart assayed what her eyes read. 'Greg's picking grapes somewhere in France,' so her daughter believed. 'Luke is busy in Texas,' reassured Sheila, but the sum total of her fads told her mother that the world was empty but for the two of them. 'What's so different,' said the old woman as the writing wavered before her eyes. Wounded though the situation, the rich man's Moll but told it as it was, no complaint. She even made her language frame how successful the Green family really were and how carefree the siblings were, though gone now from the new house in the city of humours. Where she sat now reading and regurgitating what she read Minnie hung in sorrow between here and there, her house here in the boreen and Sheila's up there in Dublin's Blackrock. As her grip slackened on the pages her mind pinpricked the names of her grandchildren, almost strangers to her.

Nose to the wind the dog stood outside the door, sniffing the air as though he could sense what the line stringing him to her inside was saying. He knew that she was getting forgetful now, his belly hinted often. He listened for her footfall but her feet were still, for she was seeing again the sadness in the letter from her daughter. It as usual had finished with the invitation to sell out the old homestead and move to live with her in Blackrock. 'Luke's all for it,' gushed Sheila.

'Me here and she up there,' said Minnie as she finished the letter for the second time. 'Her heart's in the right place, she wants to take care of me for the bit of time I've left, but I'll not budge outta here till the hearse comes. I'm all that's left when Frankie comes back. Imagine the sight of him coming dragging the suitcase, and no one to light the door with an "about time". Told her again and again I can't come, but God help her, that's why she suggested coming back home and buying the house in Blackrock. Her and me in that big posh house, it needs me like I need it. Nobody needs an aul' country woman plankin' themselves on top of them. I just want to hang on here just in case he'd come. You can't teach an old dog new tricks, and she should know that better than me. When I think of the picture of her in his wallet the evening he died, the beard of barley all stuck to it, she was the apple of his eye and he was the stone in her heart when she saw him low down in the clay. It's sad, the shock when you see the daughter so hurt for him dying, and you're so cut up yourself that you can't say the words. Aye indeed, he'd have tutored her about the rich man and the poor man's girl, the price to be paid, yes he'd tell her. Me standing there in the registry office that day, might as well've been in Timbuktu, him cool and so well groomed, so cocksure of himself, and her all fragile and in love. Me without him, her without him, the brother out in darkest Africa as they say, wouldn't it have served him better to be there to marry his sister properly but as they say on the radio, fuck all he could do, him in the sun, and her in that grey building, all polished and cold. Aye, she had the two sons and as soon as they were on their pins he skedaddled. Living out of a bag, like they say on the radio, a woman here, a woman there, she seemed broken each time she came here, the spirit sad, the kids so spoiled but grand little fellas. Her heart's in the right place, always was, the father was in her nature, her money was yours. Now where is she, without them or him. A son in Harvard, what good is that to her? Your man back-packin', she says, picking grapes. I'd have my doubts about him, he smoking like a trooper the last time he was here. 'Gran, I roll my own,' he says, the sweet smell of them, for all the world like wild woodbine, him back-packing and he so lazy he wouldn't move a coal off his foot. The nature's in them though they seemed sorta genuine, but she'll know someday, looking out the window of a posh nursing home to see if they will come. London lads born and reared, they'll not want to stop long in Dublin. Can you imagine them wanting to stay here in the boreen? Keep the blood in the place if he doesn't come back. Would she herself come? Ah! not on your nelly. She'd be like me, waiting. God knows you wouldn' wish it on her, only strong nerves could stick it here. Frankie could do it, sorta thick like myself. He could remedy this place, but how-an'-ever sure I'll hang on and see.'

Minnie sat on in her chair, the pages of Sheila's letter resting on her lap. She was remembering the prayer she once said when she begged her husband up there in Paradise to touch up God and ask if He would grant Sheila the insight to see that she was making a big error in having become engaged to the financier Luke Green. 'Pray, will you, that she'll see sense before he puts the halter around her neck.' That prayer, she now knew, had been but wishful thinking on her part: the reality was that Sheila was besotted with the man. He showered gifts upon her, he never wanted her out of his sight, his nature seemed to need her by his side, and she never thought about any other man.


## CHAPTER 70


She flew up into the sky that day, the mother did, all on her ownio, winging her way to her daughter's wedding in London. Playing the role of both daddy and mammy, she watched as her aeroplane's body left its furtive shadow on the earth below. Terrified out of her wits, she thought the plane was going to turn end over end, the curve of incline was so keen. Her face was burning in an apple-red glow as there from her crow's-nest window she fretted her gaze straight ahead or straight towards the ground. The streets of Dublin had, just a short while ago, rescued the heart of long ago inside her maverick mind when, getting off the country bus, she set about finding her transport to the airport. Now she missed Peter, her swatted man. Swatting him, the Man Above had left it all to her to forage for his less than male daughter. If only He hadn't done that swatting in the Hamiltons' lane, her father's pinion-echo would have freed his daughter never to Sloane Range, but rather to seek out a cute hoor of a local farmer and find herself a nest already furnished.

But needs must when the Devil drives, so here she sat, turmeric to her daughter's needs as her wedding day dawned. Travelling for all she was worth, she flew her jibbed way towards England. Inside the plane she had the other passengers for company but outside, and stretching away towards where the horizon mearinged with Mafia and meringues, lay the whitest world she had ever seen, and countrywoman that she was she closed her eyes for the briefest minute as she humbled herself in this work of tomboy's greenery. White white, looked back at her when she opened her eyes again. 'Janey Mac, as they say on the wireless, but you'd sink up to your oxters out there,' she told herself, the savage moving all the while nearer to London's Heathrow Airport.

As she worked her way along, where millions had waddled before, her mind was on her daughter and on the man who tomorrow would be a husband. He was fun when things were going his way but what, she worried, will he be like if yesteryear's fears should ever return to taunt him? She knew that his had been a victimised childhood, for her Sheila had said that Luke's parents split up when he was just five years old. His mother went on her honeymoon the second time round and left him to the mercy of her maid. The mother's fine heart had bought him a new rig-out for her wedding, and the rig-out had to be his mother-hen for a whole month. The maid tried to force him to wear various childish clothes, but each day he cried a child's tantrum by trial until, for peace's sake, he was dressed yet again in his wedding-day rig-out. Very fussy now, he surrounded himself with success, but he desperately needed her Sheila and she, the nurse, understood his void.

The attitude which, just a moment ago, had sympathised with a frightened boy's state soon evaporated when suddenly Minnie glimpsed her image in a long window. 'Lord bless us, but you stick out like a sore thumb,' she chided herself. Her steps, though, were bringing her ever nearer to her daughter, to the sterling-silver myselfing girl who was secretly sweating as she waited, watched, and worried for her mother.

The aeroplane which, propeller-slewing, had carried her where she didn't want to go was cooling down by the time Minnie and Sheila flung their female felinity around each other. 'You were great to come,' said the daughter to the mother as she hugged the daylights out of her. 'You came, and me only going to be married in a registry office,' streamed the girl, while where they stood, stood too the man reckoned as husband material by this girl from Moonshee Valley.

Standing where she had set it down was Minnie's new suitcase, with inside it her style from Huntstown. A heather-purple suit hinted of Holly Bog, a black hat usurped fresh bogstuff's branding, a pair of black suede shoes waited a football in London, but daddy of them all was the blouse, which she fell for that day in Huntstown. Hanging on a hanger it was, a shiny white satin blouse pleated down the front, in such a way as to conceal the fact that only a row of little mangy buttons held it fastened for decorum's sake.

That, then, was the sum total of Minnie's street style for the wedding tomorrow. She had no way of knowing what one wore in linchpin city for, green in gaucheness, she only ever before lived luxury in the Clarence Hotel. Her wasteful bridegroom had splashed out that night on white wine, but back in Drumhollow he only ever after drew springwater from the well. But as for this new fellow, this bridegroom-to-be, the fact was that in her handbag lay the hymen hoop-la, there readying itself to fund the marriage feast the next day.

Money, though, was certainly not needed from the mother-hen's handbag. Her chequebook echoed only against her key to the back door and her packet of Anadins. Luke had everything serviced for his class of wedding to his chosen girl. Decent to the point of being over-gracious, he saw the bills never came Minnie's way.

Mesmerised by the beauty of Sheila's wedding rig-out, the

mother trestled her purple number against it. Best of all, though, was Sheila's bouquet for the morning. It hessian-tied her to some white heather, the lingerie of nymphs, grabbing the mind's eye the moment the favoured flower found fat focus. It had been deposited inside the big fridge the better to remind its hidden fact that bog air can be both chilly and evocative of a heavy heart.

'Myself and himself had such plans for her.' Minnie's mind was freewheeling. A vacant stare in her eyes, she sat waiting for her daughter to enter this great grey edifice. The stairs were fanciful as her girl climbed up the wide varnished steps. Luke stood waiting on the landing, his huge frame cast as though he were a municipal statue. Bright streams of sunlight stole inwards through the stained-glass landing window. Its blue-red-green jumped across the bride's back as her husband-to-be led her into the vast office within. No organ music hailed her threshold crossing, neither did a father's arm give her something to be humble about. Ten guests marched forward to witness the marriage vows being themed between Luke and Sheila, the fortunate freedom fivers.

Minnie, the bride's mother, Hail-Mary-ed for the pair standing shoulder to shoulder. 'Mother of God,' she whispered, 'ask Jesus to give Sheila the strength to be herself despite Luke's big money.' Changing tack, she then touched up God Himself. 'Dear God,' she wheedled, 'only let him be as kind as my man was, that's all I ask and all she'll need.' She didn't even know this man called Luke, but all she saw of him filled her with nervousness, for he was very sure of himself and in his company her daughter didn't seem to know how to say no.

Looking on now, Minnie's fears were still looking out through her maternal instinct. Fresh hope she tried to engender, but with a turn of his head or the sound of his voice she fell back again to her starting post. Sheila was evidently happy beyond eaten bread, but to her mother's eyes her day seemed foreign in Luke's world. 'Maybe it's only me,' fretted Minnie, 'maybe it's me that feels out of it,' and so saying she determined to be one hundred per cent behind this couple, this sir and his mistress, this rationed man and his rationed money. Gethsemane was far distant just now as her daughter voiced 'I do' with all the love of her woman's head. The couple kissed in mock parade of affection and love; among their chosen few they fitted in admirably. Glad greetings were surrounded by cold-coloured walls so that, though supremely happy, the bride and the groom had to almost sing their bridal march by chorusing their hand-me-downs with notes of originality of threadneedled beat.

The river ran by the end of Luke Green's tennis court. The french window opened onto manicured lawns. Honesty bloomed in herbaceous borders, its rich purple easily distinguished. The menfolk drank in yardsticked freedom, the groom among them, while the bride freshened her lipstick, for her full lips had had themselves licked so often that her pink-put-upon was nesting in the corners only. Minnie counted the hairs on the bride's head as she combed her hair alongside her daughter. They chatted now, but as though they were strangers, for a singular separateness was fullblown between them and neither could help the unease that bothered there. The mother would have just loved to gather her bridal daughter into her arms and listen to her heart speaking but, as though she suspected, the bride sweetened the messaged-second by saying, 'Are you right, Mam? We'd better get back and join the others.' Minnie felt out of sorts, out of place, and out of kilter, but as they returned along the plush-piled corridor she managed to take her daughter's hand in her weathered grasp and, squeezing it to breaking point, asked, 'Will you be all right?' And turning her frank gaze towards this little countrywoman, the London gunsmith smiled reassuringly and said, 'Don't you ever worry, I'll be OK,' and giving her mother an air-kiss whispered, 'Amn't I my dad's girl, did you think I had sold out on him? Never, Mam, never!' And though her mother attempted now to describe her fears, they both laughed for the first time in London.

Fecund was the laughter around the table as guests voiced good-humoured conversation. Nobody needed cosseting except the bride's mother, and now that she had learned to laugh London-fashion she was able to be serviced in her cine-cameraed performance. Honest to a fault, her lovely daughter kept her near her. Great voices vindicated their bespoke beliefs all around the dining-room table. Minnie had never seen or tasted anything as rare as caviare, but now the blackberry clumps of bejewelled roe reminded her, here in London, of her bramble briars at home in Drumhollow. Talking to the guest seated next to her, the stockbroker from her son-in-law's house, she hummed and hawed towards his non-negotiable hearsay. Her tastebuds registering each new dish, she was really enjoying the haute cuisine from Luke's chef for the day. Button mushrooms are button mushrooms, her tongue told her, and when she sampled the dark green spinach it just reminded her of her own version of boiled spring nettles. Her family always got their share of iron, Drumhollow-style, and when she drew her findings to the eyes of Sheila they both laughed again, a knowing laugh, a laugh which came up from their very roots.

Looking on and appreciating the popular Sumerian-like Irish girl, her new husband fiddled with his lute and swore that she would be his greatest virgin, she of the night-round, she of the Sunday-round, she who silenced hell upon earth for them that linger on the edge of the abyss of death, fearful of rescue should they venture on. Noticing now his Sheila's concern for her mother, he resolved to fête his mother-in-law in his planned speech.

'Heartiest congratulations, again,' said her mother to the girl getting ready to throw her nymphs' blossoms. 'God bless you both,' she whispered into Sheila's ear.

'He already has,' her happy girl replied as, dampening down their hearts' fanfare, they clung together for a brief while.

Luke's turn was next, and foreign though her feelings she found herself saying: 'Sheila's lucky to have found you, Luke.' He, touched by Minnie's words, dressed her compliment with one of his own when he hand-picked his best humility by saying, 'I hope that I can measure up to that father of whom she talks and talks.'

## CHAPTER 71

The clock striking twelve foisted reality into Minnie O'Brien's kitchen. 'Will you look at the time,' she said, as stuffing Sheila's letter into her bib pocket she headed towards the sink. With breadsoda crawling all over her teeth she now dredged them with even more, for her new toothbrush held a special group of high bristles with which she could now excavate the valleys behind the dentures' teeth. As she scoured them they became slippery, and she had to hold on really tight to stop them sliding from her fingers. 'Musha, they can say what they like about their new-fangled tablets,' she said, 'but I'd rather my old tried and trusted soda.'

Her conversation in front of the mirror stopped while she put back her dentures, and that done, she with her two sets of teeth meeting head-on glanced again at the dangerous woman. She smiled as she looked at herself, but the crack in the glass gave her a dirty gap in her teeth. 'Minnie, you saw the two days,' she nodded knowingly, and then she laughed in a deranged, fall-away style. Her gumption, the very same which granted her the will to live on here on her own, craved now for release from its hidebound home. Her chattering eased away. Quietness ganged up on her. Unsureness struck. Bells chimed in her ears. Her eyes blurred. Thud, her body humaned against the floor, its fingers nine-nine-nine dialling. Silence took hold of her. Her hairbun splayed, its hairpins soldiering stoically. Gulliver's Mafia played on her nose. Dracula longingly drank of her blood. The occult began stringing her along. The knocker on the front door fell just once, but the honesty of it caterwauled through the house. One of her hens, a chequered Barred Rock, crowed a cockcrow, standing on the window sill. Slowly the window itself began to swim towards her. Her voice moaned 'Musha, musha, what happened?' Her hands now began glawming at her chair's legs. She began dragging her body upwards towards the velvet seat. 'Ne'er a soul about, I suppose,' she said. No, there was nobody about to have and to hold her. No, there was nothing now but the spancel there on her finger, winding in circles behind its immaculate hill. There she moaned, Peter's she-god, pain-wracked. 'God, You nearly took me that time,' she said. 'By dad You did, You nearly did. But I'm still here, have to be here, in case *magunnia* comes in the gate . . .'

Pension day arrived to find Minnie sorely tried. Her head ached from yesterday's hard knock, but following her practice she culled her mind of self-pity and began instead to prepare herself for her public.

Face washed, hair swept back and pinned in a bun at the nape of her neck, she went upstairs to fetch her overcoat, which hung on the right-hand side of the wardrobe in her bedroom. Lifting it out, she struggled into it and then the usual eulogy took place. The brooch was pinned to her coat's lapel, and struggling towards it she haughed upon it before polishing off her breath with her sleeve. Satisfied that the gemstone now glittered, her hand fidgeted around inside the wardrobe looking for her knitted hat. It was dark there inside in the cavernous interior, and try as she might she couldn't feel the hat. The scarecrow was there all right, the suit belonging to him, its pinstripes hanging there in lines of living. She knew it belonged to former days, the days when himself and herself were great together, but now when her hand touched it her senses were warmed by its serge reckoning. Peter played an integral part in keeping her company still. In fact on her bad days, the times when she heard the first faraway rumble of thunder, her notions sent her upstairs to him, to his suit, to hide there in the blackness so that the lightning, the thing which he said 'took the line of least resistance', wouldn't bother to come into the human duds-house to melt somebody who hid there inside her husband's device. Now, with that feeling still in her fingers, she trudged back down to the kitchen, and there on the hook on the door hung the thing which she was searching for.

When she had collected her pension money she folded it inside her small purse. Everything she needed could now be funded from it. Starting off in the supermarket, her buggy bumbling along behind her heels, she hungrily sought out the items of food which now appealed to her. Just the basics of life were the foodstuffs she began to drop down inside the buggy's bag, just the wherewithal for her endless mugs of tea. Bread, the plain loaf, was still her favourite baker's bread; it and marmalade together now teased her each morning from her bed. Bacon, secret from the past, humiliated her still, despite her new age dreams. Her hand stretched for it despite her not wanting the bother of the cooking. Handling tins of peas and beans she sorted out the difference: 'Peas are but poor man's greens,' she scolded, 'and beans, well beans but blow your mind, as they say on RTE.' Today she bought too a full circle of white pudding, the thoughts of how it flew at her from the frying pan not remembered now. Back rashers were now adding insult to injury when she placed them down inside beside the white pudding, but this was no time to be worrying about her fat intake, not after her mock funeral of yesterday.

Dragging her full buggy she moved towards the queue for the checkout. Neighbours made small talk with her as, hemming and hawing, they feared they might blurt out what they really thought. 'No word from Francis, I suppose,' made Minnie hand over her very soul, and the more her heart revealed its secrets the more did those doubting Thomases rely on fictional reneging. 'Of course he'll come, any day now,' they strumpeted. 'He'll just walk in, money made, the farm there waiting for him, you're a great little woman, keeping the flag flying, sure you have your son the bishop and what about your beautiful daughter Sheila, 'tis a wonder you don't go and live with her, but sure you can't really, he'll be here on the bus someday soon, you're a great little woman.' So the faces tholed the fuming figure. But saying her goodbyes and her atanarating, she waited until she got inside her own gate and then her voice felt free to make her reply. 'Shites, the lot of them. Shleeveens, every last one of them.' And so, as the hedges could hear her, she proceeded down the boreen, giving a running commentary on every denial the shites had delivered.

## CHAPTER 72

The old flower garden waited each morning for Minnie to draw back the curtains on her kitchen window. Like herself, it kept the fair side out by endeavouring each season to produce some semblance of colour, some evidence that its old resolve remained intact. It was a terraced garden, four steps leading up from the yard, four more leading up to the femoral site where her husband had placed the garden seat under the O'Briens' long-established lilac tree. For her stamina she could, this morning, thank her Maker, but the love which she had experienced in life came from one man's singular devotion, he having more than a million times told her that he and she were 'God's own virgins.'

'You mean to tell me that you never had anyone before you met me?' she had one evening asked him as she cosied up to him on the garden seat and he, like that other Peter, swore on his humbug that she and she alone had ever seen his 'leading article.'

Quaint the scene now, the fun days forever gone, the goffered hat her daughter gave her planked on her old head, as the winged woman made her locked journey up into her frigid garden. The old granite steps were stained by oxide, their lifetime's service gored by the thousands and thousands of hardy footsteps which ran up and down their wallplates. Her steps, stinging where formerly they trotted, stung their pathway towards the tree with the seat beneath. She eased herself down, her mind getting ready to fan itself into remembering. To the sound of the downpipe rattling in a breeze short-cutting round the gable-end of her home, Minnie sat, noticing the tufts of moss growing from Peter's Killaloe slates. Around the two chimneys where he had forged his lead flashing grew *tráithníns* of grass, echoing their frolicking dancesteps, the better to remind her of how she and he used waltz and foxtrot to the music of their gramophone. Paint chipped and flown left rotten fissures in the window frames, their putty long since slid away with stringy autumn. She smiled now as she remembered the days when he soft-fingered the putty for the back windows to settle in. 'Nothing is too good for my lass,' he retorted whenever she handed it to him for a job well done, and seeing as he had such gifted hands her tributes constantly flowed towards him; never certain of his everything she, credentials on show, dreadlocked him in frizzy curls of blonde faith.

The noon sun was gaining height by the time she heard the van driving down towards her house. The postman got from it and, opening the wicket gate, advanced on the porch door. He slid three letters through and listened as they plopped down on the tiles. The sound should have brought the old lady shuffling towards the post but though he listened ne'er a sound could he hear. He noticed now that the door had a chink in it, and realised that Mrs O'Brien must be somewhere about. He spotted her, then, up sitting on the garden seat, and he felt better for having checked her out. Her hand waved slightly but he didn't react, he didn't wish to give the impression that he was counting her in for another day. Sitting, her eyes watched him as he reversed his van and drove away. 'Dead only bury me,' she said, echoing to the very word and concept what the postman was thinking. She stood up and, stiff now, held on to the seat for a few seconds before straightening up and descending the steps towards the yard.

Minnie went inside, and picking up the letters she card-tricked them in an attempt to find the wild card among them. 'No sign there,' she thought as she brought them into the kitchen. Her bad sight saw the familiar bishop-plate writing on the airmail envelope and the other two were but brown-window evenings.

'Now to find my glasses,' she worried as she rummaged through the things cluttering the table. Next she searched behind the row of jugs on the seat of the dresser. Her hand ran along the mantelpiece over the stove, but there was nothing there but carbon. Her feet now headed for the stairs to find if by any chance they had fallen out on the bed from her bib pocket. She had already looked in that pocket at least a dozen times, but all she found in it was a flattened Anadin packet and a half-sucked mint, all stuck over with fibres and dust. The bed didn't yield up anything, neither did the locker. She next looked in under the bed, and got a dizzy spell which forced her to sit upon it for a few breathers. 'Sod the things,' she said for herself to hear as she returned to the kitchen, and now she gave in and sat into her armchair.

Running her hands along the sides of the cushion she eventually found the glasses, staved away for security. Now her eyes glanced at the letters on the table and, glasses held firmly, she got to her feet again. She found a flap hole on the airmail envelope, and sticking in her finger she sawed it along till the contents were looking at her. She took out the folded pages, some enclosed bills falling at her feet. 'The bishop is at it again,' she complained as, stooping down, she picked up the clean crisp dollars. 'Money from America, money for jam,' the rhyme from her childhood came to her lips. Carrying the money with her she walked to the dresser, its platters all covered in dust, but it was the teapot, standing there all stothered, which she handled. Opening its lid she stuffed in the new batch of money, in on top of the mare's nest, the gubby-voiced collection which with every letter grew more dense inside the old family-sized teapot.

Casting her eyes to heaven, the old retainer returned to her chair and began to read page after flimsy page without comment. Her son's questions, though, forced her into reading them aloud. 'Did you get the television yet? Did you ask Felix to position the aerial for good reception in Drumhollow? Did you get the electric stove, don't, at your age, be bothering yourself keeping the turf on, and the fire in?'

'Did you, did you, did you, he always asks the same questions. But sure, what would a woman like me be doing with an electric cooker, sure haven't I the range oil-fired now,' said Minnie. 'As for wanting a television,' she sneered as she spoke, 'all I need is my wireless and my paper and the rest of ye can have the television.' She rested for a while now. She wanted to think the letter through, to imagine how Brendie would look with his pointy mitre. Her mind grew faddy in its imaging. She could see the youthful bishop, handsome, ebony-hard features, serenity wonderfully oozing from his wacky smile, gold ring seven-guessing on his hand, safari-seeking God in every person's face, fracturing others' miseries by healing touch, long crozier held in his hand. She hunted his flock for him, her eyes searching out the streets for his lost and forgotten ones; she called them to his side, told them that he was her son, her God had taken him off her, played ducks and drakes with her family, chosen him as the very one He needed for the job of grating His mercy all over demented souls, the hungry-for-Him souls, the hard-luck women's souls, the hesitating seeds in souls where hunger got in the way, His festering sores' souls where He awayed plasters in order to show the blood in His body when death folded down the veins, whitening red to grey, grey to black and black to dirty dusty clay. Minnie stayed thinking about the bishop, the human-being bishop, the mitre-hatted bishop, and stressed now she voiced her worries. 'Musha,' she said, ''twas far from it he was reared, far from it it is from the day when me and Peter knelt together watching our eldest son being ordained a priest.' Now, pancaking the pages along her skirt, she flattened and folded them into a small, almost postage-stamp-sized square before tucking

235

them into her bib pocket. 'Sod the word about Frankie there,' she said as, patting her pocket, she sat back and shut her eyes.

## CHAPTER 73

His black limousine huckle-bucked its way down the long avenue from the seminary. The bourbon still lingered on his tastebuds. His joined white hands rested upon a barrel-bellied stomach. Noticing every detail was his habit, but tonight he just glanced at the black cloud scudding across the benign moon's face. Sighing with designer pleasure, he slipped a hand deep into his pocket and withdrew the Havana cigar. His fingers held the dry roll of tobacco to his nose. His silvery-haired nostrils inhaled the smell of pure pleasure. Biting and nibbling the end, he searched for his matches. He always used matches, their sulphury smell serving to associate a childish smell with a bishop's onion.

Brendan O'Brien fingered his desiccated cigar into the ashtray. The car window slipped down at his touch of a button, and out into the cold night air wafted his blue smoke. He felt the frosty air blowing inwards and, smarting, hurriedly closed the window. Veins bulged in his throat from the restriction of his clerical collar, and snarling his discomfort he jabbed his finger in a circular cutting movement. Looking back now on his day's fruitfulness he felt satisfied, for hadn't he ordained five more recruits into Christ's army.

Soft hills broke the horizon as the car drove from the hustling, bustling streets of New York City. The chauffeur took the route he knew so well. Teflon-coating his master's every yearning, he was this evening conscious of his condition and anxious to see him home before the exodus from the city got clogged up.

Upstate New York nestled His Grace in one of its exclusive retreats. There behind a high stone wall stood his luxurious plaything. The chauffeur glided the car to a halt before the steps leading up to the heavy mahogany door. He had been watching his boss's Pisa-tilt, and worried in case he might keel over in the sometimes sudden stop-start of the traffic.

The house itself was head and shoulders over anything back home in Drumhollow. When Brendan rented it he was just wanting to have a retreat to which he could come and take a break from the nightmare job of administering his section of the archdiocese. He thus always came upstate for his autumn break, a meander through his feelings, for dead of night here was something similar to the dead of night down at the end of the boreen at home. There were no dazzling neon lights here, only a solitary light on the front lawn which automatically switched off at midnight.

Up here in Peekskill Brendan O'Brien could be himself. His domestic lady came only at his beckoning. She aired the house for him and did the cooking, but it was his chauffeur who virtually ran the place for his bishop. This man was loyalty personified. He drove him when he had to, he sobered him when he needed to, he kept his own counsel about what he saw and heard and he acted as caretaker in the absence of his boss. Now, tonight, he detected his master's intoxication but bishops, he felt, couldn't be described as pissed by a son of the sod. Voicing only consideration he, Michael P. Curley, helped Brendan from the seat and together driver and dignitary mounted the steps to the door. 'So far so good,' thought Michael Curley as he set about working the wobbling man towards his bedroom. He stayed on to prepare him for bed and once he saw him safe in it he left, knowing full well the holocaust which awaited the bishop next morning.

Force of habit made Brendan forage for his rosary beads. He blessed himself in a fashion. Now with his fingers he felt for the first bead, but when he failed to locate the starting point he stretched out from under the duvet and dropped the beads on the floor. The sound of them striking acted as a stimulus to his brain, and he begged God for mercy before cosying his head down deep among the pillows and falling fast asleep.

Next morning the house was drenched in golden light. Below on the river the water traffic chugged. It was a boat's siren which nudged the brain of the sleeping Irish bishop. Feeling delicate, he massaged his forehead with cool, limpid fingering. 'Never again,' he grunted, but his grunts only served to make him uneasy and uneasiness was a feeling which seldom flowed through his certainty.

Hearing footsteps coming stamping along the passageway towards his bedroom, he resolved to be out of the bed before the knock came to his door. Throwing back the duvet he leapt himself into a standing pose. Unknown to himself, the horn rosary beads lay right in his path. His feet felt the beads slithering, but he had to stand his ground for at that very moment Michael P. Curley knocked while simultaneously opening the door of the room. 'Oh, you're up, Your Grace,' he said. 'I'll tell Mary to get your breakfast ready.' His glance took in the rosary beads peeping from beneath the bishop's bare feet. Mocking, he grinned towards it before he closed the door and started for the stairs. Thump, thump, thump went his feet on the polished wood stairs and thump, thump, thump went Brendan's sore head. This morning he felt no remorse for his binge of yesterday. All he longed for now was a hair o'the dog.

Lighting his bearded face in the bathroom mirror, he looked straight into the face of debased priesthood. Black sloes staring from a red sea homed in on him. Looking at his reflection he breathed deeply, but a fog of yeast blotted out his foolish snapshot. 'If my parents could see what became of Maggie Dempsey's miracle they'd puke,' he thought, but almost immediately came the stubbornness, the conviction that despite his being on the tear he was still a priest, a priest forever.

Mary the domestic lady served breakfast fit for a bishop. Her manner was respectful but her eyes took in their secret findings. He, though, just pickled himself with cup after cup of black coffee. Seated there as he supped, he found his eyes drawn towards the virginia creeper which climbed away over his walls, up through his shelterbelt of cypress and out across the roof of his carport. Reds fused into yellows and green into browns as the slanting morning sun dappled light on the epoch, roadrunner-like, greeting him. Lying back in his chair, he had his head almost cleared, but when the barge on the Hudson hooted its horn he had to hold his head in fury.

## CHAPTER 74

Brendan O'Brien, his confession made, tramped his steps towards his prie-dieu and knelt to pray his penance. As he had made his way towards it his hands had hung down in humility, their palms dampened by sweat. Kneeling there he began where he left off, blaming everything else for his foolish folly. His appointment to this archdiocese had hinted of his being a desert-hued bishop, for it was explained that he had served his time in seas of sand and red, African dust.

His penance said, he headed back towards his office, to his polished desk where, having resolved never to drink anything but water ever again, he tried his best not to hang a glance on the table daydreaming under three decanters. Visitors, he found, ably declined having a drink on the job, and their refusal served to keep him secretly sober. That didn't mean, though, that as he negotiated with municipal fellows or real-estated on the telephone his gaze didn't sable those three glass virgins. He always, of late, drank red wine at his dinnertime, but indeed wine was not his factory folly. His goad lay in the middle decanter, the one which housed his brandy, that bloody brandy which had now become the usurer which time and time again became his murderer.

Wanting to be at ease again, he sat there whoring his dry throat with young ideas. Really, he had hundreds of evidences by which he could justify his drinking, but today he found that every time he condemned himself, he at the same time thought of his friend from Ireland, the great friend, the great friend, the great friend, Harry Hope.

'Me and him are two of a kind,' he said to himself. 'It's just that while Harry has his tongue out for the vino or the vodka, I just want to let my ears back to the brandy.' As per usual when he thought of Fr Harry, he recalled the very last time when he had housed the poor wino.

Fr Harry Hope, the victim priest, was the very soul of treasured priesthood, but now he fell where he stood, his poor face bloated and purple as much from loneliness as alcohol. Brendan remembered the very last time he had his countryman gathered up and brought into his care. Poor Harry's dead eyes sobered from his absolute fear of this sombre bishop. The priest's collar was still on backways on Harry, but it was dirty, paw-marked, and frayed around the edges. His black stock was grey from exposure to the weather, and from dribbles which fell on it from a bottle's narrow neck. His trousers hung but barely from his hips and the fork of them hung open in a green frame. The solitary figure which was Fr Harry Hope almost breathed as Brendan sat thinking of him. He knew, as sure as he described his state, that Harry was back in the Bowery talking to his green glass God. 'That's where I belong too,' he scolded, but then a binding force somehow held his secret intact.

Marginally more humble, he lifted the telephone and checked that his secretary was present and in harness before he again waded into the bank of papers on his desk. Nobody could see his battle with the bottle, nobody but himself, and for himself he had sympathy almost to a fault.

Never one to give in to his grave voice, he worked non-stop for the whole afternoon. The desk was clearing before his eyes while outside in the next room his secretary supervised the action of the green cursor and the whining print-out as they expressed his boss's frock-coated mind.

As he worked Brendan hurled wasted efforts towards his wastepaper bucket. Gauging his aim, he rolled the sheets of spoiled drafts into round balls before gun-foddering them into the bucket. It was while he was examining the aftermath of his desk's load after load of mail that he noticed his mother's white envelope, with the word 'To' underlined before she wrote down his name. His eyes glanced for a few seconds at the noticeable shake in her handwriting efforts. But he was in a frightful hurry to read how she seemed. He didn't bother with his pearl-handled paper knife, but instead flittered his finger through the flap and withdrew what seemed like five or six pages of her little tram-tracked writing pad.

'Dear Brendie,' her voice said in a sun-following tone as she led him from mine to mine within her life. His brain had to exercise itself as he tried to match faces with their places from her news bulletin. 'Jude' he yessed to when he read that 'she now has a puck goat running with her foreign cattle. Felix's son Hugh is like a grandson to me,' he read, 'he brings me the newspaper, a carton of milk, and he'll post my letters with this one to you . . . I collect my pension myself. The walk to the post office helps me to keep in touch with the neighbours. They're all mad to talk about *The Late Late Show* and something called *Dallas* and *Density*. Some of them say I can't be alive and not want television but musha, son, the wireless is a sight more to my taste. I know you sent me the money for a television but the truth is your mother would rather listen to the news nor watch it. I often go to Mary Ann Donohoe's, didn't I tell you she's Ned Naylor's mother's, God be good to her's grandniece, to *ceilidh* and we do have to shut off the television so as I can hear myself think. God above, sure I'd not get a thing done if I had a peeping Tom like that in the corner beside the clock. Now Brendie, don't be cross with me cause I didn't buy what you told me.'

Minnie finished her letter by hinting that all seemed far from right with his sister, Sheila. 'She finds herself shut away like a sinner, afraid to come home, and if she does afraid to stay long, anxious to get back, that's as it looks to me and you know I can't do anything, I have to stand my ground in case he might wander home. Give her a yard to tell you, Brendie, the truth of how it is between her and Luke.'

The letter finished he looked again at the address on the envelope. It was now written with ballpoint pen, and now when she wrote her full stop it was just that, a full stop.

## CHAPTER 75

Minnie had over the years only ever written in a positive manner to her son on the mission fields. 'Musha, Brendie has only his beads to keep him company,' she'd tell the listening kettle as, dubbing her voice to its spout's hissing, she'd broadcast the words which he might be suppressing. Bucketfilling her notions despite her aloneness, she worked and worried about everyone bar herself. Feat upon feat she accomplished, but the five fields were never going to make a prisoner of her. Every Saturday she sold her produce, making the necessary for now, but when she sold her livestock her bank balance grew ever so nicely. Nothing to spend it on, nor anybody to buy for, meant that she minnowed now where she used plunder for a pinkeen. Even her transport held no cost factor; her upstairs model bicycle brought her from pillar to post. But each year saw her break from routine. Each springtime she'd set out for the Spring Show in Ballsbridge.

Like the swallows she'd turn up at the Spring Show, a one-woman-band ready to amuse herself. Yes, Minnie O'Brien, the woman from Drumhollow would, just for the jig of the thing, arrive each year to see how and where things were at in the heart of progressive Ireland. Not that it made a whit of difference to her and her whereabouts. She no longer needed to go through humiliation; now, her money in her purse, she could come here to this parade ground to see the animals and machinery which her late husband could only have dreamed of.

By bus to Dublin and train to Ballsbridge she'd travel, the foolish little woman, factory farming for fulfilment. Around the showrings she'd stand, watching the cream of Ireland's livestock hoofling along, their bring-and-buy things swinging between their legs. Cows or bulls, it was all the same to her: they paraded by her, each carrying their goods and chattels, dolled up to the ninety-nines, their dewlaps almost hobbling them.

Horses too whinnied for attention where, unlike the slow drudging oxen, they stunted their humour in temperamental behaviour, but did she give a damn as she stood there beside the turgid aristocracy eying their tavistock and trade. Silently, for an age she'd stand judging the cream of this year's crop of fillies or colts, the need to whisper her findings almost too much to bear, but then her hand might involuntarily touch the brooch at her throat, the touch just a gentle sigh, the unspoken thought just a Turkish delight of tenderness.

Wanting as she always did to bring home with her a haggard of hope, she'd meander around and about, in and out, the maze in her mind a plate of spoiled porridge. 'Musha, will you look at those beautiful girls,' she'd say as, stopping at the dairy stand, she'd see them serving out samples of cheeses and butters, yoghurts and milk shakes, items spreadable from the fridge or solid in the pack. Everything was there in abundance, where long ago in her whitewashed dairy there was only herself, her churn and the milk's wholesale end-product, her pounds of butter. 'The dark ages, that's what we had,' she ruminated as she walked away. 'The dark ages, that was it in a nutshell, now see what they can do with milk,' she thought. 'Sure the way it is nowadays, they can turn it into anything they damned well like, and good on them is all I have to say.'

Her feet, usually gumboot-clad, always began to hurt as she walked in her cuban-heeled slingback shoes, her tender toes all scrunched together paying the price for her heel's freedom. She, though, wouldn't heed their complaints, just rest them while she sat and ate her snack and then off she'd march them again, her eyes wider than her worries.

'Just for old times' sake,' she'd tell herself, smiling inwardly, as year after year she'd sidle off towards the farm machinery. It wasn't that she hadn't appreciated the big food stands with their pyramids of fruit and vegetables – her old fingers always tempted to withdraw a building block to detect the shemozzle there'd be when the whole menagerie'd collapse on the floor. Nor was it that she didn't admire the artistry involved in creating such pyramids of pleasantness. Yet her feet would be drawn away from them, away towards the exhibits outside, for the truth was those goods outside had evolved from her loy and pitchfork, her plough and pulper.

Like a pygmy, she'd be, when she'd at last find herself standing at the site where the manufacturers displayed that which they had dredged from their engineers' brains. Pygmy, yes, that was the measurement, when there she'd stand decoding the star turns, those huge big combine harvesters with their own thresher sited in their innards, the snazzy hay and silage balers able to make plastic parcels of hay and grass, and then the tractors with ne'er a little 'Green Acres' gobshite among them, for she had seen Eddie

Arnold's model on Felix's television the year that Felix got married. But undaunted, she'd stand her ground determinedly and look up into their high cabs as there they'd pose, from where she stood looking like the very Jacob's Ladder itself.

At the gate she had left that morning the night bus would set her down, her handbag the poorer for the outing but her mind jogged and in a state of flux. Her sell-by date was fast running out and her pillows, when at long last she'd lay her lonely findings on them, would hear her chin stubble as little mans' bristles wound themselves from their follicles, getting a head-start on death while the going was good.

## CHAPTER 76

Minnie was brusque as she ordered out the dog, for her steps had been almost tripped up by his nervous antics. The collie knew that something was afoot, and to make matters even more excitable his mistress had behaved just like this when, last Tuesday, she set off on some mystery venture. He sat at the door of the little bathroom, an air of expectancy agog in his eyes as he watched the old woman washing her face. The soap had sneaked into her left eye and so busy was she trying to flush it out with her finger that this time, through her own fault, she again almost came a cropper, not watching where she was going.

Nobody could have foretold that Minnie O'Brien would remember that today was her eighty-third birthday. It was in fact thanks to the very same dog that she discovered the significance of the number framed in biro on the calendar hanging at the end of the dresser. She had to put on the new glasses in order to find out why she had encircled this day's date, but on looking close she discovered that it was to remind her to get the dog licence. It was only as an afterthought she said the date aloud, the sound driving home the opinion that this was in fact her own birthday. 'Musha, lord, who'd have believed that I'd live to eighty-three,' she thought, and immediately struck on the plan of getting the bus to town.

'I'll be long enough in the hole,' she reminded herself as she made ready to travel. Her list written and placed in her handbag, she laid out her map. 'I've to collect the pension and buy the dog licence before the bus comes,' she planned, and as though time was against her she grew all fingers and thumbs in her hurry to get into her coat.

The dog was at high do as he backed his way, barking all the time, until he and his boss reached the road gate. 'Go home now, that's the good fella,' coaxed Minnie, but it wasn't until she picked up a stone and pretended to fire it that the dog sleeked his curving way back down the boreen. 'He'll be here large as life when I get back,' laughed Minnie, for she always had a dog and the dog always had a softie for its mistress.

She always chose to sit on the same side as the driver whenever she took the bus to Huntstown. The in-depth examination which she gave to the harvest on her right-hand side always gave better scope than the view to the left. Nothing on the left she deemed worthy of inspection, nothing but the high demesne walls around the Fortunes' place, and further along the hungry hills, their entrails torn from them by builders greedy for their groined blood. The river wound there too, but to her it seemed unhappy to be green in its gut, for though it turned and twisted it still had to bear with its journey until in under the road it coiled to come out on Minnie's side, the side where light housed a certainty and the horizon housed a promise. Today she sat in the fourth seat, looking out at the countryside of Drumhollow. Wild hurts grew still in Larkin's field. Indubitably, she napalmed the scene of former Sundays.

The sun was droll this wacky day, for as she focused her eyes dreamt up what they wanted to see. Thus was she kicking her agile mind when the girl's voice broke in on her *Gone With The Wind* play. The voice was not of this world: the structure was different, the stress silent to her ears. 'You're Mrs O'Brien, awrn't you?' the voice said, and just for the second Minnie felt that she was at home listening to the World Service. The nuances were there in this voice beside her, and turning towards it she looked into the beaming face of a stranger. Minnie was confused, but the girl said, 'You were pointed out to me last Sunday coming out of the church. You're the bishop's mother, awrn't you?' The friendly approach, attractive in its plumminess, held the old woman's senses on the alert. 'I'm a grand-niece of Maggie Dempsey, and I'm here living in her old place,' the girl said.

'You must be Laura Bewley's daughter,' said Minnie, coming over all sad and glad, and when the relationship was confirmed the pair of passengers became as old friends. Laura Bewley's daughter, Laura, filled in the details of her mother's marrying in London, 'and now here I am, her daughter, and I've just taken up a post in the District Hospital.' Minnie wept with delight as she listened to the fable told by this pretty nurse, and then she in her turn drew on her lively imagination to tell this London girl the history of the handywoman of her soused nature.

Laura met with Minnie later, and together they drank tea in Greene's Hotel. Minnie insisted that the treat was on her, and it wasn't until they neared home again that the old woman told the nurse that she was eight-three years old on this of all days.

'My God, it's her birthday and she only thinks of it now when we're nearly home from town,' scolded Laura. 'Mrs O'Brien, why, we could have had a drink, you know, a little whiskey or brandy maybe, just to say congratulations.' But Minnie was all shy in her own way, and she admitted that that was why she had got the bus to town. 'Laura, I didn't want to be doing today what I did yesterday, and musha, even what I'll do tomorrow. I just wanted to

247

be on the move, seeing folks, the day does be so long on your own. And I'm delighted that you sat beside me and musha, sure we'll be living near each other now.'

The bus chugged to a halt at the head of Laura's bog road. Goodbyes said, the girl stood and gave a final wave to the old woman before the bus moved on. Minnie's day was made for her because the girl had bothered to dilly-dally head-on with her. But to think that she was a relation of her old friend Maggie, well that put the tall hat on it! Now she had met someone who would believe her when she said she was watching out for her son to return.

Her dog heard the story of the girl on the bus, the shrill barking besides. The voice sounded the same, but the dog couldn't understand the difference in the tone of the telling. Blundering about his mistress, he worked the woman back down towards the house, scattering the hens when they reached the yard, and giving the cat a run for his money when he dared to be sitting on the flagstone outside the back door.

The following outside only made the kitchen seem ever more welcoming. The door now closed after her, the strugglings of the woman yielded to the dim quiet within. Her shoes taken off, she went upstairs to hang her coat in the wardrobe. This time, though, the hand didn't bother to rub the serge of the dead man's suit. Her head in a spin, she descended the stairs to the kitchen and sat the kettle on its hot spot. Now her body slumped itself into her chair, and before high Sunday's solo she was fast asleep, her head drooping onto her chest, nightmaring about Frankie down on Holly Bog coming towards her, lovely velvety-pink raspberries held out in the cup of his hand.

The barking woke her. There was nobody to be seen from where she sat, but a thud of the knocker on the front door set her struggling to her feet. Fragmenting her dreams, she shuffled in her stockinged feet towards the hall and porch. Her eyes still blurring her hearsay, she opened the door to find the girl standing there. It was the voice which registered first, and attaching great welcome

248

to her own voice she said, 'Come in. Musha, this is a grand surprise. I was having a doze after my day in town, and you know I'm not as young as I used to be.'

Laura Bewley carried a round tin in her hands, and when the pair reached the kitchen she set the scene by handing over the gift to the woman. 'It's only a little something for your birthday,' she said. 'We can't let the day pass without celebrating.'

A *gliondar* came in Minnie's expression. It was so long since she had heard the sound of a young woman's voice in her kitchen that she began to muss her words, her seven senses giddy all at the same time. When she tried to snap open the lid from the tin she failed, and the visitor had to do the needful. The sponge sandwich taken out, Laura laid it on its doily upon a plate. She was dedicating this human touch not only to the birthday lady but to the handywoman who belonged to this scene, to this attacking house, this mausoleum, where a hushed voice still called out the word 'Frankie'.

Laura's secret glances took in every detail of the old woman's kitchen. The neglect was only a feature of her old age. 'This place could be tidied in a few hours,' thought Laura, but she knew that she would need to bide her time.

Plying her visitor with a little drop of brandy, the old lady was treating Laura to the best in the house. The glasses clicked in birthday good wishes. Minnie slowly sipped hers, the solemn future now almost forgotten. Three times did Laura agree to another *braoneen* before terrible relief came in a mundane cup of tea, a slice of cake and a name clumsily pronounced as 'Flwanklie'.

# CHAPTER 77

At black of night the drowning took place. He stood all alone on the deck, hoping that his game would go unnoticed by either a stray passenger or a member of the crew. At his side stood the item for dispatch: like a chastised dog it almost leaned against him, chum-like trying to eke comfort or reassurance.

It was all of five years since Frankie O'Brien had left home. Looking back now, he remembered the scene as though it had happened yesterday. Footloose, he managed somehow to put distance between his mother and himself, the little, cold, tin handle of his suitcase bonding the moment by furrowing for comfort in his palm. 'Don't lose your belt,' she called after him, 'and don't forget to bless yourself every morning.' He remembered how he had nodded back in agitated agreement. Now he held on to that belt; it'd be all he'd have left to remember her by.

The swell revved in readiness the moment he picked up the suitcase, but the handle hinted for his help the hymen-hold bonding yet again. The case was full and heavy but, no need now for nervousness, he swung the suitcase away back behind him and unless he threw himself hilltop in guilt after it, he had no way in the world of foretelling where it'd land or indeed where its journey might take it.

That belt tied his bluey for many's the day. It held together the rags and tags of this oftentimes hungry gobdaw. It knew full well that he was failing here in Australia, for when he tightened its buckle it felt the thinness in his fingers, the hardship in his palms.

But hell had him fired by the time the shearing gang took him on. For all they cared he could be as thin more. Could he shear a sheep and be ready for the next, was their burning question. A shake of his head was Frankie's only answer.

It was Bob from Belfast who gave him the break. A waspish man he was, a sting in his tail if you rubbed him up the wrong way, but out here in the wilderness a man had to be able to live with himself, had each day to be his own judge and executioner, for the truth was a God-botherer was as rare out here as was a snowdrop in July back home in Ireland.

So it was in the best Protestant tradition of 'give a hand if you can' that Bob befriended his fellow Irishman. Teaching him the tricks of his trade he, a rhymer by nature, set about composing a ditty about the route which the shearer and his shears took as each sheep was divested of its wool.

'Say it to yourself and keep on saying it until you know it by heart,' suggested Bob from Belfast. 'Say it and keep saying it till your brain and hands are working as one. As you know, there's nothing to it,' he reasoned. 'You have the pair of shears and the sheep has the fleece of wool. The thing to remember, though, is that you're doing it a good turn. The heat has the sheep moidered, and only you can bring relief to the poor hoor.'

At break of dawn, it was, when Frankie O'Brien heard himself being described as fit to join the team. He had had a great teacher. By rote he had learnt Bob's ditty, the roadmap through which his clippers must travel in order to shear a sheep. As and when he got over his doubts he began to think the route ahead, and then it was, as Bob watched him release his eight shorn sheep, that he spat in pleasure, declaring this Drumhollow man 'no bloody drongo, you.'

What no one in the gang knew, though, was that the night before the dawn Frankie had lain awake the night-time long. Up overhead the moon had drawn herself up to her highest point in the heavens, and from there she milked down her echo as she listened while over and over again Frankie recited Bob's theme:

> 'Matey, start on the belly,
> Move along the first hip,

251

Clip all around the scut,
And up the backbone after it.
Shear all along the bony spine
Then open up the neck,
Run round it like a bugger
Till you reach the back of it.
Now carry on around the shoulder,
Some short clips down each side.
Back now on second shoulder,
Back on down to second hip,
Then, matey, out over the tail you go
Your sheep's shorn and that's for sure.'

To his dying day he'd remember his initiation into this greasy gang. Eight in number, they came from seven countries, only the Belfast man and he, the nobbled one, coming from the same back o'the woods. Now he, that same Westmeath man, could boast of the thousands of Merinos which he had shorn. Never now would he nick a poor sheep: no, nowadays the shorn sheep ran from between his knees with their heads held high, their only blemish the initial branded there on each one's humiliated pelt.

Australia became a playground of criss-cross journeying to Frankie and his team of shearers. Station by station they racketed along, their swags of gear light, the outback their whole universe. They could now, on average, with their mechanised clippers, daily boast of shearing a hundred and fifty sheep apiece. Standing, their backs bent, they seldom looked up, for too well they knew that hundreds, perhaps thousands, of heavy-breathing Merinos still waited their turn to be defrocked.

Frankie's years in Australia slipped by like slime through his fingers, but still the old coat belt tied his bluey. Nobody bothered to comment upon it, nobody even noticed it. A night came, though, when he cradled it for the very last time, his fingers pushing the pointed bit in through the buckle, up across the bridge in the middle and out through the other side. His hands repeated this performance at least the dozen times before he flung it, still buckled, upon the red embers of the fire. Now he watched the old withered thing burn like gorse bush, and every time a remnant fell away he kicked under the fire coals, his boot making sure that come next morning when he strode past the night's handiwork there'd be no reminders, no little harum-scarum bits of belt left funeral-beckoning to him from the hole which the fire dented in the ground.

Now the belt was gone, and with it his last vestiges of Irish nationhood. His bedroll though, could still be tied, for now he had the knack of making strong twine: now he could, by rubbing, make bush string from the fibres of the banyan tree. His handy-andy trick came one late evening when the floorboards began to fall through from their old jalopy of a truck. They had no tyings worthwhile on board, but the only Australian on the gang came to their rescue. He made bush string for them from a handily placed banyan tree. With his bushman's knife he cut deep inside its bark and, though it took some while, he eventually dug out sufficient fibre from which to make the string. The secret, he explained, was to rub the fibre with the heel of the hand up and down along one's thigh, keeping adding further fibre until the string was thick enough and long enough for the emergency on hand. As he rubbed he reminded Frankie of his late father when, with hemp in one hand and wax in the other, he rubbed and rubbed and drew and drew until he had the perfect wax-end with which to stitch the family's boots.

The wax-end, though it was but a fleeting image, came back that night to haunt him in his dreams. For the first time ever he found himself wondering about home. He knew his mother would be there, streeting the boreen, her fair hair dappled by overhanging leaves, but now he somehow felt he'd like to go back and boast to her about the great hands which she had given him.

That wax-end never allowed him to hop his hurdles. Every day now, respectable reminiscences got between him and his best

mates. 'I'm thinking of calling it a day,' he confided one night to
Bob Paisley. 'But before I hit home,' he said, 'I'd like to have a
gawk at America, and at anything else that lies between here and
there.'

## CHAPTER 78

The day ahead was going to be a red-letter day for Minnie
O'Brien, so in order to rise to the occasion she dolled herself up in
her best red jumper and her grey pleated skirt. Putting on the skirt,
though, took a great deal of manoeuvring for now, though she did
latch her eye on to a fixed flower on the bedspread, she found the
actual stooping down to pull up the skirt a job which sometimes
made her dizzy. But the job done she fixed the waistband
comfortably over her hips, and then standing there in front of the
mirror she shaped herself, it appearing as though she were young
again. Now she fetched her tights and black shoes and, moving
towards the chair, sat down to put them on. All the while she
dressed in readiness for her journey her old mind was rip-roaring
along, nourished by the adrenalin flowing through her body.

Downstairs and ready to go, she shyly took one final glance at
the mirror in the hall before she let herself out and clanged the
door shut behind her. Her dog, fed for the day, was barely able to
bark as he gallivanted along before her, wishing each time she
stopped to catch her breath that she wasn't going to turn back, for
he had fish to fry up at the road gate.

Only twice did she stop to rest on the boreen and then, newly
winded, she stepped along, ever conscious of the bus. But on
arriving at the gate she was glad this morning to be able to sit
down on the grass bank in order to compose herself before

mounting the steps of the bus. She ordered the dog home to guard the place in her absence and he, an old dog, who could not learn new tricks, just feigned interest in things inside the gate and the moment she looked away he slid between the bars and cocked his leg with gusto. Several pees, it took, before he was satisfied enough to lie down near Minnie. Camped beside her, the dog eyed his mistress, watching her as she mouthed and mouthed the decisions which she had clued into her consciousness.

The hedges flew by her shoulder, their every bush and tree lying like hairs on her head as, sitting on her side of the bus, she flogged the route to Huntstown. Clutched tight in her hands was her soft black leatherette handbag, with inside it her copy of her late husband's will, now all sepia-tinted and tight-folded. Her destination was the splendid pebble-dashed house down at the canal end of Huntstown, the office and premises belonging to the solicitor, Hubert Groan, and towards it she ever neared, her heart flittering with excitement, her mind advising her to pull the strings while she was yet able, the strings which would tie up the house and land at home for her son and keep Jude Fortune at bay until the season changed.

Stepping along through the town she glanced at folks whom she met, greeting anyone who addressed her with a 'Good Morning, heh!' Her skirt dipped below her coat, but she didn't notice. She still held her handbag clutched in a farmer's grip, and to counter each unspoken worry she had a 'how-an'-ever' of encouragement.

Entering the porch of Groan's business house, her hand slipped as she attempted to turn the knob on his front office door. Bonbons of saliva burst forth immediately from her gums as she nervously tried again. On her second attempt the door opened, and there she was greeted by the head of the family, old Hubert Groan himself. He glanced in bafflement at the woman, but she introduced herself as 'Minnie O'Brien, the widow of Peter and the present owner of my holding out back there in Drumhollow.'

Puzzled, the solicitor looked at her, but his was nothing if not the manner of a Protestant on his best behaviour. He shook the little proffered hand and pulled out an old leather-bound chair for his client. Like a queen she sat into it, her feet barely touching the floor, while he probed, his finesse such that she in fact detected nothing. Framing her address in his mind's eye, he soon had her origins, seed, breed and bishop neatly fixed before him. He now enquired as to the set-up of each member of her family while he at the same time brought his mind to bear upon the house away down at the end of a long lane. Hushed by his conversational tactics, Minnie was suddenly seized with a desperate worry, for she noted now that his questions had all to do with her son the bishop, and her daughter married and now living in Dublin, while she herself hessian-tied only the name of her youngest son to the glad violin there wrapped in a white sheet in the press of the sideboard, where she had hidden it the day after the night when, lying in her bed, she heard what Christie's of London had got for a fiddle like hers, and to the house which thermal-wrapped that respectable nugget, and great that they were the five fields, each whole and honest, they still sited there on the sunny side of the Grand Canyon.

Hubert Groan, after what seemed a respectable length of time, smiled at her in patient acknowledgement of her maternal concern, but then, freeing himself, he praised and spoke about her two successful family members, whereas each time he mentioned Frankie's name he spoke in the past tense.

Minnie O'Brien hadn't waited all those years and come this journey this morning to find herself fobbed off by this old man. Her mind stuck to her regime, and again she stressed that her last will and testament would detail her Frankie as the heir apparent. Hubert Groan still hinted that in his opinion her son must lie buried in some foreign land, but she, on seeing the track of his mind, now took on the composure of a judge when again she stipulated her desire to will her holding to her youngest son, her littlest one.

Sitting there in fierce form in the big chair, she listened as the solicitor tried again to sway her thinking. Her hand held the old creased copy of Peter's will. Eventually she could stand this man's busybodying no longer, and straight from the hip she shot when she told him: 'No, I'm not giving anything to Brendan, he was spoken for a long time ago, we gave to him when it meant going without the bare necessities of life.' Now, as though the solicitor was not even present, her mind did a re-run on Brendan's going-away trunk. It, she remembered, held beautiful new white linens, a leather-bound missal whose pages read in Latin, and the most difficult of all, she remembered now, was how she had to spend her last few shillings to buy socks for him, shop socks, her own hand-knit specimens not likely suitable for him in his new grief. Out loud she continued with her thoughts. This time she told Hubert Groan about her daughter Sheila. She described how her nurse's training was wasted when she married her wealthy husband. She didn't bother to destroy her daughter in this man's hearing, but inwardly she realised that Sheila was a different story from Brendan. Yes, her daughter had a great heart, but finding herself no longer able to nurse she was spoiled on all fronts. Dread was in fact what Minnie was now feeling for Sheila, for poor Sheila had everything this world could grant her, but in sober moments even Sheila herself knew that her marriage was a funeral set to music, the music that of a eunuch's hearing.

Hubert Groan's eyes didn't match his wasteful words, Minnie noticed, but be that as it may her shield held before her, her wainscoting fixed to her Frankie's name, she didn't mind whether or why he looked across his glasses at her. Her strand was life-sized, yellow-sanded and cracked cunningly here and there, but she could see the sweep of sea stressing before her, and from her she cast sure gaze to hint of her littlest one out there on the brackled azure world, his heart homing while his mind breasted forward in ever-increasing sure lines towards Drumhollow. Nutshelled and straitjacketed, she now sealed secret hope with her signature. Minnie O'Brien, it read, and two witnesses brought their serene gaze to bear upon her gnarled hands as she shakingly amened her task.

Determined to see her day out in grand style, she ate dinner in Greene's Hotel. Describing her strict undertaking, she healed her heart by ordering fresh salmon. Her feast brought back memories of Temple Bar, that day when he bought the grandfather clock, but even more precious was the gift which he bought from his own savings, the gold brooch with the gem of faith blinking, winking, voicing loving butter-churned ballbearings, sufficient to last a lifetime for his girl, the girl from but the bacon-slicer world of Humphrey's shop.

'Now the farm'll be there for Frankie,' she said to herself as, chewing slowly on the pink salmon, she tested around in her mouth for a sign of a bone. She was enjoying this meal, relishing a taste memory she was. She felt she deserved this treat, for she had done what himself would have expected of her.

Nimbly she walked back towards the bus terminus. On the way she bought a new frying pan, one with a non-stick coating. Back in the dark ages she fried on an old cast-iron pan, and watched one day as Brendan dropped a slice of her own butter onto the red-hot pan. That pan cracked with a sizzling clap, and she replaced it with an aluminium one, but nowadays it was buckled and inclined to burn on one side. She was dying to test out the promise inherent in this non-stick brag, and so planning she dropped into Baker's butcher's shop and bought three cutlets from a young lamb's carcass.

It was only when she was back outside the butcher's shop that she studied her shopping list and discovered that she had forgotten to buy some spray-on furniture polish, a sieve – hers at home had a hole worn through – and two plastic flowerpots for her geranium cuttings.

Her steps brought her back again to Duggan's shop, and nursing their pan she bought her items from the sad-faced woman who had recommended the pan to her. Now, her parcels cradled to her bosom, she advanced back up the street again. As she worked her way along her gaze flicked from shop window to shop window. Suddenly, she was stopped in her tracks, her eyes lighting upon a sweep of beautiful holly-green material, patterned all over in old-penny-sized white spots. Minnie was very young again. Green she loved. Holly-green she pined for, and with those big white spots, 'Why,' she said, 'sure it'll be like old times, sure I'll be able to count them like I used the pink and blue.' All those years ago, but now to her they seemed but a week since, when nursing a feed of green apples she lay in her bed, as sick as a pig, and in trying to forget her mother's dose of castor oil tried numbering the pink spots and blue spots on her bedroom curtains. Her mind back in girl's country, she walked into Waters' shop and bought the makings of two sets of curtains for her bedroom windows. Thread to match completed the order and now, her arms full of packages, she moved up the street towards the terminus.

Minnie had to make only one more call, and dropping into the supermarket near the bus stop she was noticed by a young trainee manager with an eye on public relations. She fetched a trolley, a carrier bag big enough to accommodate an old woman's parcels, and together they travelled the aisles finding tea bags, sugar, drinking chocolate, cream crackers and for the new pan's sake a packet of maple-cured rashers and a string of sausages. The young lady went the whole hog and delivered the old lady and her problems to the bus.

The plush seat of the bus was a godsend to Minnie's tired body. There she wriggled into a comfortable position, her brain creaming itself after its day's ordeal. 'Now the place will be his for the coming back to,' she told herself. 'He can stay away as long as he needs, and nobody on this earth can frame their name on his five fields.'

The bus driver helped her down the steps. He took her carrier bags to her gate. He bade her 'God bless,' and she, opening the gate, carried the shopping through and set off burdened by her stunts, knowing, with every step she took, that she would never again hit out for Huntstown or its shunts.

The clock chimed six o'clock as Minnie sat down to doze her daily oratorio of dreams. Her consciousness by day was kept alert by the battle which she daily fought to keep predators at bay. But at night, or when she dozed like now, her dreams created a field in which poppy heads lost their capsules and cast down their butter's hoard in looted pounds of practical opinions.

Moidered by sleep, she woke to the sound of the dog's barking. She went to the back door and eavesdropped on his concerns. Gestapo-like, her ears listened out for the reasons for his antics, and then she heard it, the barking of a vixen serving notice of her whereabouts and signalling messages of her intentions. She stood for an age listening, her mind cresting the now with Shelta-old findings. Then, muttering praise for her dog, she replied to the vixen's bark with a great slam of her door.

But as though it were a diversion her gaze fell on her new pan, and after washing it she dried it and settled it upon the hot plate of the stove. 'Will I or won't I?' she wondered, her hand holding a knife in the butter. 'Maybe the non-stick doesn't need any fat,' she laughed. 'Ah! but better be sure than sorry,' she told herself as she placed a small knob of butter on the hot pan and watched until it sizzled. When she placed her cutlet onto the hot fat it too began to limber up, and soon it was cooked to a turn. 'Sorra stickin' either,' said Minnie as she placed the golden-fried cutlet onto a warm plate.

Minnie's last meal of the day was simple, but she reckoned that a day on which she dined on fresh salmon and lamb must, honestly, be a nightmare.

# CHAPTER 79

The house in Blackrock was called Drumhollow. The name was Luke's idea. It was his way of letting Minnie, his mother-in-law, know that she, as far as he was concerned, was indeed welcome to come and live out her last years with Sheila.

Luke and Sheila Green's new house overlooked Dublin Bay. Its privacy was guarded by high walls and even higher poplar trees. The gates swung open on command from the Greens: even the driveway lit itself as though by magic. The hall door, set back under a canopy held high by Ionic-style columns, was of solid teak, its brass furniture polished to within an inch of its life, and its knocker, in the shape of a lynx's head, hung greatly heavy, and all-knowing in its looking. Six stone steps led down from the hall door, and there parked at the bottom of them was Sheila's love-apple, a bright red Porsche.

The house called Drumhollow was two-storied over a basement, and on the window ledge right slap-bang over the canopy sat a big black cat. Sheila had found him one day when, for something to do, she mosied about among the furniture in an antique shop on Bachelors Walk. It had been a testing day for her. She had mined disappointment that morning when Luke phoned from Bangkok. 'No, I just can't make it home for the house-warming, have to fly to Adelaide and then on to San Francisco instead.' Sheila had as usual sure-sured him that she understood, but every step she took down along the quays dramatised the build-up of her resentment. 'He's never where he's needed, what's new about that? He's never where I am, and that's for sure.'

She had taken but a few more steps when her mind was suddenly made up. 'I'll call the whole damned thing off altogether, sure what warming does the house want? Won't it only be the same as London, him touching down like a bloody bird for a drink, and me, muggins, being pulled this way and that by that shower, the movers and shakers of every good cause.'

With this new plan firmly in mind, she felt relieved when she sat down on the steps of number seven to be a child again and eat her ice-cream cone in peace. She, at this moment, was as close to that original, the girl from Drumhollow, as Minnie herself was to Pooka's Corner. As she sat there on the dusty worn steps she didn't notice anything, didn't heed anything or anyone, for she was healing, only the woman herself knew how, for hadn't she served her time to life in the fast lane, and she the red bike's owner from the boreen's end.

As Sheila licked and licked in order to catch the melting ice-cream she was just picturing the great man, Luke. She could see him now, with dark stubble hinting, bulk big and stylishly rotund, forehead frowning in flights of financial figuring, dark mohair suit designer-labelled, a cigar curling blueness from between hairy-backed fingers or wedged between a hackneyed set of teeth, lost in his own weird world of wealth and paper profits. Preoccupied, she didn't notice the blisters of icecream dropping down on her mint-green dress. No, she didn't notice, for she was gazing trance-like into a bubble in which the seat of her sorrow existed.

'If anyone could see me now,' she thought, when gradually the cold dampness of the ice-cream suggested itself. She searched for a tissue, and finding one in her dress pocket dabbed and dabbed as she tried to dry up the cream. Cantankerous now, she glanced up at the cherry-red door, wishing she could dash inside and wash away the big stain. Her dress was ruined and as she stood up to look at it she said, 'Wouldn't you swear I wet myself.' Instead of scolding herself she decided to get inside somewhere, anywhere, and hang about there until the stain dried out.

Gathering the fullness of her skirt into a fold-over pleat and hanging her shoulder bag casually on her arm, she opened the door into the dark interior of a furniture shop. All was quiet inside save for the bell which tinkled at the door. Its sound brought a lonely-looking, summons of a man out to hunt his quarry. 'Can I help you?' he asked, and Sheila, grinning her street-wisdom, said 'I'm just looking'. He backed off then, life-jinxed as he was, and she browsed at her ease. 'May I go upstairs?' she said when, approaching a few steps, she hungered to go on. Getting his go-ahead, she mounted those old back steps, and walking through an ancient doorway came upon piles of broken furniture, cracked china, old dilapidated paintings, the bric-à-brac of history all covered in dust and cobwebs. Where she leaned she caught only a glimpse of pointy ears and long, long, empty eyes. She stirred some more old frames and tried to establish what exactly it was. More movement of pieces of stolen lives had to be helped out of the way and then she saw him, the big black cat, with there in his head two black, bulging sloes in the sockets where his eyes and their pupils should be.

Sheila's eyes were trapped by his not-noticing ones. Stooping in she eased him towards her, her hot hands feeling his cold hat-in-hand plight. She began to dust him down, her one hand stroking his beautiful face, the other working itself down along his curved back until it reached his tail. His shape was perfect, just like him at home on the marmalade jar, always there long ago, sitting in front of the blazing fire, comfort personified. He also had something else about him which endeared him to her, for like him, the cat which she always drew as a child had its tail sticking out in a cosy curve around him.

Her hands were filthy but she didn't notice at all. She lifted up the cast-iron cat with the hollow insides and walked back through the doorway, carefully glancing past him as she descended the steps. 'How much do you want for this?' she carelessly asked the man. He looked at the woman, looked then at the cat, and hungry for a killing said, 'Seventy-five pounds, and Madam, can I say you've found a bargain.'

Sheila never stirred as he stood confronting her. She was feeling cold seeping through her summer dress. Heavy and getting heavier, her hands passed the cat to the man. 'Sorry, too dear for me,' she said, walking towards the door, dusting herself down as she went.

'Madam,' he shivered now as he called after her. 'How about sixty-five?' Her footsteps slowed, but went on again. Now he, like greyhounds off their slip, ran after her, baying out, 'Fifty so, how about fifty?' and concealing a smile she slowly turned and, thrusting up her hand like a point-duty garda, stopped him in his tracks with a sniffy 'OK'.

He was charm itself as he wrapped the tomcat in black plastic. His tongue loose, he filled her in on its chronology. 'From a big place up there by the Hellfire Club she bought him, my daughter did, found him at an auction there, but then she upped and married an American and dumped her cat on me.' He laughed a liar's laugh, but Sheila didn't care. She instead handed over her plastic minefield to him, and watched while he showed it to his money machine.

Mincing her words she tacked her thanks, and headed post-haste for the carpark. Desperate to leave down her load, she felt knackered by the time she reached her car. She turned the key and the boot lid flew wide open. 'Now you can purr for all you're worth,' she thought as, grimacing, she slapped down the lid on her Porsche's supper.

Her stained summer dress forgotten, Sheila drove home towards the hunting lodge behind the poplars. Kitten-silent, her car stopped, the cat still sitting upright inside the dark boot. But she was preoccupied as she lifted him from his seat, for she was in fact juxtaposing whether to site him with his back towards the road or sitting dumb-like facing forward, facing coming friend and foe alike.

Binding herself to him, her hand prying his vacant insides, she bestowed beauty, tested beauty, upon his cast-iron ignorance. Pulling up the bottom of the window, her wise hands held the cat while she tested his steadiness.

264

Beautifully firm, her big black cat sat on the window ledge looking for all the world as though he had sat there from day one. But that thought was just her plea from the inside. Now her feet whipped the plush on the carpet as down the stairs she ran to judge for herself if she had at long last brought luck to her house.

# CHAPTER 80

Sheila and her mother were two of a kind. Where they differed, though, had to do with luck in life. Sheila had had everything she could wish for bestowed upon her, the only thing missing the man of her bed. Minnie, on the other hand, had not much of the world's goodies but her man, while ever he lived, was hers and hers alone.

Nowadays, though, her wait was for another man. Near heaven's gate, she hearsed her funeral as she listened out for him. He was still alive, that she knew, for hadn't the banshee come the night her husband died, so why wouldn't she have come again if her son Frankie's soul had dared leave its camp? Yes, she knew the banshee followed the male line of the O'Brien clan, for hadn't she herself heard her on that numb night, himself cold as God on the bed upstairs, while the woman of the universal dirge circled the house outside, her ricocheting soliloquy shrilling cries of washerwoman's wailing for the testicled member who had dunnage dumped and flown away to another world.

Beavering with this certainty, Minnie had lived for freshness' sake. Each day saw her farming for the future. Her land was stone hard now for the want of sod-breaking, but the old plough lay out behind the pigsty, freckled by rust and bedded down in nettles. Her hands often touched its handles, her linseed-grasp not able to stir it from its trap. But sometimes she'd hold on, steering as though she were cutting a fresh scrape through lea ground, her yielding eyes dimmed by tears' hallucinations. Her 'Musha now, Minnie, don't be regretting,' did nothing to fine-tune her vision, for now she could in fact feel the almost-nearness of her young husband as, out of his grave, he again ploughed one foot in the furrow, one foot on the sod. Looking back, she could see his scrapes. With the keen eye of a woman she could see that each scrape was as straight as a ramrod, and as she drenched her look she could see again her children as, green in childhood, they waddled after their father, asking their whys and wherefores of him who, old-fashioned though he was, claimed to change green fields into brown utopia.

Unlike the plough, the Dublin bus acted as a living, secret summons right down through the years. She could daily hear it approach, its sound shuddering up over the Fortunes' high roadside-walls, and then with a blast of friendly greeting it'd shoot past her own five-barred gate. Assessing its sound she always heeded it, fearful that it might take her by surprise. She funded it to match the mood, noticing that in high summer it flittered past the space between the piers, its voice jaunty. She'd smile as she noted it for she had, she felt, heard it in her mother's womb. Its sound was absolute. She knew it from every vantage point. She had heard it in her bed of lovemaking, she had cringed with pain when it laboured past her scene of childbirth, she had travelled to Connecticut on it just to enjoy the rhythm associated with the driving-rod mechanism of its undercarriage. She had, she knew, milked squirts of milk hard against the bottom of a bucket just to celebrate its driving past her dull, hyphenated status. As a monument to the bus her pulper stood out, young eddies revving the blade each time she twisted the handle. Turnips tossed in by her hands emerged in fingers of foodstuff for her cows and stock. She secretly hoped that when its seated passengers glimpsed her herd, as just for an instant they would glimpse them, they would know that a human being had seen to them, even to the point of pulping purple-skinned turnips for them. Of course when grass was green and growing her fountain stood hard on stop, but come pulper-time in dead-arsed winter, down there in the open shed a human being activated that fountain, and listened to the fuming fun which the bus had as, mocking her, it sometimes slowed down to film a lonely woman hellbent on hearing her stolen child's coming, coming by way of its motor engine, coming he'd be, coming to gather her old credentials into his young arms' grasp, and he'd surely milk her tea mug for her, milk it in creamy iridescence just for old time's sake.

But winter proved that it knew her weakness; winter let her down. The bus tried hard to deceive her, tried to give her heart a boost by hinting that it had her boy, her littlest, on board, but fruitless in its set-downing all her ears ever heard was fungus drying, for the truth was that bromide had made breccia from her lifetime of hoping.

Each night, though, Minnie made a habit of recounting her findings prior to climbing the stairs to bed. Her nocturnal mask had to resemble some sort of hope. 'Musha, maybe tomorrow he'll have a letter from him,' she'd say as she wound the clock or switched off the oil burner or even dressed the old chair with maybe a fresh jumper or a bleached-white blouse all in readiness for tomorrow. 'Musha, girl, you're the right mug for bothering to be hopeful,' she might then chastise herself as, sometimes drenched by tears, she'd grab hold of the rail and begin the climb of the stairs to bed.

Blackness of night and bleakness of thought would usually envelop her nights of nothingness, for indeed her life now resembled a Drumhollow hopscotch, where kicking her hickey-stone along from field to field she'd hop, one, two, three, four rest, poppy-red rest, land-brown rest, turnip-purple rest, meadowsweet rest, rest in peace rest, REST.

# CHAPTER 81

Every cat, dog and devil joined in with Minnie as they too slept their nights away in Drumhollow, but not so the green-eyed woman in that farm next to the O'Briens' place. She never had any real interest in sleeping: the gadfly could not dream on her pillow; her yawning never kindled some shut-eye. Rather her nights were taken up hungering for possessions, hungering, no matter the human cost, for other folks' honesty be that stock or land. Nothing now challenged her more than that she should link her name to her next-door neighbour's little place. Listening the nights long her thoughts hungered, her mind hunted, and her ears listened.

Herding done, the green-eyed one always headed towards the high field, the one place from where she could zoom in on her neighbour's house and haggard. Looking hard, she'd curse the smoke which, as though for spite, vomited from Minnie's chimney. She knew that the 'moron' down there in no way felt threatened by her, her poor days spent blathering on about her youngest son, the one gone abroad, 'He'll make it home soon' her drinking song.

Mornings always seemed to het up the tired thumping in Jude Fortune's head. The long trek through the fields greedily dragged her down. The last thing she needed was to be wishing for more tension. If only she knew she should, at this juncture, be laughing at herself, now a woman of wealth.

Sitting in the breakfast room this morning, Jude dined alone. Her thoughts up there in the high field were the thoughts at her breakfast table. As she ate her fry she found this morning that she had to stop every so often, for something was bothering her, something kept tramping across her eyeline. Umpteen times did she leave down her knife and rub her hand over and back across her forehead, attempting to feel out a loose hair. It puzzled her how a hair could have come loose for she had, of late, begun to wear a hairband, finding that it kept her hair clear of her vision. She was almost finished eating her meal by the time her eyes cleared themselves, and now, pushing back her breakfast things, she sat back in her chair and rested her spine hard against the sturdy chairback.

Breakfast long over Jude continued to sit where she was, her chair shilly-shallying on its back legs. She mouthed words to herself as she slid out the form which her approach would take. Her newest idea was to go down the boreen to meet her neighbour at her worst. Her own appearance would be groomed good health in place of her neighbour's nutbrown features and butty welling-tons. She intended now to set a single plan before Minnie O'Brien, and if that first plan failed she'd negate that failure by coming up with a compromise. As it stood, she plotted, she'd secure the farm and house belonging to the old woman, but she'd be merciful in her acquisition, for she promised herself that she'd give Minnie the right of residence for her lifetime. Her brain counted on Minnie's not having too long left in this life, so her total takeover would not necessitate too long a wait. She'd make her a fair bid, give her time to consult her son and daughter, and if that plan failed, well then, she'd suggest she'd sell it back for the exact same money if Francis ever happened to blunder home.

Scarlet blouse ironed to a crease, her black skirt buttoned down the front, she dressed herself especially for the occasion. Her black patent-leather shoes shone with mirror images as she strode down the grass path in the middle of Minnie's seldom-scolded boreen. Her freedom this morning to offer such a scheme came from an inherited purse, a purse to which she added when, never one to bury her talents, she bought and sold, sold and bought, dealing in bullocks and heifers, in-calf cows and cows with suckler calves, runners and weanlings. Anything which turned a pound she prized; she had even been known to buy a stripper.

Jude attended to where she was walking. Long *tráithníns* of grass

269

snapped against her ankles. She chose to continue stepping along the middle of the boreen, for the edges were badly potholed and the bordering hedges had now become straggly ditches, with here and there a dangling-down briar or a freakish branch of hawthorn. 'Nobody in their right minds could ever wish to come back here,' she scolded as she picked her steps towards Minnie's wicket gate. The watchdog approached, barking in defence of his realm. On guard too, his mistress ran cold water from the tap at the sink and splashed it all over her wrinkles. A comb fingered through her long hair, she tucked it in its knot before the approaching visitor could reach the front door.

Jude Fortune's knock was answered by her old neighbour. Her aged blue eyes screwed up slightly as she hesitated for a moment. It wasn't that she didn't recognise Jude; rather, she sensed trouble in her visitor. But she was a hostess to her every neighbour, so she made Jude welcome and offered to brew tea. Jude said yes to the notion, while at the same time her gaze took in the general tidiness of the house. Everything was quiet and calm in the kitchen. The pendulum swung over and back inside the grandfather clock, while from the now oil-fired range old heat nudged not dependent on humouring by turf from Holly Bog.

Minnie kept the chat on a very safe plane as she served tea to her neighbour. Fresh scones, still warm, she stood on a plate and then left it down beside Jude. They no longer sized each other up; each woman knew the strength of the other, and if they failed at all it was in secretly not knowing each other's weakness. It was Jude who made the first skirmish. She asked if there had been any word from Francis, her outspoken doubt sounding its hellish death knell in the quietness.

Minnie, munching as though she missed the meaning in Jude's question, waited until she took her next mouthful of tea and then swallowed before she made her reply. 'Musha then, woman, Frankie'll be back just like the swallows out in the turfshed,' she said. 'He'll home back here when the urge strikes him.'

'But what if he doesn't?' said Jude. 'Wouldn't it suit you better to sell this run-down place to me? I'll give you a fair price, and I'll even go one better – I'll give you right of residence till the end of your days. Now Minnie, sure you couldn't get a better offer than that.'

The listening clock and the nervous old woman stonewalled for a breather, and then the answer came, but this time there was a touch of flabbergastedness in the voice. 'Listen, woman,' and this was the second time she mentioned gender, 'you didn't hear me right. I'm not in the need of selling out, not now, not next week, not, not in a month of Sundays.'

'But' – and here Jude was butting in again – 'But what, Minnie, if I say I'll buy your place and give you the security of money, and then if Francis returns like the swallows, like you say he will, I'll give you my written word I'll sell him back the whole shebang for the same money as I paid you for it. Now sure you couldn't get fairer than that, and you can even ask your son and daughter before you agree to anything.'

'Have another cup of tea,' suggested Minnie as, rising, she crossed the Abbey stage and catching hold of the handle of the teapot, wielded it towards Jude's cup. The tea fried as it poured: the spout had been too near the heat. The hand holding Jude's cup suddenly withdrew it. Tea dribbled now down on the toes of Jude's black shoes, making her suddenly tuck them back in under her chair for safety's sake.

'Musha, the oul' pot is roasting hot,' humoured Minnie, her face hiding a smile, but by the time her neighbour's cup was suitably filled the crisis had played itself out and the old warrior was in harness still.

Jude had one more skelp at her neighbour's mustered nerve. 'You know, Minnie, as they say it's not viable to run a little seed of a place like this,' she said. 'Sure look at the state of everything, all you have in the fields is docks, thistles, ragworth –'

'And big foreign bullocks,' interjected Minnie.

Jude didn't quite catch what Minnie said, but she continued, 'This place needs money spending on it, and sure, what would you be doing forking out your pension?'

Never was such a battle fought in this kitchen. Never before had Minnie to delve so deep in order to fight back fear. Tick tock, tick tock, tick tock, said the thing under the stairs as, worried now, it talked to itself. Thump thump, thump thump, thump thump, beat Minnie O'Brien's heart. Grind grind, grind grind, grind grind, grated Jude's teeth in her muffling jaws. Then when the battle seemed neutered, when everything seemed to have been threshed out, Minnie spoke. 'Not if you gave me everything you own, Jude Fortune, would I give you a clod of my clay.' Those were the words she spoke. Tripping over each other they spilled from her lips, jiving until they stung the atmosphere which surrounded the two women. Sunday it most certainly was not, but like the proverbial Bullavander, the scald of the words fried this Monday until the red blouse on the visitor, feverish though it was in colour, turned funereal, as July the month grew into January, before retort could be made by the green-eyed woman.

Minnie was human garbage after her ordeal with her neighbour. Now she brewed a proper mug of strong tea. Moustached from hurrying into the mug's depths, she licked her top lip and laughed quietly. 'Jude's asshole'll never sit on my tree stumps,' she bragged now. 'Her hand'll not pick mushrooms from my far field. The big rock in the corner of the first field covered in wild strawberries is mine and my family's secret, we threaded big juicy strawberries onto *tráithníns* and took them home with us to have with cream from the dairy, and she thinks she can own such a holy place. Jude'd flatten my orchard, she never saw children race up an apple tree to get the last red apple up on the top branch. She never saw the sick chicken whose head had been pecked raw by the others grow up into a beautiful chequered grey hen who hatched out in the first field and marched home one fine morning leading a squadron of nine chicks all feathered and fine, a present for the one whose hand had nursed her poor, sore head just a short year before.' Now she forgot to drink any more of her tea, but just sat holding the mug between her welled hands. Her mind was way down the fields with Peter and the children. Her eyes saw the mowing machine striping the ground with swathes of green sward. She listened to the cogwheel as he reversed the horses. She again showed the children how to rob honey from bees' nests. Her crab-apple jelly came from the trees in the third field; in springtime their blossoms used to flower the sky with clouds of pink-white lies. Lost in reverie, she now cudgelled her neighbour's greed with a handful of dock seed. Fighting her off, she chorused her stubbornness with the crek-crek of the corncrake, and he down there inside the gate lying on his back in the meadow, thinking he could hold high the sky with his little brown feet.

## CHAPTER 82

Looking around the stores, Brendan searched for something for his mother. Eventually his eye spotted it, a black velvet hat in Bloomingdale's window. 'Gee, that'd look swell on her,' he said. He went inside and made his way to the department where hats stood like mushrooms growing in the river field. He asked to see the black hat in the window, but the glamorous assistant had no need to leave her department: she instead drew open a deep drawer and took from it the exact replica. 'It's for my mother,' enthused the cleric in mufti, and so saying he slid his hand way back over his greying waves. The girl held out the hat for inspection before spinning it in a circle on her index finger. 'Gee, it'll sure blow her mind,' she said, and he agreed, for he felt sure that they could not both be wrong. 'I'll take it,' he said, though there was a slight hesitation in his words and she, acting on his impulse, strung him along while she tissue-wrapped the hat. Now, stretching upwards, she lifted down a round, red-and-white striped box from a shelf and ceremoniously cushioned the hat down inside the box and secured the lid. Her mind was saying 'A sale's a sale,' but her voice was uttering how great a surprise his mother would get when she opened the box. Her customer, at this moment, couldn't measure her sales talk, but his gold card handed to her of the lovely pitch, he watched as she slid his American Express right in front of her till's computerised eye.

Brendan's step was far lighter as he left the store. 'She'll look great in this,' he mused. 'Lord knows she never had a penny to jingle on a tombstone,' he smiled, 'but this from New York'll sure blow her mind, as herself back there said.' As he walked his finger grew fat and blue, and all the while the red-and-white striped box swung to and fro with his every step. He had finally made up his mind to admit to his fear of flying and, following his psychologically flying thousands of miles in his virtual reality plane, his instructor his guru, he felt he had at last conquered his fear sufficiently to allow him book a seat on an Aer Lingus flight to Ireland.

Brendan O'Brien sat down in the toilet in the gents and drank a soft-drink-sized bottle of raw vodka. He said his act of contrition at least five times. He told himself to remember what he had for years been preaching, yes, about there being a time for being born, a time for dying and the time in between for living and saving the soul. But that was then and this was now, and now the truth was he was scared shitless and ready for retreat.

Dozens of times he looked at his watch, its hands, too, balking at the thoughts of the flight-time. 'Imagine, I've a whole hour yet to put in,' he reminded himself. Remembering the two Valium which his chauffeur had given him, he headed off to get a cup of coffee. 'Take one of these Valium, the missus swears by them,' he had said as he dropped them into the bishop's hand. 'What are they exactly?' the bishop asked, and Michael P. Curley laughed as he told him that his wife took them when she flew back to Dublin for her mother's funeral. 'Just take one and I promise you that your flight won't take a whit out of you,' he said.

Boarding time announced, the bishop made his jelly-legged way towards the plane. Following along behind the passengers, he didn't even notice the duty-free. He was welcomed on board by the astute hostesses: noticing his nervousness, and guessing the reason for his tanked-up state, they led him to a safe seat by a window, he thanking God every step of the way. 'Thanks be to God, sure there's nothing to it,' he told them. 'Nothing to it at all,' they replied. 'Thanks be to God, I'm not a bit afraid,' he told the little window beside him. 'Thanks be to God, sure isn't it only an aeroplane,' he said.

Brendan O'Brien was woken up when the meals were served in this great thing of storybook stories. Kettle boiled, was the idea implied as, aprons donned, those housewives of the skies served food to their flying scald-crows. Not so the cleric with his collar on his lap. His table, when he let it down, received their little tray of freebies, but having already had his fill of vodka and Valium he could only stay alert long enough to drink his cup of jet-black coffee.

He slept all the way home across the Atlantic Ocean, no way thinking of the yawning chasm between him and the rolling sea, for sleep, the cad and cancer of all types of foolish fearing, kept him in its clasp, he never being allowed to feel the dread of dropping down to play dead for the duration as, with grim mouths opening and closing they, the big and little fish, swarmed there to eat and then gloat over the flavour of blood and guts.

'Fasten your seatbelt, please,' were the first words he recognised as he surfaced from fuzzy reality. Really, though, he felt all right. The bottle of vodka at the airport and the tablet which his chauffeur gave him to take meant that he had no great trouble in his flying, for in truth he felt brave as a baby on the plane.

275

Shannon Airport awaited the big plane's touchdown, every minute timing its approach. Its man at the control tower talked his jargon, and the plane's pilot talked his holding back. The runway waited in anticipation, it the garden of linseed touchdown, as down and dropping came the Aer Lingus St Killian, just a matter of fact its creaming down.

Meanwhile up at the plane's little window, prayed a bishop, he from Ireland as well, 'Gee, God, I'll never more doubt Your existence, if only You'd bring this bollocks down!'

Down came the landing gear from the fuselage, down came the tail feathers as well, the white fairway beckoned the direction, grip, slam, shudder, the bollocks made it, 'Swell!'

## CHAPTER 83

His hired car seemed challenging to the man from brindled city. Now he was driving on the wrong side of the road and steering from the wrong seat. The voice from the car's radio sang about 'rain against my window pane', but it had it wrong, for outside in the Irish sky the mid-morning sun shone. It was love which made the singer target the sound the rain made but he, himself, the serious listener, knew how gilded the rain could be to a man dressed in black, rescuing his love by hiding behind his collar of stone. He joined in eventually and now he was uttering ages of pain to the lilt of Tina Turner's song.

Ireland, the libido of his life, flitted by as he drove raffishly towards his home. Nothing was the same, for where he long ago saw only the backs of houses and the rooftops of towns from the windows of a train, he now feverishly noticed this new Ireland, fit to team with the best he ever saw as he was driven or drove himself around the routes of America.

He stopped en route to freshen himself up before he hit home territory. A rub of the razor, a splash of his aftershave and then a pot of coffee and a sandwich saw him right again. He didn't want to appear looking bleary-eyed in Drumhollow. He, after all, was the one coming back having created his logarithm of fame and fortune.

'Was that how it was or am I raving?' he wondered as, driving through Huntstown, he became confused, for ever since his youth this town had reminded him of the towns in the cowboy films with its straight broad street and its few shops and saloons. Today, though, it had come miles out the road to meet him. Now new housing estates crowded each side of it, a big shopping mall lined up a bit nearer the town, and where long ago Igoe's lone petrol pump used to be, there now stood a brightly painted gas station, sheltering underneath a pagoda-style tiled roof.

'Traffic lights in Huntstown, are they serious?' he said as the red light forced him to a halt. He sat there idling in his row of traffic while other traffic had to be let flow from side streets which were never known to him of the Fair Days. The Market House still stood where it had; he noticed its clock read four o'clock. 'I'm almost there,' he said as, groping, he changed gear again and moved along on his last few miles towards home.

'All had changed, changed utterly,' he thought as he drove slowly through the village of his boy's element. Lungs swelling with emotion, he glanced from side to side. 'Her letters never gave even a hint of this,' he thought. 'Where has she been?' he said, he smiling at the thought of her. 'Look, the old church's gone,' he said as he looked at the wigwam-styled structure now there in its place. Under his strict gaze the building only resembled all that he was attempting to forget. Opposite it, on the sunny side of the street, the houses had been killed off too, and now where his grandfather's huckster's shop used be hung a green-and-grey striped awning, hiding the place where the name Humphrey once rode roughshod over the name Butler.

He nearly turned back when he saw the road gate with the boreen inside. Wilderness was the concept which crept into his mind. The plain truth was crass now as it confronted him. 'Hunger would be better than this,' he thought.

He opened the bolt and the gate swung only so far. Lifting it, he edged it the rest of the way. 'God, it sure does look awful,' he thought, now back seated in his car drinking sorrow as he kindred-bumped from one pothole to another all the way down to the house.

'Gee, that sure was one helluva ride,' he thought as, having excavated a route through the jungle of overgrown hedges, he pulled up in front of his old home. Not expecting any relief here either, he was startled by the blaze of red coming from the glass porch where, all along its window ledges, grew an absolute wall of bright red geraniums. As he got out of the car his eye fell on the wicket gate. 'She has it painted the same colour as the road gate,' he thought, surprised at his mother's sense of colour, for the fact was she had themed both of the gates with her scarlet red fatwah.

'Where would the postman be going at this hour of the evening?' wondered Minnie when she heard the sound of the motor engine out at the gate. Nosy as ever, she headed towards the curtain. Her hands were covered in flour, her fingers sticky from kneading the dough, and as she carried her cake to place it on the hot griddle on the stove loose flour had dredged down on her wellingtons. Despite the floury hands, though, she drew back with the tip of her finger her white lace cross-curtain and peeped out. There she saw him, the man backing back out of his car. 'Musha then, who can it be?' she fretted, as standing where she leaned she rested her finger now beneath her chin. She knew the man was coming towards the

278

open front door, but still she puzzled. 'Mother!' the stranger called, but she didn't heed him. Now, bags dumped in her hall, he came bounding in to her in the kitchen his face the picture of happiness. She, though, just stood there looking at him, caught in her time-warp, while he, seeing his neglect, stood looking at her, his voice suddenly vanished, the drop it took leaving him dumb as a dummy.

But she, the old dog for the hard road, was first to find her feet. Walking towards him she put out her floury hand and said, 'Welcome, Father, are you our new curate?' He, ignoring her hand and her question, swept her into his arms. 'Oh! you don't know me, you don't even know me,' he said, his voice blasting out in liquid words. 'I'm Brendan,' he gushed, but she, stealing a decorous glance up under his chin boasted, 'I've a boy by that name too.'

## CHAPTER 84

When Brendan was least expecting it, she fired the question which had been bothering a lifetime. She had him sitting at the end of the kitchen table. His brown egg was boiled to a T and the fresh griddle cake was dripping in melted butter. Then it happened. 'How's Frankie, did you ever find him?' she casually asked, knowing only too well the answer.

He, when he did answer, was casual in his reply as he filled her in on the scope of his search and the number of countries in which he had sought his brother. All the while he talked he was at the same time savouring his meal, the first real food he had eaten since yesterday in New York, thanks to his chauffeur's blue Valium combined with the vodka with which he had dosed himself prior to his departure from Kennedy. Now, he had conquered his fears, that spare blue Valium was still there in case, but here he was listening to his mother's letter-voice as she coaxed him to have his fourth cup of tea. It was strong now, strong enough to trot a Clydesdale upon, yet he took it from her, his tastebuds now just tingling caricatures of his conman's delicacy.

'It's very good to have you home, but you should have warned me you were coming,' she said breathlessly at every chance she got. And Brendan, humble and growing more so, told his relic of a mother that he too was delighted that he had come, that he was sorry for staying so long away. But she wouldn't hear of his apologising. 'Sure you were doing God's work, I never ever worried about you.'

Hero that he was, his homecoming cried itself from the rooftops. Busy neighbours brought news to even busier folk. 'Did you hear the Bishop's home and his mother didn't even recognise him?' But down where the news mattered most it didn't matter at all. All that mattered there was that though the bishop had left it a bit late to be coming back in search of his mother she seemed in no way put out by his absence. No, her agenda, though equally late in its bringing about, concerned the one who homed, though he found himself distracted by a job still awaiting him, God knows where.

A night's sleep in his own bed made a new man of Brendan. His old cap still hung on the back of his bedroom door. The mirror in the wardrobe was still the same mirror he had last looked in when he returned from the missions in Africa, but now, when he stood sideways, the mirror couldn't accommodate his belly. Meanwhile his bed too felt the difference, for where long ago its springs had stretched in tautness, it now surrendered, for when he woke at sunrise this morning it almost became sundown as, scrambling, he had to struggle from the hollow which his body had overnight made in the centre of the bed.

Homecoming, though, necessitated a stroll to the river, the river of his no return. Flow how it would, he never once saw it in his nightmares. Swanking along through his golf games or deep sea fishing from his friend's yacht, the river curling and gum-sucking in Drumhollow never figured, never came between him and his dreams.

'The fresh air'll give him an appetite,' thought Minnie as she came back inside from cutting a head of cauliflower for the dinner. The moment she entered the kitchen her gaze fell again on the round red-and-white box. She desperately wanted to see what was inside, but he was down at the river living out his green homecoming, so she set upon the box and opened it herself.

Minnie's eyes fell first upon the white packing paper. Her old work-worn hands mussed it aside. And as though lifting a baby from the crib she deftly lifted the black hat. Carrying it like she would a hot griddle cake, she brought it to the kitchen table. Leaving it down on a clean spot, she fetched the crutch mirror. Now, placing the hat upon her head, she pulled the veil down over her face. Her cheeks breathed out in admiration, but when she lifted the tip of the net the better to peep at her reflection she suddenly felt frightened for herself. Frightening herself still further, she said out loud, 'Musha, it mightn't be for me at all, I'd better put it back.' But too late, the door opened from the scullery and Brendan beheld the vision of his gaunt white-haired woman, she dressed in her navy-blue crossover bib covered in an all-over pattern of blue and red forget-me-nots, with inside it a blue blouse showing and on her feet a pair of cut-down wellingtons. His eyes travelled downwards and then crept slowly up again, until his gaze freshened itself on the American hat. He began to laugh, now, at the naivety of his purchase, his howls of laughter rocking the kitchen until Minnie, swiping the hat from her head, ran to replace it. 'I thought it was for me,' she defended herself, but he just nodded and nodded. All he could do was laugh now, laughing first at himself, laughing at his innocence; he laughed too when he thought back to the wine-and-cheese charity events in New York, the thin events, where from behind just such a creation as his mother's those fund-raising women would bow towards his grace and respectability.

Minnie kept her radio's volume turned down so that she and Brendan could chat over the music as, Frankie now forgotten for the moment, she instead planned dinner for her eldest son. This today was going to be a special meal, and on that account she went to the sideboard in the parlour and sought out her best lace tablecloth, the one which Peter had bought for her for their silver wedding anniversary.

Like some undertaker she shook wide swipes until the tablecloth dressed her kitchen table. The oilcloth, the permanent table-covering, looked out through every hole and hollow trying, it seemed, to spoil the lace tracework. Her hands flattened the lace where the creases highed. Then, that done, she with great pride began to set her best willow-pattern blues upon the white luminous lesson. Her visitor didn't stir, sitting there wilting with regret. 'How could I?' worried his worries. But she was wanting, desperately wanting, to secure her late Peter's placing at this table. 'He'd be gob-smacked if he could only see me and a bishop having dinner off his cloth,' she mused, but her son was at this moment seeing the dust-shroud on the blue plates. He didn't want to be obvious, so while she was teeming the potatoes he grabbed the plates and wiped them with his sleeve. 'How's that for hygiene,' he giggled, and sat down as though he had never stirred.

As they shared this meal he was very conscious that this menu was exactly what she would have had herself. The fried bacon seemed an odd bedfellow beside the cauliflower. Her white sauce today could never make up for the loss of his favourite steak, his filet mignon, but the truth was he somehow felt satisfied after his dinner. 'You'll have a *braoneen* of lemonade to wash down your dinner,' she said, as though he were a child, and hero that he was, he sacked the tumbler of red lemonade in one wild swallowing. He had forgotten his experience in Greene's Hotel, and so was caught off guard when the lemonade erupted and peed down his nose. No dessert decorated his palate at all, no flaming crêpe Suzette, only a slice of her spotted dog washed down with a mug of tea. He hadn't for a long time enjoyed anything quite like this next-to-nothing dinner, and the best part was that he seemed satisfied, really satisfied.

When Minnie blessed herself today she was only doing what she had done all down her lifetime. She told her son of the neighbour she had in Felix Fortune. 'He's just the dead opposite of his mother, and believe me, son, you'd dread her just as much as you'd love him.' She looked the picture of alertness as she described her neighbours yet once more. Her letters to him had told of her blind-blood son, Felix, and how he fended for her despite his mother's objections. 'Ne'er the vegetable I'd have growing if it wasn't for him and little Hughie, and there's another thing,' she said, 'ne'er a drop of milk I'd have by times, only that little boy drops down with the carton. It's every second day he comes,' she said, 'and before the evening's out he'll be here.' Her history at the hands of Felix told only good vibes, but when she spoke of Felix's mother her voice took on a dead weight.

Every creature heard the news that the bishop was back – all, that is, bar Jude Fortune. Her Mercedes crept up and down her avenue, she incommunicado inside in it. Weeds now grew all along her municipality: her blunt-nosed car thinned them out wherever its tyres gummed, but otherwise the main avenue was neglected. It wasn't for want of money that the no longer tended avenue looked so, rather it was the result of a new miserliness. Now, though she each day played out her gambler's games, each stroke increasing her paper worth, she had no desire to employ any locals to scuffle and gravel her front avenue, for money had become her obsession, money was the incense through which her god glowed. Funnily enough though, the richer she became the more she watched as her old neighbour, on the other side of the mearing, grew poorer. She had of late tried to give the lone woman a hand-out, but no, she wouldn't part with her fields. Now, while she continued to watch, the lonely years filled those same fields with holly trees, not red-berried holly, but indelicate thorny trees, gravedigging and berryless. Only the snipe felt sorry for poor Minnie O'Brien, the snipe, the bird with the human voice, as plying his eh-heh-heh-heh laugh he tried all the while to prop her up till the child came home.

## CHAPTER 85

This morning the light was just seeping through the space in the drapes when Jude opened her eyes. She glanced at the quartz clock on her bedside table, its time glowing green at five o'clock. 'It's far too early to get up,' she thought. 'Sure I haven't been asleep that long.' But now that she was awake she stretched her body down the whole length of the bed, riding out her sense of physical wellbeing. Suddenly the calf of her left leg spasmed, the cramp bulging the muscle in brickwork building. 'Damn and blast to hell,' she said, 'I've that bloody cramp again,' and glawming at the duvet she scrambled from the bed. Every trick in the bag she tried, as she set about breaking the cramp's grip. 'I'd need to walk more,' she urged herself when relief did eventually come. 'Going everywhere in that Jeep has given my heart no great exercise at all,' she scolded.

The woman tested the rare morning as, not bothering with the Jeep, she set off on foot to herd. The dog was delighted, now he could trot his greatness beside his mistress. He wasn't the slightest bit interested in rabbits: he crowned his existence as a guard-dog, the night-time his for his sputnik's orbiting.

'I'll be meeting myself coming back all day,' thought Jude Fortune as, feeling lighthearted now, she set about preparing a snack for herself. The Jeep left behind she had, with stiff calf-muscle and all, walked the whole length of her vast farm, and now back home she was feeling peckish after her exertions. 'I'll have a spot of gooseberry jam on this,' she thought. 'The tartish taste might be nice on the wholemeal bread.' The jam was in a few earthenware pound jars down at the cool dark end of the shelves in the larder. Opening the doors, she glanced at the rows of jars of jams and preserves lined up before her, but stretching in further, she had just gripped hold of one of the earthenware pots when something touched the back of her hand. A whisper of a touch was all it was, yet that whisper stuck her to the floor, frozen rigid. Not for some moments could she withdraw her hand, for a thin dread had in fact gripped the mental manoeuvring of her mind. True to form though she eventually bullied herself, and withdrawing her hand she left the thing down on the thing and stood staring at the sinned spot on the back of her hand, the spot where long ago the first touch would needle. The terror was back now, there it was rind and all, its black wiry hairs growing from the dirty site on the back of her sleeping child's hand. Now she came over all hot and sweaty: her ears heard again his whispered stuff; her heart flittered in tragic beat, his weight making her own voice become stifled in her throat. Her fund of hopelessness drained back down along her fine-tuned thighs before, with a sudden jerk, she wrenched the jar off of the shelf and staggered towards the table. For what seemed an age she just sat there, staring past her terror. Suddenly she splayed her fingers in a great fanshape and, jumping to her feet, said, 'Come on, girl, the bastard owned you long enough, get back on track, it's business as usual so get a move on.'

Enemy number one, the widow on the farm adjoining hers,

limped nervously across her eyes. 'I know,' she thought, 'I'll go over later on and bring her the pot of gooseberry jam, a sort of peace offering it can be. Her house is getting shoddier by the day, you know that,' she told herself, 'and now the poor ol' bag isn't even able to go down the famous fields. So you say you'll save her the trouble, say you'll mind the set-up for her, but don't forget to rub it in about Francis never coming back, cause he can't, cause he's dead meat. Remind her again, too, of your offer to buy her out, you'll give her the money for her bits and pieces and she'll be still able to live on where she always lived. Make sure not to mention anything about her two white hopes of grandsons, wouldn't you get the awful cod if the hag left her place to either of them, but then what would they want with it, or do with it? You never know, you might get her out o' there yet, and then you could flatten the ol' house and sheds and reclaim the whole place before joining it on to your own. Won't Hugh be the bucko who'll know how to farm the whole lot. He's different from his daddy. Poor Felix was never interested. Just hand him sheets of figures, the more complicated, the better he liked it. A distant little boy he always was, but when he was handled carefully, never made too much of, never made a hardly-able of, not like that woman over there made of her kids, he turned out all right.'

As the morning advanced, so too did the green-eyed one's plans develop. She spent time titivating herself in readiness for her trip to Minnie's house. Her game the morning rallied, for now she had a goal in mind, a game of hide and seek to play.

'Have you set your agenda?' she scolded as, hiding the jar behind her back and holding it clutched with both hands, she set out to walk to Minnie O'Brien's house. 'It's eleven o'clock now,' she had reminded Lily, the maid. 'Don't forget to have lunch ready for one o'clock, cause today's the day for Felix to drop by.'

Walking where she normally drove, she had time and to spare for her rehearsal of her plan of campaign. Time and again she trapped Minnie into giving way. 'Hurry up now,' she eventually said, now her hunt was really on.

The road gate feared for its owner. The boreen chattered its teeth then to bowl over under her flat-heeled shoes. Trees swayed in whispering. The wicket gate waited. Suddenly she saw it, just a glimpse through the hawthorns, the black motor car, black playing a sunbathing game, light leppin' off of it like daggers, but in her direction. Now she stood stuck up to her eyes in jitters. Her brain said go on, but her feet wouldn't obey. Earth and sky axled, but there she stayed, holding a jar of jam. Bolting then, she shot forward and viewed the wicket gate. A big mouthful of air trapped, she pressed down the bolt and pushed it in. Turning to close it she let the gate slip from her grip and, as though travelling in a hearse, the gate slammed to, leaving its prisoner on the wrong side of the law. Reeling, she worried her way to the front door, and there her hand lifted up Minnie's brass knocker, but before she could strike her summons the door fell open and a priest stood, looking toiled inquiry at her.

Jude Fortune had got a double fright all within a few seconds, so when she beheld the visitor she became bamboozled and blabber-mouthed. Brendan stood there in the doorway, looking from eyes of long ago, but what he saw simply bothered him. Kindly, he stepped forward and, stretching out his welcoming hand to his neighbour, found he was given a pot of jam. Jude was mixed up, her co-ordination awry, her voice breathlessly mumbling as her eyes narrowed in nervous blindness. All she could think of now was the reason for her coming so she blurted out, 'The meadow field is out, cause my cattle'll break in, cause there's no fence to stop them.'

But the man put his free hand around her waist and led her inside. 'Don't you recognise your old neighbour?' he gently asked, as now his mother mosied out to see who it was. The women held each other's gaze, but it was the visitor who stressed how glad he was to see Jude. Seeing her adversary, though, made Jude assert herself.

'Father Brendan,' she gushed, 'forgive an old friend, sure I didn't recognise you,' and so saying out she thrust her hand. But too late, he had turned to lead the way towards the parlour.

Brendan's manner was, in fact, welcoming, but Jude's carry-on almost defeated his best efforts. 'Follow mother into the parlour and make yourself at home,' he invited. Jude didn't sit down though, but instead held out her hand again, saying, 'Father, Bishop, Your Grace, you're greatly changed, I didn't know if you were Francis, sure I haven't seen hide nor hair of you boys in forty years.'

He shushed her, though, by saying 'Listen here, Jude, don't be minding Bishop, Your Grace, I'm Brendan, always was and always will be.' He took her outstretched hand in his left one and, squeezing it, led her to an armchair. 'Mother,' he said, 'sit you down too and then we can have a chat.'

Minnie, looking up into his face, asked, 'What did the wan say about Frankie, is he home too?' and Brendan, not knowing that his mother was the fly in the ointment where Jude's plans were concerned, said, 'Mother is a bit confused today,' as lining her into a chair he sat down to face the two neighbouring women. He chatted easily, about Jude's life, about her son Felix, about Felix's young son, Hugh. This conversation suited Minnie to a T, for her brain was perfect on the past, but what happened yesterday could be her bogeyman.

Minnie, as usual, asked her neighbour to have tea and, the chat in full swing now, left the others talking and went to the kitchen. Her son was as a boy again while Jude took her chance to season his memories with the salt and pepper of her findings. She was over-anxious to talk, and all the time wished to highlight how very normal she was despite her shaky entry. Her voice was quiet now and her condition laid back, but Brendan couldn't help noticing her clammy face. Pretending not to notice, he suggested he'd find out what was delaying their hostess and going to the kitchen to investigate he found Minnie seated in her chair having a mug of tea and one of the cream slices which he had bought in Huntstown that morning. His humour tripped him up when he beheld the picture, and he was muted by laughter when his mother said, 'You're just in time for a cuppa, get the teapot there and pour it out before it gets too strong.' He still wasn't able to answer while, with shaking hands, he set his mother's tray. Marvelling to himself, he thought, 'If I hadn't come she'd have polished off the other pastries as well.' Now, like a man in charge of a child, he ushered his mother back to her bolstered post. She cantered before him as, stimulated by the tea, she now confronted Jude with all the verve which had stood her coldly down through the years of her woman's darkness.

## CHAPTER 86

The voice of the weatherman rose on the ether as he gave his forecast this Tuesday morning. Looking towards the Drumhollow skies, Jude Fortune sat listening to him. The lesson of the cramps forgotten for the moment, she had this morning driven the Jeep, steering it through all its ruts and raves, her big Alsatian dog galloping full out beside her, loyally trying to keep his side of the bargain.

Jude always threw a few words of praise to the dog following their foolish journeys, for the fact was her son Felix would, from his location away on the distant severity of the mearing, and come first light, have set out to herd his mother's stock. He did the herding as though he had a share in the farm's income, but nothing could be further from the truth for, when he had that job done each morning, he set off to his work in the bank, while his wife Teresa went in the other direction to her teaching job in the vocational school. There never had been any aggro between his mother and himself, for he always remembered his father's advice when he begged his young son never to push his mother to the brink, and the truth was he had to this very day kept that warning in mind, kept the reliant under his hat, never housed his new wife in Derby House, but rather moved well away to where he could still be of use and there, out of earshot, had built his own split-level bungalow.

Neighbours pillbox-spilled reasons for his actions, but none of them had ever had the gall to ask him why, or to dabble in his looking-glass. From his vantage point he watched them as they studied him, but what they could never know was that he admired and respected his mother, respected her business acumen, knowing full well that come each night she still screamed the hours away there in her never-to-be-told lemonade's mugshot.

Derby House, resting after the night's disturbance, now sunned its back for comfort. Soon that early morning sun would have the setting sweetened, the windows lit in thunder and light, the virginia creeper glossed and glowing and last night's terrible sounds buried underneath its golden skirts.

Lily, the new girl from the village, having heard the Jeep arrive back in the yard set Jude's breakfast on the table in the breakfast room. That chore finished, she set off through the house, about to open the windows for the weather. October gushed in immediately she opened each window, its air running through the house, carrying glue-smelling freshness in the makeshift hope that another night's trouble could be fended off, if it filled the master bedroom with calm air.

Downstairs Jude, as usual, sat down to eat her breakfast while she listened to *Morning Ireland*. Chewing, she suddenly stopped in her tracks, wondering if she was hearing right. The presenter, authority in his voice, its timbre unique, was telling the most God-awful news ever heard in Derby House. The articulation which this morning told the scary tidings with such skill was imparting news of the worst-ever collapse in Wall Street. As she sat listening, she who was well one moment was real dead the next, for the news of that plunge which had hurt testicles the world over was hurting her too, for, wombed-woman that she was, she had just now heard that her whole fortune was gone. Yes, it was gone, too well she knew. The entire fortune, the savings she had invested in her sacred stocks and shares, was gone, all gone, kaput, ka-bleedin'-bloody-put, but these words were not her words for she, out of her mind now, had plunged into a savage dirge, over and over again screaming, 'It's gone, all gone, down the bloody Swanee it's all gone, down the Swanee.' Staring before her, she got from the table and blindly groped towards the back door, her voice all the while wailing its slimy loss.

## CHAPTER 87

Over the fields and far away in Minnie O'Brien's house, her visitor, the Bishop, couldn't sleep for the barking of the dog. He couldn't sleep at all, dog or no dog. Great yawns broke from his jollers as he lay listening, but though on holiday he wasn't luxuriating in his bed of rest. Holy man that he once thought he was, he now lay heaped in his body of fabulous gumption. He had courted his hierarchical friends at every chance, and when promotion beckoned he was grateful for the cross. 'Terrible responsibility,' he claimed as explanation for it, but the reality told of a man who thought himself a step above buttermilk. He pontificated to his priests when he had their ear, he preached to his people come confirmation day, he visited the seminary to hesitate with the new and innocent novices, and come their ordination day he chrismed their palms to prove his right. Now he was back in his bedrocked-bed, but sleep still remained in New York. Shored by his old mother's grace, he attempted to fence his ditch. As he lined up his life for inspection he trimmed his wings, frowning only at the degree of discomfort he felt as he lay on the hard bed of dread. His face flattened out now as the bishop lay down in repose, gone the fine contour of his fair young features. Instead his pole tottered from the fullness of his cheeks, while his chins dewlapped down onto his body. No wonder his own mother had failed to recognise him, for youth had well-sprung away, as, over sixty now, he wandered from pillar to post.

The clock chimed out the hours, down where it stood beneath the stairs. Steeling himself, he counted the chimes. Six chimes, the seventh didn't come, so now he worried until he got from his bed. Praying before the crucifix, the dead figure hanging where it had hung long ago, holy smoke came from his lips. The first smoke of the day, he thought, as his cigarette smouldered in his fingered grip. Addressing his saviour, he strewed his best intentions before his lid-locked gaze, each thought gonging his sincerity. Humbly now, he begged for just one more chance, when as sure as be damned he'd play a better role to his bishop's purple.

The stairs creaked as he descended to the kitchen. Trying not to turn his holiday into a theatre of the absurd, he boiled the electric kettle. No percolator here, he spooned three heaped spoons of instant coffee into a mug and scalded it with boiling water. Just as it was, hot strong coffee, that was all he needed.

The black coffee downed, he went into the bathroom to shave his faggot's face. Punting his cheeks, he dragged his cheap safety razor down and across his countenance. That gory job complete, he baffled his hands into a bowl shape and blowing like a whale gushed the water up into his morning's findings. No set of towels hung here in his mother's bathroom, only her coarse hard luck one, and taking it up he stung himself dry.

Giving a mere thought to his Mary-land, he crossed himself in a brushing-a-fly-off-his-nose style as he set out for Holly Bog. Where he was going didn't need a man to be shaved and shorn, but nonetheless he felt comfortable, for his best face was ready to meet and greet any neighbour en route.

The flight path to Holly Bog brought him back to his bacon and cabbage days, but the path he used trot along was now no more. There were countless tracks criss-crossing but they could lead anywhere; he only stole his path from a great-licked Peggy's Leg.

'Hold on to m'hand or you'll get prodded with the thistles,' his father's voice now came back, and reacting as though he were a child he felt his hand being comforted in someone else's clasp. 'Ah! don't be such an eejit,' his better senses rendered. 'Sure isn't he below there in the cemetery, nineteen fifty-one, remember.'

Stepping along through the morning's dew, the grasses whished and swished against his wellingtons. He was feeling good, his heart happy enough with its findings at home. 'If mother was taken away from her natural environment I feel she sure wouldn't last long,' he surmised, 'and then again, if she didn't have to hang in there in case Frankie'd come, I guess she'd be gone long ago.' The mention of his brother brought him back to the days spent humouring the child so much younger than either himself or Sheila. Playing big brother, he had oftentimes had to be both father and mother to Frankie. Their rote-learnt nonsense for their games of 'tig,' 'hide and go seek' and riddles tried now to humiliate him, the words 'Indy tindy' setting him off on his search. 'How's this it went?' he said, but once he fine-tuned the words he got going.

> Indy tindy
> Terry bury
> Bumpty seedy
> Over Dover
> Dick Mullann
> Tom Thrush

293

Ear
Ore
Ire
OUT.

Now he was off, his brain busting to wrench out its canopy of wordplay. Puzzling and prodding, he got the next one to rescue itself from drowning.

Ittle attle
Bluebottle
Ittle
Attle
Out
I fell over
A bottle of stout
The bottle broke
The stout came out
Ittle attle
Bluebottle
Ittle attle OUT.

Tittering to himself, he continued along, his notions scanning the ground and realm which was trespassing on his mind. He was enjoying himself as he tried again and again to dig up dead bodies. 'Big Bullavander sitting in the hall' egged him to go on. 'How does it go?' he said as he latched on again to the first line:

'Big Bullavander sitting in the hall,
Give him much, give him little
He'll take all.
Give him water and he'll die,
Give him butter and he'll fry. What is he?'

The question tripped off his tongue just as though it too was part of the riddle, and the answer, the child's answer, coming from his

soul, was impatient in its muted shouting: 'It's a fire, it's a fire.'
Now he was hooked, now he was on to the next one:

> 'As green as grass and it is not grass,
> As red as blood and it is not blood,
> As black as ink and it is not ink. What is it?
> It's a blackberry from bud to fruit.'

The answer was far older than himself, and he remembered now
how the very first time he heard it he was puzzled, had to dwell on
it, every change in the fruit had to be reasoned out in his child's
mind. It was different, though, with the next one:

> 'One lady, two lady, three lady, pan,
> Hopster, vinegar, Irishman,
> Judy Caddie, Jack o'the laddie,
> Ink Pink,
> Sty Stow,
> Stop Stink. Out goes he.'

The names were where sense pumped at seven; sense or reason had
no business checking on rhyme. It was as he crossed the ditch
between two neighbouring farms that the next free-for-all grained
in his memory:

> 'One brightem nightem,
> Moonem shinem,
> Crossem stilem,
> Breechem torem,
> Ramem damnem,
> Et in saecula saeculorum.'

The madness of what he had just remembered made him giggle, for
he knew that his best Latin scholarship could not crack the stone on
which those words were set.

As he tramped along he grew busy trying to evince the connection, if any, between his portmanteau of druidic nonsense and where experts were at in the world of computer science and data processing. 'I'd love to see them cracking the "brightem nightem" stuff of folk memory,' he thought. 'Imagine the world's folk memory . . . could we have there in it the bedrock or possibly the core of our consciousness?' he wondered.

He was growing more fascinated by the step when, as though to mock him, out tumbled his own mother's rhyme:

'Eat when you're hungry,
Drink when you're dry.
Money when you want it,
And heaven when you die.'

'She's no joke, never was,' he thought, and now he smirked.

'What walks with its head down?' the teaser came. 'Ah! shut up,' he thought. 'That stuff'd drive you insane.' He stopped for a moment and looked all around him and then, his sights set, continued on his way.

His wellington boots, the old ones his father had last stood in, never needed a tack or stud in their soles, but since God was a boy festered fingers had tacked on soles to leather boots and shoes, and truth to tell those brads and studs did, for their lifetime and more besides, walk with their heads down. 'Gee, isn't it a strange wavelength to be on, here on the way to a bog,' he thought. Sessions would he like to have had, here where he was heading, for damned well he sensed that the stories slewing from his mind belonged to other minds, minds of people long, long buried, but natives of Holly Bog, wonderful in their time, their consciousness embedded deep in his own psyche.

Meandering paths still invited him to go this way or that, but he knew they were but cattle tracks. His was the route the crow flies, and he padded along now through places where he had played run and jump games with Sheila and the child. 'Brendie carry's across,' came Frankie's crying plea, but when he came to the place where he used to lift him and carry him across, he got the land of his life. The old board had wombed itself in the crestfallen drain, and now he was as drained as the child once was, so it took him some seconds before he could make ready for the jump. Backing, he gamely squared himself and, like an Olympic hop-step-and-jump merchant, began his run towards Becher's. Up and over he went, but if it wasn't for the young birch sapling he'd have arsed back into the bog drain. Bursting out laughing, he thought of his secretary back there in his 'Streetcar Named Desire', and the more he laughed the more he wanted to. He eventually got to his feet, his innards having just gone on a return trip to Connecticut. Big belly settled back, the better to allow bygone by bold bygone, he dusted himself down and set off for their own turf bank.

Just as though it were yesterday, his feet led him to the turf bank. There it lay, waiting for an O'Brien footfall. The face of the high-bank stared at him, a grey straggly skin coating every inch of its Fenian nothingness. The boghole, standing where it filled itself all those awful years ago, now held his gaze trapped in its silky, bonded mirror. Regrets came tooling their way into his mind. He could almost hear again his father's voice, coming up to him from the workplace down below in the bottom of the boghole. Yes, he counted again the boards of turf which they could win from their bog. In a good harvest they could cut sixteen boards of peat before yielding the vacuum to encroaching torrents of held back moisture. He looked to the line of pathways on which he used wheel his loads of brown sods. His barrow used lurch along, he remembered. He realised now that that load of turf nesting on it came from down deep in the bog – so deep did it thrive that it in fact held plans and place-names belonging to the hit-and-miss neighbours, who in their time were earmarking the very first fields ever to be farmed by mesolithic man. He stood for an age listening to the lessons from Holly Bog, and turning then sauntered back towards the road, towards that drain which in the distance waited, towards that time now when he must think of returning to the real world, the world of make-believe gone mad.

Brendan headed back on the path towards Becher's Brook, but this time he was jumping from the high side down. No Connecticut this time, for this sturdy fellow now jumping held himself to himself and landed safely the home side of the drain. His belly hinted only secretly, for now this bogman remembered how he once thought, and though his hod creaked in his ear he strode along the run-and-jump paths towards his own five fields.

## CHAPTER 88

Back at base camp, the clock listened carefully before chiming eight bells. Minnie sat up to count out the numbers. 'Musha, 'tis eight o'clock and no one up,' she chided and, grabbing hold of the bedclothes, she dyed her daymares in gumption. She forgot that she had someone in residence as she set about using the goes-under. The sound, gentle at first, flowed then in pell-mell, lilting the moment she turned on her waterworks. 'Musha, it's the late cup of tea that plays oul' Harry,' she observed as, holding on to the bedpost, she straightened up again. Now she began to ease the chamberpot back under the bed, trying not to spill the fill as she nudged it with her toe. Hustling into her clothes, she then gathered her hairpins and gravitated towards the top landing. Her eye streamlined the open bedroom door, and sluishing her slippers towards it she stood nonplussed. She looked inside at the bed, all dishevelled, but nothing came to her, nothing at all. Hairpins still held tight in one hand, she gripped the knob with the other then, shrugging her shoulders, she let go and sloothered down the stairs.

Her habits of a lifetime drove Minnie towards the stove, but realising her faux-pas, she plugged in the electric kettle to boil. In no time she had made a scalding mug of tea, her mind needing it even more than her brain. She was in fact down at the bottom of the mug and dragging on the dregs before her mind had anointed itself, and then it was that her gaze fell on the stock and collar hanging on the door. 'Ah for God's sake will you look, if I didn't forget for the minute,' she teased herself as randomly she walked towards her teeth in their glass.

Squeezing a maggot of toothpaste onto her brush, she scoured them then sluiced them and, satisfied with their appearance, brought them towards the mirror. 'That's more like it,' she thought as she settled them in her mouth again, then, remembering she had visitors, gainfully swallowed them into place.


## CHAPTER 89


Brandishing a stout stick, Brendan cut his way through high thistles in the river field. He had crossed over two neighbouring farms on his shortcut to the bog and now, back in his own terrain, he stood for a while singling out the reclamation which needed doing. The stone-lined drinking place was dilapidated, and to add insult to injury he noticed all the breaches of the riverbank where big bullocks had broken down the banks to form willy-nilly drinking spots.

He stood regretting Frankie's disappearance, for the truth was this farm needed to be taken in hand. His thoughts, though, froze in his skull for at this very instant, over on the other side of the mearing, he had just glimpsed a person dropping into the trout pool.

Torpedo-fashion he darted towards the mearing, bursting through brambles and bushes as though they weren't there. His eyes were locked on that sinister trout pool which malevolently waited, shading itself beneath a big overhanging hawthorn bush. They, as children, had always been warned away from it, for its depth held a threat even then, now though he was acting on impulse, his feet hurtling their steps towards its brink.

As though gregging him, the silent black mirror waited. Out next to him, it bordered itself with blue sky, and for devilment, right there where it was deepest floated a linnet's nest made of hair and white scalp.

Never thinking of himself he leapt in, and displacing water got a glimpse of a woman. Grabbing her, he mauled and pulled, hauled and plunged, now recognising the maenad whom his hands held. She struggled to drown him too, but his strength headed her towards the shallows. She, though, holding her death's grip on him, struggled to drag him with her, but the more she struggled the more he dragged her out. Bundling her at last onto the bank, he rolled her over on her stomach, his instinct guiding him what to do as, pressing down on her, he watched with relief as river water puked from her mouth.

The struggle of the Titans it had been, but standing there, his wellingtons full of water, he felt satisfied that he had managed to rescue his neighbour while she, stymied, struggled still, her muffled voice horror-storying the Swanee River song.

Brendan knew he had to get Jude home, had to get help, had to locate her son, but first of all he had to get her on her feet. Stooping down beside his miracle, he coaxed and cajoled her. Gradually moving her into a kneeling position, then dragging and lifting her, he managed to get her standing, she all the while muttering her mind's hell.

'So far so good,' thought the rescuer as he waltzed the frenzied woman towards her home. Looking backwards while he moved her forwards she, the drowned rat, was, he noticed, fading as a person. By the time they reached her back door her maid Lily was there to meet them, and the stir created by her mistress's bizarre behaviour in the kitchen was millimurder of the first order.

A brief and hurried phone call brought Felix Fortune driving boot to the board into his mother's yard. The tinder-box which had ever been a mystery to his boyhood's understanding grew all the time more mysterious. His mother being fished out of the trout pool was something which he could never have imagined, and now here he came, rushing to see for himself the greg which had tripped her reasoning. As he entered the kitchen, the place where she always reigned queen, he found her sitting there half-dressed and huddled, shivering out a phrased singsong about the river Swanee.

## CHAPTER 90

Every bend destroyed the speed of the car bringing Jude Fortune to St Kieran's Hospital. Felix knew the road like the back of his hand but now, desperate to follow Dr Dick Lane's advice, he drove like Sterling Moss. Grim faced, she sat beside him, but navigator to her own son she was not. No, she was never like any other fellow's mother, he only ever knew her through the warning he had heard in his father's words. 'Don't ever push your mother to the brink, son,' his daddy had coaxed him, and to this very day he had never understood why. He never could fathom why his mother screamed in the night, and though his father was dead now for many many years, he, remembering the secret between them, kept a respectful distance from her as he sinecured for his father's sake. But now here he sat beside his father's puzzle, and though he never did push his mother to the brink, a sweet lot of good it seemed he had done, for today the brink had been breached as, demented, she herself had done the pushing.

The asylum had, down his lifetime, always trestled his eyeline as it hulked inside its high stone walls always nudging for notice, as it were, despite its terrible secrets. Nobody ever came out once signed in, and nobody out ever went in by choice. Now here he sat behind his steering wheel, as though he wished to test the adage, bringing his own mother to hospitalise her in the place of hard luck stories.

The big wrought-iron gates stood wide open and welcoming as Felix drove through with his mother on to the curling devotion of avenues. Bright red salvia still filled the flower beds, while white alyssum interspersed with blue lobelia bordered their red fire. Only one bed, near the great front door, contained something different. Strutting inside its round sore was a contretemps of love-lies-bleeding, their dangling snots of deep maroon stirring in the breeze; they never stopped their thinking as they cuggered to their hearts' content inside their border of brilliant yellow tagetes.

The woman, the poor soul meant to notice the flowers, sat beside her son, her hands staging battles with each other. Her face looked gaunt and her eyes glanced every which way. Only her mouth felt any tremble of relief for, before the fact and after the fact, it spoke about the Swanee. Sounding severe by times, that mouth swirled along, for the avenues set out before this woman of graft were but tributaries to her frenetic rondo.

The hungry hospital stood there waiting. Its walls were of granite, its windows twinned and brooding. From its tumbledown of slates tall chimneys grew, and though fitted out with yellow pots, at no chimney did white smoke ooze through. Its great front door stood closed, its oakwood game and bagatelle to those snotty flowers in their collared bed. Graveyard-funded, the hospital was. An arrow brightly indicated the avenue by which the car containing the hang-dog should travel in order to reach the shotgun and cartridge ward where, on a pink Jiminy-cricket form, this hinting son was about to sign in his mother.

Witness to the march of the duds, the long flagstoned corridor drank in the sound of Jude Fortune's footsteps as, wasted between two white-uniformed women, she was led away. Winsome in greatness, she now walked to the sound of keys jangling and doors slamming shut behind her.

Felix, her son, stood transfixed as the nurses led their new admission away. He hurt greatly, his childhood's freakish mother crowned now in recognition. 'No wonder,' he thought, 'that she made such a chorrawhibble of wanting to be alone at home, and there she is now and I haven't a clue what's bugging her or what it was that bugged her as far back as I can remember.' Now he loved her in a tender way. For the first time in his life, he saw her as frail and human. He now even noticed the dowager's hump on her shoulders as, without even knowing where she was, she loitered with folks whom she would never have recognised as being worthy of her company.

Free now to stand there and stare, Felix felt satisfied that he had done his best to pretend that he knew something about his mother. But the hospital staff thought differently. They were perplexed by his not being able to give them some insight into his mother's psychosis. He seemed like an ordinary son, but for all the help he could give he might as well have been but a handyman on his mother's farm. He had heard of Stephen Foster, could even sing a couple of bars of 'Swanee', but what it had to do with his mother in the trout pool was baffling and bewildering in the extreme. Crisis or no crisis, all he had for guidance was what his father warned when they stood fishing together. His mind could still remember his father's hug when he told him that his mother really did love him and want him, but that she thought the best way to bring up a boy was to be strict with him while at the same time she secretly loved him in her heart. He told his father that evening that he loved Minnie O'Brien better but his father, he remembered now, told him, even warned him, about ever saying such a thing to his mother. 'Never push her to the brink, son,' was another sentence from that evening's fishing, and, trained by his father always to be careful near the brink of the river, he couldn't then understand how any boy could push his mammy over the brink.

Never once did Felix Fortune break his boy's silence. Never once did his mother hear about that which his father said in confidence to him. He was so afraid to be left alone with neither a father or mother that he kept his secret sadness secret. Secretly he feared, too, for his mother, an inexplicable fear, but it was strong enough to break a boy into a man at the tender age of six.

Whenever Felix hunted for love, he found a share in his next-door neighbour's house. Minnie O'Brien treated him like one of her own. She felt for the little boy when his father died, and from there out she linked her home to him. From the very first time the child met her to this very day, he had a quiet, caring friend in her. She was ever the catalyst to the little fellow's needs. His own home was big, busy and cold, while hers was sunny, warm and well-heeled in home-baked treats. Dreadful things told in his little brain, but when Mrs O'Brien hugged him and insisted on his having a scone, a helping of apple pie or a plateful of dinner, he was made to feel important, to feel he belonged even, and the softness incurred then set him up to fashion himself as a together man.

Minnie would have consoled him today if she was having a good day, if her alertness was firing on all cylinders. And strange to say, they were firing perfectly today, there in the sharpest thingumajig of her mind.

# CHAPTER 91

Brendan O'Brien hid his damp clothes from his mother as he sidled up the stairs. But Minnie O'Brien was no daw where a son was trying to pull a quick one on her. Despite her years and her human frailty, she ordered Brendan back to the kitchen. 'Come back down here and tell me where you've been,' she said as though he were a five-year-old and he, astonished by her rifle-shot, returned, knowing better than to try and deceive her. It was a long story, but he gave this neighbour a full account of Jude Fortune's actions. Now he heard the story of a nimble little woman who stood in her gap trying to fend off Jude's every onslaught. The truth will out, and when the son heard what this lone woman had done for her family and her Ottoman Empire he marvelled. Now he knew why her letters always asked if he had heard anything of Frankie.

The water was boiling hot when Brendan ran his bath, the steam almost clouding out the interior of the little built-on bathroom. Still the bath gave him relief, even his hands gypsum-posed when he lay back to evidence his planked bod. Now, his eyes closed, he lay there thinking of the words his mother had just spoken. He knew now that the woman gone to St Kieran's Hospital had played cat and mouse with his poor mother, and to make matters worse, when she wrote to seek support from him he was too busy with his own heresy to be quick enough to read between her lines of musha-musha-blotted normality.

While her son was soaking away the dampness which had dried into his body, his mother sat in her armchair thinking of Felix. She saw his boy's loneliness no longer as a terrible thorn in her notions, now she knew that her neighbour had never been a well woman and that she herself and her farm were but things of acquisition to Jude's awful needs. Fresh nursed memories trotted now past her

305

eyes, but by the time her son emerged from the bathroom they had all gone up in smoke. 'Get help to Felix,' she begged on Brendan's entering the kitchen, and sorra let up would she until he set off again for his neighbour's place. The moment he was gone her mind went too, and now she counted hours on the clock as though counting down to a blast-off at Cape Canaveral.


## CHAPTER 92


Felix Fortune drove home in the holding of the evening, the heel o'the hunt now his. He had prepared well for just such a take-over, but the thill which he now grew towards was never to be imagined. Not even a Fortune horse could be expected to know of such a thing.

Like a ball on the hop, thunder and lightning suddenly burst onto his scene, the resulting cloudburst flogging his windscreen with stair rods of torrential rain. But the brunt of his day's battle now behind him he hurried along, the entrance to his estate hungry to welcome him through.

Derby House waited and watched for this baby at large, standing with its best face on in readiness. Sadness had been wiped from its windows, and its virginia creeper was strobed now in lovely, freshly drenched leaves of red, bitter lemon, burnished pink and grim green. Heaven-scenting, whole bands of chimneys straddled its guardian roof, thieving the house of smoke, their yellow pots jungle-hiding inside their stone-grey gameplans. The huge front door, hybrid that it was, had its brass furniture polished and shining; take it from me, it read, whinging folk who in future approach my black folly must learn that the *nom de plume* Felix will

306

adorn the stolons of the deeds and documents belonging to the Fortune name.

On his arrival in the back yard, Felix found his friends standing there waiting. Teresa, his wife, and Hugh, his son, were there, chatting with Brendan. Three sets of arms waited to hug away his sorrows, and between the four of them they strayed in and around all of the reasons which might drive a woman to the chilling top of tormented thought.

The lights burned late in Derby House. Brendan saw them when he rose in the early hours. The mists of breaking dawn mimed the fog which soon would hover over the East River, but the clock striking under the stairs belonged to his here and now. The bishop's morning in New York always heralded a day of administrative pressures, but his new day here was what his ordination best prepared him for. Frank ideas meandered through his brain as he boiled the kettle for his first mug of coffee. Switching on the radio he kept the volume low and then, bringing the mug with him, he sat in Minnie's chair and drank his coffee down as far as the next thin line on the delph mug.

Dressed in his black anorak and wellington boots, Brendan eased himself from the house. The wicket gate always creaked on its spud, so he had to lift it in order to get through without creating a disturbance. Heading up the boreen then, he made for Derby House.

Arriving at Jude's house, Brendan turned the old brass knob and, putting his knee against the back door, pushed it open. In a hit or miss fashion he set off to find the way towards the east wing, the one closest to the orchard, for that was where he had seen the light burning, and there he imagined he'd likely find Felix. He lost his way a few times, but when he eventually found Jude's study he saw her son sitting there poring over ledgers, while all about him drawers hung open, doors of presses swung wide, and though daylight was pouring in he still worked beneath his mother's anglepoise lamp. 'Can a neighbour be of any help?' enquired Brendan, and Felix, all bothered and red-eyed, looked up from his quest and seeing Brendan felt relieved, for this drama in which he now found himself caught up had just begun to give answers to questions which for years had been baffling him.

Not privy to Felix's findings, Brendan offered to go back downstairs and make tea. 'Aye, would you make's a drop,' said Felix, 'cause, God above, this here is a right bloody nightmare and I've been at it all night long. Do you know what, Brendan, it's no wonder the mammy flipped, cause as far as I can figure out she's lost hundreds of thousands, and that's if it stops at that.' Brendan, starting now to understand Jude's trauma, began to feel sorry for her but this wasn't the time for holding a post mortem. Her son looked exhausted and frazzled, so with a 'come down when you're ready, Felix,' he turned on his heel and tramped back the route to the kitchen.

Down in the flagstoned kitchen the Aga cooker stood in skeletal pose, having stood there all down through the best part of a century of the history of this family. Now, down here this morning, the question was would it be of any assistance to this new tumbrel-stint. Hunting for the electric kettle, Brendan filled it and plugged it in, and just when it was about to bubble over Felix filled the doorframe. 'You don't know how good it is to get away from that mess up there,' he said, but his neighbour shushed him, insisting that he sit down and forget the pressures for a while. Handing Felix a cup of hot tea, he searched for some bread, and in a white enamel bin found half a pan loaf. 'Maybe it's a bit on the stale side,' he said, 'but then aren't we all.' His remark brought a smile to Felix Fortune's face, the first quiet smile since his mother's rebus turned frank theory on its head, for now, deutschmark or franc, dollar or pound, he knew her fortune had rebelled on her, her get-rich-quick strategy had soft-sanded and was swallowed up.

# CHAPTER 93

'God, but this sure is some swell vacation,' thought Brendan as he returned home from Jude Fortune's troubled house. Walking along through knee-high aftergrass in her lawn-field, his wellingtons seemed brand new as they glistened in the dew. 'Poor old Jude got an awful come-uppance,' he was thinking as he went over in his mind the things Felix had told him about his mother's stocks and shares. 'What puzzles me, though, is why she didn't wait to see how things'd pan out for her yesterday, but then she sure wasn't the only one,' he said, remembering how on the radio last night he had heard that back in town whizz kids in the Fulton Street Café were being offered a 'Crash Mash' cocktail if only they'd not jump from high buildings. The cocktail, the reporter said, was a mixture of Midori and sour mix and buckets o'Jack Daniels – Old Merry Wives of Windsor stuff – but now he almost laughed out loud, for, 'Where in the name of God would Jude have got the cure?' he mused. 'Sure Fulton Street's a God-awful distance away from this neck o'the woods.'

Back in his own haggard he was tripped up. 'Ah! Stocks and shares m'eye,' he scolded as his nostrils picked up the smell of bacon frying. He could just imagine the scene inside, the hot pan on the stove, the rashers on it spitting and curling as they fried in their own juices. 'There's nothing to beat that smell,' he thought as he made his way to the back door. 'It's one of those smells which you carry with you forever,' he mused.

Breakfast of bacon and egg, fresh bread and butter, with mugs of tea to theme it down, stole the morning of its groin-secret thoughts. Now, his gut filled, he nursed his belly underneath his hands while his cigar, never tired of burning, stood between his lips, almost too heavy to support. His lackadaisical stance could be attributed to sleep gone astray, but he knew that Mass time approached, his office needed saying.

Mass, when he did begin, thumb-nosed his notions, the secret hurting him parading before his conscience. 'I'm either in or I'm out,' he chastised himself, and so saying he got back in his niche, his niche where his millstream tumbled and thundered over its millwheel.

The parlour was quiet as a morgue. Religion, the word-game of the Irish, was now manifest as words teemed from his mouth. Sometimes he broadcast his testament; other times he found he almost denied his belief. In face of his only congregation he struggled, bull-in-a-china-shop, for her aged eyes were upon him, her fund of faith juxtaposing his braggart's hind. The credentials through which he played his role there and then enabled him to get going on the consecration. 'Do this in memory of me,' a God had once begged, but under the guise of bread and wine this very day he umbilically tied himself to that long-gone God, the God nutshelling now was dressed for bed there in his brandy balloon back in New York.

Light from the front window greeted the moment ahead. Candle wicks bent burning towards the bungling. Tacky flowers standing in his mother's best cutglass vase tried to scent the occasion. She, beating her fleeting heartlife, dwindled her ringed eyes on everything happening. And he, her priest son, fatherhood denied him, stood every enemy on his head the miracle to trumpet, the bindweed to greet, the freewheel to test, the fund to drink, the bread to chew, the huntsman's hands to hold it aloft, the round thing of hosts, the butterfingered hands thunder and lightning humbled, the silence of the moment broken by hump-backed whales' singing his human-voiced hysterical wonder at the bungling he had just brought about in his father's square room.

# CHAPTER 94

Brendan had been home just one week, but very likely he was now going to make his biggest move to date. He was in his mother's kitchen, nervously polishing his priest's plain black leather shoes. He got rid of some of his guilt by flinging himself into the role of Jude Fortune's lifesaver, but today was going to be different: today he was going to face the locals at the village church altar. His shoes shined to a blazing gloss, he now groomed his hair. The waves were still in cow's lick formation, but gone was the colour of former days. His long white hands showed signs of aging, and blue veins bulged silently from their backs. Their fingernails were manicured as though he were going to socialise with bluebloods in the city, when in fact he was gritting himself to be a son of Drumhollow.

Minnie was ready and waiting. She sat quietly watching her son. Her small black hat was dusty from years of sun and rain, and the hem of her coat dipped at one knee, as though she had knelt on that part of her coat for aeons of years. Her cuban-heeled shoes were polished and clean, but unknown to her, her tights sagged in wrinkles on her thin legs. Man and mother stayed silent, looking as though they were measuring each other prior to the coming exposé.

Brendan looked out the kitchen window and gazed on towards the village belfry. Suddenly, as though it were aware of the eyes fixed in its direction, the bell began to ring out the fifteen-minute call. Minnie was on her feet immediately, and picking up her handbag she blustered towards the door. Her son hesitated for another few seconds before following her out to the car. He sat her in the front passenger seat and picked his steps around to the driver's side. Together now, they drove up the boreen, he talking in a manner of speaking. But she, knowing he wasn't at all clued in to what he was saying, placed her gloved hand on his left arm and said, 'You'll do all right.' She added that she knew the neighbours, and that he'd know them better after today's Mass. Nervous now to the point of turning away and going back to his massive importance, he yet drove onwards and smiled all the while.

True to fashion, there the second-guessers stood outside the church, neighbours all, as standing shoulder to shoulder they waited and watched to find what the morning might give up for inspection. There they hung on to the last minute, their eyes searching out everything which approached, be it motor car or pedestrian. When the object of their scrutiny passed by they as one swung their gaze after it, and in chorus they then assumed hunter status as they sought to dig up some dirt. So it was when he was a boy, and so it still was today; the moment Brendan filled their sights was the moment they filled his. Easing the car to a halt, he disembarked and gave them a salute. Then, helping his mother from her seat, he headed in along with her to the churchyard where she went her way, he his.

The bishop made his entrance right on the stroke of time, his altar servers and lay ministers preceding him into the sanctuary. Together they genuflected, together they stood upright again, each now moving away to take up their place for this Mass.

'So far so good,' thought Brendan as, having mounted the steps of the altar, he turned around to face his congregation, but such was his dread of this ordeal that he couldn't help looking away down the church at the souls who to a man, woman and child, looked back up at him. 'Yes,' he thought, 'I've brought them out in droves,' and they were saying to themselves, 'He's a woeful lookin' tub o' guts.' However, when he signed himself with the sign of the cross, they did so too, and when he said, 'The Lord be with you,' they replied, 'And also with you.' It wasn't until he came to the Gloria that he stopped to take a breather, but if he did so they did too. Now his ears began to hear his own accent, sounding fake here, and the worst part of it all was the fact that, as yet, he was unable to drop his nasal twang and adopt what had once been his, and was still their, old-fashioned Jaysus-style.

It was time for his homily, and so he readied his throat. Now he introduced himself. He told his congregation that he had been away so long that his own mother didn't even recognise him when he walked into her kitchen. 'She thought I was the new priest in the parish,' he said. Hiding his nervousness, he joked about his grey hair, his American accent and, aware of the rhyme which they used say in school all of those years ago, he told them that he was the Irishman's version of a bishop. 'Remember,' he said, 'the Englishman's "Bishop supreme, will you pass me the cream"; the Scotsman's "Bishop divine, will you pass me the wine", and then we had our native son's "Bishop, ya bugger, will ya pass me the sugar". Now that job description sure fits me,' he said to the great amusement of his listeners. His self-mockery helped to bring the past into the wacky present, and soon his congregation relaxed as they sat listening to their old schoolfriend and neighbour filling them in on his pilgrimage abroad. His mother sat in her usual spot, the short seat, the one which led in as far as the steps up to the now unused pulpit. Her hands lay in the hammock of her skirt and her gaze was fixed on them, sitting there listening as though the man speaking was a missionary of old.

His homily over, the bishop returned to the altar, there to lead his flock in the Nicene Creed. Vocalising along with her neighbours, Minnie said the words of the prayer but nobody cared less than she about apostles or beliefs, for her mind was wandering again. This time was no different from ever before: she was thinking of her youngest son. Behind her closed eyes nested her image of him as he set off up the boreen towards Drumhollow and freedom.

The prayers of the Mass over, the bishop blessed his congregation. Making a last-ditch attempt to remedy his long absence, he requested his neighbours to give him time to get down to the door so that he could greet each one of them in turn.

Minnie stood aside and watched as her son shook hands and found a few words to say in greeting to each and everyone who came forward to meet him. Then, having bade his final hail and farewell, he turned his attention to her. 'Musha son, you should have done that years ago,' she said, and he, heading her back into the church to wait while he divested himself, whispered, 'Don't you think I've discovered that, what do you think I've been trying to say?' Humble pie he had just now eaten, but he wouldn't be aul' Jack Humphrey's grandson and forget to redeem himself, for too well he remembered how the locals reacted as and when his grandfather hounded them from inside the window of his huckster's shop.

# CHAPTER 95

Greeting his new acquaintance, Brendan stood outside his old neighbour's door. He had only briefly met with Laura when she had introduced herself to him outside the church last Sunday. 'I'm a grandniece of Maggie Dempsey, the woman who helped bring you into the world,' she had said that day, and shaking hands with her, he had told her that his mother had mentioned her name to him but, it sounding too good to be true, he had dismissed it, thinking only that his mother must be raving.

Laura Bewley, the girl from London, in no way steeped in kowtowing or that sort of clerical malarkey, welcomed the bishop without any reference to Your Grace or Your Lordship. 'Come in, Brendan,' she said. 'I suppose you know this kitchen better than me.'

'Well I remember it,' he replied, 'for many's the time I sat on that little stool there and ate bread and jam, and Maggie's tea was always sweetened just to my taste.'

'Well it's coffee you'll be getting here today,' laughed Laura, and so saying she set about brewing some of Bewley's best roast. The aroma of the Arabica coffee sent Brendan's nostrils into spasms of delight. 'You don't know how good it is, Laura, to smell real coffee,' he said. 'You know, the real Aly Daly, as they say in New York.'

'That's right,' said Laura. 'I've heard that expression at home, and the ra'l McCoy was another of my mother's gems, and we both know where she heard those sayings.' They laughed easily, their voices combined, one drumbeating an echo in best Bow bells singsong, the other bragging in its New York-wombed wonder.

As a moth to the flame, Minnie's name fastened itself to the coffee's aroma, her lubbard-years the topic for discussion. A salary for services rendered was the solution which her son had in mind, but Maggie Dempsey's grandniece thought differently, for she had come to the old woman, plastercast in hand, and nothing which she had created could be valued in dollars. The nurse, from her own experience, now suggested that a human being's contact was all his mother needed. She had, after all, made out this far, and Laura said her fear was that the woman'd bolt if her scene became crowded by visitors haranguing her and bringing her creature comforts which she never needed. 'I shall just continue as I'm doing,' she said. 'I shall drop in and out, she musn't ever suspect that I'm, as they say, keeping a watching brief.'

As though it had been waiting for a break in *The Winter's Tale* the phone rang just then, the sound ringing, ringing, ringing jettisoned its message into Brendan's mind. Now in Jumping Jesus' time he could never have come up with a miracle like this, and smiling for all he was worth he waited until this new pole-star finished her conversation. 'Laura, can I be really cheeky and ask you if I can call you from New York and find out first-hand how my mother is carrying on?' said Brendan. 'The weight off my mind that that'd be, I can never tell you,' he added. And Laura, the neat girl, looking directly at him was about to answer, but instead she fetched a notepad and hurriedly wrote down the telephone number of the house down the bog road.

It was lighting-up time when Brendan turned out from the bog road onto the tarred main road, and his headlights on full, he hurried to follow them. Hedgerows never seemed hungrier for notice as, hubbubed by the lights, their greenery dripped greased suspense. But, he, hot in his hour of relief, never became conscious of them. His eyes saw only the white line dividing the road as it went the distance until the hedgerows themselves swallowed it up between them.

Banishing his conscience to his old midwife's hearthstone, he returned home, his mind giddy from his discovery. Now, thanks to this modern young woman, he was going to be able to look into his mother's kitchen. The kettle, he knew, would always be in the process of boiling, the tea mug would still hang on the hook on the dresser, its high-water mark there on its insides, and benediction of benedictions, the old retainer would, thanks to Maggie Dempsey's grandniece, still be grateful for her company, just as he was this never-never evening.

His bacon saved, it was he, who, this night of nights, suggested he'd make the supper. The little bollocks of a teapot was sitting there waiting its scald but he, amen-heaving, stretched up and, as though making tea for the five-loaves-and-two-fish brigade, lifted down the old family-sized aluminium teapot from its new spot on the very top of the dresser. It was covered with dust and didn't seem as though the hand of God had touched it for many's the year. He couldn't know why he was drawn to it, way too big for his immediate needs. 'I'll wash the damned thing anyhow,' he was thinking as, heading for the sink he removed the lid, but now he stopped dead in his tracks, the cargo inside the pot flummoxing him. 'Gosh will you look,' he said. 'Look, all the friggin' dollars I ever sent,' as there they all were, gone sepia, all stuffed tightly into the brown-lined teapot.

Putting his hurt in his bread-basket, he went to bed that night a cowed man. The teapot had said its say. His grim face shuttered its eyes the moment he laid his head on the pillow. 'Me missing all those years,' he scolded. 'Me the full of a bloody teapot away,' and now, though his eyes were closed, he mimed himself, slipping banknotes into flimsy airmail envelopes before addressing them to her back home in Drumhollow.

# CHAPTER 96

Drumhollow, the village this side of Huntstown, knew that despite bad days or even tragic days, its river would twist down there where it had always flowed, as it stung its way between clay banks on its route to humble lane. Of recent times though, the river winced, for famished by age one old woman had looked into its waters and saw but death greased there before her, and shortly afterwards another woman, frightened since girlhood, had actually gunwaled over the edge and jumped into its depths, back there beneath the overhanging hawthorn bush.

Her seven senses told the old woman to back away from the river before it inveigled her into a watery grave; but the other woman, the fractured one, seven senses thundering, had never hesitated to feed herself into the trout pool, and even to cutchy down as she tried to longjump where she should have highjumped to heaven.

The river sang to itself whenever it remembered Minnie, the

woman who studied her likeness in its looking glass. But when it remembered Jude, it remembered the deranged expression on her face. Moaning where it should be singing, it strained to know what was the 'Crash Mash' which could have saved the star who couldn't wait until the morrow.

Felix, the son of that deranged woman, and avuncular to the affidavit, viewed his new address as though a stranger drinking from a pogrom's well. His had been a whetstoned boyhood where his own mother was concerned, but now he realised that she had in fact given him far more than she could spare, for now he knew that her Cyclops' eye had fed him John Smith and Jimmie Hynes together. He, even to this very day, felt hard done by, but now his eyes were being strangely immersed in his mother's hard luck story. Nymphomaniac she should or could have been, but when he henry became to her current, he better associated what she had done and for whom she had done her grafting.

Derby House, mausoleum to the Fortune family, began to free a pike each time the water in the river experienced White Nile rapids as it runned towards Huntstown. Teresa, the wife and yard-arm to Felix, taught in a school where her own son could be kindred to her vulnerable freedom. She had never slept one night in her mother-in-law's house, never knew the reason why, never hunted for a breakthrough, just got on with her life in hers and Felix's bungalow way beyond on the edge of time.

But, and every second-hand home has a but, but for but, sacred bolsters would never have held the family together. Now here they drove into the back yard of Derby House, the hector gone from it, her cultivated persona gone with her, bedraggled and mute; a freefall in the market-place had stole up on her and fingered her for destruction.

Seven o'clock was striking when the box was found in the groping end of the top shelf in the wardrobe in the room where Felix had slept as a boy. The box was a shoebox belonging to a pair of the late Michael John Fortune's shoes. Inside it, lonely for linking, lay a pair of wellington boots, little weeshy boots, glazed black on the outside, and inside them were the words DUNLOP Size 5. Her that was cold and het up, had stuffed the boots with tissue paper, and on a scrap of notebook she had written the words: 'Felix's little "bullingtons" as he called them, he had them for paddling in the puddle down underneath the arch going out into the orchard'. It was Hugh who found them, rummaging where he never could before and in the room where he was going to sleep tonight. He raced down the back stairs to show his parents his find but they, up to their oxters in trouble, barely heeded him until his gumble drew his father's attention. Felix, the human stoic, climbed the stile in the mearing anew, as the little bullingtons came back to rock him. Planking a great kiss on his son's forehead, he said, 'That's for being nosy,' and now he began lamenting in sobs of, yes, relief. 'Look, for God's sake, look,' he said as he showed them to his wife and she, when she saw the boots preserved like her own son's First Communion shoes, understood her mother-in-law for the first time, and her eyes softened now in tears. 'She really loved you, but couldn't show it, poor thing,' she said.

Hugh's find today, though, set down a marker for Jude Fortune's future days, for from here out she'd have a family; someone to cherish her, someone to come between the coffin, hungry for a funeral, and the woman who was now in no way aware of her hunger, though her belly was empty.

# CHAPTER 97

Minnie O'Brien, the woman across the mearing ditch, a fall guy echoing a fall guy to time and thought where Jude Fortune was concerned, yet managed to live vulnerably on and on. Her fun this day lay in going to town, the bishop's car humping in and out of the potholes on the boreen just but a game, a dose of sadness really, for she knew that if *he* was back he'd fill them all in with gravel. Brendan was in fact bringing her to the hospital to visit the woman whom she had never visited before, and whom she frustrated by being sane and stubborn for years back. Now it was felt that Minnie might jolt Jude's mind out of its vice, for the Fortune family were at the point of trying to establish a new persona for her.

Of the stunt Jude knew nothing as she sat yonder in St Kieran's Hospital, the epitome of her own gospel story. The single room with the sky-high window belonged to the padded cell days, but now the status was drugged differently; now it was, at a far remove, described as a rumpus room. In it she sat, the picture of stone, her eyes focused on her mind's crucible, her drugged state yelling but sinecured dumbness.

Minnie O'Brien did her utmost to talk sense into her neighbour. The method she used was the same as that which she used when her children were young and innocent. 'Poor Jude, what ails you?' she coaxed the moment she crashed up against Jude's reality. 'Where have you the pain?' she begged to know. Mother hen that she always was, she thought she had the remedy for all ills when, reaching into her handbag, she withdrew a baby Power of whiskey and set it into Jude's unco-operating hands. 'I always depend on a drop of the crathur,' she said. 'It cures all my aches and pains. Just take a mouthful before you lie down tonight and by tomorrow morning there won't be a loss on you. But then maybe it's your bowels that's wrong,' she whispered. 'If so, get the nurses to give you a few spoons of Syrup of Figs or Magnesia. I prefer the Syrup of Figs myself, sure a child could take it and no matter.' The silent one though, made no reply: visitors couldn't get through to her boneyard. But Minnie was there to cure her, and so the topics changed from white and black to black and white, yet not one word came from the enigma.

'I tried every trick in the bag,' said Minnie as she settled herself in the front passenger seat beside her son. 'As God is my judge,' she said, 'I even offered to let her have the run of my whole farm. "You can take the wire o'the gate," I said, "and let your bullocks graze the meadow field," but she never heard a whit I said, or if she did she's not able to bully any longer.'

The car was curling its way down the meritorious avenues when the question which had been forming came bursting out. 'Brendie,' she said, 'what did the nurse you were talking to say is wrong with Jude?' He made to answer her, but got distracted by a big lorry, and when he eventually managed to glance at his mother again she, question forgotten, was breaking open a blue packet of Silver Mints. She offered him one and then, popping one in her own mouth, began to suck it; lifting it with her tongue she curled it in and around her mouth, her tastebuds dreaming of good news. For all she knew, for all she seemed to know, the truth was she knew nothing of her neighbour's world. That, though, didn't stop her throwing out her historical findings. 'Do you know, Brendie, what I think?' she said. 'She's imagining she's sick, sure if I could count the times she claimed she had a pain here or a pain there, and you know it was always when she came looking to rent my whole farm, or lately even to buy it, and me still in it. Between ourselves, son, if she got what she came looking for she'd have sorra the pain. You over there in America, Sheila up in Dublin, Frankie off having a good time somewhere and me on my ownio, so help me God, trying to keep the place till Frankie wants it. I was so afraid of that woman. When all's said and done, though, I'm still here and musha, the place is still there, large as life, waiting for that fella to come home to it. Ah! but you don't know, Brendie, what it's been like, musha, it was a hoor, still is, all the time waiting, waiting to go to bed, waiting to get up, waiting for the postman, waiting for that wan to come barging over looking for the land, waiting to see which day I should go to town, maybe go in and mosey round the shops, but the oul' postman used to muck up my plans, come early some days but have nothing, only bills or maybe a letter from you or Sheila, other times he'd be late and have nothing at all, not even a lattitat, but then the bus'd be gone and I'd be stuck, maybe I'll go tomorrow I'd say to myself — are you listening, son, I want you to see how it was then.'

Brendan felt he should break in now and say his say. 'I'm listening,' he snapped. 'Sure gosh, you've told me about that postman a hundred times since I came home. I'm listening, but I can't pull Frankie out of a hat.'

'Musha, I know you can't,' his mother replied. 'But the little hat you did bring me home is a dotey little yoke. But anyhow, what's this I was saying?'

'You were talking of the postman,' he reminded her.

'Ah no, it wasn't just the postman,' she said. 'I was telling you how I put in my days. Sometimes I'd go up to the cemetery, maybe I'd be on my way to the shop or to the post office for the pension and I'd drop in to the grave, the cold oul' place it'd be, musha, at the best of times, but in the winter with all the wet leaves and the moss and the bird scour on the headstone and him down below. But I'd tell him "He's your son too," and could he not locate the child, leaving it all to me as per usual. Still, I wouldn't change places, oh lord, no. Sometimes, musha, wouldn't I take the fiddle down, you know it used always be a Thursday night when I was a child, and daddy'd come home langered, but before he'd come,

Mam and me'd have the go on the fiddle, she pulling me up where I went wrong, musha, there was the saint for you, and no big cross dangling on her chest or no gold ring, only the meanest thinnest specimen you ever clapped eyes on, there was a saint, a martyr, there slaving for him. Where was I? Oh aye, the music. I'd have it going round in my head the whole time, loved The Coulin, every time I'd play it it'd sound different, the humour in the house seemed to get between me and the strings, and of course the fingers, musha, they're stiff as be damned by times, but anyhow I'd keep at it, sorra let up would I till the tune sounded right to my ear. Ah! But Brendie, the nights was a tester, specially the winter, but musha, one night didn't I have a brainwave, left on the World Service all night. See, if I slept it didn't matter, but if something woke me or the dog barked, there wouldn't your man be going hammer and tongs at the shipping forecast, and I'd lie there trying to be one step ahead of him, Dogger Tyne Finisterre Heliogoland Fisher German Bight Faroes Bailey, I'd never be right, then maybe I'd doze off and wake up later to hear them talking of books, or even reading from one. Often I'd hear Big Ben himself, or I'll tell you what I like, the stories from our own correspondents, as they say, and their stories'd put the hair standing on you, oh! you'd be glad of the bed and musha, the roof over your head. You know, son, I didn't get your chances but I'm educated, listening to them all the nights, listening to them sometimes all night' – and now she started to laugh – 'but then sometimes, wouldn't I fall asleep listening,' she said, 'and musha, the job'd be then to figure out was I really listening as cosying there I tried to make sense of myself by looking back at the past, and musha, before I'd know it wouldn't the night be gone, and up I'd get to wait for the postman all over again.'

They were approaching the bridge just this side of Johnny Lynam's when she dozed off. Brendan had lit a cigarette with the dashboard lighter, and drawing a great pull on it he sat there holding it in until the bump of the bridge was behind him and then, opening the window, he blew his mouthful of rescue out into the rushing wind. He started to cough, but his mother didn't hear him as there she sat, her say said, her head leaning against the headrest, her voice winding itself up for its next outing. 'The potholes'll wake her,' he thought as he turned into their own cul de bag, and sure enough she said, 'Mind the briars, they'll destroy your hired car.' He smiled to himself when he thought of all she had had to say back there, but now she was right, the big buck briars would surely have the car marked if he didn't ease his way gently beneath them.

## CHAPTER 98

It was the day when Brendan went to Dublin to spend time with Sheila that the new idea came to Minnie. Like a bolt out of the blue it came, a lubbard-notion, the source wombed and weird. 'Yes,' it said, 'yes, you can do it, you can do without them now. Burn them, burn the whole lot.'

The new visitor under Minnie's eaves had brought a certain spirit into the place. Now the thunder-bird of the wardrobe felt free and unburdened. Now, today, she could even see her way to get rid of her crutch, now her serge-bogeyman was going to be set free.

The newspapers which Brendan had been buying each morning were piled in a heap in the scullery. Lifting them, she brought them out to the haggard and dumped them where the old plough lay. Tearing away pages she scrunched them into balls before piling them pyramid-fashion; the Great Fire of London was going to play mere second fiddle to her holocaust.

Returning to the house she climbed the stairs, her steps fronting her new ideas. Plans like those of this morning's vintage belonged to yesteryear. Approaching the wardrobe of her tar-barrelling-thunder days, the wardrobe which had been her dream-maker in reverse, she opened it wide and out of its dark recesses withdrew her late husband's clodhopper's clothes, limp and long from their hanging. Clutching them in an armful she carried them carefully down the stairs, her feet never missing a step until she had them landed at the place in the haggard where the incendiary was timed to go off.

It was as she scoured the workshop for kindling of some sort that her eyes fell on his old raincoat. She had, like it or not, oftentimes sat on it in the trap, or hidden under it on wet days as the pony trotted to or from town. 'That can go too,' she thought as she lifted it down from its rusty nail and, spreading it out on the floor, set about gathering wood chippings and some old dusty scantlings. She threw her finds down on to the coat and then, as though heading off to make her fortune, she gathered the collar to the coat-tails and carried the bundle to where the papers waited.

No longer careful, she heeled those chippings and scantlings in on top of her paper empire, and striking a match she, kneeling, held it cupped in her hands until the flame licked the newspaper. Up the blazes raced, witty in their ways, but the moment the fire got going nicely she gave it the placebo of her wardrobe, her old hands by force of habit having already searched them out for contraband.

The fire needed some serious encouragement, she felt, so hurrying to the shed she brought back a pitchfork. Lifting the molten mayhem, she allowed currents of air to muss the black stirabout. She was just about to add Peter's old raincoat to the now red molten lava when, like it or not, she began rifling the dirty, worn, almost threadbare thing. It was frightening to force her hand into the old pockets: anything could be lurkin' in them, she felt. But contrary to the mouse or maggot which her mind hinted at, her hand in fact withdrew something of which she, as though a dunderhead, had never known a hint.

The thing was an envelope, nearly. The address had faded and run. The stumbling block was that she needed her spectacles but they were in the kitchen, inside. Her hands withdrew a photograph. The baby was bonny, dressed in white; brown background plundered all around him, and his smile dimpled down deep in his chin. On the back, when she turned the photo over, was written in block letters big and bold so that now even she, without her glasses, could see it, YOUR BABY BOY PETER it read.

'Musha, the length he musta had it,' thought Minnie. 'His mother musta sent it to him. Oh, God be with the days when I had him,' she prayed. 'His dimple never changed on him one whit.'

She went and sat on the plough, all rusty. She began sensing something devious, but what? 'Wonder why the postman never put it through the letterbox, wonder why himself kept it outside in his coat?'

'Wouldn't ya love to know who that babby is, Minnie Humphrey,' her voice said out loud, and then she again turned over the snapshot, seeing an N there. 'But what good is an N,' she said, 'when an old woman needs a name.'

'Well he's gone now and I can't ask him,' she stammered. 'Maybe 'tis better me not knowing at all, and seeing as he never whid a word about YOUR BABY BOY PETER – well then, he'll not feel it when I burn his oul' coat.'

The old raincoat was damp from years hanging. She had to poke it with the fork till it burned, but the snapshot with the like-it-or-not inscription burned quickly, with nothing left of it nor of its letter N.

# CHAPTER 99

Minnie, ever the mocking finger to her son's conscience, was the one who freed him to mention his having to leave home again. 'Go on son, get back to your work,' she said one morning as they sat eating their breakfast. She had boiled two brown eggs, one for herself and one for her visitor. She smiled to herself as he delicately picked the spoon-cracked shell from his egg. 'He can't have learned that show-off in my kitchen,' she reasoned as, picking up her knife, she deftly slit the top off her egg with its sharp blade. They chatted in easy fashion, she about his need to get hurried in his packing, and he just as definite in his advising her to trust in Laura for her every need. 'You don't have to worry about me, you worry about you,' she said, and so saying she closed the subject of her staying here all alone, and she the downhill side of eighty. 'The only worry I have, son,' she said, 'is that the good Lord'll call me before I get to find out where Frankie is wandering, cause I know he's out there, and even though you're what's that they say, "a prince of the church" is it, I can still say something you can't, I know that our Frankie is alive, and please God I'll live to prove it. And while I'm at it,' she continued, 'and while I've time can I say something to you.' Without even a glance at the teapot, she said, 'You don't have to be buying me off, I want for nothing. As I said before, I've Gay Byrne in the morning, the Angelus at six, and if I wake at night I've the BBC World Service. Now,' she said, 'can you see why I don't want television – how could I find time to watch it? And then, too, I do be looking after Laura Bewley, you know between you and me, and you can wipe that smile off your face as well, she comes traipsing up to me whenever she feels lonely, and she has the television, you know.'

He couldn't hold it in any longer, he had to laugh. 'Talk about having the whole thing sewn up, you're a law unto yourself, isn't that what they say,' he said, borrowing one of her statements. But it was all as though he hadn't even spoken, for she just cantered on.

'The truth is,' she said, 'my days, son, are so busy that musha, I don't have time to scratch. It was ever the way with me, too much work and Christ-all time to do it in. See, I'm afraid that the bus'll stop one day and Frankie'll come bootin' it down the boreen with the brown suitcase in his hand, and me without a bit of fresh baked bread in the house to put before him. Musha, he always loved the spudcake, remember his farl had to be the biggest and the thickest? Are you listening, Brendan?' she asked as for a moment she halted, but her mind was not in need of an audience. She was in fact back in time, and scolding Frankie for going so heavy on the butter, and churning still four days away. Out loud, though, she was reminding herself to cook spudcake for Brendan. 'You'd love some potato cake before you go back,' she insisted, 'and I'll get Laura to buy me some country butter at the market. You know the ICA women make it still, even the nuns in the convent churn and God knows there's few o'them now, but let me tell you, what Laura buys is the best butter out from my own, and why, sure she's like a daughter to me. Better than my own daughter up there in Dublin like a queen in her temple, sitting looking out where second-best never never can look in, you know, son, how it is with Luke, gin-drunk on power while my poor lass is drained of notions.' Brendan, sitting idly listening, suddenly switched in to his mother's voice, and as he listened he realised that his mother was a dark horse. In Sheila's case he had always felt that his mother was the only one in tune with the fretting house, and now as he listened again while Minnie chattered on, he learnt from her that jealousy was at the root of Luke Green's problems. 'Friends never get past the door,' she said. 'Her friends, that is, but Luke feels he can bring home his golfing buddies and our poor lass has to be the perfect hostess. Now don't get me wrong, it's not that he's unkind, but musha, he can't allow her to have any life for herself. She drives down here to see me, but she can't relax, she's always with one eye on the clock and one on me. I'd prefer to see her as she used to be, but she's Sheila Green now, not O'Brien. Indeed if your father could've seen how his lovely little girl's life turned out, he'd turn in his grave, indeed'nd he'd turn anyhow when he'd think of the three of ye. One set out as a priest and came home an old man, one set out as a boy and never came back at all, and his girl set out to nurse and now she's her own best patient.' Her son sat there listening, not bothering to interrupt: his mother had her say and the fact that he sat there didn't really matter. Her grandfather clock had heard it all before, would hear it all again, for this game of waiting was murder on the heart and tinder-boxed the brain.

The morning was lousy, the rain was pouring down, the motorcar was faced up the way, and where they walked was muddy and wet. The pair, old woman and almost-as-old son, both walked towards the car, picking their steps as though clean shoes mattered. She was being brave, seeing her bishop-son off to his secret vocation in the city called the Big Apple, and he, feeling the years on him, felt like saying 'I'm going back to bed'. But neither said what needed to be said, as where they were going was not of their butting. Dreadful they felt, both frightened, but not telling each other. 'Go on, son, get back to your altar, and as they say try and find yourself,' the old woman said, and he, stepping on his tippytoes, said 'Get Laura to visit with you, and if ever you need me, tell her.' Now they had to tear themselves apart, the poor things of familiar name, she hugging her old child and he her old bones. 'Now, son, remember, no more dollars,' she said, not now needing jam and he, holding her to him, promised that he'd do as she asked. He left her where she was standing, but he had to come back again, hurriedly hugging her this time, now he almost ran in the rain. When he started the engine he said 'Damn it,' and then in the rear-view mirror he looked, snapping the vision there standing, wondering how long would it warm-blooded look. But the woman just stood there deuking, and bravely she smiled a fierce smile, a smile which indeed would frighten her in the mirror, or maybe even stop the pendulum under the eye of her clock.

'Musha, Minnie, he's gone,' she said out loud. 'God, kiss him as he goes,' she prayed, 'he's only a man, and very frightened for me. You know You'll not fail me if I'm lonely,' she continued, 'but him, didn't he look the loneliest poor divil there driving off.'

Brendan, out of sight, wiped his eyes on his big white handkerchief before closing the road gate, then, climbing up onto the road bank, he took a last conscious look down the boreen to the home of his birth. Inhaling a big breath of Drumhollow air, he jumped back down onto the road and sat back in his car. He closed the door with a great slam and drove towards the airport.

## CHAPTER 100

The Aer Lingus jet engines sucked a dreadful gasp of Ireland's air prior to taking off for the States. Inside it sat rows of wrens all whole and still, all hoping to be still whole when the beckoning lights of JFK coaxed the eagle down to hunch his hunches there where the New York skyscrapers towered, where the thunder roared in silence, where the yonders Yonkered and the great, bunty, hungering city stung humanity in a dying wasp sting until gums hardened, teeth gritted, they frolicked, revving lubbard-tunes, yonder in lingering lostness.

Blasé, but secretly bothered about taking a lift to lofty heights, and then prepared to fly even higher, sat the wren from Drumhollow, dressed in his best black. The suit to fit the mood, the mood to fit the heartache, the eyes to search the ground, the nasturtium-leaved figures flitting in the space before him, pity the humility of his mother; loneliness the greasepaint fronting his sister; hunting, the eyes of Jude; numbness, the whys of Felix; greed the winner there, animation the dress framing all, himself a witness from abroad, void his androgynous green phlegm, gradual his enlightenment that loneliness belongs to all, but he always figured on his being the loneliest, his the lynch-pinned loneliness of God's anointed one, not belonging to anyone, not freed to love anyone, not capable of being as sunny as anyone, as victim, not bleeding like anyone, dog-collared not like anyone, bishop, dressed up as freesia-scented flower, no, not lumped in with anyone or everyone but rare, rich, royal, trestled by mother church, balls between the legs like any man, putty in his Maker's hands like anyone, grand, great, gin-scrutable like anyone, bygone-ing days like everyone, breathing breaths freshly breathed by each and everyone now steaming up the porthole window, no longer clear, he like anyone, could not see clear like anyone, to look back down at anything or anyone or any crevice in any field in any country, on any bread-cake upon any stove made by any hands, work-worn hands guided by crying eyes red-rimmed now, crying still, crying mother, fine like any mother, any mother of anyone and everyone, and any man should ask why must he think him great, since any man can easily find the greater one will always be the mother-one, fighting for the right of everyone to have and hold like anyone the right to life, to be loved each and all, and best by far the female one, of everyone the stronger sex, of all the sexes the brightest one, among everyone the freshest hope, for everyone will freshly be the freedom won for everyone by she who has been threshed for aeons by every man in fear for his penis, fear for his name, by victimising her who should be king.

Looking hard ahead, Brendan found a focus. He saw his destiny framed before him. His eyes were weary from the strain of trying to read the ground of the country of his birth. Looking down filled his head with dizzying thoughts, human thoughts about his rhinestoned vocation. New York lay ahead of him, and not just New York, but dedication, reparation and castration.


## CHAPTER 101


The kitchen door opened on a knock, and Laura stepped in. Mindful of Minnie being newly alone, she came to soften the old woman's fretting. 'Am I just in time for a cup of tea?' she begged, as Minnie handled the kettle and the aged eyes glanced in welcome to her caller's plea. Together they drank and chatted, but Laura couldn't help noticing the name which triggered Minnie's conversation. She talked of Brendan, but her mind nudged the name Frankie at every chance. Her bold beauty hurt each time she saw her neighbour slip, but the chat was warm and human. Laura nudged the old woman along by telling her of Jude, but now she discovered she had fanned the fire when her neighbour began to recall the recent and lonely past. Words which Laura never knew existed in the brain of Minnie came tumbling out when she heard the name Jude. 'That woman, Laura, has been hassling me for years, she with all of her huge estate wanting my five fields. But she'll be not wanting them where she is now,' she said. 'You know I'm minding them for him.'

'For whom?' nudged Laura, and without a moment's hesitation the old woman said, 'Frankie, of course, did I not tell you about him going off on a skite and not coming back?'

Laura's laughs filled the kitchen, her comforting presence balm to Minnie's loss; voiced regrets had an audience. But when darkness came and Laura had gone home, she had to resort to talking to herself. Nodding in credible disbelief, she sat alone, finesse her very own attribute, as she freshened her mind on her own annotations. 'Listen, Minnie Humphrey,' she said. 'You gave your first mother's child to another mother, isn't that what they say, Mother Church, and musha, didn't she take him with a compliment, was he sound of mind and body, was he heir to any disease, she demanded to know, was he fit to nimble down to study, was his father's job good enough, respectable enough, could me and his dad pay his way, musha, we paying for the honour of giving, and that mother taking without knowing the awful pain of bringing him into Drumhollow, they say you forget the labour but sorra chance. But her, she took him careful only, but pain she knew never, and off he went to her from us just when he could lift us, she knew we had nothing, she took him, though, and seldom looked back, made him a priest she did, now she didn't fail there, remember the ordination, you'd think you were in heaven, he up there at the altar, remember him lying there on the broad of his mouth and nose. His father was desperate proud of him, never fear, an O'Brien to his fingertips, he should've known better, herself had changed him, had made him sort of distant like, not my son any more, but hers to do with him what she liked, not as much as a ghost of a smile at poor oul' me, I notice them things but never say nothing, cause I'm only a woman you know, not trusted, the serpent, a woman, Musha, Minnie, you're a woman all right, fending for yourself all these years, but what about your man? My man, ah! sure, Peter was one of a kind, ne'er a dishonest bone in him, well, musha, we'll leave him be, he thought he was the boss, bloody sure he was of himself, but he made me the furniture, God it was great, he'd a grand pair of hands, God bless them, nobody could better him, but he wasn't a great provider God knows. Maybe I'll drink some tea before I go to bed, by morning I'll have it all out in the open, can't talk when Brendan's about, or Laura either, they wouldn't understand how aggranoyed I get, having to keep my talk in, when like a windy day the sheets dry better out in the open, but they mean good so I'll play along. By morning I'll have the air cleared, my Brendan must be high and mighty by now, a bishop she made him, a bygoned priest, how can he save his soul

333

decorating himself by a big flashy ring? Poor me and his dad, where's our flashy ring, and his purple, his bishop's socks, what has that got to do with fishermen, I ask you, come follow me He said, and they just dropped everything and went, no purple socks, no flashy ring, and He never asked had they e'er a skeleton in their cupboard. Minnie, he's your son, then how's it I didn't recognise him, as smart as he is, he didn't know his own mother had butty wellingtons, and white hair, him with the French hat for my head, but ah! it was lovely, maybe I'll go up and bring it down and fit it on again, my head is cleared a bit now, maybe it'll look grand, not that there was anything amiss with it in the first place, atanarate I'll get it, but before I do that I'll make the tea.' And standing up slowly she sort of stretched herself as though she were snapping out of a dream and, moving towards the stove, felt the kettle and decided that it was too cooled off to bring back to the boil again.

The clock struck three, and Minnie counted with it. 'One, two, three, and my beauty sleep gone by the boards,' she said. She laughed a happy, hearty laugh and said, 'I'd give even my French hat to know where *he* is tonight.'

## CHAPTER 102

The day was well hurt by the time Minnie woke from her sleep. 'That's what you get,' she said, 'when you stay up late to chew the rag. You haven't managed to change one iota for all you've suffered and borne, but at least you'll have peace now that poor Jude is locked away.'

'One down and one to go,' she said as she thought about the future. She couldn't help wondering how she'd manage now that she had to make out on her own. Brendan had brought a verve to her being and a pep to her step, but now that he was gone she found the kitchen so quiet that she could hear the hens picking crumbs from where she had thrown them on the flagstone outside the back door. 'Why,' she thought, 'sure this is like a morgue here now, after the huffle and kerfuffle of having Brendan here.'

The postman had come and gone, and all he had for her was the ESB bill. 'Musha, for all that I use,' she said as she placed the envelope up behind a plate. She had by now dried her face, brushed her hair and was about to wash her mouth out when like a thunderstorm all hell sounded, coming chugging and flittering down the boreen towards the wicket gate. 'Jesus, Mary and holy Saint Joseph, musha, what's that?' she said as, hurrying to look out, she moved aside Laura Bewley's freshly laundered curtain. A figure was dismounting from a great monster of a motorbike, and opening the little gate he came striding purposefully through it. 'Jesus, Mary,' and this time Joseph got left out in the cold, for now she was staring at the tall figure approaching, dressed all in black, its head swollen to the size of a pig's pot, no sign of humanity there to be seen. 'It wouldn't be the divil, would it' she fretted, 'or one of them aliens they do be talking about on the wireless? Jesus, Mary and holy Saint Joseph,' she said again as the heavy knocker addressed the front door. 'I'd better answer it,' she whimpered. Standing to her full height she thoughtfully assembled herself and then, as though heathen, she plentifully walked towards the door.

'Mrs O'Brien?' the headless man said, his pig's pot now swinging in his hand.

'Yes, that's me,' she answered. But now she graced his face with a searching look. 'Ah! musha, Frankie, it's yourself, you came back!' she said as she made to hug the stranger.

'There's some mistake here, Mrs O'Brien,' the young man said. 'My name is Pete Lynam, my grandmother is Nuala Lynam from hereabouts. She asked me to drop in and ask after you. I'm spending a fishing holiday here in Westmeath.'

'Ah! musha, is that who you are,' said Minnie, thrusting out her hand. 'Nuala Lynam, y'say, and do you know, you're the livin'' image of my son Frankie. He went away and never came back yet.' She held his hand tightly as she spoke and then, drawing him after her, she said, 'Come on in, Peter, and sit down and tell me all about Nuala, sure it's only like yesterday.'

The black leather squeaked and complained with his every move as the young Englishman sat in Minnie's own chair. Soon he held a best china cup of tea in his hand. A slice of buttered barmbrack settled on his plate, but whole sentences had to be said before he could bite into the fruity bread.

At every chance she got Minnie admired him. 'Son, I can't get over how like my boy you are,' she said. 'But then I'm only raving, as you can see, sure my Frankie is now in his fifties if he's a day.'

Pete Lynam had too much breeding in him not to make allowances for the whimsy of an old woman, so he instead told Minnie all about his grandmother and his late father. 'My father died about two years ago,' he said. 'He suffered a massive coronary. I'm the youngest of five children and I'm called after him.'

'You're a very handsome boy,' said Minnie. 'I'll bet your grandmother is very proud of you.'

'I suppose she is,' he answered. 'She's at least very helpful, very supportive of me while I'm studying. You see, Mrs O'Brien, I'm still at medical school, will finish next year and then for my dad's sake I'd like to do surgery, maybe specialise in cardiac surgery,' he said.

'How long, Peter, will you be here for yet in Ireland?' asked the now settled down Minnie. Smiling broadly, the visitor told her that he had already spent one week here and still had two remaining. 'Well, musha, that's great, cause I have someone I'd like you to meet,' said Minnie. 'She's like yourself, a neighbour's child, and musha, English too. She's a nurse, one of the best there's going, and for your grandmother's sake I'd like the two of ye to meet.'

The visitor laughed. 'Are you trying to fix me up with this girl?' he said. 'Oh! Mrs O'Brien, it's just what my gran'd be up to too,'

336

he teased. 'A matchmaker, I'll tell her you are, but if you'd like me to meet this girl, well then, so I will. I can't pass up the chance to meet, as you say, "a neighbour's child".'

Two hours slipped by, but neither of the pair noticed. Minnie had the time of her life reminiscing, and Pete loved talking about his parents and, as he called his grandmother, his nan.

But now it was time to leave, and taking the old woman in his arms he hugged her, and kissing her on one cheek said, 'That's from nan,' and kissing her on the other cheek he added, 'and that's from me, for wanting to fix me up with a nice English girl.'

They laughed, comradely, as they walked out to his motorbike. 'Musha, isn't it the grand yoke,' said Minnie.

'It's more than a grand yoke, Mrs O'Brien, it's the greatest,' he laughed. 'It's a Harley Davidson, and they don't come any grander than that. I'll come again, if I may,' he said as he harnessed his helmet to his head.

'Musha, come Thursday night or Sunday night,' said Minnie. 'They're the nights when Laura comes to see me. Go on in now and turn in the yard,' she advised him, and just to please her he did. While in there he revved his furious engine, the noise imploding where only this very day she had thought about a morgue.

White shafts of light bounced off of his helmet as he approached her again. His hand touched where his temple should be as he saluted her. The visor dropped down over his face and, like a bat out of hell, he grumbled his bike's way up towards the road and then on towards Johnny Lynam's on the other side of the bridge.

# CHAPTER 103

Where the air was rare, he flew, Brendie did, lying back at ease planning on watching the in-flight movie. Discovering, though, that it was going to be a western, he switched channels. 'I've had that sort of how's your father for the whole of my vacation,' he snorted, 'and I'm sure as hell not going to live through it again.' While he didn't care a whole lot for wartime dramas, crime thrillers or science fiction, his taste could just about have lived with them, but now it was going to be music which would pan him towards the sunny land ahead. Rooting at the plugs, he suddenly had his ears filled with Mozart's 'Eine Kleine Nachtmusik'. 'Ah! that's more like it,' he thought as, settling himself, he set about absorbing the enchanting and elegant music.

He was about two hours into the flight, listening to a horn concerto, when like a drop of cold reality, a voice plopped onto his forehead. It was his mother's as, urgent and fretful, she called 'Brendie'. He opened his eyes and looked all around, but all was quiet, the noise of the engines all he now heard. He smiled at the naivety of his thinking, but now that he was fully alert, what else was there to think about but that aged woman, syphoning off the signs of death from her days, so that she'd still be alive and kicking when that pimply boy of hers saw fit to return home again.

Praying for the cloistered mother he had left behind, he was nevertheless glad that he had paralysed his fears and gone home to read the situation for himself. He was glad, too, that he had managed to spend that day in Dublin with Sheila. She had been only three weeks doing the part-time nursing, but he could see the *gliondar* of her, to have even got that much leeway off Luke was the turning point for her. 'How the bould Luke ever came to agreeing to allow her go back is something I didn't press her about,' he told his mother when he returned from Dublin, 'but all that matters is that she's back doing what she always longed to do, and the best part is, it's with his blessing.'

So it was as a fairly contented man that he sat winging his way back to work, for each aspect of his life had been dealt with while he, on the wagon, had spent his three-week vacation at home. He felt satisfied with his activities for, though his mother was failing, he could now crest her on his conscience with a modicum of ease. Thanks to Laura Bewley, he could get a bird's-eye view of her situation, and next to being there himself, was the relief of knowing that the young nurse had her neighbour under observation. He knew, too, from Sheila that a phone call from Laura would have her there within the hour, and the best part of all was the fact that Minnie need never know that her family were now worrying about her possible end. He felt happy, too, that he had been instrumental in saving Jude Fortune's life, but perhaps the best part of all of his creations was the view which he had now come to in respect of himself and his own vocation.

It happened the day when he was sitting in the field with the tree stumps. That field was situated halfway between his birthplace and the flowing-down-there river, that river which, he discovered, could be renewing or despoiling. That day, sitting there on his own, he had had to confront himself. That was the day, in fact, when before his eyes passed a sedate funeral – not his great fearless Fenian mother's cortège, no: it was the funeral of a great churchman. He looked carefully at the coffin inside the hearse. Against it lay a lemon-yellow flowered wreath with its In memoriam card framed in black, and on it in his mother's shaky handwriting was one word: BULLSHITTER.

Wandering and gliding, the gulls flew down below, examining the East River as, reading their daily office, they scanned the pages for written-upon titbits. They were wombing their dry matter, the water besides, certain of only one thing, the dreadful din going on where the aeroplanes arrived or departed from, the nearby airport.

Packed, those planes streamlined up above them, each with their complement of cargo or passengers, wasting fuel as, circling Saturday till Saturday, tiered like sticks of seaside-rock-candy, they awaited the 'come on down' from the megabusy control tower.

When the invitation did come, the captain of the Cathay Pacific airline swung his nose the better to line up his beautiful plane from the mysterious east for its touchdown at Kennedy. He, cleared off the airport's radar, made room for the arrival of the next aeroplane, the grey-bellied bird, the bird with the green plumage.

While its burn-up of fuel got on with its burning, the Aer Lingus plane circled the city of New York, holding itself high in the sky, completely oblivious to the fact that one of its passengers, the academic from Drumhollow, was sitting there in his seat, white-knuckled by fear, trying to distract himself by thinking of Lindbergh who, there outside in this very same sky, had taken off in his single-engined plane on that grey morning, in no way able to imagine that there would come a day when, in the opposite direction to the flight plan of his Spirit of St Louis, would appear an aeroplane from Ireland, a big-bellied bird of a plane, human-gutted with people, some of whom sought the evidence of a God as, jet-propelled, their plane made ready for its approach and descent onto the runway of Kennedy Airport.

# CHAPTER 104

While the Aer Lingus plane was taxiing to a halt, the passengers from the Cathay Pacific one had disembarked and set about claiming their luggage. Now they came strealing along, some pushing trolleys of luggage, others carrying one or two pieces, each and every one of them conscious of what they carried and where precisely they stored it, as they approached the counters where the customs staff waited to mark that which they deemed clear of contraband. Striding along among the stream of passengers was a fellow who had nothing to declare, for he in fact carried all that he had in this world in the holdall which hung from his shoulder. It was a long, soft, violet-coloured bag with black inserts, and attached to the steel eyelet of its shoulder-strap was a Cathay Pacific tag. This man looked almost out of place here among those passengers from the Orient, for this fellow was Irish, blue-eyed, and in stature tall and rangy.

Frankie highstepped his way towards Manhattan, on his own for the very first time. In all other instances, in all other cities, he had a mate or two in step with him. Now he was nervous in a pleasant sort of way as, with his hand stuck in his trousers pocket, he tried to create an image of familiarity with the scene, when nothing could be further from the truth. He, in fact, was really on guard, thinking of his mates' stories, thinking too of his history, an Irishman abroad feeling his way, the son of a peasant family, reared to work with his hands, not live on his wits.

All was exploding around Frankie. Lunch-hour rush hurled itself criss-cross and green-manned before him. His eyes couldn't fix on anything for long enough to form an image; it was just like an anthill in the meadowfield at home, only now he was there among the pismires, his white egg in his mouth, and he hardly knew which way or whether he was going. His feet carried him along, his bullfrog-chest heaving. Trying to pacify himself, he scolded, 'Haven't you seen crowded cities before, so why do you feel nervous here?'

Kudos of brain messages fronted Frankie's mind. He found himself comparing first impressions of New York with his first sightings of Sydney, Singapore or Hong Kong. He followed streets and avenues, cracking the layout while he idled at corners. His nostrils picked up the scent of sidewalk smells, of burning oil, car exhaust fumes and perfume proper. He, Frankie, was seeing himself in this pandemonium of peoples. His heart fastened its pumping until he too burdened himself with the wonder of his new world. He had sat in boats in blackest night and seen not a star; he had freaked the dizzy nights away in the multi-coloured hell of downtown Kowloon; his mouth open wide, he had breathed shallow gulps near golden-grassed gorges; but here today he lightly fumed in flurries of freedom in this city at the end of his rainbow.

Frankie O'Brien was a nobody in among masses of nobodies. Cranking himself along, he suddenly glanced skywards. His eyes hunked the sky, snaring a white cloud in the highest sky he had ever measured. The skyscrapers, too, measured the footage, but his white cloud rode a higher hill. It sat atop a burly black streaky billow, and hesitated just as though it was contemplating suicide. He hunted for a place to halt, and standing still he studied the débutante in white. For how long he looked he never measured, but when the woman on the ground stood beside him he jumped when her voice said, 'Can I help you, mister, help you in any way at all?' She touched his hip in a sort of jostling way, moving to face him. Her gaze rested in a saint-like stare as though she too saw a vision. That was how he saw her when he levelled on her face. Shrugging off her approach, he heeded not at all. But her voice fringed her face in some strange allure, and he couldn't help but look just a glance. She was bright in facial expression, and her

342

voice cast around in his consciousness. The chord she plucked shuddered for a while and he couldn't help himself when his tongue formed the words, 'You're Irish?' She never answered, but she walked away. He let her go, telling himself, 'She's on the game, can you believe it, and an Irish whore to boot.' He looked back at the sky. 'The bloody cloud's burst,' he smiled. He made to take a step but, as though he were a cataleptic, he stood there stock-still. He sighed in sadness and sighed in loneliness for somebody or something. Then, as though shot from a catapult, he burst after the prostitute. Vim-sweet and Vim-clean, he vied with the oncomers. He had used his women in clinical fashion, always deferential to their facial mask, and their searing need to relieve him of his spondulicks. His initiation was handled by his buddies' fresh foolery, but now he greeted an Irish come-on as though still a virgin. An Irish girl's voice in a cradle of nibblers, bit at a bait which he had not cast.

Cantering through the pedestrians, he steered this way and that. Folk froze at his mad dash. Secretly, they regarded him as the typical criminal making his getaway. But if his gaze looked frenzied it had a cause: he was searching for a girl in lime green, but he couldn't sketch more than that.

It was his crestfallen feeling which halted his run, but just as though she had shouted 'Look!' he glanced across the street, and there she was, waiting to disappear.

He caught her in a ten, twenty, thirty, forty-yard dash, and gripped her arm. 'You're the first Irish girl I've noticed in over thirty years,' he breathlessly said. 'But it wasn't you that noticed me,' she whimsically whispered, 'but my need that spotted you.' Regardless of passers-by they stood in conversation, he gripped by the accent, and she by the verity in his gaze. They were both caught in a spell of silence, earth-shattering assonance: indeed, the one greeted the other in naked need.

The mirrors gilded them in multifaceted humility. They had drinks before them which proved tasteless. His voice bell-rang in

343

her ear, while her stories nibbled at his guts. He never thought he could miss green fields from this distance, but as her voice nudged on he found himself spellbound.

It was well into the night when Frankie weaved his way back to his warm-sheet hotel. Beside him stepped the girl, about to be a tear-collector for his name's sake. All evening long she had listened to his life-storied voyaging, but by morning she knew she'd have relieved him of grey dollar bills, unrepentant, for this girl of the gutter had other fish to fry and as of now she had, she knew, this Drumhollow pinkeen in her jampot.

Bolstered by need, she met her quarried man again. He could use her, he knew, just so long as his wallet's largesse held out. The visits became regular as clockwork she, as it were, pendulum-swinging from day to night and dawn to dusty dumbbelled dusk. Now he was eulogising her beauty; he liked her 'in soft silk,' he said. 'Soft silk,' a feel to which you'd swear he was accustomed, he that only ever felt wool, wool, and more wool.

It was in a back street in Fremantle that Frankie, the woolman, had had his initiation. It was his mates who set it up for him. They left him outside while they sought her understanding, the poor woman who was going to service him.

When Frankie left the prostitute that night he strutted, like a bantam cock just dismounted from a hen, but his swaggering would be shortlived, his mates told each other, yes, Bob Paisley'd sure put the wind up him, they said.

Quietly they lazed around the fire. Frankie had just drained the billy of its dregs. It was then that the ringer chose his moment, the blazes from the fire playing round his chin.

'Did I ever tell you about my uncle?' he asked Frankie. 'I'll tell you what always reminds me of him, it's whenever we visit a whorehouse anywhere, that his ending flashes by me again.'

Bob's uncle was a Great War veteran, he told Frankie. 'He was m'mother's brother,' he said. 'Was in the medical corps at the Somme he was, got wounded, and had to be brought back from the front. Got the mustard gas he did, his arse and trunk all black, in time they patched him up good enough to go to Paris with his mates. Headed straight for a red-light house, the lot of them, the madam standing starkers on the landing. "Twelve more gentilmen, pleese," she'd call out, see she had her cubicles numbered one to twelve. And in you'd go, get the relief and out, Frankie, all bar the poor bugger George, he paid, let me tell you, for his pluggin', in three weeks he had the fuckin' shankers on his prick. Seven years it took, to reach the fat and fitty stage — that Frankie, is what they called it back then — and then in another seven he was almost a goner, cause he now had the paralysis o'the insane. The flesh it rotted off him, Frankie, the poor bugger, and not a cure in the world, some said let the mosquitoes at him and if he survived the fever then the syphilis might be killed on his dick. Always think of m'poor uncle, Frankie, as I say it's always after we visit them wans, but then sure, that doesn't mean you'll get it, Frankie, but just keep an eye on your mick.'

For three whole weeks Frankie did contortions, trying to examine himself belly, back and sides. How many times he scrutinised his willy could only be numbered in hundreds. He was conscious now of that smell in the brothel, for she that serviced his ejaculation was surrounded by a scent which, come to think of it, reminded him of something, and now he had it, the carbide in the oul' bicycle lamp back home.

Frankie O'Brien nearly lynched the mob for what they did to him that night. They laughed till they nearly died when he described his worries and the minute examinations he carried out on his cock. 'Sure, we were watching out for to see how you'd deal with what Bob told you,' they told him. 'Remember he did it to two others of us as well.'

'Soft silk,' as he now described this girl's lingerie, had had no place in his experience in Fremantle. Soft silk, though, best described the feel of this girl in New York. 'Soft touch' best described how this Irish girl-gone-wrong saw Frankie, 'soft as butter,' she surmised, but then 'What if I've got him wrong?' she worried, 'What then?'


## CHAPTER 105


In a room in the Bronx it unfolded. The invitation came from her. 'Will you come to my apartment this evening, please?' she begged, and his response brought her story from its wrapper.

'He had the apartment on the same landing as me, we often bade Hi to each other. Then we began to exchange a few words about the weather or the traffic, you know, all the usual vindication for chat's sake. We heard each other's comings and goings, my late hours home, his late mornings rising. He grew into a nice neighbour, never became inquisitive or pushy. His door was there if I needed anything, and I was there if he ran short of anything. He had men friends, I listened to their voices in conversation, or sometimes I listened to his music. Jazz, he likes, always jazz. The years, five years next week, have gone by and now he can't even answer my knock. I had to get a key cut so I could look in on him. He's all alone, all alone in this big bloody bedlam. No, you're wrong, I can see what you're thinking. You feel everyone abandoned him. But no, that's not true. When he discovered his illness he told his buddies he was going back home. They believed him, and he even believed himself. He did go home to his parents, nobody can say he didn't, but Ireland hadn't heard of his condition before — at least his parents hadn't heard, and as it turned out they didn't want to hear.' Frankie tried to speak but she pressed her finger to his lips. 'His parents as much as told him to go back to where he found it: his illness, I mean. He was back here within the week, and managed to get his apartment back before our landlord

346

managed to get another tenant. It's downhill every day since he walked back up those stairs, and so when I ask you to meet him, I want to have you ready. It's going to be hard on you. For me it's different, it's crept up bit by bit, and now I'm the only one he has to make him a cup of tea. Sometimes a little soup, but mostly it's medicine he takes.' She stopped. Frankie now had his chance to speak, but he was baffled. She was relieved, though, for now her story had been told after twenty-two months of silence. She could never tell her clients: her customers wouldn't want her sideplate of gooseberries handed to them. Now her eyes didn't even search for his response; she gazed up instead at a blister of paint near the hotel window. But now he at least knew, one other person knew of his plight, poor Pat's plight.

Frankie lay there on his side, on his side of the bed, looking at her side-face. Under his gaze, her eyes never wavered. She was still looking up, looking at that loose blister of paint, her expression composed. Lying there naked beside her, he searched down as far as his testicles as he wondered what he should do about Pat, but she, sensing his answer, was wondering if he'd flee when he saw the state of him. Suddenly, Frankie sat up and, taking her hand, gently kissed it. 'If you can be a good Samaritan,' he said, 'well then, so can I.' But she, swinging her gaze away from that god-awful ceiling, looked at him and said, 'Hold your whisht, Frankie, until you actually meet Pat.'

# CHAPTER 106

Frankie smelt the disinfectant wafting up his nostrils. Nostrils used to musk perfume, at the very least, now stung with disbelief. Here they were in New York just three weeks, no more, and now tonight they smelt behind the desperate freshness a man. He lay there grey, gas-grey and human. His flowing beard stringy, thin. Large sores fed on his establishment in hungry fashion. His reality, strong as bush-string, tried to green his welcome to this man of hers. Barely able to stretch out his hand to another, he dressed his uneasy gait with words of Irish. '*Dia dhuit*,' he whispered, barely able, and when Frankie took his awfully thin hand in his he found himself replying '*Dia's Muire dhuit.*' Ridiculous it was, them speaking their native tongue, but still the sound pacted them, this trio fashioning themselves here as Gaels.

Brushing aside his best objections, Frankie moved out of his Bronx hotel and moved into a sea-green snare. 'No hurry,' the girl had said when he whispered he'd move in with Pat. Now he felt giddy on his ferris wheel of rescue, for his heart had never before seen anything resembling that which he had now embarked upon in this caring and caring scene.

The girl grew nervous now, for fashioning a helpmate out of a customer brought its own due. Girl that she was, whore that she became, victim that she viewed her landing's neighbour, friend that she had in him, gilded sacrifice that he now told himself to pay, God-whethered that they both tinkered with, her angst her hopelessness, hysters of gingham-clad shoulders his vulved nothingness, her gibbet his hanger-on to life, freedom from his hacking cough bought by her body comfort, grace her spiritual gift to him, as basking there he bristled by night and blessed her by day for working those God-awful hours in that God-articulated brothel of

348

dishwashing, dirty-ashtray-emptying and, worst of all, her vying with her mates to get the biggest tips in the bar, that swanky bar where the well-heeled ethnics gathered to sip black Guinness, bystanding there in indirect invitation to be greeted with a 'howya' instead of a 'hi'. Moidered by her deceit, freshened by her being able to get relief for him through drugs, antibiotics and paingrinders, she made use of clients who made use of her, but he was never to know her sources. He tried, God knows he tried, but body blows broke his flying questions, and relief brought him the gibbet, decorated once again in yellow gingham, filleted especially for his mind.

The arrival of this Irishman nurtured new, ham-pink life into Pat. He now had someone near at hand but, determined to be as handy a man as need be, he made ferrets run in search for strength to enable him to act as normal for normality's sake. Frankie grew to bonding, just as sure as that Monroe dress did to flying, yet he was daily touched by the girl's constant giving. Berry by berry, he watched as she fed the sick man, coaxing him to eat her strawberries and cream, meant to freshen Pat's memories of home. Together now the three reminisced: testing each other's memories, they had no need, now, for playing the radio or watching hired-out videos. No, that'd be far too noisy, in this thurible of suffering; all that mattered now was that the days could be lifed for Pat. Playing word games then, they were back in their childhoods, back at the national school, though two of them had third level education. 'What's the Irish for robin?' It was Pat himself asked the question, and here in the Village was tossed out the word *spideog*. 'But what about his red breast?' he tested. Long searching winnowed the pictures on school walls at home. 'Well *dearg* is red,' the girl said. 'And *broinndearg* is redbreasted,' she added. 'Well how about the word for bog?' teased Pat. 'Ah! sure, that's easy,' said Frankie. '*Portach* was a bog last time I was home,' he said. The game this evening was simple, yet it was terrible, for nobody was giving anything away, and neither was Pat. It was when Frankie and the girl were least expecting it that he brought out the word. 'What's the Irish for dying?' he said. 'I know the word for dead is *marbh*, but the act of dying, you know, from day to day and inch to inch, give's the word for that?' Poverty set in, so much so that they all stopped in their tracks, and nobody tried to translate the furnished words – nobody, that is, except Frankie. He now greened his *raison d'être* by lifting Pat up high onto his pillows, and hesitatingly asked the question which no one else would ask. 'Pat,' he said, 'is there something bothering you about dying?' He looked hard now at the dying which was creeping ever nearer to this almighty man. Ten o'clock struck on the old colonial mantelpiece before Pat answered. 'I'd like a priest to look in on me,' he whispered, sort of, and now that he had it said he felt his voicebox freed. 'Yes,' he said, more to himself than to the others, 'yes, I'd bloody well like to be anointed, and then I'm more than ready, more than willing, to meet Him face on.' Zoo-caged on the bed of boredom, he now bestirred himself. He looked about him as though searching for someone. 'I don't know ary a priest, do ye?' he said, and with those words he had thrown the fat in the fire.

Her business contacts were her own numbing business, so she couldn't name a name. Frankie, thanking his lucky stars, knew he couldn't be expected to know anyone. His brother was a priest, he told them, but where he was or how good he was he didn't know. It was frail Pat who grew possibilities in the disinfected air. 'Nobody I ever heard with your name,' he said. 'Nobody in this neighbourhood, that is, except he's a bishop.' Frankie giggled. 'What's this fella's name?' he asked. 'Maybe I'm related, nothing but a bishop, no less.' Pat hesitated for a moment, trying to recall the name. 'I think it was Brendan, if I'm not mistaken,' he said. 'Go on, tell's more,' said Frankie, but all the sick man could offer was a copy of the *Irish Echo*, showing this man newly returned from holidaying in his homeland.

Frankie sat stone-quiet, letting his eyes examine the photograph. Yes, he could recognise the bushy eyebrows and the cow's lick waved hair. 'Arrah, go on, yer only coddin', arrah go on, yer pullin' me leg,' he found himself saying. 'It's him, it's bloody well him,' he said to Pat. Forgetting himself, he jumped up and threw the paper in the air. 'It's Brendie, I'll be damned if it isn't Brendie, and he's a bishop, no less,' he said. Suddenly he copped on again to his surroundings. 'I'm sorry to be leppin' like this and you so ill, Pat,' he said, 'but then you've only yourself to blame.' Excitedly now, he spoke of his whole family, and sure of at least one member he was talking like a gramophone run amok. Nothing could be done tonight, but come morning this priest-problem of Pat's was going to be solved.

## CHAPTER 107

The phone rang on the bishop's desk as there he sat, up to his eyes in paperwork. He thoughtlessly gripped it and, holding it to his ear, said 'Yeah?' There was a split second of silence, then down the line came words: 'One lady, two lady, three lady, Pan/Hopster, vinegar, Irishman.' Where he sat listening now he screamed, 'Judy Caddie, Jack o'the laddie, where in hell are you, Frankie, I can't believe it's you.' Now he sat there, the phone still at his ear, interjecting at every chance. 'The Plaza, of course I do. Yeah, I know, the UN buildings. Oh sure, sure. When did you arrive? God, we've been searching the world. In New York, beside me. God, it's great to hear your voice. Oh yeah, the minute I heard it, you didn't have two lady out before I knew. Yeah, you never forget. Oh God, if only you knew how good it is. Listen Frankie, don't stir whatever you do. I'm on my way. Yeah, just a few minutes. Yeah. That'll all hold. Aye, I know. But listen, hang on there. Look't, I'll say goodbye. I'll see you, Frankie. Yeah, wait in the foyer. Yeah, yeah, the front hall. See you Frankie, bye.'

The phone banged down, he started from his desk, and it was then he saw his secretary standing at the door. 'Were you in on this?' he asked, and they both laughed. 'Now that's him, that's the bould Frankie, and if I don't get there quick the bugger might disappear again. You just hold everything for me until I get back.'

He was like something on speed as his cumbersome body hurtled through the hallway, making a beeline for his car. 'The Plaza, you know it,' had said Frankie 'near the UN buildings.'

'Do I know it,' thought Brendan. 'If it was in downtown Mars I'd find it. Only be there when I come,' he prayed.

The staff in the Plaza Hotel were about their business, completely unaware of the drama about to be staged here in their foyer, where a man sat, reading, a big bloke minding not at all the comings and goings, for he was hiding his interest behind his newspaper. Then a cleric came through the revolving doorway, breathless from hurrying. He stood for a moment, his eyes scrutinising the man seated there. 'Yes, he has the right height,' he was thinking, but the bloke behind the newspaper only needed to spot the black trouser legs and the two long shoes to know that he had found Brendie.

Jumping to his feet he made for his brother, his two arms flung open wide. 'Brendie,' he said, 'the minute I saw the two shoes I knew I had found you.' They stood, sort of awkward, there in the foyer, the pair of referees, each thinking through the thoughts of childhood.

Respectfully they hugged each other, slapping one another's backs, but the voices which they wound around each other were flibberty-gibbet and folly to their respective hearing. 'God, it's great to have you back,' Brendie kept telling his brother, and when Frankie replied his enunciation was in turn but the first cousin once removed of his brother's American twang.

In the bar they time and again ordered and reordered their beers:

they had a lot to talk about and a lot of territory to cover. Brendie talked constantly about their aged mother, but Frankie, not having seen her in over thirty years, was finding it hard to believe what his brother was spelling out for him.

The conversation eventually moved away from Drumhollow and on to themselves. Now, though, they were not in a bar in Manhattan but back competing on Holly Bog. Neither could be seen to yield to the other, for now it was as though they were back stacking turf, except that the sods comprised their successes and their ventures. Not an inch did they yield to each other, but the very mention of their sister, Sheila, changed all that. Tears filled their eyes as Brendan told Frankie of Sheila's marriage to Luke, and of the lonely life which she and her two sons led, while he, the man of money, traversed the globe always sure that, like the fly caught in the spider's web, his wife would be there at home waiting to welcome him back.

All the while they chatted, Brendan noticed a certain uneasiness about Frankie, but so glad was he to be here sitting opposite him that he made no comment about what he was thinking. So it came almost as a relief when Frankie blurted out the question which all the time had been bothering him. 'Brendie,' he said, his nervousness making his speaking voice slightly slurred, 'there's a reason for me looking for you, nothing would have discovered you for me, if it wasn't for a friend's wish.' And so he filled his bishop-brother in on the awful needing of a blessing for his friend, Pat. 'The poor fella is dying and he knows it, and do you know what he wants, to be anointed. He's under the doctor but he knows he's going, and he said "If I was anointed I'd be ready to meet Him face on." Will you come and anoint him, cause I sort of guaranteed him that if I found you, you'd come.'

Minnie's priest-son grew uncomfortable. His nimble mind began setting up obstacles. He was suspicious of the whole set-up between Frankie, some girl, and some dying man. 'His own priest'll be glad to serve him,' he voiced, going on then to excuse himself by

353

highlighting his great responsibility. 'I won't come myself, but I'll send one of my priests to look in on your friend,' he said. 'Just give me his address and I'll know his parish.'

'I'll send one of my priests,' said Frankie, as he scornfully imitated his brother's voice. 'You'll not send one of *your* priests, because I'd rather Pat die with dignity than get the pushover from a pup like you. If Mammy or Daddy could hear you refusing to console a poor dying man they'd shoot you, and do you know what, I'd even help them.'

Brendan attempted to explain his position, but Frankie was only interested in his friend's need for a blessing. 'Come off your high and mighty big job, and see your vocation for what it's supposed to be,' begged the wayfarer, 'and make up your mind fairly smartly, cause I'm in a hurry and I want help.'

Brendan sat there, all composed. He was a dab hand at giving folk the put-off, but with Frankie it didn't work. This tinker, tailor, soldier, sailor had seen too much of life in the red raw to be baffled by a fella who had shared the same back bedroom for all those ghostly nights in Drumhollow. Niggling his brother so created a strain where shortly before had reigned brotherly love, but Frankie was a hoor's ghost for always getting his own way as a child. Now he was trying the very same tactics again. He stood up suddenly and held out his hand to his brother. 'I'll just tell Pat that you're away,' he suggested. 'I wouldn't have the heart to hurt him, and he on his deathbed.' He turned as if to go, but Brendan was playing like a fisherman in deep swirling waters. 'Don't be so bloody hotheaded, Frankie, you'd swear nobody cared but you and that girl you mentioned. It's not that I don't want to help,' he said, 'but you seem to forget I'm a bishop now, and a bishop has other jobs to do.'

Frankie was from foot to foot, exasperation riding shotgun across his face. He cut across his brother's reasonableness and said, 'Cut the bullshit, are you coming or are you not? I'll give you the address if you're coming, and don't send a messenger, cause he won't get past me.'

Brendan asked for the address, and when he saw where it was he decided that someone must be very careful, because Christopher Street wasn't the usual hang-out for bishops. He smiled now a kind of cute-hoor, streetwise smile, calculating all the while what he was being roped into, and yet freshening his vocation at the strict expectation of his brother's grand spirit, he felt himself drawn, inexplicably drawn, to this soul who called him.

Frankie was better at studying the landscape than his brother. He saw the expression changing from cool businesslike to gleam-in-the-eye style of thinking. Now he assessed his brother's mind and said, 'Brendie, come any time tonight or any time in the morning. But don't delay,' he suggested as, giving his brother a big hug, he was gone, gone as though he had scored a motza.

As Frankie made his way back to the Village he was as happy as he could be. He began now to rehearse the news he was bringing. 'Pat,' he would say, 'you wanted some priest to anoint you, and a priest you're going to have. Maybe even tonight, or failing that he'll be here in the morning.'

## CHAPTER 108

The room was sorted and beautifully tidy. Flowers, white lily-of-the-valley, stood in a dark-green vase, their clusters hanging down in awe at the grace of this man here waiting for death to claim him. Janitors, they perfumed this room-setting in fine-tuning with the desires of the spirit here present. They were standing in their bottle-green vase on the table where the girl's hands had set them, wanting, as it were, to let a dying man get the scent of nature's message to him. Where she lung-filled the man, she set candles, one spaced on either side of his bed, burning in anticipation of his death-wish being granted. They weren't beeswax candles or blessed candles, but they were all she had, and now they flickered and flamed in absolute unison with Pat's heartbeat.

A sea of white engulfed the dying man. Pillows piled high enabled him to sit up and sometimes glance around him. His eyes plied between the two Samaritans, just about able to appreciate their joint preparation on his behalf.

Hours ticked by, shedding themselves like petals around his bed. The clock in the kitchen area chimed nine and, as though synchronised, the doorbell picked that very moment to ring. Frankie didn't even wait to find out if the voiced announcement would come from his brother; he was down those stairs like greased lightning, and flinging open the door he saw him standing there. 'I knew you'd bloody well come, I knew you wouldn't fail me,' he said. Leading the way, he headed for the stairs, but before taking even one step he looked back at his brother and said, 'Wait'll you meet this man.' The bishop said nothing, just tramped up those flights of stairs after Frankie until they reached the floor on which Pat had his apartment.

He merged with the bedclothes, particularly his beard, a straggly white affair, just lying there stacked on top of the white bedspread. His pale lips moved as the priest entered. '*Fáilte romhat a athair,*' he abled himself to say. Brendan stooped towards him and said, 'Pat, I'm very pleased to be here to help you.'

Frankie's job done, he left the priest and the player together: only they momented now. Closing the door after him, he crossed the landing, and pushing in the open door went in to her apartment. The girl sat there on her divan bed, her head bent, deep in thought. His rubber soles plucked on her carpet, the sound grating to her ears, and now, lifting her head, she looked at him. 'Thank God he came,' she whispered. 'If he had to die without a priest, I think I'd pack in God for good.' Her words were the same as the gospel story, but she was a twentieth-century whore simmering in the cauldron of man's indecency towards women. Frankie was feeling moved too, nearly, greased by his mates' use of women, he almost found himself bragging about his own sexual conquest and its aftermath. He stood near the door awaiting developments. 'Do you want to meet my brother?' he asked, but his question sounded laden with doubt. She shook her head. He hid his relief by standing even nearer to the crack in the door. He moved the moment that the doorknob rattled, and was out on the landing when his brother emerged.

The bishop closed the door quietly after him and, as though regretful of preconceived ideas, grasped Frankie by the arm and said, 'I'm very glad you told me about Pat.' Their voices low, they crossed the landing, and the girl could hear them going back downstairs.

Her job was almost sorted out, but still she went back to his bedside. Bending over him, her hands caressed his buckled fingers and her pearl necklace dipped down, touching his branded beard. 'Pat, are you happy now?' she quietly asked, and as though he didn't hear her he didn't reply. She blew out the yellow candle butts and stood there watching the smoke curling and twisting. It was then he spoke. 'Remember I told you,' and his voice was faltering, 'I told you that when I told my father I was home to die, he told me that when I had the dinner eaten I was to go back to the dog that bit me? And ever since, whenever his words came back to haunt me, I'd at the very same time see the hurt face of my mother, broken in bits at the justice dealt out by a bully. And now you ask me if I'm happy. Why wouldn't I be, and I after experiencing a miracle? I'm happy and I'm unafraid and you're the girl to thank.' He smiled a fraction and closed his eyes again. She walked away, her voice gone, and closing the door of his room left Pat to rest. Now she could hear Frankie tramping back towards her, and looking down towards him she put a finger to her lips.

357

# CHAPTER 109

The casket, desperate in its loneliness, freed itself suddenly and sauntered between the plush, maroon-coloured curtains into the inferno within. Pat's body, fire-hindered by grace, lay inside, as important as any bishop's and as unimportant as any tramp's. His grim death had been placid, and the moment of expiry just a huge gasp. The bishop was seeing to his funeral service, and standing there as mourners were Frankie and four other neighbours from the apartments on the floor beneath Pat's. But lying low and well in the background shied she of the night, the girl from his home country, the friend who asked nothing but gave all that was required so that a rejected man might die in dignity. Nobody here really knew her except Frankie and Pat, but now, her job complete, she but fretted for Pat's ashes.

The morning mist hung free on the briars, scrubs and ferns. She tramped upwards hindered by huge fillets of rock. Still, determinedly, she bore onwards and upwards. Her eyes scanned the highest point. She tried to imagine how high he would go. She stopped occasionally and looked back down, the better to measure how high she had come. Human worth lay as sadness in a plastic urn in her haversack. Hunter Mountain was his favourite spot in this state, and she planned now to join him and it together. Tiring, she stopped for a moment, and it was then she saw it – a sunny glade in between huge chunks of weathered rock. 'I'll bury it here,' she thought, and searching around she found a sliver of stone. Her hands dug in primitive humanity and now, the hole deep enough, interred the urn in the mountain grave. Using her bare hands she scooped the earth back into place. She smoothed it with the sole of her shoe, and standing back now for a little day, she thought final thoughts before bowing her head towards the Catskills' grave, and descending the mountain again.

## CHAPTER 110

'He's coming home, the child,' she said, the musha-comforter not needed now. 'He's coming home, the child,' she said, and the clock stuck on its tick. 'He's coming home, the child,' she said, her thumbs not churning now. 'He's coming home, the child,' her grim voice said, for sand in her eyes, the raven's book read, her soul heard the dead-bell now.

Nobody would dare say that that phone call from New York had come too late to matter. Nobody had the nerve to nil her response. Nobody knew how heavy or how grumpy the news made her feel, for when Minnie O'Brien did hear that Frankie was alive and in New York and heading homewards, her Hy-Brazil gave out signals which only she could yes.

At nine, when the wind was trying to warn her, she missed the sign, for she couldn't see its fingers pointing at something which wasn't there. At nine the rain reckoned she'd feel its sign but, used to getting drenched on Holly Bog, she didn't feel its attacking drops as fact, and fiction bore down its plea, the better to herald its warning. At nine she echoed her husband's truth when he swore to her that she and she alone had ever seen his 'leading article'. Now at nine, she thought she heard that motorbike again, but the wax in her ears dumbed the signal and each time her late husband's grandson, throttle out, wuff-wuffed that long ago deception, she but heard inside her head the yin and yang of her own blood coursing through her veins. At nine she swore she could smell something like incense, but foible that it was, she missed its signal, her senses ignoring the scent. Sniffing vacantly, she now felt funny, and taking a paper hankie from her apron pocket she attempted to unclog her nose by blowing furiously into the tissue's soft Fenian fold. At nine she tasted druidic butter from her butter-churning days, ginseng it really was, but the sign of the times was not hers to notice. Now instead, left to her own devices, she just curled her tongue all around her mouth, tasting naught but her own saliva.

Cackling for all she was worth, the guardian now redundant had time and to spare for her game of holy hell. Propped up in bed, she rectified the whole family's faults. 'They were drilled too much and frightened too much,' her voice said to the mantelpiece. 'The game's up now, the child is kinda coming back.'

'I'll bet Brendie and himself have had a bleddy good fight by now, each blaming the other for staying away too long, but I know them of old, when the shouting and roaring'd be finished I'll bet they go off and have a tightener, maybe in some posh restaurant suitable for my son with the three hats.' Now she screamed laughing. 'What do you think of that?' she asked the black mantelpiece. 'There they are,' she added, 'my children, the green fools, in that big drunken night over there.'

But she was raving, so she was, for if Minnie Humphrey-that-was could have got on her broomstick and steered her way over Manhattan, she'd have seen 'Rent-a-priest' and his brother 'Rent-a-whore' choring as together they saw off a Donegal man's soul to paradise, and as if that wasn't good enough for a country pair, the 'Rent-a-priest' was off again, this time answering a tip-off from an Irish-American police officer. His message on Brendan's answering machine said, 'One of your boys is down in the Bowery, get your ass down there and pick him up before we have to.'

# CHAPTER III

It was one of those cold, frosty evenings in New York City, the air folded between the skyscrapers ravishing the flesh on folks' faces. He felt cold inside his fur-lined jacket, and the steam from his breath had dampened the scarf which he had curled around his neck and across his mouth. He kept his hands in his pockets and his fingers clenched inside his fists. Along the street in front of him ascended clouds of steam. Lights, myriad in colour, lit up the confusing swirling steam in a medley of blinking reds and lilac-blues. Pondering on the telephone message, he knew he'd find his man down here in the lane of the stunted. Harry Hope, the philosopher of the class, now hung out here with his drop-out nobodies.

True to his notions of his joined-up Jesus, Brendan worked his way in and out among the pedestrians, on or around the manhole covers, sometimes stopping and standing stock-still as he hunted in the Mafia-necked lanes, looking to see if he might spot a figure in black.

Brendan the bishop, mad at his friend for once again letting down the church, strode smartly so as not to draw the winos onto his case. He was in mufti, he thought, but somehow the sharpers down here caved insights like animals. Still, it had to be done, he just couldn't bring down the archbishop on top of him. He'd find his old buddy, bring him home, sober him up, dust him down, hell if he wouldn't, and he'd find himself doing the same thing come next month, or maybe he'd even get by for three. Same story, though, since he found out about Harry, the young man who lay prostrate beside him on Ordination Day.

Glancing into the great hubbub of this forge, he eventually found what he was looking for. It was the singing which caught his ear, the two women fulminating through the cold dead air. In an archway they drew on their jolly humour to sing out in words of lily-white longing. 'Oh Danny Boy, the pipes, the pipes, are calling,' raucoused the American voices as, with attempted encouraging language, they hoped that he'd manage somehow to lift himself up. The man in grey-black, though, lay prone, the empty vodka bottle clenched in one hand.

Brendan sat on his hunkers and glanced sideways at the flattened face of the priest. Shaking his shoulder he whispered, 'Harry, can you hear me, it's Brendie O'Brien.' The figure never budged. Now the bishop used his strength, and catching hold of the drunk, lifted him up onto his knees and prodded him for memory. 'You might as well be talking to the dead,' he told himself as, looking about him, he searched for a place where he might prop up his charge. Half dragging and half lifting, he worked the priest out from the archway and into the dark underworld. Now he propped Harry Hope against a wall and stood back for a breather.

The down-and-out priest didn't know day from night nor dog from devil, but as he sat there he somehow managed to lift his head and stare into the eyes of the sober one. Brendan didn't heed the look, too preoccupied sizing up the dirty, stained stock, the paw-marked, frayed collar, and most of all the green part of Harry's once black trousers.

It took three people to load Harry Hope into the cab, and then it took all of Brendan's resources to prop him up and hold him in his seat until the hall door of his residence came into sight.

He had to put Harry Hope in a kneeling position when it came to showering him, a bath out of the question, he sensed, for his friend was gone past the head-above-water stage. He had searched out some of his clothes for Harry, deciding then on giving his friend the lovely bottle-green v-necked sweater which his sister Sheila had bought for him in Arnotts that day when he went to Dublin.

Next morning saw Harry Hope up with the mushrooms, his load

of drink slept off, only his shakes to deal with. Two mugs of thick black coffee under his belt now, and the realisation that he would be soon rubbing noses with a bishop, fairly brought him to his milk.

The morning outside looked lovely and sunny, but inside where he now sat the room felt chilly. He had retrieved his breviary from down inside the lining of his anorak where it had, over the months, burrowed through the pocket, and nowadays slid and sloothered all around the bottom of the padded jacket. Down now where his hands wouldn't shake the bejaysus-words off the flimsy pages, he set the book, the table at least steady, and began turning his blinded mind towards the wonderful likely God of his imagining. Liberty was his as he read his salutations to his being. There he sat, for all the world a fullblown sinner, but the voice hinting in his ear told him that the lily finds its opium in the drunk's leftovers. Thus was he sitting there thinking when his Mother Teresa of last night burst into the room. Stuttering, he was blubbering something about his mother dying. At first Harry couldn't decipher what his old pal was on about, but eventually the story outed itself, and none better was there in an emergency than this man whom Brendan had picked up and sorted out on so many occasions.

## CHAPTER 112

It was Laura Bewley who discovered Minnie O'Brien, sitting there in her chair, an expression on her face the likes of which in her years of nursing she had never before been privy to. 'You'd swear she was on something,' she thought. 'You'd swear she gave up the Lyons tea and has gone instead on that ayahuasco stuff.' Pleased beyond words, that's how Minnie's face looked, and despite Laura's best efforts, sorra talk would she.

Teresa Fortune, Felix's wife, gripped her next-door neighbour under each arm and, backing up the stairs, pulled and lifted in order to allow for the greater weight which was on Laura, as thumping together they brought the old woman up to her bed. The burden left down, they rested, the thunder pounding in their insides, her thunder transferred. On her back they laid her, her head gently placed on her pillow, the room green in places where white spots didn't hailstone. The bun feast which their old patient had had the day she bought the material for her two sets of curtains was not theirs to know of, and the joy it gave her each morning, provided the sun shone through where her needs lay, God alone knew, for the green cotton material with the big spots was only fit for a summer dress, but Minnie made from it a dotted drubbing.

It was from the Fortunes' hallway that the two phone calls were made, one to the doctor in Huntstown, the other to Minnie's daughter, the nurse, Sheila Green. The message to the doctor was urgent, but the one to Sheila was couched in careful language, for it held a double-barrelled shotgun to the Hill O'Down, the Hill O'Down where the clock had hollered its tingalingaling the Thursday before the Friday when, up at five o'clock, ten past in fact, she that was now in green-grassed meadowland, white gunsmoke bobbing up here and there, had gone to the depot to collect the linchpin, the pin which until today had stolon been, and now was about to die to hasten home a child, a son of sodomy, a libellous funeral to attend, and her in the hearse, a bungler's mother, and stung so her corpse would not rot now, the nimble hour, or ever.

Hearing Sheila's voice on the line from Ireland sent a quiver of tension wellspringing down Brendan's straightness of spine. He knew the moment he heard it that something had happened. Sheila seldom bothered to contact him, for her husband's network kept her in thrall, his wish her command, his bull her cow's myth, his prison of a mansion her house on death row, but now her voice begged him to act. 'Come at once, for God's sake come, and bring Frankie, she's calling for Frankie, she calls and looks towards the door.'

The traffic was actually fairly thin on the ground as Brendan went in search of Frankie. The cab dropped him in the Village the minute he humiliated himself. In no time at all he tried the bell beside Frankie's name, but no voice replied on the intercom.

Brendan read the name of the next apartment's resident, and now he pressed her bell. The wait was eternal, the years following each other in minutes, until after what seemed like forty years a girl's voice said a pleasurable 'hello'. Now he couldn't get his words out, his brain wouldn't function, wouldn't numb itself long enough to let him articulate his sentence. He wanted to explain that he was desperate to speak to a man now occupying the apartment on her floor. 'I'm his brother,' he bellowed, 'and I need to speak to him urgently, very urgent like, you see.' Now he was adapting his boyhood's phraseology, and found himself explaining like, just as he did when he was, say, ten. 'My, I mean his, you see like she's mine too, my, our, mother is dying, you see,' and having managed to get that much said, he was starting to taste the saliva coming pumping from his gums. 'His mother is calling for him, like, where, do you know, is he?' The girl's quiet voice cut across his moiderdom, and she said, 'Just hold on a moment and I'll come down.' He tried to compose himself, but his lip was trembling, just like it was the day he drove away from his lonely mother. Standing there, he felt almost as alone as he knew she was on that day back home in Drumhollow.

The door opened, and the girl pleased his pleading look when she told him that 'yes,' she knew his brother slightly, and thought that she might be able to help. 'He gets in around six most evenings, and maybe I could give him your message. I'm sorry for your trouble,' she offered, and he consciously noted her phrase of condolence. He was too upset to linger, but he stressed how urgent it was for Frankie to get home. He gave her an envelope, explaining that it was an open airline ticket for his brother. 'His mother is mentioning his name constantly, you see,' he stressed but she, the girl with the grey eyes, reassured him. 'He'll get there, I'll see to that for you, Father,' she said. His gratitude was effusive, but he steered himself to go. Then he looked back again at the girl. 'Please tell my brother that I'm on the Aer Lingus flight tonight.' Thanking her again, he dashed away.

The departure lounge that night was criss-crossed by folk going about their business. Brendan sat stony-faced, seeking his new brother among the crisis throng. He sensed that the girl would get the urgency of his message over to Frankie, so he didn't give up hope until he felt the engines of the plane roar into action. He even stared out of his small window, glancing back to see if by any chance there happened to be some person chasing after the plane. He didn't see the comic touch within his action, for, crazy with great feelings of sadness, he just wished to have Frankie with him when he got home.

## CHAPTER 113

Frankie O'Brien had fully intended going home to cook a meal for himself, but his eye read the advertisement telling of the big fight programme at Madison Square Garden. His interest in boxing dated back to his young days when he followed the career of the Brown Bomber, the 'long count' fight decision in the Dempsey versus Tunney fight, and most of all he remembered his father, ear glued to the old steam radio as he called it, trying to hear the fight commentary from the BBC. 'In New York, and didn't go to Madison Square Garden?' he could almost hear his father reprimand, so he bought a hot dog and a beer and headed for the fight night. His seat was spot-on for a good view, his companions on every side of him talked and chatted as though from the one big family. The buzz from the crowd was electric, and the fights hadn't even started.

His programme gave him all the names of the teams taking part tonight, and as he looked on he could swear he recognised some of the trainers. His memory came from nights chatting in bars or around camp fires, but the fights tonight would be for real. He was looking forward to the spectacle of glove bombarding body and head bombarding glove. He felt he owed himself the experience, so he settled down for the night's entertainment, secretly pretending that his father was sitting beside him.

As the fight night progressed, he watched amateurs scoring humdingers with a great left hook or a right cross, but he was really looking out for the heavyweight pairing, for he knew that they could soon be world heavyweight champion material, and then his own boast would be that he knew them as amateur Golden Glovers.

The sound of the stadium's voices buzzed through his hearing as he walked out into the night air. He was bowled over by the events of the tournament. 'That black man who won the heavyweight fight had all the cut and jib of Muhammad Ali,' he was thinking as he sauntered along, for the moment forgetting all his own hang-ups about being on your guard in any big city. The boxing tonight had revived memories from his childhood, of the kitchen at home, the wireless there near the window, whistling and spitting and fading just when the fight was exciting. He smiled now as he remembered the old oil lamp with the green bowl: the glass chimney used to blacken on one side, mostly. He used have to carry home the oil in a can from the shop, the paraffin always managing to get on his hands. He smelt his palms now, more in memory than habit, and then he smiled, noticing where he was as those nutshelled memories began surfacing. 'I'll have to get back there soon,' he thought, and now he grimaced as he totted up his years away. 'I'll just give here a week or two more,' he said, 'and it's home, bucko, then, your travels are through.'

He noticed the card pinned to his door while he was still climbing the stairs to his apartment. 'Please give me a call, I've an urgent message,' was as far as he had got before her door opened and she strode out. 'What's the urgent news?' he asked her, but she made him come into her room and there she sat him down. Now she led up to her news, her voice smoothing the vital message. 'She's constantly mentioning your name, nobody else's, Frankie, only yours,' she gently told him. But it was all no good, for his whole composure collapsed. 'And I was just thinking of her, and I after leaving Madison Square Garden,' he said, talking to himself. The girl, though, remembering her promise to his brother, filled him in on what was now of most importance. She told him of his brother's travel arrangements, but now, looking at the clock, they both knew that he was too late for that night's flight to Ireland.

Night hesitated for hour after hour as he sat at Kennedy Airport. He was trying to catch even a flight to London, and maybe from there get home in time. Rescuing his freedom from his birthplace had led him in his odyssey to the ends of the earth. Now, if his mother could just manage to breathe a little longer, he'd get to the end of his journey and hear her name him, her youngest, 'the child'.

# CHAPTER 114

It was a night in druid entity, God thin-looking in the bed, avoidance His game, the October month well near gone, when Minnie O'Brien's priest-son harum-scarum-like staggered to her bedside. Crossing her five senses with chrism, he begged forgiveness for any or many sins committed by either or all of the stumbling-blocks. Starting at the eyelids, he moved to the nostrils, then down to the lips and, seeing as they should be closed tight, worked her lubbards together with the little finger of his left hand before he thumb-signed the chrism with his right hand. The palms of her hands were next for anointing, the two hands white on the backs, buns of veins bulging, but turned over as though mushrooms frying, the hands' palms indicated lines and lines of life, theming teeming traces, thin and Sibyline in greatness, but he traced his cross on those palms, funding his vincible faith in his bungler's blessing. Last sense of all was foot-sore and tired. The feet, soles in dreadful, thrashed, frenzied footwork, were last to be blessed with holy oil. Technically they didn't have to be anointed, but this son, ravishing ad hoc immediacy to his dying mother, sought mercy for her, the likes of which could only be found in paradise.

Conscious one moment, unconscious the next, Minnie dallied the days of dreadlocked design. Her voice emptied her longing from her heart so often that, to her assembled family, she seemed as though she was just holding out for Frankie to come. Sometimes a great anxiety ructioned, it seemed, and sitting up in her bed she ably churned her butterchurn, spade-clapped butter, caught flying sods of mushy turf, or so it seemed, and looking on, the helpers from those days churned with her, but as though questioning a dumb spastic, began moving more and more into lateral evidences in order to fit the meaning she meant onto her clues as, bolting the door when the horse was damned near gone, they saw things they had never bothered to see before, when she was in harness and pulling their dray all the stolen nights and days of their banyan tree's eminence.

Umpteen times was the woman lifted up onto her pillows, the handlers looking at each other in exasperation. Assiduously they settled her, and just as assiduously did she undo their settling. Sometimes she recognised them, her eldest son and only daughter. 'Ah, ye're very good to come and stay with me until I get up again,' she cackled. 'He'll be here now anytime, have ye the kettle boiled?' she'd ask. 'Ye know how much he liked the grub. When he was back then, he thought the munging came from being stuck here with his mammy, but he'll have learnt, he'll be able to tell us all about his travels. Australia, y'say, Down Under, isn't that what we learnt in school,' she said, and now she laughed and chortled until she hung a lip and went to sleep again.

She'd have laughed her sides sick if she could have seen herself near the moment of death. 'Musha, musha, musha, will you take a look,' she'd likely say. 'They hadn't time to fart with me when I was the star turn here, but now that the time has come when I wouldn't hear a fart even if they farted, I declare I have them both. Doing much better, I am, than when poor Peter snuffed it, look musha, I have a bishop, no less, to prepare me to meet the Man Above, and I have my poor lovely girl to nurse me and then, when the time comes, to get me ready for the worms.'

'Was it a night such as this that the clock came home here?' wondered Sheila as, hours spent attending to her mother, she now took a rest beside the stove in the kitchen. She was granting stillborn glances at the clock under the stairs as it waited, its pendulum stilled and its twin black hands stuck on the figures nine and stringent twelve. The neat nurse, the girl of the hooked auncels, herself, almost, in mourning, looked now at the dour face of the clock, and listened as one admonished to the voice working itself down the Peter O'Brien-made stairs from the hybrid fig lying dying in the bed upstairs as, praying and doubting, the fig's nuisance bossed down in the mud and cried up in the stars: 'He's coming down the boreen to me, coming now, but late as ever, coming soon,' she bragged, but shyly 'coming nice and clean and quietly. Coming stealing through the meadows,' those she guarded, though she wondered. 'Coming winding through the gateway, coming quickly through the haggard.' Minnie, he's coming, says the mother's brain, hurry up her secrets' strain. 'Hurry Frankie, hurry home, hurry now, hear me moan. Hurry son, hurry please, my heart's leppin' like the fleas, hurry son, remember the hens the fleas hopped from as though a flock they sneezed. Hurry Frankie, by land or sea, hurry, hurry, between you and me there's still some time to go before that last long bell at the church-porch door. It's coming, Frankie, coming fast, coming carting a grained, brown box. I'm afraid He's coming, son, coming nearer, looking careful, sorta tearful. Come home quickly, come on son, I can't wait forever, come on, come. He's coming never, Minnie *a ghrá*, he's coming never, never at all, he'll not get here before the *lá* when I must answer His beck and call. Frankie, Frankie, come to me, come in a hurry, come and see, I can't shut my eyes for fear for you, for fear you'll come and no one in to welcome you with *fáilte* word.' Minnie bombarded her worn-out brain, welcoming Frankie before he even came, by fretting in flurries like windblown snow, she bullied and bolstered her heartbeat slow. 'He's coming,' she said, her voice winding down. 'He's coming,' she said. 'I felt His finger, son, He's coming,' she said, a hotness dreaming her ear. 'Minnie,' it breathed, 'Minnie, I'm here.' She closed her eyes in sweet relief, her hands lay streeted, cold and neat, her thumbs didn't twiddle or churn or wind, her musha-word silent, the mega-Messiah died.

# CHAPTER 115

The road gate was being eaten alive with rust. Hillocks and blisters of paint bubbled up on each and every bar of it. Drops of scarlet red hung like dewdrops from its old ruins — she who painted it last didn't wait to brush it in or blend it on. But it wasn't Minnie's handiwork with a paintbrush which was the problem as Frankie looked at the situation. No, it was the spudstone which had stopped him in his tracks. Long years of opening and shutting the gate meant that the eye of the stone had worn down in depth to such a degree that the spudstone itself had split into two halves, and therefore the back-style of the gate had no well in which to pivot.

Frankie had to lift the gate the last few feet in order to have a gap wide enough through which to drive his Hertz-rented car into the boreen. Inside the gate, inside in this nonentity of a little road, he felt almost claustrophobic, for the freedom which had been his in the great wide beyonds of Australia was gone, and all he was seeing here before him was a maggot of pathway, wrinkled from years of hardship, its gummy ground gridlocked under dead brown leaves, while overhead, where the sky should be, he glimpsed scrappy overhanging hawthorns, writing on the drumbeaten heavens, their leaves all forlorn in their fewness, unkemptness their put-on wonder.

He swallowed nervously as he scuttled his car forward, big potholes testing his labouring-man's driving. At only breakneck speed he drove, his Fenian mother needing him to give an answer when next she called out his name. Despite his desperation, he couldn't help noticing the quietness in this wherewithal of a boreen, for gone were the old thoughtful sounds of cartwheels. Now all he could hear was his engine as it purred and baffled, this reclusive Sunday at the end of October.

He was composed when he drove into the yard. He had the feeling that he had got home in time. This thought made him sturdy, almost, and to cap it all he now had that boreen and its horror-story behind him. Tomorrow, at first light, he'd gimlet his eyes into every old nook and cranny, but that'd wait. Now, echoing, was bone upon bone, questioning in his creature.

When he ran into the funeral kitchen he was balked by his brother and sister. Seeing the stricken appearance of their luckybag faces, he knew the worst: knew that he had left it all too late, and all for his thirty pieces of uniqueness.

'Ten minutes' became his mantra words, as he yearned for the clock to go backwards. 'Ten minutes' more, and he'd have redeemed himself. 'Ten minutes', he fucked them, dreadful the wails coming from him, the brother and sister beckoning him, the one fore and one aft cushioning him as he mounted the shabby stairs to a corpse's room.

Hungering towards stylish death, he was flabbergasted by the horribleness of his eyes' witnessing, for there, waking on her own bed, lay a figure with whom he could not establish a link. This corpse, this mother, the Fenian, was a stranger to him, a withered fig on his branch, and as he stood there now he could feel nothing but disgust, for the stand which he had set himself had never imagined a coming home to something which in no earthly way resembled his beautiful, fair-haired mother with the blue-blue eyes.

Next to nobody could feel more isolated than the adventurer back from foreign fields. He saw his folly out to his own satisfaction, but now he demon-dangled in dreadful misery, hellish misery, and to his cost, now found that hell has a slippery welcome for the new arrival to skate upon.

Nobody could measure Frankie's heartbreak. His mother had been destroying him, calling for his company while he, seated in a ringside seat in Madison Square Gardens, was rescuing memories of his father. Now he was back to walk alone, though hundreds bore down on him; brine was the taste in his trebling of grief, becoming lonely was soldiering inside his forehead, and all danger now past, he covered his eyes at the thought of his hod's load of denial.

The sound of the dead bell ricocheted around his conscience as he knelt in the chief mourner's pew in St Peter's Church. He had tried to comfort his sister, but his words hiccuped in human frailty. Praying automatically, he never prayed one response, for despite his bishop-brother's best Manchestering liturgy, he only saw before his eyes an old dead woman being foisted on him. As the Requiem Mass furnished the body in the coffin with grandiose dragnetting he held his breath, yes, held his breath in awe, for from his youth he remembered herself racketing on about the gain to be gained when heterosexual grinding realised such as he. Dying, her Sunday-best boy, nine o'clock that she died, was ten minutes late for her Bren-gun blasting. Never thinking the story through, fever set in. Now she was gone, gone to her graveyard's partner, only their likenesses remained to grow up, then down, then up again, beneath or around her banyan tree's host-planted stems.

It was at the behest of their mother that Sheila's two sons volunteered to join their Uncle Frankie and his neighbour Felix Fortune to negotiate the way towards the burial plot in the cemetery. The thunder at the church now over with, the four men of the Apocalypse carried the coffin towards the grave. All devoutly the dream had unfolded as the bishop, thurible swinging, incensed the Sten gun prior to her transfer to the graveyard. Now a sprinkle of holy water every which way, and the sign of the cross for good measure, the bishop lustred the coffin with his final blessing. A clay crate before her, a clay crate behind her, clay in every Stygian stitch of the vacancy in the hole where she now lay, and lingering, the crowd gathered at the graveside waited the final decade for decoration at the end, as green grass the clay waited to grow, the earthworms to fodder, there in Drumhollow graveyard, where woman of women all, the Fenian-heart-stopper Minnie Humphrey-that-was joined her husband-that-used-to-be for ever and ever, amen.